The ants on his lips, his eyelids, all over his face, and some moving down to the tender flesh of his neck—all of them began to bite.

He tried to twitch, to move his face, shake them off . . .

He was tempted to push at them with his tongue. Force them away. Maybe he could blow them off . . .

But that would mean opening his mouth.

That's what they wanted.

PRAISE FOR MATTHEW J. COSTELLO
ACCLAIMED AUTHOR OF *MIDSUMMER* AND *WURM*

"A LOT OF HORROR WRITERS ARE GOING TO BE LEFT CHOKING ON HIS DUST."
—Rick Hautala, author of *Winter Wake* and *Cold Whisper*

"COSTELLO IS SOMEONE TO WATCH AND READ AGAIN!"
—Edward Bryant, *Locus*

"UNEXPECTED TURNS AND TWISTS . . . UNPREDICTABLE."
—*Science Fiction Chronicle*

"TOM CLANCY MEETS JOHN CARPENTER!"
—*Scars*, The B. Dalton Horror Newsletter

"SPARKLES WITH NERVE-WRACKING SUSPENSE."
—*Rave Reviews*

"HARD TO PUT DOWN, IMPOSSIBLE TO FORGET . . . ONE HELL OF A BOOK."
—Joseph A. Citro, author of *The Unseen*

"WE'LL BE SEEING A LOT MORE OF MATTHEW J. COSTELLO!"
—*Blood Review*

Books by Matthew J. Costello

BENEATH STILL WATERS
MIDSUMMER
WURM
DARKBORN

DARKBORN

MATTHEW J. COSTELLO

DIAMOND BOOKS, NEW YORK

To Rick Hautala,
friend, writer, time traveler

DARKBORN

A Diamond Book / published by arrangement with
the author

PRINTING HISTORY
Diamond edition / February 1992

ISBN: 1-55773-660-X

Diamond Books are published by The Berkley Publishing Group,
200 Madison Avenue, New York, New York 10016.
The name "DIAMOND" and its logo are trademarks
belonging to Charter Communications, Inc.

PRINTED IN THE UNITED STATES OF AMERICA

10 9 8 7 6 5 4 3 2 1

Will Dunnigan woke up.

And for one terrible moment he didn't remember ever falling asleep, didn't know where he was, didn't even know what the hell he could be doing *here*, inside this car—

It wasn't his car.

He knew that.

Breathing the stale air, hearing the sounds outside. Horns honking through the streets, faint voices from somewhere behind him.

His own breathing.

Then—not a gift, but more like a curse—he remembered where he was.

And why he was here.

He looked at the dashboard clock.

Will watched the clock. He licked his lips.

It's not too late, he thought. I'm not late. In fact, he thought with a weird satisfaction, I'm early. Even though I fell asleep, I'm early. Always did like being punctual.

I have lots of time now.

11:03.

Will pushed his thinning, sandy-blond hair off his forehead. And he looked out the windshield, all steamed up by his breath. He rubbed his sweater sleeve through the dewy window, clearing a smeary arc.

So now he got a good look at the freak show. Right outside.

Right there, ladies and gentlemen.

And while he watched, he leaned over and checked that his door was locked, that all the car doors were locked, be-

fore he let himself just stare outside, safely sitting in the dark
car.

He heard his breathing.

I'm breathing much too heavily, Will thought.

But then . . . who wouldn't?

Will didn't want to take his Toyota tonight. It wouldn't be
fair, he reasoned. No, not to leave Becca with both a missing
car and a missing husband.

Not fair at all.

The car got the shopping done. It got the kids to their ballet
classes, their piano lessons, soccer practice . . . the too-busy
routine of suburbia, the stuff that constituted the good life.

All of it now light-years away, galaxies removed from here
. . . and now.

Funny. What time can do.

Time and circumstances.

Will cleared another smear on the part of the windshield
facing the passenger seat. Now he could see the street sign.
He was parked just a bit back from the corner of 28th Street
and Madison.

Nice neighborhood to live in, he thought. Real nice.

If you like crack dealers, and hookers, and homeless
wraiths who shambled around as if they might discorporate
in the blinking of an eye.

And then there were the horny cruisers who trolled these
streets—so busy during the day and now abandoned to these
new-age horrors—searching for a moderately cheap thrill.
Some of them had kiddie seats in the back of their station
wagons . . . model fathers.

Will saw a tall black girl standing across Madison Avenue,
right in front of the bank.

It was as if she had materialized. She wore gigantic spike
heels that raised her to true Amazonian heights. A tight
leather skirt. Straight jet-black hair that had to be a wig. Her
short half-jacket exposed a flat-as-a-board midriff that gobbled the silky white color of the tungsten streetlamps.

She saw him.

Sitting in the car.

Dirty little man, she probably thought.

Will looked away, but not quick enough.

The hooker crossed the street, moving toward him like a lioness, flashing brilliant white teeth as if she were saying:

I could eat you right up, babe. In one quick gulp. No problem.

She hurried across, dodging a mad cab that flew right past her.

She walked up to the car, and then she paused. She looked up and down, checking for signs of John Law. Solicitation was still—officially—a crime in this city. It was still on the books. *Officially*. But after midnight, the blocks around here became a regular *Satyricon*, filled with sexual wonders and nightmares that had to be seen to be believed.

And Will guessed that those who sampled such pleasures weren't too troubled by AIDS. Life's too short . . .

The hooker stood right by his window. She smiled at him. Big, open—

The better to—

She tapped the window, signaling that he should roll it down and get the transaction going.

Will smiled back.

An ineffectual grin that he hoped said, "No, I'm not shopping tonight . . ."

He hoped she wouldn't assume that he didn't like her.

That she wasn't to his taste. He didn't want to get her mad.

She shouted through the glass.

"Hey, baby . . . wanna go out?"

A euphemism. Will shook his head, and smiled some more.

But the giantess leaned close to the window. She stuck out a long, dark tongue and made a licking motion with it. "C'mon, baby!" she said. "You'll love it."

Will couldn't hold the smile on his face any longer. He shook his head and turned away.

The woman cursed at him. A fusillade of fuck-yous, then, storming away, teetering on her giant heels, she turned and delivered what she must have thought was the ultimate blow to some creep from the hinterlands of Westchester or Suffolk.

"Fuckin' faggot!"

And when she turned and said that—with cars, and then a growling bus gliding past their intimate street scene—he saw something. Just below her chin. Bobbing up and down as she yelled at him.

An Adam's apple.

A TV hooker, he thought. Or a pre-op transsexual, working her way through the college of hard knocks, saving her nickels and dimes for that big operation.

If the crack man doesn't get it all.

He *does* have sticky fingers.

Will looked at his hands.

Gripping the steering wheel.

Holding on as if it were a life raft.

He shook his head, disgusted with himself.

What the hell am I doing? he wondered. If this little encounter rattles me, then, shit, what's going to happen later?

What's going to happen when I have to go out there?

It was cold, but he felt icy beads of sweat on his forehead.

And you *are* going out there, he told himself.

You are.

And not just for that he/she hooker, not just for all the others, wandering around, blundering their way through the night, not knowing what the hell they were up against.

They don't read papers.

No, not just for them. You know that.

It was more than that. Much more.

He let go of the steering-wheel heel.

Look, Ma, no hands.

He felt as if he might float away, that the roof of the rented Toyota would explode upward, and he'd be sucked out. Sorry, sir, this car wasn't meant to cruise at ten thousand feet.

Again, he heard his breathing. He thought: I sound like a three-pack-a-day nicotine fiend, battling emphysema . . . pneumonia.

Or maybe, maybe it's just a goddamn death rattle.

He turned and looked in the backseat.

Will saw the black leather attaché . . . more like an old school bag. He leaned over his seat and pulled it to the front, onto the passenger seat. He stopped and checked the rearview mirror.

A few headlights, but nothing that looked like the outline of a police car.

Will opened the bag.

The bag's buckle felt cold, and when it snapped open, a musty, ripe smell erupted from inside the bag. Old leather and a sweet food smell, a bit of apple, perhaps a sandwich . . . drying things, all leaving their imprint inside the bag.

He pulled out the book. It was on top.

Black. The leather was cracked. It felt heavy, leaden in his hands.

God, I'm so tired, he thought. If I could just get to a bed somewhere, just eight hours. Eight hours of real sleep. That's all—

And then he felt for the other things.

The jar, clear, shining, catching the light. He wedged it into the crack of the seat. Then the yellow pad, filled with page after page of notes, suggestions.

And then—hard, metallic, and a bit more reassuring—the gun.

I've never fired a gun, he thought as he quickly took it out of the bag and slid it onto his lap. He let his hand stay closed around the handle. His finger touched the trigger—ever so gently. Just testing that it would, in fact, give when he pulled back.

It was, he was told, a .45-caliber pistol. The beefy sporting-goods guy who sold it to him said that it would punch a good-sized hole in someone.

"About the size of a baseball." The man grinned. "Great for target shooting," he added when Will looked up at him.

Will bought a box of bullets. There were twenty, maybe thirty shells. More than enough.

If they do anything at all.

But he felt better having the gun.

Then, at the bottom, he felt the last thing, wrapped in black velvet. His fingers traced the outline, feeling the bumps and curves, and the way the velvet caught at the calluses on his hands, the way it caught at his chewed fingernails.

He didn't pull that out.

No. He smiled to himself. That would dispel some of its mystery, its power. Now, wouldn't it?

If it has any power.

And if it doesn't?

I'll die. And worse.

I'll die painfully. It might last a few seconds, but it would seem as though it lasted forever. A lifetime of pain, terrible, horrible agony.

Forget the Inquisition. Forget the good old Spanish priests who really knew how to party. The fun guys who'd take a pregnant woman and stretch her on a spike-filled rack and then hoist her up by her ankles and let her fall to the concrete. Until she confessed her sins . . .

Forget the Salem witch-hunters who left people chained and naked while vermin came and chowed down on their extremities.

That's *nothing* compared to what will happen to me, Will thought.

And he pulled back his hand from black velvet.

He looked left. The driver's window was fogged up. He wiped at it.

The store across the street had closed.

A few minutes ago—or was it an hour, two hours?—it had been open. He didn't remember.

It was a fruit and vegetable store. He remembered brilliant floodlights outside the store, hung from a green awning. They illuminated the bright, inviting display of sparkling lettuce, and bloodred tomatoes, and plump squash, and grapes of every kind. Oriental men in white coats bustled about, checking the produce, weighing selections for customers.

Now all the produce was gone. The store was dark. The men in their white coats were gone. The awning had been folded back into itself. Corrugated riot doors covered the windows.

I wish they were still here, Will thought.

To keep me company.

He looked back across Madison Avenue, and the black hooker was gone. Scooped up by some lucky, if unsuspecting, soul about to taste the duplicitous pleasures produced by sexual camouflage. Will saw another girl, a different professional, standing across from the bank. She was chunky, with waves of synthetic blond hair.

Probably young. Probably much too young.

Where do they come from? Will wondered. And what could possibly make them come out here, to stand here, night after night, in the cold, in the rain?

Has life gotten that nasty, that tough?

A white Cadillac, with incongruous pink pinstripes, took the corner and pulled up to the girl. A tall black man in a leather coat got out. The man talked to the girl and gave her something.

Will watched, in the darkness of his car. Feeling like a spy, a voyeur. They don't see me.

But I see them.

He watched the girl take whatever it was the man had proffered and bring it up to her nose.

She kicked her head back. And she grinned. A nice big grin visible from all the way over here.

Thanks. I needed that, her smile said.

The pimp got back into his duded-up wheels and made his whitewall tires screech as he pulled away.

Just putting another dime in the meter.

Keep his girls running.

As simple a concept as the donkey and the carrot.

Will heard a noise from behind him.

Shit, he thought. Goddammit. His hand closed on the barrel of the gun and then moved around to the handle. His heart raced, and he scolded himself.

Stupid, absolutely dumb! I should be checking the rearview mirrors, watching all around. I can't get caught up in the street theater.

I can't screw up, not tonight. Even if that *is* what I do best. I can't screw up.

Not tonight.

He turned around just as his hand felt the gun handle.

And if it's a cop, Will thought, what will I do then?

What if he starts looking in the car? What if he sees the gun? There were supposed to be cops all over here.

Supposed to be . . .

But it wasn't a cop.

It was—yes—a homeless person.

When I was a kid we called them bums, he thought. Mom used to warn me. Stay away from the *bums*. And when I went to the city, to Manhattan, I'd spot them on the subway platforms, ghostly, raglike creatures, one hand bent in a permanent cup shape, searching for a coin.

And Will learned to keep his eyes off them, to move away.

Sometimes there'd be a blind guy with a dog, stumbling through the subway car. Looking up at nothing, rattling along with the car. Stumbling this way and that, sometimes falling into people. Excusing himself to the embarrassed passengers in their seats. While the blind man held his tin cup at the ready. Right below his neatly lettered sign that read:

I am blind.

Please give whatever you can.

Praise God.

And then there were the cart men, the guys with no legs. Will never asked how they lost their legs. He didn't want to know. It might be catching . . .

They were the scariest, those legless people who seemed so full of energy, waving pencils at people as they hurried by. So scary, as if they could threaten to turn you into one of them, and *you'd* become a cart person if you didn't give them something, anything.

Now they were all called homeless.

And now there were committees and action groups, and people said it was our responsibility to do something, that it could happen to anyone.

He had been right as a boy. You *could* turn into one of them.

Nobody cared if a lot of them preferred the streets to the shelters, that they actually liked rustling through overflowing mesh garbage cans for discarded McDonald's buns and stick fries. They liked living in the underworld.

And they still scared him.

Will watched this man shuffle next to the car. He was of indeterminate age. He might be twenty. He might be seventy. He had a beard that surely carried the leavings of countless grisly interactions with food and God knows what. He wore a regulation brown coat, flapping open to the breeze, probably covering layers of clothes.

They wore all their clothes when it turned cold, layer upon layer upon layer.

It was easier than carrying them.

But this fellow also dragged a cherry-red Bloomie bag filled with his life's treasures. The man stopped before he got to the corner. He put down the bag and then looked around, waving back and forth as if a good stiff breeze would blow him clear off his feet.

He didn't see Will.

The man dug at his groin, pulling at what must be a bunch of zippers.

He was only feet from Will.

Who kept watching him, fascinated.

This is like bizarro television, Will thought.

The human circus.

The man finally hit pay dirt. He arched away from a pillarlike protrusion of the office building and urinated. The wind caught the steamy smoke . . .

At which point in the show, Will turned away.

Will kept looking away, giving the man time to move his act on.

Can't blame him, Will thought. When you gotta go, you gotta go. And where the hell are you supposed to pee in the city? There are no toilets in the subway—they're all locked up.

Though you'd have to be crazy to venture into one of those halls of horror.

In Paris, they had WCs right on the street, discreet cubicles where you could relieve yourself.

In Manhattan, you checked for the cops and let go.

Just like a dog.

If you can make it here . . . Will's mind hummed.

When he looked back, there was nobody there. The man had moved on, disappearing around a corner.

The sideshow had, inexplicably, ended.

No hookers. No homeless people. No crack magnates.

Will felt cold. Creepy.

As if he were being watched.

He looked at the digital clock.

Hoping it wasn't midnight. Not yet. I'm not ready.

11:15.

Plenty of time.

Imagine, all that *activity* in just ten minutes or so . . .

Imagine . . .

And now he knew that he still had plenty of time.

Lots of time.

To sit and think.

And now—without anything to watch—to do what seemed unavoidable.

His constant activity now.

Unavoidable. Incessant. This thinking . . .
Always searching for the way out, the escape hatch.
The fucking way out.
And never finding it.
No matter how many times he let himself do it, no matter how many times he forced himself to remember . . .

St. Jerry's, 1965

"Dunnigan! Will you come off it? Have a smoke, for Christ's sake!"

Tim Hanna turned to the rest of them and grinned, as if to say—for the umpteenth time—What the hell is wrong with *this* guy?

But Will Dunnigan shrugged and took a sip of the Coke, too cold, too sweet for so early in the morning. The communal plate of fries—greasy, covered with a disgusting smear of ketchup—was more than his stomach could handle.

It didn't bother anyone else, though. His friends all dug into the plate as if it were perfectly normal to be chomping on french fries at 8:15 in the morning.

"Come on, Hanna," Will said. "Just get off my case, will you? I don't want one of your goddamn cigarettes. I don't want to smoke, and that's the end of it, okay?"

Now Tim pulled at the cuffs of his sport coat—they all dressed in sport coats and ties, regulation dress for St. Jerry's. And Will watched Tim lean across the table, close to him, until Will felt manic intensity, the power of Tim, who, at five feet, was the shortest of them all.

And Tim said:

"Dunnigan, when are you going to stop being such a fuckin' pussy?"

And everyone laughed.

This time, even Will laughed. It was all in fun. Tim was his best friend, maybe his only real friend. And the language, all the ranking out, was just the way they talked.

It didn't mean anything.

Will, never one for the sharp comeback, sipped his Coke. Then, looking at the clock, he said, "Five minutes, guys."

13

And a flurry of hands darted to the fries, eager to leave no greasy prisoners to Mr. Kokovinis's dumpster.

Ted Whalen looked over at Will. Whalen seemed older, slicker than the rest of them, Will always thought. Maybe he *was* older. Whalen's straight hair was combed completely to the left, flat against his forehead.

Whalen made a disgusted look at Will.

That's in earnest, Will knew. Because Ted Whalen didn't like him. No, he put up with him because of Tim. But Whalen made no secret of his distaste—his dislike of Will.

Will seemed to feel himself shrivel when Whalen looked at, past, *through* him.

"Don't fucking worry, will you, Dunnigan?" Whalen said, snapping the word "fucking" like a whip, his voice filed to a nasty edge. "Gately doesn't care about some fucking seniors missing the first bell. Jeez!"

Will didn't say anything.

He learned that it didn't pay to argue with Whalen. Whalen was too quick on his feet. And then, even Tim would start laughing at him.

And that was something that Will really couldn't stand.

"We better go," another voice said. Quiet. Even quieter than Will's. It was Michael Narrio, who was what Tim crudely called their "token wop."

Narrio never had much to say. He didn't laugh much either, he was just always *there*.

Narrio played trumpet in the band. He was good. And then everyone heard him fine . . .

One ketchupy fry remained when the Kiffer—Jim Kiff— came flying through the luncheonette door.

Everyone turned and looked at him.

Sometimes Kiff made it to school, and sometimes he didn't. He had arrived last spring near the middle of the junior term. He had some trouble at another school, grades maybe, maybe something else that he never talked about. At least not to the group, not to Will.

Kiff had an uncle with connections and he ended up at St. Jerry's. From that first day Kiff just glued himself to the group.

He wasn't in any of the things they were. He didn't run track, like Whalen. He didn't debate, like Tim did, and

Will tried to. And he would have nothing to do with something as corny as the band.

"Screw extracurriculars" was Kiff's motto.

Kiff, they all recognized, was crazy.

When they went drinking at the Oak Leaf Tavern in Germantown, where the old barkeep and his wife from Deutschland didn't bother the nice, well-dressed boys for IDs, Kiff always went too far. He'd drink more beer than anyone else, and then—God—shots of real whiskey, matching the old farts, the regulars, whose big asses barely fit on the barstools.

Then Kiff would start talking to them. Arguing with the Germans about—*unbelievable!*—the Nazis. Asking them flat out:

What did you do during the war, Wolfgang?

On some Mondays, Kiff showed up at school with a black eye. Sometimes he laughed about it.

Sometimes he didn't.

Kiff—the Kiffer—scared Will. He was out of control. Wild. Dangerous.

"Guys," Kiff announced breathlessly, scooping up the last fry. His tie, speckled with stains, dangled from his neck, knotless. His too-bright red hair was askew, totally wild and uncombed. Kiff had, Will guessed, about two minutes to get his tie on before he'd catch hell from his homeroom teacher.

"Guys, you won't fucking *believe* what I've found." He leaned over the table, his loose tie trailing through a puddle of Coke, a dollop of ketchup. But he was flying. He didn't care.

"Go on," Tim said. "Stun us!"

"We gotta go," Michael Narrio said. The quiet, dark-haired boy started pushing against Will, urging him to slip out of the booth.

Will checked the clock. "Oh, yeah," he muttered to Narrio. But he kept an eye on Kiff as he got up.

Kiff backed away, brandishing his fry. "Hey, don't you want to hear what I found? It's going to blow you guys right out of the water."

We have to hurry, Will thought. We've got to get moving. St. Jerry's wasn't a place where you screwed around. They'd suspend you even if it was a week before graduation.

The Jesuits were tough. Soldiers of Christ. God's storm troopers.

"Sure, Kiff—but hell, can't it fucking wait until lunch?" Tim said.

Kiff finally popped the last shriveled fry in his mouth. He reminded Will of the scarecrow from *The Wizard of Oz*. He always looked as if he were ready to fly apart, all loose stuffing and wobbly legs.

"Yeah, sure, Hanna. But I *can't* tell you this shit at school." Kiff leaned down close to them all. "It's too fuckin' *cool* to tell you there. Some schmucks might hear it."

Will picked up his books, held in a tight bundle by a rubber book buckle that looked stretched to the breaking point.

Kiff was always coming up with weird tales. Like the time he told everyone he was screwing some housewife in his apartment building. He swore he was doing it, swore it on a stack of Bibles, honest to God . . .

Nobody believed him, though.

Certainly not Will.

For a lot of reasons.

They all started for the exit. Mr. Kokovinis moved to their booth, muttering to himself, pissed off at their slobby mess, but too interested in the four or five bucks they dropped there every day.

"I'll tell you here, right here, after school." Kiff grinned. The toothy smile revealed less than gleaming teeth. His stringy red hair looked as though it needed a wash.

Tim Hanna pushed open the door. "Sure. There's nothing happening this afternoon."

He looked at Will.

"Is there, Dunnigan?"

Will shook his head.

Kiff grinned some more. He clapped his hands together. "Timmy . . . Will . . . guys, you won't fucking believe it . . ."

And of that fact, Will was reasonably sure.

Will started hurting toward the end of the English class.

He felt sick.

Not that this particular class was bad. If anything, their teacher, Mr. Scott, had made Will's four years bearable. He could survive Latin, Greek, and even the religion classes knowing that an English class with Scott was coming up to save the day.

Scott seemed old, almost ancient. He was like a morose Falstaff, larger than life, with a slurred accent like sounded vaguely British, but always impressive.

Mr. Scott heaped scorn on his students, and that only seemed to make him more popular.

"Mr. Hanna," Scott bellowed out now, slouched dramatically in a chair, his black robes covered with a fine dust of chalk. "Would you be *so kind* as to read us the third stanza of the Donne?"

"Right," Tim said, smiling. And Will saw that his friend was momentarily lost. Will tilted his book up and pointed at the right poem.

"Er, yes," Tim said. " 'Batter my heart, three-personed God—' "

"Stop," Scott bellowed.

He stood up. The teacher's eyes were blue, filled with a fire that seemed half mad. "Now, what exactly do you suppose John Donne is asking God for here?"

The teacher waited.

Scott could wait for a long time.

Will looked at the clock.

He felt even sicker.

"Mr. Dunnigan. Would you be so kind as to favor us with *your* answer?"

Caught coasting in the ozone, Will thought.

"It means—well—Donne's asking for help, to be made strong . . ."

Scott favored Will with a Cheshire-like grimace. "Yes. And do we know why?"

The teacher looked around the room. A farmer searching for errant sheep.

A few hands shot up.

Tim looked over at Will.

He made a fist and worked it up and down. Will didn't catch on. And then he did.

The universal symbol for choking the chicken. Or self-abuse, as the padre in the confessional referred to it. Will grinned.

"Mr. Syzmanski," Scott said.

Charles Syzmanski gave his answer in a high-pitched, almost feminine voice.

Syzmanski's announced plans were to enter the priesthood.

Not everyone was sure that would be such a great idea for old Charlie . . .

"He's asking for release from his sexual obsession," Charles sang.

"Very good," Scott purred. "Sex, gentlemen. A great romantic poet, and here he is devoting his brilliant talent to warding off the demons of *sex*!"

Scott shook his head, his great mane of white hair flying. "What a *waste* of his gifts . . . and I'm sure that you gentlemen have no such problems . . ." Scott made a sardonic grin.

"Now, let's look at John Donne after he's *undone*. Page three-twenty-one, gentlemen . . ."

Will looked at the clock.

This was worse than the dentist, this awful waiting. He supposed that some of the danger, some of the fear, was just in his head.

Yeah, that's probably all it was, he tried to reassure himself.

But no. Not after what had happened last week.

Not after last week's gym class.

They're out to get me, Will knew.

Though I'll be damned if I know why.

What the hell did I do?

And though he wished the clock would slow to a crawl, the minute hand seemed to fly to the 12.

Then—a horrible moment—the period bell rang, loud, absolutely piercing.

And Will had five minutes to hustle to his locker and then get down to the gym.

High noon had arrived.

Henkel, the gym teacher, didn't like him.

At least, that's what Will supposed. The squat, bald-headed man—surely he doesn't have a *real* college degree?—always had one beady eye open for any sign of Will Dunnigan screwing up.

Those moments were not too hard to find.

Will lived with the fact that he wasn't fast, wasn't strong, wasn't coordinated. "Sports" was a nightmare word to him. Sports equaled failure. And gym was his own personal arena of embarrassment.

Even Tim and Mike Narrio seemed to distance themselves from Will in gym class. He was too sorry a case to get tangled up with, Will knew. Later they'd talk and laugh, but not about gym class, not about his pathetic performance and the incessant way Henkel picked on him.

Henkel was also the football coach. He was married, rumor had it, though no one ever saw a Mrs. Henkel. Will imagined the little Mrs. with a matching bowling-ball head and even beadier eyes.

Now, it wasn't long before Will had his blue and white gym outfit on, and his sneakers—cursed shoes—before Henkel was screaming at him during the class's warm-ups.

"Come on, Dunnigan. Can't you do even one good push-up?"

Cue laughter. *Everyone laughed.*

Even, Will knew, his friends.

And there were ropes to climb. Nearly everyone climbed up these cargo ropes, climbing and kicking as if they were monkeys, as if there were *nothing* so damn easy in the whole world.

While Will, tall but without any real strength in his arms, kicked at the rope, feeling the rough strands dig into his hands. I'm a dead weight, he thought.

He grunted. He felt the sweat pouring out of him. Inside his head—inaudible to Henkel—he cursed Henkel and this forty-two-minute period in hell.

But he didn't move.

And then—within moments—Henkel was there, screaming in his ear, nice and loud. The old marine drill instructor in him coming out.

"*Come on*, Dunnigan, move it. Move it! You're pathetic! Use your legs, pull with your arms."

And then, just to heighten the embarrassment, Henkel would fit his palm under Dunnigan's ass and shove.

"Too many Twinkies," Henkel grunted, playing to the

other boys. "Gotta trim down, Dunnigan, if you want to get up the rope."

Dunnigan nodded. And took it. I *have* to take it, he knew. What else can I do?

It never occurred to him that he could do anything to stop Henkel's torment.

But as bad as Henkel was, there was something worse about gym.

Though Will eventually figured out that—in some sick way—they went together.

There were jocks in the class. A bunch of gorillas from the football team, already working toward the big hubba-hubba Thanksgiving game with Brooklyn Tech. Half of them couldn't get *their* big asses up the rope, but Henkel didn't bother them. No way. They did practically nothing during the class. They threw a few baskets, sat on the stage.

And they watched Henkel work on Dunnigan.

And that was the bad part.

They watched, and they waited until later.

Because after the class, everyone stripped down and went into the showers. Everyone was bare-assed, the jocks clustering together, so damn easy for them, laughing, grunting, proud of their animal noises.

While Will tried to get in and out as fast as possible. Just a sprinkling of water.

Last week, he had felt them watching him. D'Angelo, a hairy monkey who was bounced out of the regular classes in his sophomore year, started taunting him. Called him "Candy-ass Dunnigan."

D'Angelo got some of the others going too.

And with the water streaming off his face, Will thought: I could be in deep shit here. They could be out to—

What?

He didn't know.

And he didn't want to find out. He ran out of the shower, tufts of soap suds still clinging to his ears.

Dunnigan remembered that fear. And now he slid off the ropes, giving up any hope of climbing them.

"Laps, Dunnigan!" Henkel screamed at him. "Give me some laps."

Will nodded. This he could do, even if he'd feel the air

burning his lungs as he padded around the gym floor, feeling kids watch him. His friends—suddenly distant. And the others . . . just watching.

Smelling fresh meat, he thought.

And all he could think about, as he went further and further into oxygen debt, was the showers.

When suddenly, beady-eyed Mr. Henkel wouldn't be around.

Will wanted to get to the showers fast, hoping to get a free nozzle close to the lockers, close to escape.

But Henkel had him do one more lap while everyone else trudged away.

And is it my imagination, Will thought, or are D'Angelo and the rest hanging together, looking at me?

Will felt as if he might just be able to keep running. Anything would be better than going into the lockers.

"All right," Henkel shouted disinterestedly. "That's it."

Now Will had to follow his class.

And by the time he got to the showers, he saw that there was only one nozzle free. All the way in the back.

I'll make it fast, Will thought. Just get myself wet, get my hair wet, so Henkel doesn't get pissed off and send me back in.

He walked past his friends, back to the free nozzle. He turned on the water.

An ice-cold spray shot out.

Someone had turned the nozzle all the way to the left.

D'Angelo and his buddies were there, and they laughed.

Will backed out of the water, gasping, shivering now. He leaned in with one hand and twisted the nozzle the other way.

And he waited, looking straight ahead. Can't look at them, Will thought. That would be like a signal. Okay, I'm expecting it. Come on. Do whatever the hell you're going to do.

The water turned to luke and then hot. Will twisted the knob a bit and stepped in.

Real fast, he thought. Just get wet and—

The water was warm, soothing after—what, a dozen laps? It dribbled over his head, covering his ears, his mouth. Muffling the noise of so many showers. The other kids talking.

When he felt something.

On his back. Then right on his ass.

A slightly *warmer* stream.

He jerked his head out of the spray. The noise, the voices were there, surrounding him.

He turned quickly, a sick feeling growing in his stomach. What the fu—

He turned. There was D'Angelo. A stupid grin on his face. Laughing. Like a mechanical clown. Heh-heh-heh. Grinning, looking at his buddies.

Will looked down.

D'Angelo's prick was shooting a stream of piss right at him.

"Shit!" Will yelled. He backed away.

And now D'Angelo couldn't stand it, couldn't fucking stand the comedy of it. He doubled up, convulsed with how funny it all was.

Will jerked backward and banged against the metal soap dish—always empty—driving the thin metal into his back.

D'Angelo just stood there, laughing, grinning.

Everyone was watching.

Everyone.

And the only sounds were D'Angelo laughing and all that water hitting the tiles, swirling into pools, then rushing down the drain.

And it didn't matter anymore.

It didn't matter that D'Angelo was built like a human tank, all blubber and muscle, with a neck like a telephone pole. All Will felt was everyone watching him, and the horrible laughing.

What the fuck do I have to lose? Will thought crazily. *What the fuck—*

He leaped at D'Angelo. He grabbed at that bull neck. It was so thick that Will's two hands couldn't even close around it, but he grabbed it as hard as he could and squeezed.

And then—a moment of inspiration—he brought his knee up.

Right into D'Angelo's groin.

And all the while Will screamed at him.

"You fucking bastard, you lousy, shit-eating—"

He saw D'Angelo's eyes bulge with the sudden, completely unexpected pain.

But then, after that terrible burst of adrenaline, he saw D'Angelo's face change.

Here was a guy who every weekend smashed into the big black monsters from Power Memorial. He'd had half a dozen guys fall on him. Regularly. And then he'd stand up, good as new. No problem. He had his face smashed, his legs crushed, his head banged like a punching bag.

D'Angelo sure the hell isn't scared of me, Will knew.

And—while everyone started whistling, calling, screaming for the wonderful show to continue—

D'Angelo moved, quickly, smoothly, with an animal strength that absolutely terrified Will.

3

Will felt Tim watching from the sidelines. Everyone was watching. Sure, everyone liked to see a fight, even one as obviously mismatched as this was.

For a second he could see the absurdity of it all. All these naked guys standing in the shower, their weiners hanging out, watching a gorilla who enjoyed his work.

The metal soap dish cut into Will's back. He felt the steel edge break his skin. He groaned. But then D'Angelo's meaty hand covered his mouth, ending the sound.

Such a giant hand, hard and fleshy.

Then Will felt the edge of D'Angelo's palm slip up toward his nose.

I won't be able to breathe, he thought. I won't be able to breathe and no one will know.

They'll just think that I'm struggling to get away from the Big D.

That's what everyone called him.

The Big D.

And when Will and his friends sat in the luncheonette, they joked about Big D and how it stood for ''big dope.''

Will felt a quick punch to his side. Fast and hard, and suddenly his eyes filled with red fireworks.

I'm going to throw up, he thought.

His eyes were fixed on D'Angelo's. And D'Angelo's eyes were dumb, animal eyes . . . with just a hint of amusement. *This was fun.*

They reminded Will of his dog's eyes. Kind of dull. Empty.

And what do my eyes look like? Wide, terrified?

Is that giving the monkey an extra kick?

Another rap, and Will felt the wind knocked out of him.

Will kicked at D'Angelo's legs, scraping at his hairy shins with slippery wet feet, trying to get his arms up. But D'Angelo had both arms pinned with a forearm block that pressed Will's ass right against the shower wall.

Everyone was quiet, and Will realized that something real serious was going on here.

This was more than just a joke, more than a nasty prank.

This was about settling differences.

The differences between the jocks and the other kids who didn't give two shits about heroics on the home field.

This was fucking primitive.

And the sick thing—the really *sick* thing, Will realized—was that if D'Angelo removed his pan-sized palm from Will's mouth, he knew what he'd do.

I'd beg.

I'd do anything to get the killer monkey off my back.

D'Angelo's hand had slipped toward Will's nostrils. Up. Over. Closing them.

D'Angelo didn't mean to do it . . . did he?

And Will kicked.

It was like being underwater.

I can't breathe, he thought. *I can't fucking breathe.* I'm gonna die.

And then there were more punches, just to hasten the process, and more, until—

A voice.

Henkel.

Barking out one word, just one word, at first.

"Hey!"

Please, Will thought. Move your ex-Marine ass over here. Please.

"Hey, D. D! Hey, let him go. What the hell are you doing?"

Then Henkel, shorter than D'Angelo by a foot, was right there, grabbing at D'Angelo's leaden arms, pulling on D'Angelo's elephantlike torso. Tugging at him, yelling loud now for other kids to, Jesus, come and help him.

And then some of D'Angelo's friends trudged forward—Will saw their faces, smirking, perhaps sad that it was all ending.

D'Angelo's hand popped off Will's mouth.

Will sucked in the air.

"Now, what the hell's going on here?" Henkel shouted, looking at the two of them. "What are you two doing?"

Right, thought Will as he doubled over, chugging the air. As if I'd start anything with that human tank. But Henkel had his favorites.

Of which I'm certainly not one.

"What was it, Dunnigan? What were you two doing here?"

What an idiot, thought Will. What is this guy using for brains?

D'Angelo backed up only a few steps.

He still wore that same grin. As if he were thinking it wouldn't take much for him to lift up Henkel, move him aside, and come back to play with Will.

"This animal—" Will said.

Realizing—only then—that it wasn't just the shower water running off his cheeks.

I'm crying. Goddammit, I'm crying in front of everyone. That was the worst, the absolute lowest.

"Hey, hey, hey!" Henkel said, turning to him, waving a meat-bone index finger that showed he descended from the same evolutionary offshoot as D'Angelo.

There were humans, and there were these geeks.

"None of that," Henkel scolded. "Watch your language!"

Then Will saw an incredible thing.

Henkel turned back to D'Angelo and actually put an arm around his shoulders. Patted his oxlike back. "Go get dressed," he said. Then, as if the physical education teacher realized that he had a crowd of kids watching, he said:

"The two a yers are going to detention today."

Yers? What kind of word is that? wondered Will.

D'Angelo stopped. "But, Coach, what about practice?"

Henkel raised a hand. Such a fair and impartial man.

"Detention first," he said, looking at Will and the other kids, and then he turned back to D'Angelo. "And *then* practice. Now, everybody clear out of here before you miss lunch."

And Will stood there a moment.

Marveling.

The whole thing had taken only minutes. But it seemed as if he'd been in this hell, this shower, for a lifetime.

He turned to walk out, to leave with his friends, to the corner of the locker room where they had their lockers.

But they weren't there.

They had left already. Quickly.

Leaving Will behind.

He saw them at lunch. His friends, but he quickly looked away.

He swore he saw Whalen lean forward and say something to the others that made grins bloom on their faces.

They were all there. Tim. Narrio. The Kiffer.

But if they're my friends, Will thought, angry at being left to fend for himself, maybe I'm better off hanging alone.

So he took his tray of pureed mystery meat on toast points and a big slab of what was dubbed "Boston cream pie," and went off to the side, where the freshmen—looking absolutely juvenile—sat.

For now he didn't want to talk with anybody.

It was before the last period when Tim came up to Will just as he slammed his locker. Tim pushed back his glasses and stood next to Will.

"Hey," he said. "You okay?"

Will nodded.

Great. Wonderful. Nothing like getting pissed on by the star fullback who then tries to kill you.

Will nodded and then turned to go to their last class, Latin 4. Cicero was wrapping up Caesar's last campaign. Gripping stuff . . . especially in the original.

Tim grabbed his arm to stop him. Will shrugged it off.

"Hey, wait a second," Tim said. "Christ, Will, don't go getting all bent out of shape. You had a fight." Tim leaned close to Will, had to actually stretch up to say something in Will's ear.

"He's a fucking Gamma-minus," Tim said, referring to Aldous Huxley's alphabetical classification of humanity from *Brave New World*. Will and his friends were sure that they were the Alphas—the smart ones who'd someday buy and sell D'Angelo and his goony friends.

Will smiled, despite his anger.

Tim could do that. He could always make Will laugh.

But then he forced an angry mask back onto his face. "We're gonna be late," Will said.

The hall was empty, except for Father Ed, the youngest teacher in the school. He played guitar. Took them to the soup kitchens of the Catholic Worker.

A real Red, Tim pronounced. But Will thought that the priest was okay.

"Are you mad at us?" Tim asked. "Are you mad 'cause we didn't help?"

Will stopped. "Some help would have been nice."

Tim let his arms fly out, gesturing dramatically. He was the school's best debater, a state champion. He knew how to take the podium and use it.

"Sure, and can you see *me* up against that monster? He could fucking pick me up and bounce me against the ceiling. Besides, Narrio had already gone for Henkel to get help—"

"He did?"

"Sure he did."

But Will remembered being left there afterward . . . being left all alone. They had abandoned him to his shame, he thought. His friends didn't want anything to do with him. *Nada.*

Or maybe I'm reading that wrong, Will thought. Maybe they were just hurrying to their class and—

And he thought of Ted Whalen, his hair slicked down by the shower. Making a joke that Will was sure was about him.

Maybe I'm just paranoid, Will thought.

"Give me a break," Tim said one more time, giving his black-frame glasses another push.

Will nodded. Then he smiled, just a bit. "Okay," he said.

"You're still coming this afternoon—to the luncheonette?"

"Right after detention." Will grinned.

Tim spun around to see Father Ed come up the hall.

"And we'd better get to fucking Latin class, Dunnigan," Tim whispered, "or our ass will be grass."

And for a moment, Will felt a bit better.

Detention was conducted in Father Gately's small ante-chamber—a dark, windowless room done in a spooky black-ish wood, filled with glass-enclosed book cabinets that held oversized books that looked as though they had never been read.

Ever.

Gately was, according to the popular wisdom, insane. What other kind of priest would make a career out of discipline?

The headmaster might run the school, but Gately, the Prefect of Discipline, *owned* it.

The seniors joked about Henkel. By their fourth year at the school, some of them could probably beat up the bowling-ball-shaped man.

But *nobody* ever joked about Gately.

And the priest with a face that made Boris Karloff look handsome had a wicked sense of torture.

Like now, Will thought. He had set D'Angelo and Will facing each other.

So Will had to sit there, look at D'Angelo, and just imagine all the things the Big D might want to do.

Gately gave orders to sit up. Nice and straight. Any slouching, and he'd have us on our feet, Will knew. Maybe with our arms out. Holding some books.

He was a fun guy.

Used to be a boxer, the rumor mill said. Before becoming a Jesuit. Good career preparation . . .

Will tried to look around at anything but D'Angelo's pug-nosed face. Anything.

Is it my imagination, Will thought, or is D'Angelo breathing heavy, snorting? Making weird piglike noises.

He heard Gately typing inside his office. The minutes crawled.

And you could do nothing, Will knew. No homework, nothing.

But then—a welcome relief—the phone rang and Will heard Gately talking. The silence had been horrible. Gately spoke, a whispery garble. His voice had the vocal consistency of sandpaper.

He heard Gately push his chair away from his desk, the legs screeching on the polished wood floor. Then Gately opened the door wide to his office.

The Prefect of Discipline cleared his chain-saw throat.

Will imagined that the priest might hawk a louie in his direction.

"You may go, D'Angelo. Mr. Henkel wants you on the field."

Great, Will thought, the creep does ten minutes' time and I still have fifty more. Can't let anything interfere with football. No, sir, sports fans, the big Thanksgiving game is only weeks away.

But D'Angelo made an unfortunate mistake.

As he stood up, still staring at Will, he smirked.

An ugly sight if ever there was one.

And Gately didn't like that.

The priest suddenly moved across the floor with all the speed and grace of a leopard. With pinpoint accuracy, Gately's hand shot out and grabbed at D'Angelo's hair. There wasn't much of it. Crew cuts were out and there was a neat forelock, a sheaf of long greasy strands that Gately's hand closed on.

For a second Will thought that the hair would just slip through the priest's powerful fingers.

But no. The grip was much too strong. Too solid.

Gately held, and now he rattled D'Angelo's head back and forth, faster and faster. The football star looked like Wile E. Coyote after getting hit by one of the Road Runner's cannonballs. The small, pudgy head—not much space for a brain cavity—wobbled back and forth, faster and faster, a blur.

"Do you find something funny about this, Mr. D'Angelo?" Gately said through clenched teeth.

Bite him, Will thought. Open up your gummy old mouth and lower those vampire-priest's choppers right on the asshole's neck.

But Gately was content to just put D'Angelo's brain through his own blending process. Back and forth until—when Gately let go—D'Angelo stumbled forward like a top. The fullback threw out one rhino leg to break what might turn into a fall.

His hands fluttered, helping him balance.

Then D'Angelo looked up at Gately.

And Will thought: He's going to kill him. D'Angelo is going to kill the priest!

But D'Angelo just looked down, and them mumbled the only word Gately ever wanted to hear.

"Sorry, Father."

"Now get out of here!" Gately growled, the voice rich
with phlegm and bloodlust.

What a cleric! Will thought.

And D'Angelo staggered out of the prison, humbled.

Will guessed D'Angelo would think twice about gunning
for him later. Not with Gately around to mete out such cre-
ative punishment. Gately turned to Will, who made his face
as flat and impassive as possible.

Maybe he'll let me go early too, Will thought.

But Gately just shook his head in disgust.

The priest walked back into his office.

A big Regulator clock, just within Will's peripheral vision,
clicked.

It was 3:20. Will had forty more minutes of this garbage
before he could leave.

To meet up with his friends.

And hear what had Kiff—crazy Kiff—so damned excited.

Not knowing how everything about this day was falling
together, in a certain way, like the clock he watched, pushing
him toward something that he'd regret for the rest of his life.

4

It went silent the minute Will opened the door to Koko's Luncheonette.

One minute his friends were all laughing and talking. And the next, they stopped.

As if their actions had been frozen for some picture.

School chums. Senior year. Fall 1965.

And Will wondered if maybe he should have gone home.

He let the door slip through his fingers and it slammed shut.

Mr. Kokovinis, over by the counter, talking to two men squatting in front of coffee cups, looked up.

But then Tim said, loud enough for Mr. Koko himself to look over and shake his head, "Hey, Dunnigan! Get your butt over here!"

And it was all there, in Tim's words, his tone of voice. An acceptance, a sense of *moving on*, past whatever had happened that day. Will smiled, trying to pick up the mood tossed off by Tim as if it were a gently lobbed tennis ball . . . to be picked up and returned.

He walked over to the booth, which was engulfed by a cloud of smoke.

"What the hell happened?" Tim said. "Old Gately make you stand on one leg?"

Will grinned and he sat down beside his friend. "No, but he sure the hell let D'Angelo off the hook." Will shook his head. "Football practice. But at least Gately gave D'Angelo's head a good rattle before letting him go."

"The Deadly Gately Blender! Great."

Now Will looked up at the others. Narrio was smiling, listening. Mike never had much to say. But Whalen still wore his usual disgusted look that seemed less a pose and more the outward sign of one nasty kid. Will looked around, over to the counter and Mr. Koko, then back to the others.

"Where's Kiff?"

Whalen took a drag on his cigarette and sneered. "Gone to check something. Told us to wait here. For *you*." Whalen rolled his eyes. "Who knows what the hell he's up to . . ."

Narrio nodded. "I have to go soon."

It seemed as though Kiff's great surprise was petering out. But then Tim tapped his arm.

"Whoa. There he is," Tim said. Will turned around and there was Kiff, dodging the traffic on Ocean Parkway. He looked demented, waving at them in midstream, grinning a giant smile surrounded by his mess of freckles.

A strange-looking guy, that was for sure.

A car nearly hit him and Kiff banged on the hood—they all laughed—and Will saw him yelling something, his mouth open.

"What an animal," Whalen muttered.

Then Kiff ran the rest of the way, up to the door, and on into the luncheonette.

He came over to them, barely able to contain himself, so excited because of his secret.

"Will, Tim, Whalen, Mikey . . . great! You're all here."

"Hail, hail, the gang's all here and all that good shit, Kiff," Whalen said. "Can you please get on with it?"

Kiff raised a finger—a lecturer pausing in midthought. "Let me get a Coke."

He flew over to Mr. Kokovinis, who looked spooked by Kiff. He recognized a crazy person when he saw one. The man went to the fountain, pulled up a Coke glass that was still wet from a recent washing. (If plunging the glass into semi-soapy water and then dunking it under something almost equally soapy for a rinse could be called washing.)

Mr. Koko pulled back on the spigot and Coke gushed out.

"I can't believe we're sitting here, waiting for him," Whalen said. "Watch, it will be nothing."

Kiff grinned at them, then his face looked surprised. He dug into his pants pockets, pants held up by a belt but still the cuffs dangled to the floor, scraping at it. Kiff went over to the jukebox.

Tim slapped Will's arm. "What? He's going to play music?"

And sure enough the machine—normally quiet—kicked into life and the Beatles' "Help" thumped out of it.

"Oh, groan," Whalen said.

Kiff picked up his drink from Koko and swooped toward them, sending some of the Coke sloshing over the side.

And Kiff sat and licked at his hand.

"What's with the fucking music, Kiff?"

Kiff took another lick at his wrist.

"God!" Tim said in mock disgust.

Kiff reached out and squeezed Will's wrist, and then Tim's.

And that made Will think about some of the things he thought about Kiff. Some of the things the others said about him, half joking, when he wasn't there.

Will wondered just *how* strange Jim Kiff was.

Kiff grinned, feigning shrewdness. "I don't want anybody else to hear this, guys." His face looked serious all of a sudden. "*Anybody* . . ."

Kiff's face looked just too weird, like the guy in Dracula who gets to feed on bugs, overjoyed at discovering an errant moth.

Will turned and looked out the windows of the luncheonette. The sky had turned cloudy, thick with gunmetal-gray clouds. It might rain, he thought. Maybe I should get going, hit the subway, beat the storm.

But then Kiff began his story.

"I was at Scott's home for my advisor's meeting—"

Will nodded. Every senior met with one of the three advisors for college counseling, career guidance, and all that other bullshit. The lucky ones got Mr. Edward Scott. The others got somebody else.

"Hope you kept your fly zipped while you were there," Tim said, his voice louder than even John Lennon's wailing.

"Oh, fuck you, Hanna," Kiff came back.

In the great world of postpubescence, Will knew, everyone was suspected of being homosexual . . . especially a male teacher who lived alone.

"Anyway," Kiff said, struggling to regain the momentum of his story, "old Scott got drunk."

"What else is new?" Whalen said.

Kiff turned to Whalen. "He was plastered. You saw him. You were there just before me," Kiff said.

Whalen nodded.

"Get on with it, Kiff," Tim said. Will saw Mike Narrio look at his watch. Narrio's parents were Old World. Real garlic eaters, Tim joked snidely. And they liked their Michael *home*, doing homework, practicing his trumpet.

Will and his friends were doing their best to be the bad influence in his life.

"I mean, he was blotto, gang. I was pretty well wrecked too . . . Jeez, we were mixing sherry and brandy."

"He let you drink with him?"

"Sure, he was too far gone to care."

Whalen spoke again. "All right, so you had a few drinks with old Scott. Tell us something that we haven't all done."

Will looked at Whalen. Thinking: I've never had a drink with Scott. There was something about Scott that scared him. He might not be homosexual, but he was pretty damned eccentric.

Whenever Will spoke to Scott he thought: We're not in Kansas anymore, Toto.

"But that's just it, Whalen, my man. He passed out. Flat out in his living room, muttering garbage about William Blake and poetic realism and throwing the cup at the altar."

"Oh, no. Not *that* shit!" Tim said, laughing. He dug out another cigarette. Tim was loving this. This kind of event—people completely out of it—was Tim's element.

Except—except . . . Will didn't remember Tim ever being out of control.

"What shit?" Kiff said.

"Scott has this thing," Tim said. "The Church's teaching on yanking the crank—"

"Beating the meat," Whalen added, grinning.

Kiff looked lost.

"You see, Scott says that the Church is out to lunch, because it compares the onanistic act of spilling one's seed with dumping a chalice of consecrated blood onto the ground. Drives him nuts."

"I never heard him say that," Narrio said.

Tim shook his head. "Last year, Mikey. You were out of class that day. It must have been National Pizza Day."

Everyone, including Narrio, laughed.

"Yeah, well," Kiff said, trying to regain the floor. "He was out, gone. So I decided to nose around a bit."

"You what?" Will said.

Kiff turned to him and Will smelled Kiff's foul breath. The guy needed a refresher course on human hygiene. Coke, fries, the occasional Devil Dog. But was there any toothbrush action in the guy's routine? Will doubted it.

"I looked around his house. Why not? It's filled with books, papers, all sorts of neat stuff. A really great wine cellar."

"Jeez, you spied on him!" Whalen said.

"Right!" Kiff grinned. "And guess what I found!"

For a second, no one said anything. Because, Will figured, nobody had an idea.

"I got it," Tim said. "You found his mother, in a wheel-chair. All dried up . . . Norman," he added, laughing. "Norman, put me down!"

Will laughed, but he saw that Kiff wasn't enjoying this. His story wasn't getting him the respect he felt it deserved.

Kiff made a fist. "No, Tim. That's not what I found. I found a closet. And then, behind the closet, a fucking secret door!"

Tim raised his eyebrows.

And Will saw Whalen look up.

Narrio looked at his watch—quickly—then back to Kiff.

He had their interest *now*.

"Go on," Tim said.

"Yeah, a secret door right behind his little wine cellar. It looked ajar—as if he had just been there and had the door open, and was too fucking drunk to close it. I opened it. But I couldn't see too well. There was no light. But I reached in, and then I felt what was there."

Kiff waited, letting everyone hang there, blowing in the breeze.

Will thought he heard a rumble outside. Damn storm is coming, he thought. And I've got no raincoat, no umbrella . . . nothing.

The song on the jukebox changed. The Rolling Stones jumped in with "Get off My Cloud."

Seemed appropriate.

"My eyes got used to the dark. It smelled like hell in there. And I could just about make out that there were books, shelves of them . . ."

"And?" Tim said, licking his lips, smoke whispering out of his nostrils like a sleeping dragon.

"Tim, it was fucking unreal." Kiff looked to the others. "I pulled a few of the books out. And damn, he had something called *The Book of Enoch*. The fuckin' *Book of Enoch*. Do you know what the hell that is?"

Will expected everyone to shake their head no.

But Whalen nodded.

"Yeah? So? Big deal," Whalen said.

Kiff reared back. "What, Whalen? *The Book of Enoch*. How many copies are there in the whole world? Three, four?"

"So? He's a book collector," Whalen said.

Will couldn't wait anymore. "Would someone mind telling me what *The Book of Enoch* is?"

Kiff turned to Will, grabbed his arm. "Just one of the most ancient books of alchemy and occultism ever, Will, my boy. It's called the fucking Black Bible. Shit, it's still on the Vatican's top ten proscribed list."

"But can you dance to it?" Tim said.

No one laughed.

"And what else?" Will said.

"There was a lot of books. Some of the spines felt as if they'd crumble away in my hands. But I saw two more titles that I knew. Two more major books in the world of the occult—A-number-one tracts for the old dark forces."

"Shit," Tim said, "you sound like Father Williamson having one of his visionary attacks in the middle of mass."

"Don't laugh, Tim. These are *incredible* books." Kiff licked his lips. And Will—for the first time—was scared of Kiff.

He looked *gone* . . .

And where Kiff was, Will didn't want to follow.

"So what's the big deal?" Will asked, knowing just how unconvincing he sounded.

Mr. Kokovinis started over to their table.

Kiff—with eyes in the back of his head, apparently—shook his head to Will and started slurping at what was now an empty glass of soda.

"You-a boys want some more?" Koko said none too pleasantly. They always overstayed their welcome for the one soda they bought.

Kiff popped up. "Another round, barkeep," he said.

Koko shook his head and walked away.

"Hey, I gotta go," Narrio said.

Kiff shot out a hand and imprisoned Narrio.

And Kiff—crazy, wild—told him to wait. It sounded like an order. An order to them all to wait.

At least until he heard Kiff's plan.

And Will listened, thinking, What the hell does this have to do with me?

Not knowing that the answer to that question was *everything*.

5

Nobody had any Coca-Cola left by the time Kiff wrapped up his pitch. And Will watched Kiff sit back, just like a carnival huckster, to wait for the suckers to take the bait.

Kiff made his plan simple, so simple that it was hard to find a reason to say no. Mr. Scott has these books, he explained. And these books have ceremonies, rites, for doing things.

Cool stuff.

"So let's get one and try it," Kiff said.

The jukebox went quiet.

"How?" Tim said, dropping his cigarette butt into the dregs of the Coke.

Narrio leaned over to Will. "I gotta go. I should have left—"

Kiff's voice cut in, loud, pushing away Narrio's nervous squeaks.

"That's the great part," Kiff said, looking around as if Mr. Kokovinis might actually be interested in this nonsense.

And that's what it was, Will knew. Nonsense. The occult, the spirit world, black magic.

Cue *Twilight Zone* music, or maybe the even eerier wail that opened *One Step Beyond*.

Just bullshit, stuff to talk about on hot summer nights, hanging out on the corner. Looking at a yellow moon. UFOs. King Tut's curse. And is John Dillinger's prick really in the Smithsonian? Bullshit. That's all it was . . .

"Scott's rehearsing *Hamlet*. And"—Kiff fairly sputtered in excitement—"it will be a long rehearsal, until six, at least."

"Oh, Christ. I know where this is leading," Whalen groaned.

"What we do, guys, is go over there and"—Kiff took a breath—"break into Scott's apartment. I know how to do it and—"

Tim laughed. "Right. Breaking and entering. Just what I need on my records before I apply to Princeton. Right, Kiff. You got a *real* chance."

"No. Tim, Will—*guys*. It's no big deal. Scott's basement apartment has a back door. I saw the lock. It's a piece of cake."

"You notice those things, do you?" Whalen said.

"One of us can watch while another gets in. We won't even take the fucking book. We'll just copy down the instructions—"

"Yeah," Tim howled. "How to summon a demon. God!"

"I gotta go," Narrio said. And this time he pushed hard against Will.

Will stood up.

Maybe it *was* time to go.

"Wait a second," Kiff said. "We can *do* this. Test the forces of darkness," he said, grinning. Kiff slapped a fist into his hand. "Hell, we can do it this Friday, instead of going to the stupid dance."

That Friday was St. Jerry's monthly dance, and they usually all went, even though only Tim ever had a date, his steady. If he was to be believed, he was getting it regularly.

"Not go to the dance?" Will said. "And do what?"

Kiff stood up, his shabby trench coat flying around his body like a cape.

"We'll do the fucking ceremony. We'll try to summon a spirit." Kiff paused. "Or are you guys too punk?"

"Oh, yeah," Tim said. "I'm *terrified*. Absolutely frozen with fear, Kiff. Why the hell don't you—?"

"Then do it, Tim. You always have the big mouth, the big ideas. So let's do this."

Tim shook his head. Will thought he was going to say something. But he didn't.

There was a rumble outside. Then another. Will heard the tiny specks of rain hit the glass.

Kiff waited. Whalen lit another cigarette. Narrio picked up his book bag—the only one of them to actually use an official St. Jerome's book bag. Bags were strictly for douchy freshmen.

"All I need is someone to come with me now—to help me

get inside. Scott's out of the way. Then we can make plans for Friday." He paused again. "That's it."

"I suppose," Whalen said slowly, smiling, "that you can get us some Old Grand-Dad too . . . just in case your other spirits fail to materialize."

"Damn straight I can," Kiff said.

"I can't go with you," Tim said. "I have to go with my old lady to meet my old man in the city."

Will knew Tim was lying.

"I—I'll come Friday," Narrio said, "but I have to go now. My—" He walked to the door.

"That's okay," Kiff said sympathetically. Everyone *knew* that Narrio wasn't the right person for Kiff's plan.

Will and the others said goodbye to him as he hurried away.

The door to the luncheonette slammed . . . and then there were four.

"*I* sure as hell can't go with you," Whalen said. "If I don't catch the five o'clock train, I'm fucked."

Whalen was prisoner to the Long Island Railroad time tables. He lived somewhere out on the island. In a real big house. He had to catch the right train.

It was his convenient excuse.

Then—like a play, as if it were scripted—Kiff turned to Will.

And Will thought: Why didn't I see this coming? What the hell is wrong with me that I *didn't* see this screaming toward me from miles away?

"Will, can you come?"

Then all eyes were on Will.

Like before. When he was in the shower.

Will shook his head. "I really should go. I mean, there's the calc test tomorrow. And, shit, it's raining."

He watched their eyes, but they weren't buying any of his excuses. They saw right to the heart of the matter.

"Hey, c'mon, Will. You're the only one that *can* go." Kiff waited.

Will licked his lips. His throat felt dry and tight. "I—"

"C'mon," Kiff pleaded.

"Forget it," Whalen said.

A script. A play.

"Forget it, because he doesn't have the balls for it. Isn't that true, Dunnigan?"

Whalen looked right at him, his grin wide, a mouthful of teeth.

"Screw you, Whalen."

"Got—no—balls—" Whalen said again.

The rain came down a bit harder.

Will looked outside the window.

"Shit. There's time. You can still get home for dinner," Tim said. "Your parents don't give a shit . . ."

Will nodded.

"Maybe—if you're too scared—it's better you didn't do it," Whalen said.

Will looked at them.

"Okay," he said. "I'll do it."

Kiff slapped his hands together.

And before he knew what had happened, he and Kiff were outside, walking through the light rain, the heavy splats matting down his hair.

While the others—the sane ones, Will thought—were on their way home.

They started out walking, but once they were across Ocean Parkway, the rain turned nasty. The occasional spritz gave way to a steady downpour that Will's all-weather coat didn't do much against.

His hair was sopping and the rivulets ran off his nose.

"Couldn't we have done this tomorrow?" Will shouted through the curtain of water.

Kiff's long red hair was, for once, all going in the same direction. Right down his forehead, nearly covering his eyes.

"I don't know if Scott's rehearsing tomorrow," Kiff yelled back. "And that would just leave us Friday." He shook his head. "It has to be today."

Kiff reached out and tugged at Will's sleeve. "C'mon," he said.

Will hurried, but he pulled his cuff away. He didn't like being touched by Kiff. Kiff was okay in the group—barely—but one-on-one, he was an unpleasant experience. Too weird.

Maybe dangerous.

They passed the Ocean Theater. It was still showing *The Sound of Music*. The posters showed a giant Julie Andrews surrounded by a bunch of squeaky-clean kids.

Kiff ran ahead and stood under the marquee, getting protection from the rain.

"Damn, it's raining like hell," Kiff said.

Will pulled his books from out of his coat, checking to see how they were doing. There were times, he thought, when a book bag might be helpful.

"Stupid-ass movie," Kiff announced, looking at the poster. Will nodded.

"Did you see *Thunderball*?"

"Yeah," Will said. "That was—"

"Yeah, really great. That rocket pack? When Bond blasts off? Bitchin' movie . . ."

Will looked around. There was no sign that the downpour was letting up. Kiff lit a cigarette.

"I think we should get going," Will said. "It's getting late."

"Sure, Will . . . we'll keep going."

And like crazy people, Will thought, they ran off, splashing through the growing puddles that gathered in the cracks and curves of the sidewalk, running all the way to Flatbush Avenue.

And on, past a grungy candy store with a giant faded Breyer's ice cream sign, until they came to Carroll Street, lined with rows of neat brick homes.

Thick trees guarded each side of the road.

The leaves—still on the trees—sheltered them from the worst of the rain.

But now Will smelled the ground, the car oil brought to life by the sudden splash of water. The smell of garbage cans, empty but marked by years of messy spills, sitting in narrow alleyways leading back to tiny backyards.

"Okay," Will said, feeling better now that the incessant downpour was off his face. His shirt and his sport coat were soaked near the top, a ring of dampness that was creeping its way down.

Kiff came close—the small of his breath, the unhealthy look of his skin—much too close. "It's the sixth house down, Will. Now listen," he said, putting a hand on Will's shoulder.

Stop touching me, Will wanted to say.

"We walk down there, as if it's nothing. Scott always has students coming to see him, even ones that have gone on to college. Nobody will think anything. We'll turn down that corner, right to the back door."

"And then—?"

Kiff smiled. "Leave the rest to me."

Then he turned and led Will down the block. They passed the protection of one big maple tree. Fresh drops hit Will's face. And then on to the cover of another tree, until they came to—yes—the sixth building.

Jim Kiff took the turn into the alley as if he had done it a thousand times.

"Here we go," he whispered to Will.

Too many James Bond movies for the Kiffer, Will thought.

The alley was dark, almost black. The stale smell was strong here, overpowering. He heard noises. A TV blasting in the house to the left. The smell of food cooking. Garlic. Onions frying.

Then they came to the backyard.

"Just walk right up to the back door," Kiff hissed.

Will nodded.

There was a small patio in the back, and one chair. A statue, a fountain of some kind, stood surrounded by overgrown ivy. But one arm of the fat cherub statue was broken off, and the fountain listed to the left. It was speckled with black and moldy green.

Is this where old Mr. Scott comes out to do his reading? Grade his papers? Will wondered.

He turned back to the door.

"Get close," Kiff said angrily. "Somebody might look down. Block me—"

Will leaned over, watching Kiff. He held a piece of wire. A straightened paper clip, it looked like. Kiff kept fiddling with the lock. Then cursing. There'd be a hopeful click. And then Kiff would say *shit*, or *damn*, or any one of the other powerful words from his special litany.

"I thought you said that you *knew* how to do this."

"I do. Just shut the hell up."

Will shook his head. It was time to bail out of this afterschool activity.

A car went up Carroll Street. Slow, almost crawling, its engine just kind of lazily roaring up the block.

Just the way a cop car would do, Will thought.

Immediately he imagined the cop car. Moving slowly, maybe called by a suspicious neighbor, some old biddy who spent her day looking out her window for robbers and commies.

And then, as if to confirm his suspicion, he heard the car stop.

"Oh, shit, Kiff. There's somebody out there."

The car had stopped. Still Kiff fiddled with the lock, making it rattle hopefully. But nothing happened.

A window opened. Will heard it.

From a house down the road.

There, right there, Officer, Will imagined someone screaming.

Of course, the cop would shoot to kill.

"I'm splitting," he said.

But Kiff was too fast.

His hand shot out and grabbed Will's collar. Kiff was long, lean—the definition of "wiry." No one had guessed he was strong.

But now he was manic as hell and this thing, this crazy garbage that they were doing, obviously meant a lot to him.

"Don't—freak—" he said slowly.

"Hey, I've—"

"If you run out there now, and there *is* someone there, they'll fucking see you. Maybe it *is* a cop," Kiff said with an evil smile. "He'll nail your ass." He took a breath. "Besides, I almost got this."

Will nodded.

He looked back at the cherub in the garden.

Except, it wasn't a cherub.

No, its one intact arm had something up to its mouth. And there were these two bumpy ridges on its head. Sort of like horns. And then the legs—

A different sound sputtered from the lock.

"Got it!" Kiff said.

He twisted the door handle.

And the door opened. Creaked open, louder, louder than the rain spattering, louder than the car that sat on the street, its engine quiet now, clicking, cooling.

Kiff pushed the door wide open.

He stepped in.

And when Will didn't immediately follow—

When Will just *stood* there and watched—

Kiff, grinning from ear to ear, as he said, "We're in, Will."

And as much as he didn't want to, Will walked inside the basement apartment.

6

Kiff just stood there.

"What's wrong?" Will asked.

"Nothing. It's just—"

He heard Kiff breathing, and Will looked around. He saw they were in a tiny kitchen. There was a cereal bowl on the table, crusty with Cheerios. A coffee cup, with just a cold, filmy mouthful left. A small white stove and refrigerator. It felt damp down here.

"What is it?" Will said.

"I thought I heard something."

They both held their breath, and Will craned his neck, turning slowly from right to left.

Because if Kiff heard something—someone—then, boys and girls, we're not alone, Will thought. And if we're not alone, then we're in deep—

Screech.

They both heard the sound, and they both jumped into the air.

Before they saw the grayish blur zip across the cracked, yellow linoleum floor.

Screee-eeek, the mouse squeaked again, suddenly stymied by a wall that offered no hiding places, and it drunkenly darted back under the refrigerator.

Kiff laughed. "Just a goddamn mouse," he said. Then he nudged Will. "Shut the door. Everything's cool, Willy. Just fine."

Will gently pushed the door shut and heard it click closed with terrible finality.

"Let's do this fast," Will said.

Kiff nodded. "Right, sure." And Kiff walked out of the kitchen. "C'mon," he said.

Will followed him. They entered a dark passageway—too tiny to be called a hall—and then on into Scott's living room.

It was black, with just thin bars of gray light sneaking into the room from the windows.

"I can't see anything," Will whispered.

Kiff raised his hand. The old pro. Trying to steady the newcomer.

"Just keep cool, Will. Let your eyes get used to the darkness. We can't risk putting any lights on."

Will heard a sound coming from the front, from the stairs leading to the apartments upstairs. Kiff shot him a look. He raised his hand again, signaling him to stay still.

They waited and listened to the steps, labored, slow steps, plodding down toward them.

The footsteps stopped just outside Scott's door.

Will backed up.

Closer to the passageway. Closer to the kitchen.

If that door handle turns, I'm getting the hell out of here, he thought. As fast as I can.

But then he heard the creaking sound of a door being opened—the front door. And whoever it was—they were gone.

"Okay," Kiff said. "We're all set."

Will looked around, marveling at the wonderful clutter of Scott's room. There was a couch, more of a love seat. And an easy chair, a heavy, uncomfortable-looking thing with a high back. But mostly there were books.

They were *everywhere*. On the chairs. On the floor, scattered like crumbs from a giant's table. Stacked against the wall, leaning against the fireplace. And, of course, on the shelves that ran all the way around the room, leaving only space for the windows.

And papers too, scattered piles, probably Will's last paper on *Moby Dick*. Will could imagine the teacher sitting in this dark room, this temple of books, poring over papers while he poured himself another sherry, and—what?—railed against a fate that led him to devote his life to reading the scribblings of sophomoric sophomores.

There was, he felt, something unsettled about this room.

"Okay," Kiff whispered, "can you see okay?"

Will nodded.

"I'll tell you where the books are—and you can go get it, the big black book, while I keep watch."

Will turned sharply. "What do you mean?" he hissed. "What do you mean *I'll* go get it? Why the hell can't *you* get it and I'll keep watch?"

Kiff came close to him, his smell, the strangeness, all but overpowering in the tiny living room. "Because I know how to look out. Will, I've done this shit before and—"

"Oh, yeah. Where?"

Will figured Kiff was just arranging it so that he'd be closer to the door. And where will I be? he thought. In Scott's back room, rummaging through his stuff. Shit . . .

"Listen," Kiff said. "I can check the front and the back doors. I know which way Scott comes." He paused. "I can keep my head, Will. You go get the book."

Kiff's washed-out blue eyes glowed in the gloomy room.

And yeah, sure . . . Who knows? Will thought. Maybe Kiff's right. And the sooner I get the book and do this stupid thing, the sooner we're out of here.

"Damn. Okay. Tell me what to do."

Kiff pointed to the small door that led off the living room.

Is there fate? Will wondered. Or is it just my dumb luck that I ended up here, doing this?

Or was it in the cards all along?

Because this morning I sure as hell wouldn't have guessed that this is where I'd be at five o'clock.

He moved into Scott's bedroom.

And now he felt the creepiest. It was one thing to break into someone's house, to walk through their kitchen, their living room.

But their bedroom?

God, he could even smell Scott, the heavy cloistered smell of sheets that needed changing. A wineglass sitting on the end table, probably lined with a dry, reddish crust. There were no windows in this room. No light. Just the pitiful glow from the living room.

Kiff had said he couldn't turn on any lights.

Which means that I won't see shit, Will observed.

Everything was marked with shades of blackness.

It felt like a tomb.

Will rubbed his cheek. He looked around for the closet.

He heard something moving. But this time he didn't jump.

Old Scott needs a cat, a good mouser to clean up his apartment.

The mouse was there, out on the floor somewhere. Will heard the squeak.

"Okay," Will whispered to himself. "Where's the closet . . ."

He turned around.

And there it was, behind him.

As if it were waiting for him.

He almost laughed.

He went to the closet door, turned the handle, and pulled it open. The door squeaked and he stopped.

He had arranged a signal with Kiff. If Kiff saw anything, if they had to get their ass in gear and get the hell out of there, Kiff would whistle once.

But if Kiff whistled twice, it meant that something had happened, that it was already too late. Everyman for himself. Women and children overboard. Rich stockbrokers into the dinghies, and fuck the *Titanic*.

Will listened. But beyond the door's noisy sound, there was nothing.

He pulled the closet door open.

And the rows of wine bottles caught the small bit of gray light. Will could barely see the bottles, black, looking like rows of battleship guns, ready to fire.

He reached out and touched the bottles. He felt the dust gather at his fingers.

And the secret compartment, boys and girls—he thought— is right behind the bottles.

Somehow.

He let his fingers trail all around, looking for a way to move the wine cellar out of the way and expose the hidden treasure.

"Shit, Kiff," Will said at last, hissing loudly. "I can't see anything. And I sure as hell don't see how to get at your secret door. Are you sure you weren't imagining all that shit?"

He heard Kiff run back to him.

"Damn, Will. Can't you—?" Kiff ran his hands through the rows of bottles, feeling the edges, looking for some kind of latch or something.

Will stood back.

Time to make an exit, he thought.

"Where the hell—?" Kiff said. And then Will heard a rattle. And the rack of bottles moved, swinging out toward him. "There," Kiff said. "I've got to get back and watch. Just get the book!"

Kiff vanished.

It occurred to Will that the secret door was pretty well hidden. It wasn't, he thought, something that you could just *stumble* upon.

It was as if Scott had left it open that afternoon Kiff was with him.

And forgot to shut it.

Will pulled open the wine rack a bit more. The bottles rattled against their berths. Now there was a narrow entrance into the closet, with just enough room for him to squeeze in. He took a step.

Thinking: There's got to be a light in here.

And: Fuck Kiff. Fuck him. I'm turning it on.

He felt the wall, searching for a switch. He reached over his head. There was no string. But then, as his hand flailed at the air, he felt the beaded pull chain of a ceiling light.

He turned it on.

The bulb was brilliant, blinding.

"Will," Kiff hissed from outside. "Will, what the hell—?"

Screw you, Will thought.

Now he looked ahead. At the shelves, at the books in front of him. He reached out and touched them.

And he knew they were the oldest things he'd ever felt.

Some of the titles were so worn away that the raised letters were lost in the splintery leather bindings. A few books were encased in thick plastic, hermetically sealed against any more destruction.

It's just his collection, Will thought. A bachelor teacher's passion. Old books.

But then Will tilted his head and read some of the titles.

"Will! Shut the damn light off!" Kiff said.

Le Mystère des Cathédrales . . . De Occultus Philosophia . . . Gate of Remembrance.

Well, sure enough he's got *all* the classics here, Will thought. Where's *Ivanhoe* . . .

He saw a book called *Experiments in Time*. He noticed the author's name. T. W. Dunne.

Close to my name, he thought. Close to Dunnigan . . .

He pulled the book out.

And moving the book, pulling it from its place on the shelf, seemed to stir up the odors, the ancient smells of the books.

For a second Will didn't think he could breathe.

The smell was feral, the way an animal might smell.

After it has been sealed up in your closet for a decade or two.

But he kept pulling out the book. He opened it.

The pages were tissue thin. One page was filled with Greek. Another with Latin. A third with what looked like hieroglyphics . . . at least, he saw the telltale oblong circles of cartouches.

He turned the page and he heard it tear, a gentle sound, the paper was so thin . . . sere. And this page was in English.

"On the Manner of Displacements," the section was called.

He read a few words, forgetting for a moment his fear. This was amazing stuff, he thought. These books were strange, incredible.

And he wondered: How much damage did I just do by ripping that page? Is the book worth less now?

He read the first paragraph. It read like some long-winded preamble, something Thomas Paine might have written, working his way up to *Common Sense*.

Then, in the second paragraph, Will read an amazing statement.

"This work is constructed to aid the alchemist in his pursuit of that which the Lord of Light would deny us. For when the paths of time are open to us, there will be no gods."

Right, thought Will. Exactly my sentiments.

"Will!" Kiff hissed again.

Will started. Had Kiff whistled? Was someone coming? And then his fear was back. He felt surrounded by the bottles, the books, the twisted bed sheets of Scott, the smell of worn clothes strewn on the floor.

He closed the book and put it back.

He ran through the other titles until he came to a large black book. He found it on the bottom shelf.

Yeah, Kiff had called it *The Book of Enoch*. The Black Bible.

It wasn't nearly as ancient as some of the other books.

Will grabbed it, and he squirmed out of the narrow closet, shutting the light off as he left. He ran out to Kiff.

"Got it," he whispered.

Kiff was at the window, pushing the blinds out, leaning close to the pane.

"What the fuck were you doing in there?"

"It was interesting. He's got some really weird books—"

"Okay—you come here, watch through the window. I'll find the right page." Kiff turned to Will, and Will saw that he wasn't smiling anymore. His face was grim, worried.

It wasn't fun for Jim Kiff anymore. This was serious stuff now.

Will handed him the book and went to the window.

Kiff squatted on the floor. Will glanced at him and saw him take a piece of paper and pencil out of his pocket. Then Will went back to looking out the window.

He saw an old lady coming up the block dragging a small wagon filled with groceries.

Will paid no attention until she stopped and started coming up the steps to the stone house, to Scott's building.

"Someone's coming!"

Kiff got up and went beside Will. "It's probably just the old lady who lives upstairs," Kiff said. They both watched her drag her cart up the stone steps, slowly, struggling for every step. And then she disappeared, into the foyer. But they heard her now above them. The wheels of her cart squeaking, the sound of her feet moving on the wood floor.

Kiff put a finger to his lips.

They waited, listening to the rhythmic tattoo of the woman pulling her heavy load up the stairs.

"Okay," Kiff said.

He went back to his sketch. Will took a quick look at it.

He saw a star surrounded by a circle. And squiggly symbols outside and in the points. But he quickly looked back outside.

And saw someone else walking up the block.

A man, dressed in a raincoat, holding an umbrella. He wore a hat pulled down low.

Will couldn't be sure.

But . . .

The man came closer.

And then, shit, the man looked up a bit . . . nearing his house. His home, and—

Will knew it was Scott.

"It's Scott!" he said, not whispering. Will let the bent blind slap shut. "Oh, shit," he said.

But Kiff didn't move.

"Almost done, Will. Hang on . . . almost—"

Will danced away from the window. Jeez, he thought he'd piss, he was so scared.

He imagined where Scott was. On the bottom steps, right now! Maybe digging out his keys, walking down to the basement door. Getting close to the door.

"C'mon, Kiff, get the fucking book back. Get it back!"

Closing the umbrella. Opening the door to his apartment.

Screw it, Will thought. He turned to run.

And then, suddenly, Kiff, all gangly arms and legs, was up, his face still deadly serious.

This is all real for him Will saw. This is a real fucking thing for him.

Will backed into the kitchen. Thinking: I can get away. But if he gets Kiff and Kiff talks and—

I should have heard the front door open by now, he thought.

Kiff shot up.

"Got it," Kiff whispered, running into the bedroom to put the book back.

The front door should have opened, Will thought, reaching for the back door. Sure, because—

And then he knew that Scott wasn't coming in through the front door.

No.

He was coming around the back.

And I nearly went out there. I nearly ran right into him.

Kiff was out of the bedroom, running into the kitchen.

"No," Will said, pulling Kiff away. "He's coming this way."

And now they both ran, as fast as they could, to the front door.

Kiff turned the handle. He yanked the door open.

But a chain slapped it shut again.

Will reached up and undid the chain. And then it flew open.

He heard the back door open. He and Kiff slipped out the door.

Then—oh so gently—Kiff closed it behind them.

They stood there, listening a moment, as if to run outside would only get Scott's attention.

But then Kiff went out the front door of the brownstone building. He pulled up the collar of his trench coat.

Will did the same thing.

They went out, and up the steps from the basement apartment, running as fast as they could.

And with each giant step Will felt as if he were getting younger, regressing back to ten, then nine, then eight years old, when he and his friends would ring people's doorbells and then run away, laughing hysterically. As if that were the funniest thing in the world.

And this time, he did the same thing, laughing, and gasping for air, following Kiff, who was yelping, spinning around in the rain, screaming . . . now that they were a good block away.

"We did it, Will! We fucking did it!"

And Will laughed some more, feeling that yes, they certainly had done *something* . . .

7

By the time Will hit the subway, the IRT was filled with commuters, gray-faced, gray-suited men whose eyes darted left and right searching for a seat.

Will found a vacant strap in the cattle car and held on. His wet clothes dried tight to his skin.

But when he thought again of running from Scott's apartment, and Kiff waving his precious piece of paper around as if it were a map to a gold mine, he had to smile again.

It had been crazy . . . fun.

The stations roared by until, when he saw the Church Avenue platform, the train emptied a bit and he got a seat. He thought of his homework. He had at least three hours ahead. Maybe more.

Finally the train reached the end of the line.

His stop.

Flatbush Avenue.

The doors whished open. The subway cars gave out a great pneumatic sigh of relief.

And Will got up to walk the ten blocks to his house.

He had to use his key to get in the front door.

Mom started to keep it locked. Someone was robbed, she said. Only a few blocks away. She never had a name for the victim. No details. Just that—someone was robbed.

He didn't argue with her.

The hall light was off as he went up the stairs to the top floor of the two-family home. And he stepped carefully on the carpeted stairs, quietly, remembering what he had been warned about ever since his first steps.

Be careful of people's heads! his mother said.

Don't make so much noise for the people downstairs.

As a little kid he had imagined that the downstairs neighbors—
a nice, quiet, old couple with grown children—somehow had their
heads attached to the floor, the stairs. They felt every squeak,
every wild leap Will made.

His mom worried about that kind of thing.

She worried about lots of things.

At the top of the stairs he saw a crack of light escaping
from the kitchen. He pushed open the door.

His mother turned. She smiled. He felt that she forced her
smile. As if saying, I'm in terrible pain, but I'll smile for
you, sweetie. There you go . . .

"Hi, Mom," he said.

"Will," she said breathlessly, as if she were just about to
collapse. Catching her breath. Her hands were clenched in a
fist. They were always that way. She was just holding on. A
metaphor for her life. It's a white-knuckle flight, he thought.

"You're late, sweetie. What happened?"

"A debate meeting," he lied. It came easy.

At this point in his life he knew that his parents had no
real connection to his life. There were lots of things that they
had no reason to know.

They were in one world. And I'm in another.

At least, he hoped he was.

"Where's Dad?"

The woman's face fell. Noticeably, almost theatrically.

She nodded toward the living room, through another closed
door. "He's—he's in there. Watching TV."

Will put his books down on the table. He smelled spaghetti
sauce. That was good. Something Italian was in the offing.
That would go down well. He nodded to the living room too.
"Still no luck?" he asked.

She shook her head. And then, as if digging up some
strength from deep inside herself, she said, "Dinner will be
ready soon."

Will nodded. And, reluctantly, he walked in to see his
father.

The man sat in his chair, a faded easy chair perfectly po-
sitioned to see the color TV. They had bought the big RCA
set just three years ago. It was one of the first color sets on
the block. His father was so proud, even if some of the shows

did turn up with purple people and grass that glowed an unhealthy green.

That was way before he lost his job.

Before the Best Foods chain sold out to Western International. The new chain was based in Seattle.

And poof! He was out of a job.

It had been five months now.

"Dad . . ." Will said.

The TV was on. The man was there. But there was no light on.

"Oh. Will," he said, turning in his seat. The words came out slurred—just a bit—but enough to tell Will that today's edge had already been shaved off.

Then he heard his father's hand fiddling with the lamp, searching for the switch.

"Wait a second . . . where the hell—?"

The light came on. And Will saw him, unshaved, dressed in casual clothes that looked like a suit of defeat. Here was a man that belonged in a crisp suit, with his *Journal-American* tucked under his arm.

The shot glass on the lamp table still carried a glistening smear. The tracks weren't old.

He probably killed it before I came upstairs.

"How are you, son? How was school?"

Will smiled. "Great, Dad. Just super. Mom said it's almost dinner."

At the word "Mom" Will watched his father's face fall.

I wouldn't have wanted to be here today, Will knew. In fact, things might still get pretty bad tonight. A few more shots, a few funny faces from Mom, and it could be one of those nights.

Will looked over at the TV. The news was on. Color footage from Vietnam—wherever the hell that was.

A stupid police action. Some unlucky G.I.'s dodging bullets in a rice paddy.

And that's the top news story? Will thought.

He looked back to his father. "C'mon, Dad. C'mon, let's eat."

And Will was tempted to go over and help his father up.

* * *

The next day, the subways ran slow and Will got to school late—missing everyone at the luncheonette.

So it wasn't until just before physical science, with Father Ouskoop, that he heard Tim's idea.

"If I'm going to give up getting laid," he said to Will, "then *I* want to pick the place where we try this horseshit."

"You saw Kiff's sketch?" Will asked.

Tim screwed up his face. "Yeah. It looks like something my kid brother would draw. It has to be a pretty retarded spirit that would respond to that invitation." Then, as they walked into the classroom, Tim leaned close. "But what the hell. Kiff can get some booze and we'll get loaded."

Will smiled.

They found seats together.

"And I've got the perfect place. You won't believe it."

"Yeah?" Will said.

The classroom was constructed like an amphitheater. The seats curved around the lecture platform where Ouskoop displayed the wonders of the world of science, without even a hint of the showmanship of Mr. Wizard. Mostly, Ouskoop scrawled incomprehensible equations on a blackboard. It was definitely grade-B science. It was a known fact the St. Jerry's kids didn't do so well at science and technical schools. Too much religious mumbo jumbo, not enough test tubes.

But Will was going to try—that spring—by applying to MIT.

Ouskoop waited for the class to settle down.

Will plopped down and Tim sat next to him.

"Where?" Will said.

Tim turned, shielding his mouth with his hand, about to answer.

But Ouskoop, despite glasses with Coke-bottle lenses, quickly spotted Tim talking.

"Mr. Hanna," the science teacher called out in a whiney, singsong voice, "I think you'll get more out of this class if you find another seat—away from Mr. Dunnigan."

Ouskoop grinned.

"Groan," Tim whispered. He got up and moved away from Will.

"There," Ouskoop said. "Now, we are attempting to deal

with the problem of inertia. Does anybody remember the first law of thermodynamics?''

And Will started taking notes on the laws of the universe, instead of wondering about where Tim planned to have their séance, or summoning, or beer blast, or whatever the hell it was going to be.

Ouskoop went quickly, too fast for Will to understand what he was talking about. The teacher flew right past the second law of thermodynamics, erasing sketches from the board that Will had only half copied. Nothing stopped the mad professor-priest.

Nothing, that is, until he spotted something odd—at the back of the room.

Will barely noticed that Ouskoop had stopped lecturing, so fast was he scribbling notes.

Ouskoop just stood there, down below, in the arena.

His bald head had just a few wispy strands of hair that were uncombed, as if unnoticed. Ouskoop grinned some more and pushed his thick glasses back on his nose.

By now nearly everyone knew that the priest had stopped teaching. And Will looked back in the direction Ouskoop was studying.

And Will could easily see who he was looking at.

Jim Kiff was in the last row, near the corner of the room where the top row curved to the door. He was out of the way, almost out of sight, slumped down in his chair. And Kiff had his physical science book open wide in front of him.

As if it were the best damnedest thing he'd ever read.

Ouskoop didn't say anything.

Someone hissed in Kiff's direction. A few kids laughed and Ouskoop looked around at them, as if saying: It's okay to laugh.

This *is* funny.

Until finally, like a sub coming up for air, Kiff looked up, his eyes just peering over the edge of his book.

Then he looked left and right, as if wondering what everyone was doing looking at him.

''Mr. Kiff,'' Ouskoop sang out.

Tim looked over at Will. His face mouthed the words: What the fuck is going on?

Will shrugged.

But he guessed whatever it was, it probably wasn't good.

Kiff started to sit up straight in his chair. He started to close his science book. But it didn't seem to want to close.

"Mr. Kiff . . . you seem terribly engrossed in what you're reading back there."

A few more laughs in the class.

Ouskoop looked around at his audience. He took a step off his platform heading toward the bleachers.

"I wonder if you wouldn't mind sharing whatever wonderful thing you're reading there?"

Kiff sat up.

He cleared his throat.

"Well, Mr. Kiff, would you?"

Kiff cleared his throat again. "No, Father," he said.

Everyone laughed. Except, this time, Ouskoop. "What do you mean, 'No, Father'?" Ouskoop took another step. He placed a foot on the first step leading up. "It wasn't a request, Kiff. What are you reading"—a bit of grin returned—"up there?"

Will looked left and right, knowing that nearly everyone was enjoying this, grateful that Kiff had derailed Ouskoop's train of thought. Already this had been good for a solid five minutes of wasted time. And it was still going strong.

Except Will was surprised to see that he felt worried for Kiff.

After yesterday, Will knew that Kiff didn't work the way normal people did. As Tim might say, Kiff just didn't give a fuck.

So why should I give a damn? he wondered.

"Mr. Kiff, I will come up there and *take* whatever it is you're hiding behind your science book. Now—what is it you're reading?"

And Ouskoop started up the steps slowly.

Shoot-out at Black Gulch.

And Will knew who'd win. In this place, such competitions weren't even close.

"Er, Father," Kiff said, with an altar-boy politeness that sounded completely out of character. "I was reading a novel."

Kiff had closed the science book, and Will thought he saw Kiff slide something onto his lap.

Ouskoop kept moving up the steps.

"Well, I'd like to see that novel anyway, Mr. Kiff."

Kiff looked around.

As if he were searching for a fire escape.

Kiff sniffed the air. Rubbed his red hair, redistributing the fiery-red strands in yet another random manner.

"Hand it over, Kiff," Ouskoop said, his voice hard, demanding.

You don't screw with the Jesuits, Will thought. These soldiers of Christ were trained in the Inquisition.

Kiff looked real uncomfortable.

His face was beet red. His freckles vanished, lost in the glow.

Tim turned to Will and leaned across a bank of seats.

"He's dead meat!" Tim hissed.

"Hand it!" Ouskoop said, no longer the slightly dotty and discombobulated teacher. "Now!"

Kiff took a big breath. And then pulled the book slowly from his lap. His face, if anything, turned redder.

Will saw a black cover. And swirling letters. But he was too far away to make out the name of the book.

But that was no problem.

Not at all.

Because Ouskoop read out the name of the book aloud.

"Fanny Hill," he said, as if it were just another discovery of Newton's.

(And Will wondered: Were John Cleland and Newton contemporaries? Maybe old Isaac had a copy of *Fanny* sitting on his bedside table.)

Then, with a great flourish, Ouskoop read the subtitle.

Perhaps he's not familiar with the work, Will thought.

"Memoirs of a Woman of Pleasure." Osukoop read it slowly, almost poetically. And the voice, the words, hung there. Filling the room, echoing off the walls. Nobody was laughing.

Ouskoop was real pissed.

Even Will sat up in his seat.

Ouskoop looked at the book. He actually thumbed through some pages.

Be careful, Padre, Will thought.

And then the priest looked back at Kiff while smacking the book into his palm.

"Mr. Kiff. Report to the headmaster's office." Ouskoop looked down at the book. "And bring this trash with you." The teacher took the last few steps between him and Kiff. "Bring this," he said, smacking the book on top of Kiff's head, "and tell—" Smack. "Him." Smack. "What."

How many words left in this sentence? Will thought, wincing.

"You. Were. Doing."

The last word got an especially big whack.

Will thought he saw a tiny wet spot glistening in the corner of Kiff's eye.

Maybe he's hurt, Will thought. Or maybe he's just scared.

Will imagined that the school didn't look kindly on those who read pornography during class.

Ouskoop threw the book at Kiff, who tried to catch it. But it slipped away, flying past him, tumbling to the floor. Kiff crouched to get it, and one of the jocks—with a big shit-eating grin on his face—handed it to him.

"Now, Kiff. Get going," Ouskoop said.

Kiff stood up. And, Victorian erotica in hand, he trooped past Ouskoop, looking straight ahead.

Color-coordinated for the first time, his red face matching his red hair.

"Now," Ouskoop said, still on the steps, turning back to his blackboard. "I believe we were looking at the conversion of energy . . ."

And without missing a beat, the class was back in the wonderful world of force and mass and acceleration.

Showtime was over.

When Kiff didn't surface at lunch, Will's worst fears were confirmed.

"They're going to fucking suspend him," Tim pronounced. "You can't do that in class and get away with it."

Today's luncheon menu included a choice of ravioli and green salad, or cheeseburger and french fries. By the time you got to be a senior, you knew better than to take the ravioli.

"Suspend him? Are you sure?" Will asked.

"What else are they going to do? Give him detention? Keep him in for lunch?" Tim shook his head. "No way. He's gone for a week at least."

"What about tomorrow?" Mike Narrio said, pushing aside his half-chewed burger and eating his fries and ketchup.

"That will be no problem." Tim pulled open three ketchup packets and used them to completely cover his gummy cheeseburger and the fries until the platter looked like a crime scene. "I'll call him tonight. Tell him where we'll meet." He looked up at everybody. "No problem."

Will's mouth was full. The burger and bun offered an overwhelming dryness. They quickly soaked up whatever saliva there was and then only a quick mouthwash with Coke could force the food down.

It was a cheap meal. But it was nearly inedible.

Whalen came over, mugging at his tray.

"I can't believe they give us this shit three times a week," he said.

Will waited.

Whalen had goaded him into going with Kiff the other day, and he wondered if Whalen would say something about it. Like "Nice going." Or, "Shit, you *do* have balls."

But all Whalen did was make a disgusted face at his burger.

"Tim thinks that Kiff's getting suspended," Narrio said to him.

"Serves the asshole right," Whalen said. "You know," he said, between chews, "it would be funny, *if* he hadn't been caught. Anyway, we're still on for tomorrow?"

"Sure," Tim said. "And I've got the greatest place. We can booze it up and no one will see us."

Will felt someone watching him then. He felt eyes on his back . . . like when you're in a car and you know someone's watching you. He turned.

He saw a table off near the back. D'Angelo and his friends. Laughing.

He saw D'Angelo looking right over at him, and Will turned his head back.

He still wants a piece of me, Will thought. What the hell did I ever do to him that he wants to screw up my life so badly?

"A good place?" Whalen said, chomping down. "And where's that?"

Will looked at Tim as he leaned close to them.

Tim didn't say anything.

But he grinned. And then he flipped open his notebook.

He always did have a taste for the dramatic . . .

And there—in big block letters—were two words.

Manhattan Beach.

Will shook his head.

Thinking: Now, where the hell is Manhattan Beach?

So he asked Tim.

And Tim told him . . .

11:35

8

God, was *that* the sound? Will thought, sitting in the rental car.

The bag had been repacked, neatly, tightly, then latched shut.

He listened, hearing the swirl of horns and engines outside.

Am I hearing it here? he thought.

That clicking sound. Just like—

But then he knew he wasn't. It's just the clicking of the traffic light, that's all, suddenly clear in the silence, as the streets began to empty, and the night people took over.

The corner just across Madison Avenue was *filled* with hookers now, stepping around in their heels like skitterish colts. Like any herd, a few checked for danger, leaning out into the street, searching for a blue and white cop car.

And if a cop car was spotted, they scattered, like roaches startled by a light flashing on in a tenement kitchen, interrupting their late night feast.

They'd vanish.

Some of the hookers would crouch behind cars. Some walked down Madison Avenue. Just out for a stroll. Others brazenly crossed the street as though they were housewives hurrying home to a nice dinner with hubby.

The cops couldn't be bothered with the hookers.

But he knew they'd noticed him.

These were strange days in Manhattan.

And the cops were on the lookout. Not for whores.

But for guys like me, Will thought.

Already a cop car passed him, slowing a bit, but then taking the turn at Madison for the rest of its loop. But then another car came—or maybe the same one came back. And this time it stopped beside Will's car.

He kept looking straight ahead.

He thought that they'd get out.

Shine a flashlight inside his car. In the backseat. The front. They'd see his bag. And they'd think it was suspicious enough to make him get out . . . yeah, to search the car.

But then the patrol car pulled away . . .

Now Will licked his lips. He heard the damned clicking again and it startled him. He grabbed the steering wheel.

I'm not cut out for this, he thought. I don't have—

He looked up to check the rearview mirror. The cars at Fifth Avenue were stopped at a long stoplight, a light that took forever to change.

And amid the bright headlights, Will was sure he saw the outline of a cop car. The little glass dome on top . . .

Maybe the same cop car.

And this time they'll pull over, he knew. This time they had to.

Even with all the cops doing overtime. With all the crazy, sick headlines

The *Daily News* headline . . . just two words this morning. *Horror City.*

Horror City, Will thought. Got that right, boys. Fucking-A, you got *that* right.

Yes, even with all the cops pulling double shifts, the reduced, tax-starved police force was spread thin.

Will guessed it was only ten to fifteen minutes between loops by the cop cars. But that time could be an eternity.

That time could last forever.

And the cops were smart. They weren't going to get out of their car unless they absolutely had to.

The light changed.

And Will made his decision.

I can't stay here. I've got to get out.

He fumbled for the door handle on the driver's side. But he stopped himself.

They'll see that, he thought. They'll see it pop open. See me get out. They'll remember that I had been sitting there. And they'll see my little black bag.

He hurriedly slid over to the passenger seat, popped open

the door, and crawled out of the compact car. He pulled the bag behind him, catching it in the door latch. But he yanked it hard and then slammed the door shut.

He took a breath.

The cars were coming down the block. Some of them just horny men, the cruisers moving up to the pussy take-out window next to the bank.

And what disease would you like, sir?

He walked to the corner and turned right.

Keep walking, he thought. Just keep moving.

And all the time he felt the cops watching. He knew that they just had to be digging out their guns, calling up for reinforcements. They were ready to haul his ass into the 27th Street station, only blocks away.

And then he told himself:

Quiet. You're just feeling paranoid. Remember paranoia? Remember smoking dope in college? Remember buying a suitcase filled with amphetamines from some country pharmacist and driving down the Northway in the middle of the night—

Thinking that every state trooper in the world was watching you.

Remember paranoia?

More steps. Keep walking.

That's all this is.

They're too busy to worry about you.

Horror City. Remember?

And by the time Will reached the corner his breathing was almost normal. He shifted the bag from one hand to another while he paused at the corner.

It felt so light in his hands, so powerless.

He heard a sound to his right. A rustle of paper. A guttural noise. He turned. Somebody was at the corner, backed up into one of the recesses of the office building. Another rustle and Will saw a brown bag rise up, out of the indentation. Catching the light.

Somebody enjoying a nightcap.

Will looked back, trying to decide where to go.

Because he knew it was much too early.

He had hoped he'd be able to just sit in the car. Safe and

comfortable. Sit and wait. Now he was out on the streets.
And the streets were not a friendly place.

He looked left and decided to cross Madison. I'll make
my way down to Park Avenue, he thought. It's well lit . . .
lot of traffic, a lot of yuppies making the run up from SoHo
to the First Avenue bars.

But as soon as he started down the block, he wondered
whether this was such a good idea.

There were no stores, nothing open on this block until the
corner. Just warehouses, and dark façades zippered with metal
riot shields.

He heard every step he made.

Cars in the distance.

The creaking of the leather bag as it swung back and forth,
back—

Halfway down he felt lost. Park Avenue was a million miles
away, and he had just passed the point of no return.

More steps. More creaks.

And then another sound.

Just behind him . . .

He stopped.

So much like a movie, Will thought.

Wondering, at the same moment, why am I sweating? Why
do I feel all itchy and sweaty when it's cold out? Damn cold.

He listened.

Thinking: I fucked up. I let myself get spooked and now
I'm out there and I'm the one being followed, I'm the one
being tracked . . .

Will turned.

Half expecting a big leering face to be there, right in front
of him, to go: Boo! Looking for someone?

I've got my knife. Want to play mumblety-peg? And *I* go
first.

No one would see me here, Will thought.

It could all be over so fast.

He looked . . . and there was no one behind him.

"Shit," he said. He stayed there. A car went by, a big
purple car, some Impala or Buick that was an easy dozen
years old. Blasting music, thumping, pounding sounds that
made Doppler-like shifts as the car screamed by, the Spanish
rhythm rising, swelling, then trailing away in the distance.

But no one's following me, he thought.

No one.

So get a fucking grip on it and start walking.

He turned around, facing Park Avenue again.

He shifted the bag to his other hand.

The stuff inside shifted.

He fought to get his breathing under control. Nice and steady does it, he thought. One breath after another. Just take it easy. That's all. That's—

Wait.

Oh, I heard something then, he thought. Oh, yeah, I damn well *know* I heard something.

He kept walking. Park Avenue was only a bit closer now, still miles away.

I could run, he thought. Tear off down the block and—

He turned and looked over his shoulder again.

He wished he hadn't done that.

Because this time someone was there.

Someone not too far away.

And Will—

Still walking, still putting one foot in front of the other, wondered:

Where did he come from? When I looked before, no one was there. And now.

Will moved faster, not yet running, but picking up speed. Running was the wrong thing to do. He thought of a gazelle, cautiously stepping away from a cheetah, slowly, knowing that if it ran it would be all over.

He looked back again.

And he fell. Something tripped him.

His knees slammed hard onto the sidewalk.

His hands splayed out to break his fall, landing in something wet. He hoped it was water. Maybe some rain.

Except it hadn't rained in a week.

It felt oily, greasy. He turned.

The man was running toward him.

A lean, dark shape. A skullcap pulled low on his forehead. His sneakers white, too white, catching the light.

I could get the gun, Will thought. I've got a few seconds. I could pop the latch and get the gun. That's why I brought it.

But as Will got up on his knees—both of them throbbing from the pain—and stood up, he knew he wouldn't have time.

"Yo, man," the voice called out. "You okay?"

Up, and then Will started running.

"Hey, I gotta ask you something."

Pumping now, and Will wished he'd kept jogging in the morning. I used to have wind when I jogged, he thought. Wind and stamina and my heart was probably in real good shape. I haven't run for years now.

"Hey, man!" The voice screamed, real close now, gaining nicely on Will.

I'll never make it, he thought.

"I said wait a fuckin' minute, I got somethin'—"

But then the corner was nearly there. And at the corner, there was a light.

It was someplace, a store, something open.

Will looked at the sign.

Chock Full o'Nuts.

A coffee shop.

Please be open, he begged.

"Hey!"

Will reached the door.

A black waitress, oversized and wearing a tiny starched orange cap that was much too small for her great tuft of black hair, looked up.

The door didn't open.

It's fucking closed, Will thought. But then—amazingly—the doorknob turned.

It wasn't closed at all.

And he stepped in, pushing the door behind him.

He heard music on the radio. Not too loud, but it was there, amid the overpowering smell of coffee and hot dogs turning on a rolling grill.

Will stood there.

The woman looked scared.

"I think—" he said. "I mean, there's someone—"

He turned and looked out the window.

There was no one there.

"I—" he said to the glass.

"Can I help you, sir?" the waitress said nervously.

Will turned back to her. It had to be near closing time.

She must get a lot of strange customers, even here, at the corner of Park and—

What street am I on? That would be important to know. To figure out how long I can stay here . . . hide here . . .

If I can stay here.

"Can I help you, mister?" the waitress said, a nasty edge creeping into her voice. " 'Cause if you don't want to order something, then you gotta leave. No loitering allowed. And we don't have any public rest rooms so—"

Will took a step. All the stools—red-topped, looking like giant mushrooms—were empty. He took the closest one and sat down.

"Coffee, please. And—"

Will looked around. What else could he order? What would sound normal?

He saw just a few hot dogs, brownish orange, shriveled, turning on the silvery grill. And small cakes, wrapped in plastic, but sitting under a plastic dome just the same.

"A hot dog," he said.

The woman nodded. She pulled up an odd bun. More like a slice of bread folded into a U shape. She fitted it into a cardboard holder. She forked one of the hot dogs and then pulled it off the fork with the bun.

She placed it in front of him.

Then the waitress poured some dark coffee into a heavy orange cup. She placed the cup in front of him and then balanced a spoon across it, a metal bridge from one side of the cup to the other.

He nodded.

"Thank you."

He reached for the spoon.

And the waitress backed up a step.

"Hey, are you all right?" she asked. "What happened to you?"

Will looked up. "What? What do you mean?"

He stirred the coffee, and the smoky swirls streamed left and right.

"Your hand," she said. "It sure looks like you did something to your hand."

What is she talking about? Will wondered.

Then he let go of the spoon and looked at his hand.

It was red.

Covered with a thick red smear. As if someone had painted it.

He opened it and closed it. Some of the smear cracked. Peeled. Flaked.

It's blood, he thought.

The wet spot . . . on the ground.

I landed in a little puddle of blood.

He looked up at the waitress.

"Can I—can I wash up? I—"

She looked about to say no. Get the hell out of here. Nobody liked blood these days. Blood no longer just meant that something bad had happened.

Now it meant that something bad could still happen.

But then she nodded. And she pointed to a stainless-steel sink near the back wall.

And Will got up and walked over to it.

Later, when his coffee was gone and he'd chewed up his hot dog as much as he was going to, the waitress said, "I have to close up."

A car was outside. A man waited outside. The woman's husband, she explained.

Just in case he got any ideas . . .

Will nodded.

He dug into his back pocket. He put down five dollars.

Cheap at twice the price, he thought.

Got to get a grip on it, he thought. Can't get freaked again. Can't—

"Thanks," he said. "Thanks a lot."

And he pushed open the door and walked out . . . thinking:

This has got to look like that Hopper painting. The lonely coffee shop where it's always the Hour of the Wolf.

He went out the door.

The woman's husband watched him carefully.

Will smiled.

And then he turned left, onto Park Avenue.

And when he got to the corner, he looked at his watch.

Midnight.

It's time, boys and girls.

He thought of Becca. The kids. Sleeping, so distant from all this. As though they were living in another world.

And Joshua James, he thought, sitting with his family, inside my house . . . and what—

Praying? Reading? Thinking? Sleeping?

Watching Johnny Carson sputter through another monologue . . .

Will walked. He passed a card and gift store. Party Time Gifts. The window was filled with Halloween stuff. Witches on crepe-paper broomsticks and articulated skeletons that could hang on your door. Little ghost candles.

Halloween has gotten big, Will thought.

Too big, if Dr. James was to be believed.

Too fucking big.

And Will stopped a second.

There was a clown face in the window. A big toothy grin and giant pie-plate eyes. And the lips making a big "Ooooh."

Weird.

But not as weird as the grinning rigor-mortis face of Steeplechase, he thought. An amusement park . . .

Steeplechase. The Funny Place.

And as much as he didn't want to, as much as he knew it wouldn't be good to think about it, not now, not here—

He did.

Because now it seemed as though it happened yesterday.

Funny idea, that.

When, in actuality, it was still happening . . .

Friday

9

Friday took forever.

It was the day favored by the teachers for their quizzes. The regularly scheduled Latin quiz vied for attention with a bimonthly full-blown calculus test, a real mother . . .

And Father Ouskoop—perhaps in retaliation for Kiff's leisure time reading—dished up a pop quiz.

Dubbed a jap quiz, in memory of Pearl Harbor.

Before lunch, during study hall, Tim passed Will an atlas. A pencil was stuck into the oversized book marking a page showing the coastline of Brooklyn. And there, circled right at the edge, was a place called Manhattan Beach.

Manhattan Beach was right next to Brighton Beach—a place that conjured up images of bathhouses and apartment buildings. And right next to *that* was Coney Island, on a spit of land that clearly was really once an island.

Good, Will thought. So now I know where Manhattan Beach is . . .

Will nodded and passed the atlas back to Tim.

Was the adventure still on? he wondered.

Because Jim Kiff was nowhere in sight . . .

Will got the story on Kiff as he went down to lunch.

"A full fucking suspension," Tim said, whispering in the stairs lest some back-robed spy would swoop down and visit the wrath of St. Jerry's on them. "He's really done it this time."

"What a crazy moron," Will said.

Their steps echoed in the stairwell. The cafeteria clattered open below them and Will heard the swell of voices, the banging sound of bowls being scraped and dumped, and the dull clink of cheap silverware. The greedy torn wrappers of dozens of Devil Dogs. "So what about this afternoon?"

"No problem," Tim said. "I spoke to him and he's all set. Kiff's going to meet us at West End Avenue, near the subway stop." Tim leaned close to Will as they both neared the food line.

"We'll score some bourbon and then head out there."

"Great," Will said, smiling.

But somehow—looking around, seeing the goofy signs about tonight's dance—he wished he were gong there. Kiff's plan had sounded like fun. A crazy adventure, the kind of thing you should do when you're finally a senior. But now . . . well, he'd just as soon go to the dumb dance.

That won't get me suspended, he thought.

And down deep—admit it, he thought.

You're scared.

He picked up a plate of fillet of something, and a side dish of shoestring fries that tasted like real shoestrings. Then he and Tim searched for Whalen and Narrio.

Will spotted them, at a back table, well away from everyone else.

Whalen didn't look happy. He was leaning forward, talking at Narrio, who kept slipping fries into his face.

One at a time. Nice and methodical . . .

"Looks like problems," Will said.

They walked over to the table.

And Will turned to see if anyone was watching him.

They're always watching, he thought. The fucking jocks . . . Or is it all just in my head?

He looked around. He heard laughing. But no one seemed to be looking at him. Will shook his head. Gately stood near a side door, a wooden Indian. His long face was drawn and pinched and his massive arms were folded in front. He spent the lunch hour scowling at everyone.

Will got to the table.

Whalen looked up at Tim, then at him. "Shit. Narrio says he's not going," Whalen said disgustedly. "He says he has to go home."

Tim did a wonderfully dramatic double take. Will saw Tim's eyes go wide in horror. He pushed his glasses up, off his nose. His mouth opened—too stunned to speak.

Then Tim sat down in the seat next to Narrio and pulled it close.

Mike Narrio went on shoveling the fries into his food hole. But he was getting down to the last Indians . . .

"What!" Tim said, the horror thrillingly real.

Will—almost relieved, thinking that *now* the trip would be called off—saw Whalen look over. But Whalen wasn't grinning at the scene.

He looked genuinely pissed.

"What's the deal, Mike?" Tim said to Narrio. "It's all arranged. Kiff is going to meet us. No problem. We'll get some booze." Tim leaned forward and then he stuck his moonlike face right in front of Narrio. "And we'll summon the spirit of Boris Karloff to join us for a late night swim."

Narrio grinned.

He never said much. And he wasn't breaking stride today.

"He's a pussy," Whalen whispered disgustedly, taking a quick look to see where Gately was posted. But they were safely out of earshot of anyone. "A real mama's boy," Whalen sang.

That was probably true enough, Will thought. But he didn't like to see Tim and Whalen ganging up on Narrio.

And he saw Narrio's face change. His square face was usually so open, so complacent. Now Will saw the face visibly darken.

"It's time to cut the fuckin' apron strings, Narrio," Whalen went on.

Will saw Narrio clench his fists. He was a squat, compact guy, with chunky hands that probably had more strength than baby fat.

Narrio wasn't smiling anymore.

And Will thought: He's doing the same thing . . . Whalen's doing the same thing to Narrio that he did to me.

Pushing. Goading. And Will knew that Whalen was someone to watch out for.

A guy like that could be dangerous.

Looking over the cliff edge . . .

Go ahead. You jump first.

"Forget it, Whalen," Will said. "Ease up. If Narrio

doesn't want to come, he doesn't have to." Will hesitated. "Maybe we should all bag it."

Tim spun around. "Hey, Will, don't you cop out." Tim grabbed his arm. "It's all planned." And now closer, planting his grinning face in front of Will's. "I gave up getting *laid* to go with you guys tonight."

"Sure, right." Will laughed.

"Fucking pussy," Whalen whispered to Narrio.

Narrio stood up.

Ready to move.

As though he were going to jump right over the table, grab Whalen's tie, and drag him across the table.

A new side of Mike Narrio.

"Hey, forget it, Whalen," Will said. "Just ease up, will you—?"

"And now you're punking out too?"

Will shook his head. "No, it's just—"

But Tim was between them, and for all of Whalen's taunts, Will knew that only Tim could get the trip back on the road again.

"Hey, Mikey," Tim said, his voice low, thoughtful. There was a good reason Tim was a New York State Champion debater. "C'mon. We're fucking seniors, and winter's coming, and all we'll have are the stupid dances and playing cards in Whalen's basement. And do you know how warm it is out? It's going to be great tonight. Warm, like"—he leaned close, grinning—"goddamn summer."

Tim held Narrio's arm.

He'll be great in the courtroom, Will thought.

Yes, ladies and gentlemen of the jury, even though my client *did* murder a half dozen people, he has recently seen the error of his ways . . .

And Narrio looked over and nodded.

"Okay," Narrio said. "I'll come. I just don't want to get home too late."

Whalen made a disgusted noise.

And Will wondered . . . just what the hell are we in for tonight?

As Cicero might have scribbled: The augurs are not good.

But Will didn't know the half of it . . .

* * *

They flew out of school, trench coats open, ties loosened, unbridled, grinning and laughing as they made their way to Ocean Parkway and the subway.

They took the steps down to the underground tunnel two and three at a time.

Everybody was up now, Will saw. Everyone was excited. There were no problems. Even Whalen seemed to have lost his snarl.

A few people waiting on the platform looked at them. A black woman clutched her bag of groceries tighter. An old man stirred on his plastic seat.

The woman in the token booth didn't grin when Whalen said something to her, something that had him doubling up with laughter.

Tim came over to him. "What the hell did you say?"

Whalen leaned against a metal girder, right on a Chiclets machine. "I asked her if she got to ride the train for free."

"Pretty hilarious," Will said, rolling his eyes.

But Whalen was still laughing, and then they all were, filled with the giddiness of the moment. Freedom, that's what this is, Will thought. School is out, and the great weekend yawns ahead. And not only that! No, tonight there will be mystery, magic, the powerful elixir of booze.

And by Monday they'd all have tales to tell.

Something to keep them going while they plodded through the drudgery of more tests, more quizzes, more questions about college, the future—

What the hell.

Tonight existed apart from all that.

"It's coming," Narrio said.

Will heard the distant rumble of the train. He stepped to the edge of the platform. He didn't see anything. He just heard the low roar, an underground rocket coming at them from miles away.

Then, yes, the two white lights.

He spun around. The station lights at the other end switched from red to green. It reminded him of that scene in *King Kong* where Kong watches an elevated subway race at him, reminding the big ape of the prehistoric horrors he battled on Skull Island.

And then the metal monster was there, amazingly able to stop at the station from its bulletlike trajectory.

They waited a few seconds for the doors to whoosh open.

And then they tumbled into the car.

It was one of the old cars, with wicker seats and straps that felt like porcelain. The rectangular placards above the lights offered career training in refrigerator maintenance and the opportunity to learn something called Speedwriting.

U cn lrn hw to rd n rt lk ths!

Will looked at his friends. There were plenty of empty seats, but they stood there, grinning. Tim hit Whalen on the shoulder and said, "Got any matches?"

Whalen nodded.

Will said, "Hey, you can't smoke in here."

"Screw it." Tim laughed.

And the train roared out of the station, moving east, toward the ocean.

Toward Coney Island.

On the way there, Tim told them a story.

He spoke loudly, nearly drowned out by the incessant clatter and rattle of the train.

If anyone else on the train heard him, they didn't give any sign.

"I was reading last night," he announced loudly, "this book called *The World of Mystery and Magic.*"

Everyone nodded, squeezing together, closer to Tim.

"And I found this wild story. In some of the medieval cathedrals the fuckin' priests used black magic." He paused, letting everyone imagine the possibilities. "Not only were they diddling with the local virgins . . ."

Everyone grinned, always pleased to joke about earthly passions and priests.

"But they worshiped the devil . . . or some of his good pals."

Tim waited, making sure that he had everyone's attention.

Will smiled, but he looked at some of the other passengers. They watched him and his friends with funny looks. And even though Will was sure that they couldn't hear what Tim said, he saw the worried look on their faces. A woman with a small boy, a tall, pretty woman, seemed nervous.

The boy looked up. He pointed at them, and Will smiled back.

As if to say: We're okay. We're not bad guys, lady. Just having some fun.

But the woman pulled her child close to her.

"So these crazy priests made pacts with Satan himself," Tim announced portentously.

"Whooa," Whalen said, laughing. "What else is new?"

"Hey. C'mon," Tim said. "It's in this fucking book. So what the priests had to do was *give* a virgin to the devil, or one of his demons. And the way they did that—"

The train screeched to a stop, rattling all the boys one way, and then back the other. Stoogelike, they nearly bounced their heads together.

Tim waited, and some people went off—the woman and her son—and a few others. Two schoolgirls dressed in tartan-like skirts and blue blazers got on.

Tim nudged everyone.

As if, Will thought, we need nudging.

But when the girls turned around, Will saw that one was worse than homely. Glasses and zits do not for beauty make. The other girl was okay . . . kind of skinny, but okay.

Tim screwed up his face and pronounced his judgment on them. "Forget it," he said.

"Woof," went Whalen.

Narrio laughed.

As if any one of us would walk over and actually talk to the girls . . . even if they were knockouts, Will thought.

The subway started again.

"Two more stops," Whalen said.

But Narrio, always so quiet, cleared his throat. "Go on," he said to Tim.

The noise of the train again masked Tim's words, and he continued.

"Well, the old priests lured sweet young things down to their chambers and trapped them there. They'd give them wine, maybe mix some sleeping powder in it. Then they'd screw them—in the name of evil."

"Right. 'I screw thee in the name of evil!' " Whalen laughed, holding his finger in the air, like the scarecrow explaining that the square of the sides of triangles equals the square of the hypotenuse.

They laughed. But then they quieted down again, wanting to hear the end of Tim's story.

Tim always had the absolutely best sick stories.

He was a connoisseur of strange war stuff . . . weird tales of Japanese maidens who'd tease and torture captured G.I.'s until some sumo-sized monster with a machete entered the room to cut their wangs off.

Tim *liked* those kinds of stories.

And, Will admitted, it was fun hearing him tell them.

"Yeah, so the priest had his way with the virgin. And when she was deflowered, she was sealed up in the wall, in the very bricks of the cathedral . . ."

"Like the Cask of Amontillado," Narrio said.

"Very good," Tim said good-naturedly. "Go to the head of the class."

Will cleared his throat. "Dead?"

"What?"

"The girl . . . she was sealed up dead?"

Tim shook his head.

"No, bozo, alive, of course. That was the *whole point*. She had her mouth covered—"

"How?" Narrio asked, no longer smiling.

Tim grinned. "Some were gagged . . . but some had their mouths sewn up."

"God," Narrio said.

Another stop, and Tim waited while the car whistled and wheezed.

"Almost there, boys and girls," Whalen said.

"But why?" Will asked. "What was the point?"

Tim shrugged. "Who knows? Part of the deal with the devil. I guess it has to do with all that god-awful terror, all that fucking fear. You know, just getting diddled by some fat old priest is bad enough. But, man! Being buried alive in a church? Somehow, the virgin's fear must have made the black magic work . . ."

Now Whalen leaned close.

"You know, I read something like that . . ."

Will had the image in his mind—effectively conjured by Tim. He saw the priest fitting the last brick into the wall, closing the small chamber where the young girl—probably no older than those schoolgirls sitting at the other end of the train—writhed in her chair.

And she probably tried to scream . . . and only tears came.

"Yeah," Whalen said. "There's an old town in Denmark that was attacked by Vikings or somebody. I don't remember. And when they stormed the town, climbing over the walls of the fortress town, they discovered that the wall was filled with bodies, young boys and girls—"

"Nice," Will said, starting to feel a bit woozy.

"Every year the town added a body. It was the same kind of thing, some deal they had with the *dark forces*."

"I guess it didn't work," Tim said.

Whalen shrugged. "Maybe they stopped doing it.. I dunno." Then he laughed. "It's like a mortgage. Once you get involved in the deal, you have to keep it up."

Then why the hell are we doing this? Will thought.

But he knew the answer to that.

Because we don't believe any of this crap. And this is how we show we're above it all. Above religion. Above superstition.

Like taking a dare.

The train stopped again. The schoolgirls got up and left. But not before the less homely one turned and looked back at them.

She smiled. Interested.

"Forget it, sister," Tim muttered to them.

They all laughed.

The girls left.

"We switch next stop," Tim said. "We gotta take the Coney Island el for two stops, and then we meet Kiff."

"If he's there," Will said. "If he doesn't have too many loose wires."

"Fuck it. He'll be there, Will. Don't worry about it."

Narrio was still crouched forward, as if Tim or Whalen were still telling spooky stories around the old campfire.

He said something.

"They did this stuff, with the virgins and everything"— Narrio paused—"to make the magic work?"

"Yeah," Tim said. "Sure."

Narrio nodded. "They were like—what? Sacrifices?"

"Right, Narrio," Whalen snapped. "My, aren't we sharp today?"

Narrio grinned. A bit. There had been too much fun and laughing for him to deflate entirely. But Narrio's face clouded over again. Will watched him, curious, wondering what he was going to say.

"Well, we're doing the same thing. Right? We're going to try and summon a spirit, right?"

"Getting nervous, Mikey?" Whalen scoffed.

And for once, Will appreciated Whalen's tone. This was all for grins, okay? thought Will. A goof. A story to tell everyone back at school.

Our trip to the Twilight Zone.

"B-but then what are we going to do?"

"What do you mean?" Tim asked.

Narrio rubbed his chin. He had a shadow there, a real beard that could use two shaves a day.

"Those were sacrifices. Are *we* going to sacrifice anything?"

Will looked at Narrio's eyes, dark, almost squinted. There was still a hint of a smile on his face. But it was fading, fading—

Until it was gone.

And Tim exploded, laughing, punching Narrio in the side, coaxing back a full-blown grin.

"How the fuck do I know? Goddamn Kiff has the"—he put his face right in front of Narrio's—"fuckin' instructions."

Everyone was laughing.

"But don't you worry, Mike." Tim made a sweeping gesture with his hand as if he were a fat lady swearing off another piece of chocolate layer cake.

"We won't lay a finger on any virgins."

"Speak for yourself, Hanna." Whalen laughed.

And then, with the laughter mixing with the screeching dead-end stop of the train, Will saw that they were there.

10

Kiff was there, dressed in scruffy civvies—no sport coat and tie—with a nasty-looking puss on his face.

"Looks like he's really hurting after being kicked out," Tim said.

The lanky redhead waved at them from across Ocean Parkway. Will followed Tim, who was running across the wide avenue, with Whalen and Narrio behind.

"Where the hell have you been?" Kiff said.

Kiff was dressed in faded, worn khakis and a plaid shirt that looked as though it belonged to his father. He wore dingy sneakers that were coming apart in three or four places.

He doesn't look like us, Will thought. From high school senior to bum in one day.

"What do you mean, a-hole? We're here, so let's get going."

Kiff's face fell, and Will knew he had bad news to tell.

"I didn't get us anything," he said.

"What?" Tim said. "What! You didn't get any booze? Why not?"

"The old fart wouldn't sell it to me." Kiff gestured across the street to a small liquor store. "He did other times but, damn, today he wanted more ID."

"Great," Whalen groaned.

Tim looked really upset.

"I wish I had known, Kiff. I could have lifted something out of my old man's supply. But now—shit . . ."

"There's another store," Kiff said, "right off Shore Parkway. We could try there before we go down to the rocks."

Rocks? Will wondered. What rocks? I thought we were going to a beach . . .

"Okay," Tim decided quickly. "We'll try that."

There was a sound above them. Whalen looked up at the elevated subway. Then he turned and said, "There's a train coming, guys . . ."

"Let's go," Kiff said, grinning again, and he led them up the stairs to the subway—the el—taking awkward, giant steps. Will and the others were slower, carrying their books bundled by tight elastic straps or, in the case of Narrio, dragging his heavy book bag. Will guessed that they all had brought the absolute minimum number of books needed for the weekend.

But they had to bring something.

They got to the platform just as the subway train pulled in.

"Come on," Kiff yelled.

There was only one working turnstile, so they had to wait for the machine to swallow their tokens, and then turn and spit them onto the platform.

Kiff hurried onto the train and held the pneumatic doors open.

"Come on!" he yelled.

Will pushed his way through the sluggish turnstile. He saw the engineer looking down, watching what was holding up his train.

But then Whalen—the last—got through and darted into the car just as Kiff let the doors whoosh shut. Will leaned against a placard advertising the World's Fair that had just closed. The orange and blue was faded, and the globular Unisphere looked dopey.

The train lurched away, sending them all reaching for poles and straps on the nearly deserted train.

Deserted, Will guessed, because who'd take the Coney Island train on a windy fall day? Who wants to go to the seashore today?

He plopped down on the street grinning, a bit breathless, and he faced the windows that looked out to the sea.

It was choppy out there. The sky had turned gray . . . not exactly threatening, but all the blue was gone, replaced by a full gray-white haze. The water looked even darker than the sky, except for the white tongues of foam that dotted it everywhere. He saw a few large boats rocking in the water.

Some ships have to wait out there for days, his grandfather had told him.

Grandpa knew about these things. He had worked at the Brooklyn Navy Yard, building ships, big ships. Until one day he wasn't watching and a girder went flying right at him.

There was a closed coffin at the funeral.

And Will's brother, Danny, said it was because Grandpa had been cut in two.

In fact—

Danny seemed to enjoy telling him that.

"Cut him right in two, Will. And that is why they won't open the coffin."

Danny was away at Georgetown University. Spending more time with the Jesuits.

And Will was just as glad.

Except when Dad got bad. Real bad, dark, and lost and—

"Hey, look!" Kiff yelled, swinging from his pole as if he had already been drinking.

"There's the parachute jump."

The great metal structure, looking like the skeleton of a giant mushroom, floated past them. It was the tallest thing outside, taller than the housing developments, taller than the roller coaster. It even looked taller than the new Verrazano Bridge. The parachutes were clustered near the top, the head of the mushroom. Will saw the silk chutes—real silk, it was rumored—fluttering in the wind.

"Too bad it's not open," Tim said.

"Yeah," Whalen echoed.

The train stopped.

The Coney Island stop.

Right next to Sleeplechase Park, in front of the immense white building.

Steeplechase. The Funny Place, the sign said.

The building was mostly glass, like a giant greenhouse, with the wood frame all painted white. It was a giant building, strange and bizarre, unlike anything else. And inside, there were giant wood slides polished to a glistening patina by decades of fannies sliding down them. And colorful giant cylinders that turned as you tried walking through them.

Will remembered being real small and watching his dad try to crawl through, laughing, falling . . .

It scared him.

And people fell on each other, tumbling in slow motion as though they were human laundry. And when you came out, there was a chaos-loving clown with an air hose. He shot a spray of air at the girls, sending their skirts flying above their waists.

Steeplechase.

And there were rides, like the huge metal horses that sped around the outside of the building. A carousel with balls, is what Danny called it. The rearing horses slid on metal tracks, oh so fast, too fast, as if it wasn't safe to go *that* fast.

And it probably wasn't.

People had gotten hurt. Some said Steeplechase was dangerous. And the parachute jump was part of it. That *had* to be dangerous.

Even the sign, the symbol of Steeplechase, looked dangerous.

Will looked at it now. The big face above the word.

As the subway clicked and wheezed, ready to push on to the next station.

It was a human face. But only just. It was a man with an acorn-shaped head. He had his slick hair parted right in the middle, left and right. It looked like a misplaced moustache, oversized . . . weird. And he had a grin, a terrible grin that went literally from ear to ear. All teeth. And big fat red lips.

Mad, Will thought.

That face looked absolutely mad.

The train started again.

And Kiff was quiet. "Hey, look," he said.

Will saw Tim get out of his seat to see what Kiff was pointing at.

Will half listened.

"Shit, they're tearing down Steeplechase," Kiff said. Now he turned back to look at Will and the others, his face red, flaming with indignation. "There's a sign that says 'Demolition—Fall 1965.' "

"What?" Will said, not really hearing everything Kiff said. He got to his feet, but already the giant white building and the surrounding outdoor rides were streaming away, vanishing . . .

But he could see the big word—"Demolition"—running

right above the entrance to Steeplechase, covering the top of the letters where it said "The Funny Place."

"Oh, no," Will said. "That stinks."

Things weren't supposed to change, Will thought. Some things are supposed to stay the same . . . so you can get older and go away, but when you come back to your world, your life was still here.

But he was learning that it wasn't like that.

It all fades away. Faster than you can imagine.

"So they're going to tear the place down," Whalen said. "It's a fire trap anyway."

Will felt as if he'd like to smash Whalen then.

Whalen grinned at him. A self-satisfied smirk.

I sure as hell don't like him, Will thought.

Not at all.

He shook his head and turned back to the window. The train passed the new aquarium building, still looking unfinished, with great planks of wood crossing the craters made by wheelbarrow ruts and dump-truck tires.

"We get off the next stop," Kiff said. "And then we'll see how lucky we are today."

And Will looked at Jamaica Bay, just to the east.

Filled with small white flecks, white specks that made the sea look alive . . .

"No, Tim, you wait out here. You'll only screw it up if *you* go inside."

Whalen shook his head at Kiff. "Can you two just fucking do it so we can get going? I could use some antifreeze." He laughed.

And Whalen was right, Will thought. It was cooler here by the water, almost cold. The wind blew steadily, and they weren't even at the water yet.

The small liquor store was just ahead . . . while they argued outside of it, looking about as inconspicuous as five underage, potential customers could look.

"If I go in first," Tim said, "I can bullshit with the guy. Okay? Distract him. And then you"—Tim said, pointing a finger at Kiff's chest—"show up to buy a bottle of Old Grand-Dad."

Kiff shook his head.

If they screwed this up, who knew where they'd find another liquor store. Will looked at Mike Narrio, holding his book bag tightly, as if he'd gotten onto a wrong bus.

"Give it a shot, Kiff," Will said. "Tim can bullshit with the best of them."

Tim grinned. "Exactly my point."

And then Kiff nodded, reluctantly. He gestured for Tim to lead the way in. Kiff followed while Will and the others backed away, down the block, the wind at their backs.

Whalen put up his collar.

"Damn, it's cold," he said.

They waited.

After a few minutes, Narrio said, "What do you think is happening in there?"

Will shook his head. "I dunno . . ."

They waited silently a few more minutes. No one came out.

And no one went in.

What *is* going on? Will wondered.

Yes, ladies and gentlemen, it's the liquor store to hell. Next stop, the drunk tank at Red Hook prison.

"Shit," Whalen groaned. "What's keeping them?"

The door opened.

It was Tim.

But he only came halfway out.

What the hell is going on?

Then Will saw Tim turn back, talking to somebody inside. The owner, most likely. Talking, gesturing. Tim smiled.

Then he grinned, waved, and walked away from the store. The door shut noisily behind him.

He kept walking, as if he didn't see the three of them crouched there, awaiting the results of the quest.

"How did it—?" Will started.

"Come on," Tim said. "Start walking, follow me." He spoke through clenched teeth.

Now we're behind the iron curtain, thought Will. A dozen spies have their Uzis and telephoto lens trained on us. And one false move . . .

They reached the corner.

"How did it go?" Whalen insisted.

Tim didn't turn to look at him. Instead he checked the highway.

But there were no cars here. Who'd come here? What in the world for?

There were just some tiny, squat homes, some with window boxes and dry flowers, and others with white paint peeling, flaking off the side, littering the overgrown grass.

Lampposts, telephone poles. Ye olde liquor store. But that was it.

The next block was short. Just half a normal city block. The side facing the highway had a few more homes, even smaller. The color scheme seemed a bit off. A purple door here. A striped mailbox there. One turquoise wall surrounded by a washed-out white.

A dog barked at them as they walked past the line of small houses.

And behind the houses was a field. There were the remains of a baseball backstop, but it had been claimed by the tall reedy grasses.

It was a forgotten park. Unused, unmowed.

Because—thought Will—there are no kids here.

They've all been taken by the liquor store man.

Finally Tim turned to them. "I don't know how the fuck Kiff did. Okay? I talked to the guy about what a dumb-ass politician LBJ was, how what the country really needed was Barry Goldwater to kick some tail in Southeast Asia. The guy was a vet. Flags and shit all over the store. Fought in the Big One, as Dobie Gillis's Dad used to say. World War II. He agreed with me. I was just keeping the guy preoccupied. But Kiff took forever to find a bottle."

"What's his problem?" Whalen said.

"Beats me, but I think it's a pretty simple job to find a bottle of bourbon and bring it to the goddamn counter. Anyway, I asked the guy how to get to the aquarium. Just more bullshit. Then Kiff finally came to the counter. The guy kept talking. Starts in on how great it was JFK got his brains blown out. Didn't deal with Kiff at all. Jeez, I had to go . . . he was talking me out of the goddamn store. I don't know what happened."

"Great. So now what?"

"On the way out I kinda nodded to Kiff . . . toward the water. If he gets something, he'll follow us there."

"And if not?" Whalen asked.

Tim grinned. "He'll still follow us there. But then we'll send him out to find another store."

Will trailed behind them, listening to Tim. And Narrio was even further behind because—Will saw—Narrio kept looking back to see if Kiff was coming, if Kiff was following them down to the water.

But the streets were empty, absolutely deserted.

The dog even stopped barking.

Will looked ahead. He saw the ocean now, but nothing else. The road that ran from here to Sheepshead Bay was high, above the beach.

Tim hurried, his walk breaking into a run.

Will picked up his pace too . . . until he got to the edge of the road and saw that there was no beach.

No beach . . .

Because the beach was covered with a jumble of rocks— great, flat slabs of concrete. It was a cracked highway that ran from the jetty—where the bay met the ocean—and on toward the bay, as far as they could see.

"Where's the beach?" Will asked.

The wind was in his face, blowing continuously, clear and clean, but laced with the salt water, the tangy taste of the ocean only yards away. Waves kicked drunkenly against the rocks while an occasional big surge sent a thin geyser rushing straight up into the sky.

Tim turned to him.

"There is no beach," he said. "It's all like this."

"And what is this?" Whalen asked. Will saw Whalen's eyes squint against the constant wind.

"It's a walkway," Tim said. "It's a fucking promenade. There used to be a hotel here, a monster . . . forty years ago, maybe more. Manhattan Beach used to be a resort and it had this big sidewalk running from Brighton to Sheepshead Bay."

No one said anything for a few seconds. The wind echoed in Will's ears. Then . . .

"Well, what happened to it?" Narrio asked.

And everyone laughed, laughing at the way the question sounded, rolling so flatly and quietly out of Narrio's mouth.

"Look at the water," Tim said. "Right here, Jamaica Bay meets the Atlantic, Mikey. And when a mother of a storm hits, it can get real nasty. The people around here probably get their houses flooded out a couple times each year."

Well, thought Will, that explains the low-rent look to the neighborhood.

"My old man said that there was a bitch of a hurricane in 1939, the same year Adolf started playing Risk with Europe. The hurricane hit Long Island and Brooklyn straight on."

"No shit," Whalen said.

Will looked out at the water, all bubbling and foamy, and so close. But he stood on the tilted chunks of concrete walkway, above the water, as if he were on the prow of a giant ship.

No, thought Will.

Not a ship.

More like a raft.

Adrift on the sea.

"Yes, Whalen. And the storm blew salt water two hundred miles away. Two hundred miles! To Vermont and New Hampshire. It ruined the apple crop, lifted houses up and tossed them miles away. And," he said, taking a properly dramatic pause, "it did this . . ."

He gestured to the concrete walkway.

And—as Will turned—he saw something.

Just out of the corner of his eye.

Something small, and blackish gray.

Barely there—almost in his imagination.

Except—except . . . he got a *real good look* at something long and snaky as it disappeared between two big chunks of concrete, swallowed by the open crack.

"Hey," Will said. He licked his lips. "Hey, guys, I think I just saw a rat." He turned to Tim, who looked like the commander of this ill-fated vessel. "Are there rats here?"

Tim shrugged. "Beats me. I guess there are." He looked around, sniffing the air, as if that would tell him something. "Sure . . . I guess there'd have to be. Sure. Probably water rats."

"Oh, great," Whalen said. "Now we're going to get our butts chewed by rats. I always did want rabies."

Will saw Narrio look around, holding his bag as if it were a weapon. And Will felt more and more empathy with Narrio. An early evening might be in order . . .

"You don't bother them, and they won't bother you," Tim said.

Everyone considered the wisdom of those words until they heard a voice . . .

Above them, from the road.

Kiff.

Looking down at them.

He was grinning.

"Hey!" he yelled. He had one arm behind his back. He waited until everyone was looking.

Will looked up, but he also checked the crack that the rat had entered. It was a black hole.

And it would get blacker as the sun set . . .

Wherever the sun was in this cloudy sky.

"Hey!" Kiff yelled. And then he pulled his arm out in front of him and hoisted his prize, a brown bag, which he held aloft.

"Shit, the a-hole will probably drop it," Tim said.

But Kiff reached over with his other hand. He looked delirious, mad with excitement. And he pulled out his treasure, the amber-brown bottle that was—Will realized—the only spot of color amid the gray stone and the gray sea and the gray sky.

Kiff held it high.

"Success!" Kiff yelled.

And with a whoop he bounded down to them.

11

Kiff leaped down, taking awkward, lanky steps that would be comical if they weren't so spastic.

He's going to drop the bottle for sure, thought Will. But miraculously Kiff landed next to them. He pulled the intact bottle out of its bag.

"Way to go," Whalen said, sounding almost sincere.

"I even got four cups." Kiff grinned. "That old man in the store was half blind. He asked me if there wasn't some-thing *else* I needed. I could have bought *two* quarts."

"Let's keep that store in mind," Tim said, reaching out and taking the prize from Kiff. He unscrewed the cap cere-moniously.

Kiff handed out small wax-covered cups that seemed more suited for Kool-Aid. Will held his and waited his turn.

The wind nipped at his ears and he heard the constant churning sound of the ocean. So close, but held back by the jagged crunch of rock.

Tim poured himself the first taste. He moved the half-filled cup under his nose, savoring the aroma as if it were a rich bordeaux. He wrinkled his face in approval and then chugged the bourbon in one gulp.

"Perfect," he said.

Whalen stuck his cup under the bottle. "Hit me, Tim," Whalen said.

Everyone was *up* now, Will saw. Everyone was feeling real loose.

Will took his sip. The warm booze trickled down his throat, burning with such a pleasant warmth, pushing away the wind, the water, the cold gray clouds. And Will thought:

This is fun.

We're going to have a good time tonight.

But he thought about the reason they were here. The whole point behind coming to Manhattan Beach.

Supposedly . . .

The crazy bullshit reason.

To put ourselves between the devil and the deep blue sea, he thought, smiling to himself.

And he turned and looked around, seeing the ships waiting at the mouth of the harbor, darker now as night came closer. And further out, the Barnegat Lightship, a welcome sight for ships trying to find the harbor. He kept turning, watching the hypnotic dance of the foaming water. He saw the strip of land directly across from them: Breezy Point, ending in a bony finger of rocks that stretched out into a rough, hungry Atlantic.

I've been out there, Will knew, in a sixteen-foot boat rocking back and forth, up and down, until my cookies weren't the only thing that I was in danger of tossing.

He thought his brother, Danny, was going to fly overboard. Danny was, like Dad, three or four Rheingolds south of okay, and his grip on the side of the boat looked tenuous.

And Will's look was scared. Dad was no sailor, and Will remembered his father screaming at Will, yelling right at his face.

Hold on, for Christ's sake. Will you hold on to the goddamn boat?

Will thought for sure that the Coast Guard would have to save them. But somehow, his father got the boat past the worst of it, back toward Jamaica Bay.

And when they got home, Mom wanted to know where all the fish were that they had caught.

No one told her that they had almost lost Danny.

Will kept turning around, taking another sip of the bourbon. He saw the desolate-looking Riis Park Bridge. No one was taking it to the beach today. Nobody was running away to their Breezy Point cabanas this weekend. He saw two lights, one on each tower of the bridge. They blinked on and off, probably to warn the airplanes streaming toward La Guardia.

"Another shot?" Tim said, startling Will.

"Oh, sure," Will said. He gulped the last sip and Tim gave him a full cup this time.

Will didn't worry about how bombed this would make him. That didn't seem important.

He turned back to the others. They had found perches on the rocks, holding their dainty white cups with the fringe of blue flowers as though this were a picnic.

"Hey, how are you doing, Willy?" Kiff yelled.

Nobody called him "Willy." He hated that. But right now, Will didn't give a damn.

"Super, Kiff. Great."

He saw Mike Narrio smiling, looking—God!—as if he was actually starting to relax.

"How's it hanging, Mike?" Will said to him.

Narrio laughed and tilted his cup to Will. "Straight down, Dunnigan."

And everyone laughed, as Kiff, the sommelier, the wine steward of Club Atlantic, went around refilling glasses.

The bourbon was moving fast.

Will felt the first shock waves of the alcohol.

He found himself laughing at something Whalen had said, something about one of the sumo-cooks in the cafeteria, a woman with arms shaped like meaty hams.

Laughing at fucking Whalen, he thought. That's a first.

But Kiff—who always seemed so goofy, so ready to laugh—was quiet. He had his shirt collar up as if he were cold and he hadn't said anything for a few minutes.

The booze seemed to be taking Kiff somewhere else.

But then he saw Kiff get up.

Tim was down by the ocean taking a leak right at the water's edge.

A streetlight—the only nearby light—came on. It was half a block away, but it might send a bit of a glow their way. Whalen was telling more funny stories to Narrio, who laughed his ass off.

Kiff walked over to a big piece of shattered pavement, the biggest in sight. He pulled a sheet of paper out of his pocket—

Oh, yeah, Will thought. The paper. From Scott's apartment.

And Will shook his head. Why the fuck bother? he thought.

We're all relaxed, having a good time. Maybe we can hit a movie later. Get some late breakfast at a greasy spoon.

But Kiff held the paper up, catching the glow from the streetlight. He dug in one of his front pockets.

"Shit," Will heard him say. Then Kiff worked his bony hand into the other pocket. He pulled out something black, in three or four pieces.

Will started to take a sip of the bourbon, but his cup was empty.

He walked over to Kiff.

Kiff knelt down on the stone with the paper in his hand.

Tim came up behind Will.

"What's he doing?" Tim asked.

Will shrugged. But Kiff heard the question. He looked up, his face serious, determined.

He's scarier this way than when he's acting like a madman, thought Will.

"I'm drawing the circle," Kiff said as he made an oblong shape with his arms. "It's got to be nine feet in diameter, but I don't have a fucking ruler."

Tim laughed, and grinned dopily at Will. "Me neither. I guess we'll just have to fucking estimate!"

"Or use my wang!" Whalen said.

And Will laughed.

As a sudden wave exploded behind him . . .

Kiff had trouble getting everyone to quiet down. Narrio was giggling, laughing at everything the suddenly happy-go-lucky Whalen said to him.

"You have to stand on the circle," Kiff said, talking over the wind and the waves. He looked ridiculous, a skeleton man with red hair, holding his pathetic piece of paper in the air as it fluttered.

"Or we'll be blown to Oz," Whalen said, and everyone laughed.

Everyone except Kiff. Kiff looked at them, but his washed-out blue eyes were invisible in the dark. He was at the wrong angle to catch any light.

Will grinned. The bourbon was—what?

Gone? Nearly gone? And he felt good. Happy. As if this was the greatest place in the world, right here. As if he could jump in the water—it had to be cold, just had to be—and swim to France.

"If you don't want to do it, then screw you," Kiff said. "We won't do it."

"Great!" Whalen said.

But Tim spoke. He wasn't laughing.

And that was odd, thought Will. Isn't this hilarious . . . absolutely the funniest thing ever? Why isn't Tim laughing?

"Hey, come on, guys. This is why we came here. Let's do it."

He sounded serious.

How could he sound serious? Will thought. This whole thing is one big goof, isn't it? Just for grins.

And we're already grinning plenty.

"Okay, okay—Christ, Hanna, you know how to interrupt a party." Whalen got to his feet. Narrio was still sitting, squatting like an Indian on the stone. "C'mon, Mikey," Whalen said, reaching down and pulling Narrio. "Up and at 'em."

He jerked a hysterical Narrio to his feet.

Mikey's gone, thought Will. Mamma Narrio's boy has lost it.

"Okay," Tim said, "we're listening."

Kiff gestured out with his arms, quieting the natives. Whalen was still giggling. Narrio rocked back and forth on his feet.

But Will heard Kiff, listened to what he said.

"You each have to stand on the circle, at the tip of one of the star points . . . the tip. It says that you're not safe if you move off."

Whalen hooted like an owl. Everyone broke up.

Everyone fell off their star points.

Ooops.

But then, like rowdy Cub Scouts, they hustled back to their assigned places.

Will looked down. The white concrete was tilted so that it caught whatever light was here. And he saw Kiff's handiwork.

The irregular circle was filled with a five-pointed star. The lines were wavering, but it was definitely a star. Inside the star were symbols, looking like Arabic squiggles, a Greek cross, and other scrawls all looking properly exotic.

Will found himself staring at one of the symbols. It looked like a key but it ended in a dagger point. Something about it fascinated Will, as if he had seen it before.

He shook his head.

Probably from an old Hammer horror film.

Curse of the B Movie.

"Once I begin the ceremony, once I start chanting, you can't move. Not the slightest! The demon—if it desires—will make its presence known to us."

"How?" Tim said, as if that was a reasonable question.

Probably in the form of a cop doing a quick zip by the beach looking for nuts like us, thought Will.

"I don't know, Tim," Kiff said with the best professional tone he could muster. He sounded like a stumped Mr. Wizard.

It was all crazy . . . absurd.

Whalen exploded in another volley of repressed laughing. Narrio collapsed into him, giggling.

"Doesn't look like such a good night to summon the demon world," Will said, gesturing at them. Whalen and Narrio—an easy audience—collapsed some more, but then Tim turned to him.

And grabbed Will's shoulder hard.

"Hey," he said, "let's just fucking do it, okay?"

Will smiled at his friend, his best friend. But Tim didn't smile back. And Will saw that his friend was not a happy camper.

The alcohol has taken him someplace not so friendly, he thought.

"Okay," Will said, trying to sound chastened. "Can you tell me something, Kiff? Just who the hell are we trying to contact?"

Kiff nodded. He took a breath. "He's called Astaroth." Kiff said the next words with relish. "It says that he's the Grand Duke of Hell, the *numero uno* Adversary."

More giggles, but Will asked another question. "Adversary of whom?"

"Of God, of course. He's also called 'The Handler,' since he's so adept at handling human contacts."

Whalen laughed. "That's reassuring." Still laughing, he

turned to Will. "But I don't know why we'd like to contact this sucker, do you?"

Now Will laughed until he heard Tim say, "Hey, c'mon, Dunnigan . . .''

Will took what he hoped was a sobering breath. "Okay, I'm ready. Let's do it.''

Tim nodded, in the darkness.

And Will checked that he was standing right on the point of the star, at the edge of the circle.

Kiff said, "Okay . . .''

And then he began.

Everyone tried not to laugh, Will guessed. Will knew that *he* sure was trying. But it wasn't long before Kiff was a few syllables into his chant, the all-powerful words from *The Book of Enoch*, before the suppressed laughter was a dam ready to erupt, ready to wash them into the sea, rolling and laughing.

"Bagabi, laca, bachala . . . meisto lamal, cahi, meisto . . .''

The sputters turned into giant belly laughs.

"What the hell kind of language is that?" Whalen said between wipes at his eyes.

Will laughed some more. His stomach hurt. He had to piss from laughing.

But Kiff only repeated it. And again. And again. Until the laughter eventually faded.

The joke grew sour.

Kiff paused.

The waves smashed against the stone. Will felt a tiny salt spray touch the back of his neck, chilling him. This wasn't fun anymore, he thought. I'm cold. And his stomach was starting to feel as if it were moving in time to the water.

Put a hold on a late breakfast later, he thought.

He imagined poached eggs sitting on toast, looking like rheumy, diseased eyes. And then he'd poke his fork right in the center and all this yellow goo . . .

Kiff started his chant again. Louder, his mouth spitting out the words.

Enough of this shit, Will thought. I've got to sit down. I've got to get out of here and—

Kiff spoke English.

The same rhythm, the same sound, but now in English.

"Come visibly and without delay," he said. "In a human form, not terrifying . . ."

English, thought Will.

But then—

It was back to the gibberish.

Will looked at everyone. They were standing still. Where had all the laughs gone? Will thought. We need some laughs. Why won't Whalen say something funny and cutting? Why won't Narrio fall down, so goofy and convulsed with how damn funny this all is?

He looked away.

And saw someone.

Further down, standing on the rocks, right near the water's edge.

"Hey," Will said. But then there were two people there. And—it was hard to see, there was no light. But—

Someone was watching them.

Will looked back to Kiff. "Hey, guys . . . we're—"

"Come . . ." Kiff said.

Shit, Will thought. We'd better get out of here. Better . . .

He looked back at the people standing away from them, watching, what the hell . . .

They were gone.

Will looked at Whalen.

He seemed to rock on his feet, on the stone that was tilted forward, right toward the sea.

He watched Whalen rock back and forth.

Whalen's going to fall, tumble forward, Will thought.

Will went to take a step toward him, to catch him before his head smashed against the rock.

But first he looked back, out to the darkness again. There was nobody there. Probably just a shadow, thought Will. He looked down.

At the circle. At the rock.

At the point of his star. His feet were planted right on the tip.

Whalen rocked like a stalk of wheat being blown by a wind that couldn't make up its mind.

Will raised his hand.

"Meisto lamal . . ." Kiff said.

But Will didn't move.

And Whalen fell forward, his chin smashing against the stone with a crack that made Will wince. And Will saw blood gush out of the cut, more blood than Will had ever seen.

"Shit," Tim said, kneeling down beside Whalen.

Kiff was still chanting.

"Cut that crap," Will said.

Narrio still stood on his star point as if unaware that anything had happened.

Will crouched beside Whalen too. And with Tim's help they tried to pull Whalen to his knees. They got him up into a doggie position. Whalen's chin dripped blood, but Will saw that it wasn't a bad cut, just a bloody one. A small flap of skin hung open, bit it didn't look like anything that would need stitches.

Whalen looked up at them. "Guess I chugged a little bit too fast. I just—all of a sudden—"

And Whalen looked up, out to the sea, as if he had just seen the most incredible thing. He opened his mouth wide . . .

And proceeded to shoot a spray of vomit that must have reached the water's edge.

Will—no steady sailor at this point himself—felt his own stomach go tight, ready to join the party.

But he took a breath of the suddenly full and too-sweet air, and he was able to steady himself.

I guess the fun part is over, he thought.

But, once again, he was wrong . . .

12

"I'm okay. No problem, really." Whalen looked up and around. He wiped at his chin, grinning, as if he had just been splashed with a messy wave that broke too high.

Mike Narrio laughed. Everything was so damn funny to Narrio again, even Whalen wiping puke from his chin.

Will shivered. The wind shifted a bit and he smelled his friend's vomit, splattered across the rocks. Whalen held his tie against his chin. The flow of blood seemed to have been stemmed.

"Maybe we should bag it," Will said. "It's getting cold out here."

Will saw Kiff standing there. Looking disappointed. The streetlight sputtered, flaring into increased brilliance. Will saw the dots of Jim Kiff's freckles. Then the light shriveled to a paler glow.

Let's get out of here, Will thought.

"Hey, no," Whalen said, forcing a hearty laugh. "I'm fine. No problem." He reached out and took the bourbon bottle from Tim's hand. He held it up to the milky light. "There's still a few more drinks here. And we can always hit that friendly liquor store again." He turned to Kiff. "Right, Kiff? Right?"

But Kiff was staring at the circle, at the trail of upchuck, at the sea.

"He's disappointed that nothing happened," Tim said. "No demons . . ."

"Hey," Whalen said, standing up, "you call what happened to me nothing? I'd say I did a pretty good impression of a volcano."

Will smiled. Whalen was trying to bring himself back from

108

the land of the dead. And Will felt his own stomach start to settle. Then, incredibly, Whalen reached out—

Don't do it, thought Will . . .

And grabbed the bottle again and took a slug of bourbon.

"Hair of the dog," Whalen said.

Will groaned.

"Shit," Kiff said to the stone.

And Will knew that Kiff, crazy Kiff, had thought that something might actually happen.

He's somebody to stay away from, Will thought. No doubt about it. Jim Kiff is certifiable.

"Let's go," Will said. He took a step, climbing from one flat piece of broken stone to another.

But Tim waited.

Tim stood there, in his shadow, and said, "Wait."

Narrio laughed. He was so drunk that everything was funny to him. Whalen gave Narrio the bottle and Narrio took a slug, nearly killing the bottle.

Oblivious to whatever taste might linger on the bottle.

"I've got an idea," Tim said.

"Breakfast?" Will said.

Breakfast didn't sound like such a great idea. But it would get them away from here, off the rocks, away from the sea, and—

"No." Tim took a step up to the rock next to Will. And Will felt the others watching Tim, the next scene to be played out.

"What's that?"

"Let's go to Steeplechase," Tim said.

"It's closed," Whalen said, laughing. Narrio howled.

Tim barely turned to them. Instead he kept focused on Will. "No. It's going to be torn down. One of the great places in the world about to vanish."

"Like Ebbets Field," Whalen added.

"Yeah," Tim said, "like fuckin' Ebbets Field. And once it's gone, you'll never see it again."

Will knew where this was leading. And he didn't like the direction. He looked out at the sea, looking for some escape route, some way to end the night, get back home. Turn on *The Tonight Show.*

Crawl into bed and sleep until noon.

"So what . . . they're tearing it down."

Tim grabbed him hard. "There's nothing like it anywhere, Will. We could see it, at night. A private fucking tour. It would be the highlight of our senior year."

Tim always cursed when he argued for something. Sometimes—in the middle of a debate on nuclear nonproliferation—Will thought Tim might lose it.

As if he'd say, screw the Affirmative's plan. It won't fuckin' work.

"I don't know," Will said.

Then Whalen, the rocky sailor, was there, grinning ear-to-ear.

Trying to regain his land legs.

"I'm game," he said. "Why not?"

Sure, Will thought. Whalen was trying to reclaim some respect after his little show. He'd agree to anything just about now.

"How about you, Mikey?" Whalen said.

Narrio laughed.

"Great," Narrio said.

"Kiff?" Tim said.

Kiff looked lost, deflated. But he looked up, still grim-faced, and nodded.

In a few seconds a big decision had been made. And then the potato was passed back to Will.

"Will?" Tim said.

He shook his head.

The water was black and oily. The streetlight made a tiny sputtering noise, as if the bulb was on its last legs. "I don't know."

"C'mon, Will. Don't be a pussy." Tim came close, pushing his body right up to Will's. "We'll run in and right through the place. Then we'll go for some food . . . promise."

"I'll pass on the food," Whalen said, laughing, echoed by Narrio's braying.

"What do you say?"

And Will said, "Okay," thinking . . .

Thinking . . . that if nothing else, at least we'd get off the rocks.

He turned and led the way, quickly, up to the road.

* * *

They were halfway to the subway station, past the empty field covered with tall grass that blew in the sea breeze, when Will stopped.

Froze in his tracks.

And he remembered.

"Shit," he said.

Tim turned to him. "What is it?"

"I left my books back there," Will said.

Because I wanted to get away so badly.

Tim nodded. Somehow, the others had all remembered, even drunken Narrio with his worn St. Jerome's Preparatory School bag.

Tim nodded. "Uh-huh. We'll walk slow," he said. "And meet you at the subway."

Right, thought Will. While I turn and walk back to the rocks, to the water.

All by my lonesome.

Whalen, without hesitating, turned and started walking away in the direction of the station. "Get a move on, Dunnigan."

The others followed, while Tim nodded, as if it was okay, and said, "We'll see you there."

Will turned. To look at the water, the dwarf houses, the eerie field, abandoned and dead.

He took a breath.

And he started running.

For a second he thought that he had come to the wrong spot. It all looked different, the slabs of broken concrete, the water crashing over them. The lines of streetlights, spaced so far apart.

Except—no—this was right. The nearest streetlight glowed more dully than the others. And he saw the stone with faint markings, the circle, the pointed star.

That seemed like years ago.

Now it was there, like a child's scribble on the street or sidewalk, dotted with clumps of Whalen's vomit.

Where are my books? he thought.

I've got to find my books.

He stepped down onto the rocks.

Splash! The water smashed right next to him. He stood right by the water's edge. The black water that sent a tiny phosphorescent spray into the air.

Will came down here so that he could turn and look up, searching for a lump that he'd recognize as his books. There was no color here. Just gray and black.

If my books are in the shadow of one of the stones, he thought, I'll never see them.

He looked all around. He saw the bag from the liquor store. He saw the bits of charcoal that Kiff had used. Some cigarette butts crushed into the stone.

But no books.

Until he took a step forward, and something caught a bit of light. The buckle part of the thick rubber book strap. Just a bit of light, but enough to catch his eye.

He took a breath.

Salvation, he thought.

And he walked straight to the books, hurrying, eager to get the hell out of here, not watching where he was going.

He got to the books, and he picked them up. They felt cold and alien in his hands.

Of course . . . they'd been sitting here, in the dark, in the cold, covered by a thin wet spray.

He turned to leave, still hurrying, taking big steps.

He stepped into something slippery, and one shoe, a brown loafer, slid comically.

Will felt his knee buckle.

What the—? he thought.

But just as he was going to put down his hands to stop himself, he saw what he had slipped in.

Whalen's upchuck.

Spread all over Kiff's demonic artwork.

Will gagged.

He didn't put his hands down. That would have been too gross. But he was able to stop his legs from moving. Stop them. And then he moved his unsullied foot to another rock and pushed himself up, and away.

The light sputtered.

He took another step, another, hurrying still.

Got to get up to some flat pavement. This is like something

from Wonderland. A road gone mad, right by the ocean, and—

He turned and looked back at the pentacle, the circle.

He took another step.

And the shoe, still coated with a tiny veneer of gummy goo, slid on the stone. His leg slid, moved, and—

Went down.

He felt the edge of the stone, and his leg fell into some kind of hole.

He turned around to see what was trapping his leg.

I've fallen between the stones, he thought, into the crack between two stones.

But it was worse than that.

He had slid into a hole, a cavern made by one rock lying askew on top of another. His foot hit bottom. It twisted. He felt pain as rock rubbed against his anklebone, trapping it.

The light sputtered.

Will looked up at it.

No, he thought.

Please.

No.

I'm all alone.

There's no one else here. There's no one for blocks . . . I could be on another planet somewhere. Another world—

No . . .

The light sputtered.

And then it went out.

13

He tried to yank out his leg quickly.

Just get it the hell out, he told himself, and keep moving.

The road was only yards away. There were more lights, houses. Just get your leg out . . .

But one tug told him that it was wedged into the hole.

Good thing the tide's not coming in, he thought.

He looked at the ocean.

Or is it?

As if in answer, a wave splashed noisily only feet away.

He reached down with his hands, palms down, and pushed against the edge of the upper rock. He kicked with his free foot. He grunted.

He felt the skin of his trapped ankle scraping against rock.

It hurt, but he pushed some more, and the pain grew, turning sharper, and he knew that he had torn his skin.

And his foot still wasn't moving.

I've got to twist the leg somehow. Work it out. Try another angle.

After all, it got in there, didn't it?

It got into this—so it has to come out.

He looked at the hole.

He remembered this hole.

I do? he thought. How could I remember this hole? What on earth—?

And through his alcoholic haze, he did remember. Getting here, and seeing something move, something fat and gray. Disturbed by their coming.

But now he was alone. And it was dark.

Will chewed his lip.

Oh, no, he thought. Oh . . . no . . .

He imagined it moving down there, hearing his foot scratch at the rock, and—yes—maybe even smelling the blood.

And it might come a bit closer, its tail snaking this way and that, cautiously, nervously.

But when I didn't run away, this bleeding thing . . . Why, the rat might . . .

"No!" he yelled, and he twisted his foot, grunting, pulling as hard as he could.

Pushing his hands against the stone.

He felt more skin being torn, the pain sharp, biting, as the skin was peeled away from the bone.

But then his foot moved.

Great, he thought, and now his leg flew up, out of the hole.

His foot came out.

But—

His shoe slid off, back down into the crack.

"Oh, shit," he said, standing. He rubbed at his ripped ankle and felt the blood. It wasn't bad, more of a scrape. It would hurt to walk but that wouldn't be so bad.

He stared back at the hole.

Leave the fucking shoe.

Yeah, he thought, his decision process surely affected by the Old Grand-Dad.

Leave the shoe and get on the subway and keep going.

But they were new loafers. And just how would he explain that to his parents?

We had a wild dance, Mom and Dad. Real wild. Great time, but I lost my shoe.

I've got to get it, he thought.

I've got to reach in and pull the damn shoe out.

He nodded.

Then he tried convincing himself that it was no big deal. The rat was probably nowhere in sight, scared by the noise, all their laughing. Yeah, the chunky rat was probably long gone, down to Sheepshead Bay where he can munch on fish heads and dried chum from the day's party boats.

Will knelt down.

He was breathing hard.

He tried to decide which hand he'd use. Left or right?

As if he were trying to figure out which one he'd be less likely to need the rest of his life.

But, Will thought, speed is called for here. Do it fast. Snatch the shoe, yank it up, and we're home free.

He leaned forward. Now even the stone was black in the darkness. There was no moon, and the stars were washed to a yellow dullness by the clouds and smog.

He took another breath.

He stretched his hand into the hole.

Deeper, deeper, his fingers bunched together.

Lest he touch something he didn't want to touch. And further.

But he felt nothing.

He didn't even touch the ground.

It's deeper than I thought.

Will moved his hand back and forth in the hole. He opened his fingers—just a bit. He felt nothing. The shoe was still lower.

He leaned forward, pressing his shoulders tight against the stone, letting his face press against the speckled concrete, until, finally, his fingers scraped at something.

Sand.

Great. I can feel the bottom.

Now, where the hell is my shoe? Where the hell—?

He felt the tip of the shoe. And he flailed at it with his fingers, trying to move it closer, until he felt the open end and the heel . . .

Until he could close around the shape and bring it up, and . . .

And it slipped from his fingers.

He grabbed it again, a practiced hand now. Squeezing the shoe tight.

He pulled it up.

When something slid across the back of his hand. Slowly. Like a cold wet strand of spaghetti.

He wanted to scream.

He wanted to jerk his hand up.

But then I'll drop it again and I'll have to start all over—

He held on, feeling the tip of the shoe hit some rock, turning it, easing the shoe over.

The snakelike thing slid off his hand.

Will heard a chirp.

Almost like a bird. Then again, another chirp. And—

Bristly things touching his fingers, poking him. Hard, bristly—
Oh, God.

He yanked his hand out hard, not caring if the damn shoe
fell back in.

He yelled.

A low, guttural sound, a scream of revulsion.

But the shoe came flying out, up into the air.

Will rolled back from the hole.

And for the few seconds he sat there—watching the hole,
watching if the rat would climb out, disappointed, hungry—
he thought he heard something.

Thought he heard it . . . because he knew it couldn't be real.
Couldn't be.

I'm just hearing this because I'm scared. And it's cold and
my heart is beating a thousand times a second.

My ears are ringing.

So I'm not *really* hearing this, he thought.

But it sounded like . . . clicking.

Clicking, chattering . . .

The sound of teeth, hundreds, thousands of teeth, clicking,
chattering, quietly at first, then louder and louder, until it
was a chorus of chattering, clicking *teeth*.

"Oh, God!" Will yelled. He brought his hand up to his ears.

He heard his name.

He took his hands off his ears.

"Will, what the hell's taking you so long?"

He turned. And he saw Tim . . . Tim's shadow, at least,
up on the road.

Watching him.

"I—I—"

Well, what was it? he thought. What is my big problem?

"I got stuck. Between two rocks—"

"C'mon, dork. Everyone's waiting."

Will nodded. He slipped his foot into his shoe.

Stopping for a second, thinking that his toes would meet
something. But they didn't.

Then he picked up his books and ran up to his friend.

14

The rattling of the subway train did little to ease Will's queasy stomach or his confused mind.

What happened back there? he wondered.

I fell into a rat hole. I cut myself.

He reached down and touched his ankle, the thin crust of blood now meshed with his dark blue socks.

But what of the chattering, the clicking?

Sounding so much like teeth.

The wind. Must have been the wind.

Or a rat's nest. Or—

Who the hell knows . . . after half a bottle of bourbon?

The subway wheezed into the Brighton Beach station. Tim had been sitting on the other side, watching the dark ocean and square apartment buildings roll by. But when the train stopped, he got up and came over to Will.

"What's the matter with your leg?" he asked.

Will looked up, smiling. "Nothing."

The train lurched forward again. Tim sat down. "I can't believe I gave up getting my rocks off to hang out with you dorks," Tim said, grinning. Will smiled back.

Then Will asked, "Do we have to go to Coney Island? Shit. It's getting late." Will paused, licked his lips. "It's a stupid idea."

Tim turned and looked out the window.

Kiff was laughing at something that Whalen said, which, of course, set Narrio off again.

If a transit cop comes in here, he's going to haul our asses right off this train, Will thought.

"Why not?" Tim said, still looking out the window. They had a clear view of the lights of the apartments, the houses ending at the blackness of the sea. "It's early. The dance would have another hour to go—at the least." Tim turned and looked at him. "Don't worry about it."

Will nodded.

But he did anyway.

And all too soon, they were at the Coney Island station.

They went screaming down the stairs, hooting and yelling.

But when Will got to the bottom, to Surf Avenue—the main strip of Coney Island—he saw that their high spirits weren't appreciated.

There were men down there, some black, some Hispanic, a few whites. They all had small, dark eyes. Hungry, nasty eyes.

They hung around on the corner, leaning against the wall of a place that sold—the sign yelled—CORN ON THE COB! In big puffy red letters.

The men were talking.

Looking at us, Will thought.

He felt as if he had just fallen into the bear pit in the zoo.

"I don't think we're in Kansas anymore, gang," Kiff joked.

"Just keep fucking walking," Tim said. And to demonstrate, Tim stormed off, out, across the street as if he had an appointment with his stockbroker.

Will hurried to follow, not wanting to get caught in his wake.

Then, from behind him, he heard Narrio.

"I want some corn."

Will looked back. Narrio stood on the corner, digging into his back pocket for some money.

Whalen was halfway across the street, looking back, laughing at Narrio.

"Will you get him away from there!" Will hissed, just loudly enough for Whalen to hear. And Whalen ran back to the sidewalk and hooked Narrio by the collar of his trench coat.

"Jesus," Will said when they came abreast of him. "Narrio's got the street smarts of a puppy."

Whalen laughed at that.

They passed a bar, and Whalen said. "Shall we try our luck?"

Will shook his head, but he saw Whalen stop and look in.

He heard the song thumping out . . .

"I Got You, Babe . . ."

Sonny and Cher. America's favorite rock and roll couple, *Time* magazine insisted.

Yeah, thought Will. And by next year they'll both be history.

Will was stopped, just behind Whalen. "Hey, c'mon, Whalen. Let's keep—"

But Whalen studied the bar, sizing it up to see whether they could troop in there and actually get served.

Will looked at the name of the bar. McCann's. It seemed as if every sleazy corner in New York had a McCann's. Sandwiches and booze. Booze and sandwiches. And more booze. Until you didn't care whether you had a sandwich anymore. As long as there was booze.

He thought of a joke.

What's an Irish seven-course dinner?

A potato and a six-pack.

Cue laughter.

Too fucking true, he thought. Too—

He saw eyes looking out of the darkness.

"You got me, and I got you . . . babe . . ."

"Hey, Whalen, c'mon. Let's go."

So dark inside. Just a bit of a glow over where the bottles were, and reddish lights over the trays of steaming meat. Real meat, or just an amazing simulation?

Let's go get a sandwich . . . and ten shots of Canadian Club, with chasers, please.

Will looked up at Tim, still trooping away, leading Kiff further down the street.

Into the dark part of town, Will saw.

"Hey, Whalen, give it up. We'll get something later."

After we leave this ghost town.

And Will looked back the other way, to see if any of the corn-on-the-cob men, the lean and hungry men, were doing more than watching. He looked to see if any of them were following.

But they weren't.

"I'm going to catch up with Tim," Will said. "And you can do whatever the hell you want to—" And Will stormed away, leaving Whalen and Narrio frozen outside the bar, sizing up their chances with all the discretion of plastered sailors wobbling outside a whorehouse.

Will hurried up to Tim and Kiff, and then he heard steps behind him as the others abandoned their quest and followed Tim.

"What the hell gives with the streetlights?" Will said.

There were two lights out on this block alone, and another across the street was flickering feebly.

No one answered him.

They walked past a crumpled figure collapsed in the doorway of a building. A neon sign, off for centuries, said *The Shore Hotel*.

The perfect place for your Coney Island stay . . .

"I didn't know it had gotten this bad," Will said to Tim. Of course, nobody he knew ever went to Coney Island in the summer. It was a beach for the masses, the great unwashed herd, as Tim called them. But now the place looked more like a penal colony.

"Just keep your wits about you, Willy."

Will looked over his shoulder again. A few blocks back there were some bright lights, and a crowd in front of Nathan's purchasing the world's best hot dog. But down here . . . this was the edge of the world. The bottom of the universe.

And ahead, down the next block, was Steeplechase.

He saw the giant wood and glass building, catching the light from the washed-out streetlights. The word "Demolition" was pasted right across the name, right across *George C. Tilyou's Steeplechase Park*, cutting off the top of the words *The Funny Place*.

It didn't look too funny now.

The big face, the big leering face, was nice and clear.

Tim started crossing the street.

Will turned. He saw a police car down near the corncob joint. But it turned right and disappeared.

It probably doesn't want to linger here. No, sir, not where there's any real problems. Just take a cursory peek and slip back to the world of normal people who stay at home on Fridays and watch Jack Paar.

Tim picked up his pace, his short legs hurrying them to

the giant building, and the amusement park surrounded by a massive fence.

Whalen came up to him. He looked excited, back to normal. The fresh air seemed to be doing him some good, Will saw. "What's the plan, guys?" he said.

But Kiff danced in front of them just as they hit the curb. He put his hands out dramatically, stopping them. "We can't just go in this way," he said. "But there are doors around the side, big doors. That's where we can break in."

"Are there dogs?" Will asked.

"What?"

"Are there dogs, I said. You know. Guard dogs."

Narrio burped.

He's not long for holding all that shit down, Will guessed. Best to stay out of his firing range. He took a few steps away.

"Shit, Kiff, do they use guard dogs inside? Big German shepherds? Doberman pinschers? Understand?"

Kiff looked at the fence and into the park. The rides were still there. Most were shrouded with heavy tarps that made them strange, misshapen lumps. But a few were exposed, as if ready for a late night party. The kiddie rides were here— the small boats, tiny Model Ts—right near the front of the park.

The real stuff was further in.

"No," Kiff said. "No. I mean, why would they have dogs? The place is going to be torn down. I—"

Tim cut him off.

"Let's just go around the side and see what we can see."

"Punking out?" Whalen said.

Will shot him a look. Ah, yes, Whalen was back to normal. The cut on Whalen's chin made him look like a gangster.

"No, Whalen. I can hang in as long as you don't puke at us again."

Everyone but Whalen laughed.

Whalen came close. "Fuck you," he said.

Tim yanked Will away, down the block. Down to the side of the Steeplechase building.

And that seemed to decide it.

But as they walked that way, Will cocked an ear, listening

for the sound of a dog growling . . . behind the fence . . . or inside the building itself . . . waiting.

Waiting, Will thought, for such fools as us.

It was like a garage door, all splintery. The ground was dotted with white flakes of paint and tiny chips of wood. The wind blew from the ocean, carrying the dull, thundering roar of the waves. It made Will shiver.

The garagelike door was bolted with a lock the size of a horse collar.

The street was dark. Just two lamps. Spaced too far apart to take any of the funereal gloom out of the side street.

And Will remembered a rhyme:

Up the narrow alleyway,
Down the dirty street,
To the place where a man lives
Who wants children to eat.

"Hey, no way," he said, watching Tim handle the lock. And he thought: What are we doing? Isn't this breaking and entering? And aren't I getting to be an old pro at that? Is this how you get to be a criminal?

Or is this still just a prank? Just normal teenage high spirits?

That's all, Officer.

He looked back to Surf Avenue.

Someone was crossing the street. A man seemed to stop, to slow. Pausing halfway across.

"Someone's watching us," Will whispered.

"Fuck him," Whalen said. "He can't see us."

Will looked back.

Whoever it was had vanished.

"We can get this off," Whalen said, fingering the lock. "No problem."

Tim turned to him. "Then do it!"

Whalen grinned. "The bolt is attached to the wood, and it's rotting away. All we need is"—he looked around on the ground—"some kind of—"Whalen walked to the curb and then went further down the block. "Look up the other way," he ordered. "Up toward the road."

Kiff started toward Surf Avenue.

"This is crazy," Will said.

Tim looked at him.

"You don't have to stay if you don't want to." He said it flat, without any feeling. And it made Will feel like shit. The criticism was right there . . .

I want to punk out again.

"No, Tim, it's just—"

"Hey!" Kiff yelled. "Is this any good?" He held something up and waved it in the darkness.

"What is it?" Whalen yelled back.

"A wire hanger," Kiff said.

"Forget it."

"Dork," Tim said, laughing.

Will nodded.

He hoped that they didn't find anything.

The waves seemed closer. Was the tide coming in? It was *roaring*, a repetitive drumming on the beach, just a hundred feet away.

"I've got something," Whalen said. He ran back to them.

"I gotta take a piss," Narrio said absently.

Tim turned to him, grinning. "Then go piss."

Narrio walked away from the group. Out of the corner of his eye, Will saw Narrio huddle close to the building wall.

"This should do it," Whalen said, brandishing an oddly curved stick. It looked like a piece of driftwood. It looked like—

Whalen quickly stuck one end of his prize between the curved loop of the bolt and the metal latch of the door. Whalen started pushing against it, using leverage to pry the bolt off the door.

"It's giving," Whalen said.

Will heard a siren in the distance. I almost hope it comes here, he thought.

Save us from this.

"Yeah, it's *moving*."

Narrio came back.

Will looked at the stick.

It turned in Whalen's hands, twisting just a bit as he pressed harder, and—

Will knew what it was.

"It's a fucking bone," he said. He stepped back.

Whalen looked up at him. Then Tim turned and said, "What?"

"The stick—it's a goddamn bone," Will repeated. "It's someone's bone. Damn. Look at it." He felt his voice rising. "Will you look at what you have in your hands?"

Now even Whalen stopped. He let go. He backed away. The bone was wedged in the lock, sticking out at a severe angle.

"What the hell?" Whalen said.

They all studied it. Will saw the indentations of the joints . . . the anklebone connected to the kneebone . . . the kneebone connected to the—

What bone was this?

"What the—?"

"It's probably just a dog's bone," Tim said. "Go ahead, finish up," he ordered.

But Whalen didn't move. In fact, it looked as if the more convinced Whalen became that it was a bone, the further back he stepped.

"Shit," he said.

What happened next happened fast.

Tim went to the door. He grabbed the bone. He threw all his weight against it, pressing hard, flush against the door.

There was a splintering noise. Then the metal bolt flew off one door and slapped against the other. The heavy lock dangled, useless.

The door creaked open a few inches. And Will smelled something inside, a warm, sweet smell.

Tim tossed the bone back into the street, where it landed with a dull sound.

A wave broke. Closer, closer . . .

"Now let's get the fuck inside," Tim said.

And—for some reason—it seemed like a better idea than standing out in the street.

15

Tim pulled open the door. The bottom edge ground against the sidewalk, and the hinges creaked, and more of that smell gushed out.

Old wood, Will thought. That's what the smell is.

And Tim disappeared into the building, into the darkness.

Kiff followed him. He made a spooky owl sound.

"Ooooooo!" he howled. Narrio and Whalen crept in.

Another wave broke as if lapping at the boardwalk.

And then Will went in.

It was pitch-black.

"Pull the door shut, doofus!" Tim said to him. And Will reached behind him and grabbed at the metal handle.

The handle was cool, a curved piece of metal maybe a hundred years old. How many hands have grabbed that handle? he wondered. And how many of those people are dead?

"What now?" Will whispered.

Tim answered in a full voice. "There's no reason to fucking whisper," he said. "Who the hell are we going to wake up?"

"Maybe there *are* guards," Will said. "Or dogs."

"Christ," Whalen said, "he's back on that again."

"I see another door," Tim said.

Amazing, Will thought. Because I can't see anything. To prove that fact he held his own hand out in front of him. And he wriggled his fingers.

Nada.

But then—while his hand was still suspended in front of his face—he did see something. His fingers were catching some light.

Light that came from ahead.

"No," Tim said. Will heard him take a step.

"This is really creepy!" Kiff said.

"Not a door. It's a stairway, leading up."

"Great!" Kiff said. "It will take us to the amusement area
. . . the slides . . . all that neat stuff."

Will didn't see anything amusing about their current position.

Now, as his eyes adjusted to the darkness, he could barely
make out Tim, Kiff, and the others, shuffling toward the stairwell, pale gray in total blackness.

"Anybody bring a miner's hat?" Whalen quipped.

Everyone laughed.

That's nervous laughter, Will thought. I know fucking nervous laughter when I hear it, and that was it!

Then he heard steps. Tim going up the stairs. Then the
cautious, trudging steps of the others. And Will wondered—
banging his foot into the first step, waking up his injured
ankle—is it such a good thing to be bringing up the rear?

Is that a good thing?

He remembered the old Abbott and Costello film where
they meet Frankenstein's monster, and Dracula, and just about
every other monster. There was a scene where they're all in
a line and one by one they get snatched.

Will let his hand flail out behind him. He groped around.

His heart was beating wildly in his chest.

He licked his lips.

And then he had a weird thought. I'm scared. Sure, I'm
scared half crazy. But then . . . I'm also excited. He felt the
thin handrail as he went climbing up, his hand sliding along
the metal.

This is damned exciting!

And it was getting lighter and lighter. Less black . . . more
gray.

Somewhere, right above us, there are windows, letting in
light.

It's just there, Will thought. Just ahead of us.

"Holy shit!" he heard Tim yell.

"Fan-fucking-tastic," Kiff squealed.

Will grinned.

This isn't so bad, he thought.

We're inside.

With no dogs. Not even the smallest yelp.

Inside the great Steeplechase building.

"C'mon," he said, nudging Narrio, just ahead of him, to keep going up the stairs.

Not so bad at all . . .

In fact, it was marvelous.

The roof was mostly glass, an endless checkerboard of glass and wood. A cloudy light, more of a glow, filtered down from there, a mixture of the streetlights and the dull shine of what must be the moon hidden behind clouds.

It was just enough light so Will could see where they were.

He looked around, soaking up the very strangeness of the experience. To his left he saw the great open barrels that spin around. And he thought: I've been through them countless times. To his right were the spinning disks, different sizes, designed to spin at different speeds. You tried to hold on until the centrifugal force sent you spinning away, laughing, holding on to the legs of a perfect stranger.

If you were lucky, a girl rolled on top of you.

And further away, Will saw the outline of a rope bridge that shimmied and shook, left and right, trying to knock you over the side into a pool of foam rubber.

Will was grinning from ear to ear.

Who cares if the place is closed and dark?

"This is great," he said.

Except—everything was quiet now. Usually there were the voices, the sounds of a thousand people. Laughing and screaming. And the engines were quiet, the big machines that made the barrels turn, and the wooden dishes spin, and the bridge shiver.

Now there was no sound.

"Sure is quiet," Will said.

And—in answer—Kiff hooted and ran into one of the barrels.

But it was no challenge.

He came running out and then pointed behind them.

"Hey," he said, "I'm going to try the slides."

Steeplechase was famous for its slides, giant wooden slides that gave you a nasty burn if you tilted to the side and let your arm drag all the way down. You could tell who caught a bad slide from seeing the kids with big red blotches on their arms and knees.

You could get hurt on the slides.

The stairway to the slides was barred by a small gate. But Kiff ran over and jumped the gate. He tore up the stairs. Narrio followed.

Will turned to Tim.

"This is great," he said, "really—"

But Tim wasn't there. Will looked around, expecting to see him running across the rope bridges or inside the barrels.

But he didn't see him.

Whalen was grinning, watching Narrio and Kiff, now nearly at the top of the slide near the roof of the building.

And at the top, through the great glass panels of the side wall, Will saw shapes.

Horses . . . lined up, just beside the slide.

The steeplechase horses, ready to race on their rails, ready to gallop around the outside of the park.

"Watch this!" Kiff yelled. And then crazy Kiff took a flying leap off the edge of the slide, a full gainer, and he was rolling down the slide, spinning out of control.

Halfway down, Kiff's smile vanished.

His arms were getting burned by the wood.

He landed like a human pretzel at their feet.

Will laughed. He looked around for Tim. But he didn't see him. Where the hell was he . . . ?

Kiff popped up.

"Damn . . . shit . . ." Kiff said. Then, for good measure, "Damn!"

Now it was Narrio's turn. And he went sliding down with a loopy grin on his face, his arms folded in front of him, squealing all the way.

He caromed into Kiff's feet, nearly knocking him over.

"Hey, watch it," Kiff said.

"Sorry," Narrio said insincerely.

Maybe I should try the slide, Will thought.

But Kiff, rubbing at his wounds, ran over to the gate, wanting to brave it again. Narrio followed him.

And Will decided to just watch them one more time.

He watched them take the steps, two, three at a time. Right to the top.

When Kiff got to the top, he checked the slide, getting ready for his leap. Narrio was just behind him, right next to him . . . when he turned . . .

Narrio saw something.

"I'm all set," Kiff announced, the fierce daredevil.

Narrio moved away from Kiff.

What's he doing? Will wondered. And Will took a step closer to the small gate, to the stairway.

"Here we go," Kiff said.

Narrio moved to the side. To a door. Leading out of the building up there, right by the Steeplechase ride, out to the horses . . .

Will heard that door pop open. And he saw that Kiff heard it too. Kiff stopped and looked at Narrio.

"Kiff," Will said.

Then, turning to Whalen, he said, "What's Narrio doing? Where is he going?"

"What?" Whalen said, as if he hadn't heard or hadn't seen Narrio.

Kiff looked back, ready to go on with his jump.

"One," Kiff said.

But Will saw Narrio go through the door. There was a landing there, a platform next to the horses. Right, Will remembered. That's where you got off the horses. And you came right into the fun house there. One breathless experience after another, one thrill—

"Two!" Kiff yelled.

Will took another step, getting a better angle. What's he doing? thought Will. What the hell is Narrio doing?

Through the door. Touching one of the horses. Touching its head.

Climbing on top of a horse.

Will jumped over the fence.

"Kiff! Get Narrio the hell away from there. Stop!"

Did he say those words? Or did he just think he said them?

Because Kiff just yelled, "Three!" and flung himself into space, onto the rolling, wooden hills of the slide, while Will ran up the stairs.

As fast as he could, the steps creaking, the wood of the slide squealing as Kiff slid by him going the other way, sliding down.

The creaking.

The clicking.

Will almost stopped.

Almost froze on the steps. Because here it was again.

The clicking, the chattering.

Like crickets, but only louder.

Sharper. Teeth.

First faint, but then louder and louder until it seemed as if the sound filled this giant room . . . as if the racket was echoing off every pane of glass.

Narrio was on one of the horses, sitting on it.

Will got to the top of the stairs, breathless.

You're out of shape, Dunnigan, Henkel yelled. *You're out of shape! Drop ten. Do some laps. You're disgustingly out of—*

Will gasped at the air and ran up the stairs, toward the door.

He grabbed the handle.

To the door leading outside, to Narrio.

Narrio looked at him and smiled.

The door wouldn't open.

Narrio, the little Italian cowboy.

Yippee-tie-yay.

Will grunted and pulled at the door.

''What's wrong?'' Whalen yelled.

The clicking grew louder.

Don't they hear that? Will thought. Can't they hear that sound?

What is it? he thought. What could it be?

The door was jammed.

Or locked.

But then—how did Narrio get out?

Narrio rocked on the horse.

And Will thought he heard a different kind of click.

His hand froze on the handle.

Another click—no louder than the thousands of others— just different. . . .

And easily found.

It came from the bottom of the horse, from the post that held it locked on the single rail it traveled.

Narrio laughed, holding on to the metal stirrup.

The face was on each door. The wide toothy smile. The slicked-down hair. The poached-egg eyes.

The twisted symbol of Steeplechase.

The latch holding Narrio's horse popped up. And then the horse started sliding away.

Narrio's smile faded.

He tried to slide off.

Not a good idea.

Because the horse picked up speed, hitting an immediate downhill that sent the horse speeding away, to the other end of the building, toward the beach, and sea, and the waves.

Narrio nearly fell off.

Through the closed door, Will heard Narrio scream.

Will pushed his face against the glass. Narrio's horse soared up one side of the hill and then turned the corner of the building.

And Will couldn't hear him anymore.

He'll come around the other side, Will thought, looking across to the other side of the building.

And Narrio will be able to jump off there. If he moves fast enough, if the blotto fool thinks.

Will ran over there, thinking, What's the big deal? What if he goes on the ride all the way, what's the problem?

He heard Whalen behind him, following him, finally aware that something was wrong.

"What did he do?" Whalen called from behind Will.

But Will didn't answer. He had to get to the other side before Narrio went sailing by, without a drunken idea about how to get off.

Will got there, to the other side, to another door, another platform, another door that wouldn't fucking open.

I'll smash the glass, he thought. I'll yell at Narrio.

And then he saw what he must have known, must have seen before—but only in some dank corner of his subconscious.

The rails, the four rails for the four horses, came to an end.

They just ended.

In thin air. Right there, next to the platform.

Somebody had taken them down already. Started taking Steeplechase apart.

Part of the demolition.

They ended.

And now Will heard the scream again, closer, louder . . .

As the insane clicking, the sharp sounds, mixed now with Narrio's screams.

Will pulled against the door.

Surrounded by the din, the sound of a million teeth chattering in the frozen darkness, a million crazy, jabbering hungry teeth about to eat them all alive . . .

16

Narrio galloped toward Will.

His face twisted sadly to the side, as if he'd had a stroke, as if all the muscles in his face were gone. Even from yards away, Will could feel those dark eyes locked on him, begging him to help.

He looks sick, thought Will.

And Will screamed at him.

"Jump off the horse! Jump off the goddamn horse!"

I said the words, thought Will. I really did. I screamed at him. Then why isn't he moving? Why the hell isn't he doing anything?

The horse's eyes were frozen into the wild, frenzied excitement of the race. Its front hooves were perpetually up, ready to leap over the next fence, the next stream.

Narrio flew past Will.

And Will thought of smashing the glass. Reaching out and grabbing him. Yank Narrio right off the horse.

Except—he saw that Narrio's hands were locked on the metal stirrup, holding on for salvation.

"Jump!" Will yelled.

One last time.

As Narrio sailed by, unaware of what was ahead.

Goddamn you, Will thought. Why wouldn't you listen, why wouldn't you jump off the horse and—

The clicking was deafening.

I'm going crazy, thought Will. I've drunk too much and I'm going mad . . .

Like that gibbering idiot in the Poe story.

Screaming about that heart, still beating, under the floorboards . . .

There was a wrenching sound. Metal scraping against metal.

"Jesus," Will whimpered.

A prayer this time.

Another wrenching sound. And *there*—Narrio's scream.

Will watched it happen.

At first, Narrio and the horse sailed together, a wild leap into space as the rail ended. It was like the diving horse at the Steel Pier in Atlantic City. The horse climbed up, high above a giant tank at the end of the amusement pier, while some fat announcer in a spangled suit made lame jokes.

And when the horse finally dove off the small board, its legs shaking—so scared—its eyes were terrible to look at. They were so big with fear that they looked as if they'd pop out of its head.

A beautiful girl rode the horse. She held on tight, pressing her lean thighs against the sides of the horse.

She smiled. The horse looked insane.

This was like that.

Narrio's scream echoed from down below.

And Will had plenty of time to watch it all. It took forever to happen. Forever. He watched Narrio separate from the horse, still trying to hold on to the stirrup, but then the horse's heavy body pulled away.

Mass times acceleration.

Equals force.

Ouskoop demonstrated the principle with steel balls and an inclined plane. Different masses move with different force.

Then Narrio was flying free, the scream swelling, sounding pitiful, horribly sad. He knows what's going to happen to him, thought Will.

Plenty of time for that. Plenty. And Will watched the way Narrio's body landed.

Narrio's head was up. As if he were straining to get back to the rail. His hands were in front of him, like a kid trying to stop himself sledding too fast down a snowy hill.

But just below Narrio was a shed of some kind. It had a tin roof, a roof that protruded around the top of the building.

The horse crashed to the ground. The sound, the shattering sound of the metal carcass exploding against the ground, made Will shiver.

But then Narrio flew into the shed.

And the roof, the flat piece of metal, hit his neck.

Narrio's body smashed into the building. There was a sick dull thud, the sound flesh and bone makes when it smashes into something. The sound a rotten tomato made when he threw it against old Mrs. McDaniel's door at Halloween.

It went *splat*.

The roof sheared off the head.

The snapping sound was sudden, electric. Narrio's head tossed up in the air. A free ball, in play, spinning around and around. Still with that same lopsided look, still not too happy about what was happening.

Will saw the face move. It didn't know that it had no body.

"Jesus," Will whispered again.

Around and around, until the head careened off the top of the metal roof. There was a bang, a thud, and it rolled away.

Mike Narrio's ride not yet over.

Will backed away.

He looked around.

The clicking stopped.

It's just in my head, he thought. *Just in my fucking head.*

For a second, it was as if it hadn't happened.

He turned and saw Whalen, sweating, bug-eyed. Almost funny-looking . . .

And then Kiff, standing there, mouthing words, trying to say something, but Will didn't hear anything. Nothing at all.

Just the water now. And the wind whispering through the building. Whistling and wheezing the way it does in a cheap horror movie.

Oooooo!

And then—coming behind Will—he saw Tim.

Where's Narrio? he wanted to say. I've just seen the damnedest thing. So where the fuck is Narrio?

But that was *just it*.

Narrio was down there.

Something happened to Narrio.

Things were different.

And as Will looked at them, he thought: Now there are four of us . . .

* * *

They gathered by the shed, even though they knew that Narrio's head was somewhere yards away. Sitting in its own blood, in the darkness.

We don't want to see that, Will thought.

The body had smashed into the shed and then bounced backward so that now the stalk stretched out, pointing to the sea. A steady steam of red spread from it.

"Oh, God," Kiff said. "Oh, God, poor Narrio, poor fucking Mikey."

The stream just grew and grew.

So much blood in a body.

And Will looked up. There was a new smell now.

This sweet metallic smell mixing with the wood and oil.

To the left, one of those freaky faces looked down at them. The Steeplechase man. Happy at their plight. Happy at everything.

Sorry, Michael, Will thought, apologizing. I guess we shouldn't have come here. I guess we should have gone to the dance. And you could still play your trumpet. And laugh at Kiff's dumb jokes, and bust your ass studying calculus because it's such a bitch for you.

"Should we get him . . . his—shit! His head?" Whalen said. His voice came from miles away.

"What?"

"The head. Should we get it, bring it here?"

The stream was closer to Will. He stepped back a few more feet. It looked black and shiny.

Will laughed. What a stupid idea, what a silly idea. Yeah. We'll go pick up the head and try to put it back on.

Make Mikey as good as new.

His eyes stung. And Will wiped them. Why do my eyes sting? But he felt that they were wet. Wet, and when the trail ran down to his upper lip, he tasted the salt.

He turned away.

There were sirens. A few blocks away.

And when he turned away, he saw Tim. In the shadows with Kiff, pulling him aside, talking to him, whispering.

What's going on? Will wondered. What the hell are they doing?

"Man, I don't know," Whalen said, still considering what he should do. "Maybe we should—"

Kiff shook his head. Will heard Tim raise his voice. His arm held Kiff, tall, lanky Kiff, close to Tim's head.

Will took a step.

Tim looked up to him. Tim's glasses caught some dull reflected light.

Maybe he thinks I'm responsible, Will thought. That I could have saved Narrio.

But I couldn't, he thought.

I couldn't.

More sirens. Louder, closer.

Tim walked over to him and Whalen.

While Kiff stayed in the shadows.

"It's all worked out," Tim said. His voice calm, in control.

Will sniffed. His nose was running. He wiped at it.

"What do you mean, 'worked out'? What are you saying?"

Tim nodded. "It's okay."

"Okay?" Will laughed. "You gonna put Mikey back together again? You going to make him come back to life? What the hell do you—?"

Will was screaming.

And Tim came up to him and grabbed Will's jacket, his prep school blue blazer. Tim grabbed it hard and shook him.

"We're *all* fucked if we stay here. You understand? *We're all fucked.*"

Will was crying. Thinking: I want this over. I want this not to have happened. I want this to be yesterday, so I can decide not to do it. Please, God, please.

And he felt sick with himself because he didn't care about Mike Narrio now, he just cared about himself, about his terrible feelings.

Tim plastered his face right in front of him.

"We've got to get out of here. You understand—?"

Will shook his head.

He understood nothing now. Nothing.

Tim backed away.

And said: "Kiff said he'll stay. He'll stay and say it was just him and Narrio. Just the fucking two of them. He's suspended already. He'll fucking do it, Dunnigan."

Will looked over to Kiff, standing in the shadows.

"What?" he said.

And thought: What is this? Kiff's life is halfway in the toilet. So he'll take the complete plunge?

"We've got to move!" Tim said.

"Kiff?" Will said. "Kiff, what—?"

Kiff came out of the shadows. His face was milky white marked by the thousand specks of his freckles.

"Go," he said. "Get the hell out of here."

Whalen grabbed Will's arm.

"C'mon. We're leaving."

Tim and Whalen backed away, cutting through the park, back into the building.

Will stood there.

"Kiff," he said. "You don't—"

The sirens were there.

"You better go," Kiff said.

And, asking God to forgive him, Will ran away.

17

There was a ten-block walk from Will's subway stop on Flatbush Avenue to his family's house.

The streets were empty, deserted for his walk. He was alone, carrying his books, the strap all rubbery, the metal clasp cool.

Schoolbooks. Big test next week. Gotta study.

Big test. And maybe a funeral.

He walked slowly.

A car gunned its way up Avenue H. He heard somebody making out with a girl in a doorway. Heard their voices, low and sweet. He looked at them, and kept walking.

I'm back from the dance, he thought.

He imagined unlocking the front door and making his way quietly upstairs.

Hoping that his parents would be asleep.

Because if they woke up, they'd ask him.

How was it? Have a good time? Enjoy the dance?

And he'd have to smile and say yeah.

A real nice time.

His steps echoed on the deserted streets. The trees, still full of leaves, rustled as he walked by. He kept taking deep breaths, trying to purge his lungs of the air, the smells of the water, the wood, the sweet smell of blood.

We didn't look at Narrio's head, he thought.

We should have looked at Narrio's head.

Because, because . . . now.

Yes, now I'll see it for the rest of my life. Imagining what it looked like. For the rest of my life.

No one woke up when he got home.
No one asked any questions.
That all came later.

18

With a macabre sense of timing, the police interviewed them just before the funeral, right at the school.

One by one they were taken in, Tim first, then Whalen. Will sat outside the headmaster's office waiting for his turn.

They had their story. There will be no problem, Tim had said, as Will left that night and got onto the subway.

Now when Tim came out he walked straight ahead, and Will wondered whether he had cracked.

Whalen came out crying.

Then they called for Will.

The headmaster's office was filled with books, a dark red mahogany desk, matching red leather chairs. The headmaster, a small man, stood at the back. He introduced two men, detectives, who sat in the front.

They smiled at Will. Will immediately forgot their names.

They asked him about that night.

Will started talking. Slowly, carefully.

One detective, a rumpled-looking man in a too-small brown suit, flipped through a spiral notepad.

"You—you saw Jim Kiff buy the alcohol, son?"

Will nodded. Then he shook his head. "No, I mean we were outside. Kiff—Jim Kiff went inside and bought it."

The other detective, a young guy, cleared his throat. "And you drank it down at Manhattan Beach?"

Will nodded.

"You finished the bottle?" the rumpled man asked.

Will nodded again.

"Could you please answer aloud," the young detective said, frowning. "For the record," he said, smiling a bit.

"Yes. We drank it there."

Now the rumpled one nodded. "And can you tell me what the drawings on the rocks were about?" He dug a sheet of paper out of a folder. He passed it to Will.

Will looked at the circle, the star.

But they had their story about that too.

Sure.

It was a game. A drinking game. Something involving walking straight lines after drinking a lot.

Will handed the paper back.

The rumpled detective looked at his partner and then at the headmaster.

"Will, please be very careful to tell all the truth, just as you remember it."

Will turned around to Father Bryant. His face was locked in a grimace.

I may be in deep shit over this anyway, Will thought.

It wouldn't be the first time that a St. Jerry's Prep senior got his degree from Midwood Public High School.

"Yes, Father," he said.

"Will, what happened after you were finished drinking? After you finished playing your game?"

Will cleared his throat.

"We left the beach. And—and I wanted to go home. So did Tim . . . and Ted Whalen."

"But Jim Kiff and Mike Narrio didn't?"

Will shook his head, then he remembered the detective's instructions. "No, sir. They had drunk more than the rest of us. They were pretty high. Kiff wanted to go to Coney Island, to do stuff . . ."

And Will thought about the men, the corncob men that saw them at Coney Island. Maybe they'd be found. Maybe they could be witnesses. And the police would learn that there were five of them at Coney Island. Five of them, walking up to Steeplechase.

The rumpled detective nodded.

"So what did you do?" he asked.

Will looked him right in the eye.

"I went home, sir. I went home and went to bed."

The rumpled detective pursed his lips. He looked at the sketch of the pentagram inside the circle. He slid it back inside his manila folder.

Then he smiled at Will.

"We may have more questions for you later, son. But that's all for now."

Will sat there for a second, unsure of what to do. He turned to Father Bryant. "Should I go?"

The steely-eyed headmaster came forward.

"Yes, Will."

Will got up.

"I will see you and the other boys tomorrow," the priest said.

Will nodded. Tomorrow he'd find out what was going to happen.

He walked out of the office, straight to the school chapel, where his class was already seated, waiting for the funeral service to begin.

Will didn't see Whalen or Tim during the service, though he was sure that they were there. And he didn't see Kiff.

Because Kiff never came back to school.

It would be a long time before he ever saw Jim Kiff again.

And he and Tim and Whalen weren't kicked out. They were given what was called an in-school DA—disciplinary action. They were forbidden any involvement in extracurriculars. They were forbidden to speak with each other. They ate lunch at a special, supervised table.

And even when that ended, they didn't talk to each other.

As if the last thing in the world that they wanted to do was talk to each other . . .

Will started getting to school just in time for classes, and then leaving as soon as the day ended.

No one bothered him anymore. Not D'Angelo, not anybody.

Everyone knew that there was something wrong with his story. All their stories.

He didn't cry at the funeral. He couldn't imagine that Mike Narrio was really in the white box with gold handrails. Mike Narrio was still at Steeplechase.

And hearing Narrio's mother wail, her terrible keening filling the small chapel, was too horrible to allow Will the solace of crying.

He knelt and stood, and sat and knelt again, staring straight ahead, listening to the Latin mass, staring at the coffin.

Thinking: He's got his head back now.

Only one time did Will feel as if he might snap.

At Communion, when the entire school received.

And while Will sat in his pew, awaiting his turn, Mrs. Narrio came back from the railing, the host still in her mouth. Her husband supported her. She walked funny, with a small limp, as if there were something wrong with one foot.

Will kept staring forward.

But the woman slowed. She slowed, and she stared at him.

Right at him. Will felt beads of sweat on his brow.

Will turned just a bit.

To see her looking at him, her face a mask of horror and hate.

Her eyes were dry now.

No more tears, Will guessed.

Then she moved on.

And Will tried to breathe, to make the air flow in and out of his lungs evenly.

But he gasped at the air, filled with the smell of incense, the smell of hundreds of small votive candles, the stifling smell of boys' wool suits and scented vestments.

Later, he'd think of this as the moment that he lost his faith.

While Father Bryant rambled on about Michael's life, his love for his parents, his church. What a *good* boy he was. How he liked playing the trumpet.

Will waited for the celebrant to criticize just one thing . . .

Michael's choice of friends.

But that hoped-for penance didn't come.

And, after a while, Will imagined that he was alone inside the chapel. Just him and the coffin and the priest rambling on, forever, into eternity.

They gave Mike Narrio his own page in the yearbook.

He smiled out from page 3, under the heading "Dedication."

Will didn't need the picture to see Mike as he was, or what happened to him.

It was the sixties.

And a lot of things were about to happen to Will.

But Mike Narrio, the beach, that night, were always there, in Will's thoughts, in twisted nightmares, well into college . . . and beyond.

Until it all started again.

12:08

19

I've been tricked, Will thought. I got nervous and hid inside that coffee shop and now it's way past midnight.

I lost track of the time.

That's ironic, now, isn't it? Lost track of the time.

He stopped at the corner of Park and 30th, just up from the black building, all dark glass and steel. The black glass and steel building gobbled all the light.

Will shifted the bag in his hands. There was no doorman outside. It was an office building.

Except people came and went all the time, working around the clock. Industrious people, people trying to get ahead, to crawl above the rat race.

Will knew that. James told him that.

And he's in there, James said. *I saw him.*

Will looked at his watch.

He pressed a small button, and a tiny light illuminated the LCD face: 12:09. And then . . . 12:10.

He's in there, Will thought. If I haven't screwed up, if I'm not too late, *he's in there.*

Twenty-seven years later . . .

Three times 3 times 3.

And that equals 27.

A cube. A perfect number.

Mathematically pure.

That was more of the irony, Will thought. Three to the third power.

Twenty-seven years . . .

He heard steps behind him.

Will spun around, trying to snap out of his reverie.

It was just another hooker. He knew that just to look at

her. Didn't have to be a rocket scientist to see that. She walked up to him, dressed in ultra-tight shorts, shimmering yellow. And a tank top that exposed her midriff. Full, red lips.

Will looked at her.

And guessed that she couldn't be more than thirteen, maybe fourteen years old.

"Hi, babe," she said. "Want to go out?"

Not much older than my daughter, Will thought. For one terrible second he imagined her out here, part of the chain of money and coke that ran from this corner to the giant blow plantations of Colombia.

Will moved his bag from one hand to the other. It felt heavy, a constant drag on his arm. Heavy, heavier. He looked back to the building. No one came out.

And no one went in.

She took another step forward, her legs coltish and lean. "Whaddya say?"

Then he saw her look down at his bag. Good, he thought. She's not a total idiot. She's dimly aware that there might be something bad going on out here, that there's—

"What's in there?" She grinned. Nervous. "Homework?"

He nodded, thinking that he must look like any other forty-year-old guy with an attaché, looking for a cheap thrill, trying to chase away those midlife blues.

There's only one cure for them.

Only one . . .

She licked her lips. "We can have a nice party," she purred. More steps. And Will found himself backing up, against the wall. Another quick turn to check the building. A van blocked his view, then it passed, slowing, another potential customer checking out the action as the girl worked hard to sell herself to Will.

I should just tell her to get lost, Will thought. Take a hike. Tell her I'm a cop.

I'm shopping for something else tonight.

But he saw her eyes, still clear, still not completely fogged up by whatever hellish life she was leading.

Will walked closer to her. His bag swung on his arm.

"Look, don't you know what's been happening out here?" The girl squinted her eyes as if struggling to make sense of what he was saying. "Don't you read the papers? Don't you know what could happen to you?"

She grinned.

"All I know, honey, is that my man"—she turned, and pointed toward Madison—"is right down there, right there, watching over me." She smiled. "I'm protected."

Will nodded.

"Protected," he mumbled.

"Yeah," she said, "I'm—"

He turned back to the building.

Maybe James was wrong. Maybe we have this thing screwed up somehow. He looked at his watch: 12:15.

Unless . . . unless I'm late.

Like the White Rabbit, tumbling down a hole to the best little tea party in hell.

He turned back to the hooker, someone's little girl, all grown-up. Launching her career.

Making a name for herself in the Big Apple.

She was gone. He didn't see her, and he couldn't hear her. She's a ghost. A phantom hooker. Down the street were half a dozen dark cars. Maybe one of them had her pimp, watching over her trade. Maybe not.

Maybe she simply gave up.

A cop car came down the block. Slowly. Cautiously.

His paranoia snapped back into place. I've got to get out of here, Will thought. He tried to decide on which way to walk. The understaffed, under-the-gun cops might decide to pull him over for questions. And then look inside his bag.

Is this your gun, sir? And this bottle, would you mind telling us what this is, sir? And here, in the bottom of the bag, could you tell us—?

Will turned and walked down Park Avenue. Damn! he thought. I won't be able to see the black building. I won't see him come out, see him melt into the streets . . .

He kept walking, looking over his shoulder, searching for the peaceful blue and white colors of the cop car that terrified him.

He passed an electronic teller. Ready to spit out money for those postmidnight moments when you're a bit tapped out.

Will looked back again. He saw the nose of the patrol car at the corner of 30th Street. Go straight, he ordered. Keep on going, Officers. He took more steps. Another look. The car edged closer to the corner until Will was sure that the two cops must have a clear view of him.

Shit!

He kept walking.

He listened to his steps. Counted his breaths.

One. Two. Three.

He turned around.

Thinking:

The light must have changed by now. But the patrol car was still there, and he cursed himself for looking again, alerting them.

I'm here, he was saying. I'm here and I'm nervous.

Looking pretty suspicious, don't you think?

Now he picked up his pace. Twenty-ninth Street was just ahead. He walked into a breeze. A steady gust blew from the Battery, up through Chinatown and SoHo, and all the way to Harlem. An Atlantic breeze slicing through the stone canals of the city.

He was nearly at the next corner.

Nearly there, and he had to risk another look back. Just to make sure that the patrol car had really continued across Park Avenue, trolling other waters, out of the way.

The cops should be his allies. But not tonight. Not here.

He looked.

Just as the patrol car took the damn corner, slowly, tentatively, a big cat spotting an undersized gazelle.

No, he thought, got to get away. He walked briskly to the corner . . . he reached 29th Street, moving further away from where he needed to be.

Near the black building.

If I'm not too late . . . if it isn't already too late.

He took the corner, and he was swallowed by the darkness . . .

Will kept on going down the gloomy block. Past closed restaurants, and than an import shop, and a hotel with no lights anywhere. Was it closed forever, or merely sealed up to keep the streetwalkers and their johns at bay?

He was alone on the block.

All by his lonesome.

It's past midnight.

Do you know where you are?

He didn't want to walk this way. The breeze had been cut off, and now he smelled the street, the sidewalk. The stench of years of garbage and food and spit and oil and droppings from hundreds of air conditioners groaning to keep the horrible city heat away. Now silent, braced for winter.

He sniffed.

His bag swung from his arm.

He turned.

Will watched the patrol car fly down Park Avenue, picking up speed. They weren't interested in me after all, Will thought. I'm just jittery. Paranoid.

Maybe crazy.

It was a possibility.

Three times 3 times 3. The number danced in his head.

He stopped.

I have to go back, he thought. I have to go back to the black building and wait for him . . .

If I haven't screwed up, if it isn't all screwed up . . .

He stood there.

And then he heard a sound . . .

It was a voice, soft, plaintive, calling out from some stone steps leading to a basement, to a small restaurant.

But Will just stood there a second.

He licked his lips.

Probably just a wino rolling around in his perpetual lost weekend, fighting off hordes of imaginary—and perhaps real—vermin.

But he listened to the sound.

It was a woman's voice, raspy, full, as if—

He walked closer to the side of the building to the steps leading down.

He leaned over the edge of the railing.

And he saw the entrance to the closed restaurant. L'Auberge Savoie.

He saw the girl. The confident hooker he had seen only minutes ago . . . only minutes ago . . .

Lying at the bottom of the stone steps, all crumpled up, one leg bent back at a sick angle, her head tilted backward.

The red of her lips had spread, and now her chin, and her neck, were filled with red blotches.

Not lipstick.

She had her hand crossed in front of her midriff. Her cute, sexy midriff.

As if she were holding something there.

"Help . . . me . . ." she wheezed. All of a sudden she was a hundred years old.

"Please."

She moved her head a bit, so that her eyes could see him. Will nodded, and moved to the steps, hurrying now, wondering why he had hesitated.

Knowing that he was too late.

He's out.

Out *here*, in the streets. Anywhere, everywhere.

And now I may never find him.

He squeezed close to the girl.

She extended a hand to him, reached out to him.

Which she shouldn't have done. Because now her insides were all open.

She had been neatly filleted. The skin of her flat stomach had been cut with a cross, up and down.

Another bit of irony? Will thought.

Then peeled back until everything inside just hung there, exposed.

James had told him he might see this.

"You might see the Ordeal," he had said. "Don't let the signs, the works, get to you."

But it got to him. It got to him *good*. Will froze, unable to take her hand.

Even in the sallow pit by the restaurant door, her viscera glistened with a slimy life that was at once horrible and depressing.

"No," he whispered. "Put your hand back. Put it on top of your—"

Will smelled something. The blood, of course. And her perfume. Yes—but there was something else, wasn't there?

Sure, there was another smell.

"If you get that," James said, "if you're lucky enough to smell something, anything, of the emanations, then move!"

Right, thought Will. Move.

Do what the man says.

Get up and get out of here.

"Please," the girl said.

Will thought he saw her try to speak. She opened her mouth. Her tongue moved. But the smells—they were definitely there—suddenly overwhelming.

There was no breeze down here, nowhere for the vapors to escape.

He sucked them in.

There was a squishy sound from the girl's innards. A coiling and an uncoiling.

A pit of snakes.

Will reached out for the wall.

I've got to get up. Get up, turn around, get out of here.

"I'll get you help," he lied.

But the girl's eyes flashed.

You can't lie to the liar.

Never works. Never has. Never will.

Her other hand came off her midsection, exposing the perfect symmetry of the dissection performed on her. The girl's bloody hand closed on his.

"I said—I need some fucking help," she screamed, a hissing belch of disgusting air flowing over him. He thought he'd faint. He gasped, choking on it, coughing and dragging phlegm up from his throat.

Then there was the sound.

As if he only heard it yesterday.

Chatter, chatter, the nasty, busy little sound of teeth. Clicking away, thunderous, echoing off the cement walls of their intimate alcove.

A bloody bubble popped from the girl's midsection, and another, and another . . . louder, mixing with the clicking sounds, a regular party.

He tried to jerk his hand away.

Her grip was strong. The only way that hand is coming off is if I hack it away.

Another great bubble popped from the girl's viscera. And then a shape squirmed out, a weird offspring released by the grotesque cesarean section.

Will started yammering, "No, no, no!"

Losing it. All gone, he thought. All gone.

I fucked up.

His bag, his stupid dumb bag, was next to him, sitting there, while this—

Head. A bulbous Uncle Fester head squirmed out, and then Will saw two eyes, dripping the girl's blood. They blinked open. They looked at Will.

The smell was beyond anything Will had ever sensed.

His stomach spasmed and clenched—fistlike, fighting to expel anything inside it.

But James had told him to eat nothing.

Nothing. No food. No liquid.

And so Will just felt the sick tightness in his midsection and around his chest.

Arms now dug out of the girl's midsection, two, three, maybe more, crawling out. It was hard to tell. Then a gigantic membranous tissue, a panel, wing, a flap of some kind, jutted out of the thing's back.

Will jerked away, yelling at the thing.

But he felt something hot on the wrist where the girl held him. He looked down. He saw that her fingers had all melted together, blurring into some kind of flipper shape. And now those fingers were melting against his flesh, joining him to her.

The Uncle Fester head groaned.

A mouth. The thing has a mouth. At least it has a black opening.

It had only taken seconds.

Will kept screaming at it.

No. No. No.

Over and over.

Until he heard James's voice again.

Right there, in his ear, above the bubbling and the clicking.

James had looked in Will's face and told him clearly, calmly:

"Turn away from it, Will. That will be your only chance. Turn away."

The burning was worse. Flesh melting into flesh.

The red-black membrane spread above him, above the head, the girl, whose body rocked left and right with horrible spasms of this hellish birth.

Will closed his eyes.

Did he feel his bone rubbing against the girl's bone, joining?

He turned against the wall.

He closed his eyes.

The clicking, the chattering . . .

The teeth were everywhere. The universe was teeth.

His other hand felt the bag.

"God help me," he said.

And he opened his eyes . . .

Kiff

20

It was the last cookout of 1992, the last time you could wear short-sleeved shirts and a baseball cap. The last time you could sit outside and feel the sun on your face and hope that winter would never come. The last time you could imagine that there was no such thing as snow and ice and dark, ugly clouds.

But Indian summer was no summer at all, and the deceptive warmth of midday gave way to long shadows that sprouted too early on Will Dunnigan's backyard lawn.

The breeze carried the smoke of the barbecue away too quickly, as if eager to be done with this nonsense.

Will pressed down on the burgers, cruelly squeezing juice out of them that splattered down to the gas-fed pumice stones. A small blanket of flame came to life above the stones and licked at the sizzling meat.

Will liked tending the barbecue, though he eschewed the usual accouterments of chef's hat and goofy apron.

Give the chef a kiss!

Will knew why he liked it, and so did Becca . . .

He picked up his beer, a warmish Coors Light, took a sip, and looked at Becca. She was sitting with a bunch of their friends gathered around her. She was laughing and making them laugh. Two things that she was very good at.

Becca was, they both recognized, the complete opposite of him. With all her natural exuberance, her openness, her warmth, Will was at the other end of the universe.

I'm the yin to her yang, he'd joke. And that was true enough. She thrived in social situations. The more the merrier. She put everyone at ease, made absolutely sure that everyone knew the name of all the other guests. She'd introduce people two and three times, until everyone felt like old friends.

Parties and picnics were her natural element.

And then there's me, Will thought.

Though his few personal friends from Legal Aid wouldn't say so, Will felt handicapped in any crowd larger than two. The social wheels just don't spin for me, he thought.

Which was why he liked tending the grill.

It gave him something to do. People might come over and jokingly ask *the chef* how things were coming. Stand there a moment and inhale the aroma of charbroiled burgers blackened to a primitive state of carbon. But Will could squeeze and flip the burgers, and generally keep busy.

His daughters played hostesses. Sharon, the older, walked around with tacky little wieners wrapped in dough that she insisted just had to be served at the picnic.

She wore a long dress and no shoes. Her brownish-blond hair caught every bit of sunlight God was sending down.

And she was beautiful. Will ached with love nearly every time he saw her like this, at a distance, as if she were someone else's kid.

And thought: She's my daughter.

There's something halfway decent I turned out.

He took another sip of his beer.

Then there was Beth, named for Becca's mother just a year before she died.

Except Beth, at six years old, was no Beth. More of Larry . . . more of a Moe.

She had no interest in the long dresses or beautifully combed hair. She tended to mutilate her Ken and Barbie, removing legs and heads as her play bordered on the Frankensteinian.

And what gift did Beth have.?

That was easy. Laughter. It didn't always come when they appreciated it. More than once they stormed out of a restaurant, fed up with Beth rocking in her seat, laughing at the food, or the service, or the other patrons.

She had a thing for bald-headed men.

Made jokes about their egg-shaped heads.

Sharon would laugh or grow embarrassed, whatever was

her ladylike wont for the day. While Will often felt prisoner of Beth's wicked, out-of-control sense of humor.

Which left Becca to do the disciplining.

Will flipped the burgers. This first batch was nearly ready.

He tried to signal Becca, to let her know. She was talking to some of the teachers from her school.

Will waved a spatula.

Someone patted him on his back.

"Calling in the reinforcements?" a voice said.

Will turned around. It was Brian Vann.

Invited at the insistence of Becca.

"You never know," Becca had said. "You might leave the public defender's office and want to start a practice. Brian could *help* you."

Will tried to explain that you don't start a practice at forty-one. Doesn't happen.

I made my bed, Will tried to explain. Public defending is dirty, cheap-paying law work. It serves the public good but you'll never get rich.

Hell, even with Becca's salary, sometimes it was hard to make two ends meet anywhere near the middle.

How was I to know that the eighties were to be the decade of greed? Missed that boat completely. I always did have a proclivity toward the unfashionable.

"Hello, Brian," Will said. Will looked at Brian's Molson bottle, the dark green glass hiding its status.

"Need a fresh one?"

Brian shook his head. "No, just grabbed this one myself. So how are you doing, Willy?" Brian asked, with the concerned, forthright expression of someone who wanted, in intimate detail, the exact status of your life at that moment, from the bedroom to the bankroll.

Will turned back to the burgers.

"Good. Keeping busy. Handling a few interesting—"

"I bet. Say, did you read about John?"

John Fortier was another neighborhood lawyer who was, from all appearances, doing extremely well. He was also at the picnic, sitting and listening to Becca.

"No."

"He's been made a full partner in his firm."

Will nodded. Trying his damnedest to be disinterested.

Brian came closer.

"The grapevine has it that he's going to be good for half a mil a year, minimum."

Will smiled. "That's great."

Super. Fantastic. Best fucking news I heard all day, Will thought.

As if to confirm that fact, the pleasant part of the day faded as a puffy cloud, a rogue cumulus patrolling the blue ceiling, blotted out the brilliant sun. Gooseflesh rose on Will's arms, encouraged by the ever-stronger breeze.

"Getting chilly," he said. To Brian. To himself. He wasn't sure.

Then he turned to Brian Vann, alighting at last on a strategy to make him go away. "Could you ask Becca to come over? We're about ready to go here."

"Oh, sure," Brian said. And then Will watched him hurry over to Becca, interrupting her in midlaugh.

She looked over at Will, and he guessed that he must look like a forlorn figure, standing by his Gasjet grill, a reluctant soldier in the suburban army.

"Oh, sorry," she said, walking up to him, her smile now gentle and sweet. It was a special smile that, for all of Becca's social graces, he knew she reserved only for him. "I was just talking about my new principal . . ." She made a small laugh.

"That's okay." He pointed down at the grill. "These suckers are ready."

"Gotcha," she said, grinning more broadly. "I'll get the paper plates set out."

"What a smart girl."

Her hair was darker than Sharon's, but it was long and—for these days—unusually straight. She felt no need to crop it to the size of a beanie or whip it into a frenzy of exotic curls that—in another era—would have been called tawdry.

And though she was a bit rounder than when they got married fifteen years ago, she looked appealingly sexy. As he liked to joke with her . . .

I guess we'll keep you around.

The truth of it was more simple.

Without her, he'd be lost.

To his work, to his thoughts, to his dreams.

To himself.

She's my lifeline to the planet, he knew.

"Don't *boin* the *boigers*!" she said. Her best imitation of a Brooklyn accent.

An accent that he had lost somewhere between skiing in Vermont and four years of college in Massachusetts.

He smiled and started shoveling the meat patties onto a big metal tray.

"Hors d'oeuvres?"

He looked up. Sharon held her tray of pigs in blankets as if it were a gift from the Magi. She was twelve going on forever.

The only time Will felt hopeless, defeated by life, was when he thought about the future.

What kind of world will she and Beth get?

It's not just a case of it being *different*.

The world had become a jungle. Dangerous, hostile, thick with vile things that could take her sweetness and squeeze it right out of her.

We should move to fuckin' New Zealand, he thought.

But then—he had just read a story. They got crack there too. Some local politico helped finance a crack operation run right there, out of Christchurch.

"Oh, cocktail wieners," he said, gushing. "My fave." He snatched one and tossed it into the air.

"Dad-deee!" Sharon said, horrified by his gaucheness. But she was smiling, laughing at his trick.

He nearly missed. But he caught the end of the mini-frank and gobbled it like a cormorant tossing back a squirming herring.

"Dad, that's not how you eat them!"

"Oh, no?" he said in mock surprise.

Sharon shook her head in disapproval.

But Will was saved from a real scolding by Becca, calling their guests to the suddenly set picnic tables.

And he left his post, and carried his spoils to his well-lubricated guests.

"What do you think, Will?" It was Brian Vann again, attempting to lure him into the discussion.

Into a discussion about a subject Will knew nothing about. He looked at Becca, feeling her eyes on him, knowing how uncomfortable he was.

Vann recapitulated. "You see, the SEC claims insider trading, since the corporation counsel did have prior awareness of the sale. But the CEO countered with the fact that his counsel had only heard *speculation* about the possible sale, among a number of other possibilities. It's a judgment call, the legal team claims. All perfectly legal."

Will winced. Why is he doing this? he wondered. Is he trying to embarrass me?

"It's way out of my field," Will said, wiping his mouth.

Brian was at least four Molson Goldens on his way to lugubriousness. He pressed on.

"But that's exactly what I mean. You're out of the corporate rat race—"

We all know what that means, don't we? Will thought.

"You'd have a good legal opinion on the matter, as an outsider."

Will nodded, feeling the trap close, irresistibly tight.

Vann waited. Then he said: "So what do you say?"

Will cleared his throat.

Stand back everyone and hear the lowly paid, onetime idealistic public defender speak on a matter that he has no knowledge of.

Crack I know. I knew four different ways to process the shit, a dozen ways it can be brought into the country. I know how a human mule forces the condoms full of raw cocaine into his stomach, making, for once, their dumb-ass lives finally worth something.

And I know about guns, not that I've ever fired one. But I know what people in the inner city favor as a weapon—a police magnum, if they can get it. But any compact 35mm handgun will do. I know how many drunk drivers are on the road each Friday and Saturday night and how many of them are tooling around in unlicensed cars without insurance.

I know about men who beat women and children. Every day, until something really bad happens and they sit there, shaking, talking to me.

They got rights too, I tell myself.

And sometimes all I want to do is blow them all to hell, all of their fucked-up, twisted lives, filled with drugs and weapons and pain and stolen cars.

Blow 'em the hell away.

While I pack up my family and go . . . where?

Not New Zealand.

A town called Alice? Down under . . . and sinking fast. Or Ireland, where the potato famine reigns eternal? Or Japan, where the stressed-out businessmen read S&M comics like Rapeman?

Mars. Ice Station Zebra?

Face it, kiddies, there's no way out of here.

Despite what the Joker said to the Thief.

"Well," Will said slowly, realizing that everyone was listening for one of his infrequent excursions into the chatter of human concourse called conversation, "I think that if anybody is dealing stocks, bonds—junk or otherwise—and they have any inside information of any kind and they use it . . . well, I think that you can probably get their ass thrown in jail."

Will took a slug of his now putridly warm beer.

He realized that there was silence.

Wrong answer, he guessed. That wasn't the answer that everyone was clamoring to hear.

Brian nodded. Then, as his look of dismay melted away, he forced a big grin onto his tanned face.

Aruba, Jamaica.

That's where the big bucks take ya . . .

"Right. Sure, Will. With the right prosecuting DA, with a crackerjack government lawyer." He paused for effect. So that everyone could realize the unlikelihood of that happening. "But with the best legal help money can buy, I don't see how any company would have to spend more than a few minutes worrying about it."

"Not that we'd recommend it," Fortier, new VP with stock options to burn, added.

People laughed at his witticism.

Which Will didn't see as a witticism at all.

He rubbed his eyes, retiring to his role as ex-chef and member of peanut gallery.

When he took his hand off his eyes, he saw Becca looking at him, her smile small, and sad now. Knowing what he was feeling.

Which is what? he thought. What the fuck exactly am I feeling?

He looked at Beth playing with the other kids, tossing a Frisbee with a hole in it, running around, dashing in between the long shadows of the house.

What am I thinking?

That I have to do something about my life. Make some time for friends. Do things . . . play golf, racquetball, something to shake me out of my funk.

And maybe—go on, he told himself, admit it . . . you've been thinking about it . . .

Maybe ask for some corporate work on the side. Some legal stuff, a handout from Vann that would bring some extra money in the house.

So they could upgrade one of the cars.

Maybe finish the family room that still looked like a garage.

He smiled back at Becca.

Here I am, he thought.

This is my life.

And—for some reason—I don't feel too happy about it . . .

He got up to clear the table. Becca didn't stop him. She understood.

He just hoped that nobody suggested that they move inside, and let the picnic roll on into the evening.

But like a lot of his wishes lately, that one didn't come true either.

Becca combed her wet hair, pulling the brush through in smooth, gentle strokes with her head tilted to the side.

Will picked up the remote control and flicked to the National League play-off game. It looked as if the Mets were about to go down to another loss to the Cubs. Then the series would be tied 3–3.

"Was it terrible for you?" Becca said.

Will grunted, kicking off his sneakers, undoing his jeans, watching Frank Viola trying to pitch his way out of what had been a disastrous inning.

Take him out, Bud, Will urged the manager.

Another pitch. A ball. And then—the telepathy worked as Bud Harrelson oh-so-slowly crawled out of the dugout and ambled over to Viola.

A tad too late, Will thought.

"Well, was it?"

Will turned to her.

"Was it what?"

"Terrible. The picnic."

He shook his head. "No. It was fine." Then—a look of concern—"Did something go wrong? Something happen?"

She shook her head. Her robe slipped open a bit. The kids were sound asleep, exhausted from all the playing and partying that kept them up past their bedtimes.

He looked at Becca and was glad that this unfortunate ball game was nearly over. He considered a shower.

"You seemed really—uncomfortable, when we were eating."

He turned back to the tube. Bud Harrelson called John Franco in from the bullpen. A good choice, though his relief work was a bit off these days.

"No. It was fine. Just talk. The usual."

She got up. He saw her out of the corner of his eye as she walked over to him. She draped her arms over him and pressed herself close. He smelled her hair, the wonderful clean smell. She leaned up and kissed his cheek.

"You made wonderful—"

Another kiss.

"Burgers."

He smiled.

Franco's first pitch was a ball.

"Shit," he said.

She reached down, in front, rooting into his underwear.

Will grinned. "Come on, John," he said. "Throw something with a little action on it."

Her hand grabbed him, squeezing him with an authority. But now he enjoyed teasing, watching the game while she worked on him, pressing against him.

Franco threw a strike.

But it didn't seem to matter anymore.

"Hmmm," she murmured against him. She was up on her tiptoes. She took a swipe at his ear with her tongue, tracing a wet line around the outer lobe and then down his neck.

She pulled at him, hard, then gently, letting her fingers work an ancient magic.

Who cares about baseball? he thought.

He shut the tube off with the remote and turned to Becca just in time to see her slip out of her robe.

* * *

Later, in the dark, he turned away from her. He looked at the window, heard the rustle of the trees outside. The tiny squeaks of air trying to whistle their way into the house.

Becca threw her arms around him and pulled herself close. Sleep came fast for her now, and—while still breathing a bit hard—Will knew that this would take him away, a perfect moment, in just an instant.

And he lay there, suspended, detached, feeling safe and warm for the first time today.

Loved, protected.

God is in His universe.

And all is well with the world.

Slowly, like a helium balloon freely drifting away, higher and higher, into a perfect sky, he lost hold of consciousness in such a blissful, dreamy way . . .

But the phone rang.

Shocking, hard, the jangling bell sound tearing through his peace like a knife.

It rang.

Becca's arm slipped away.

She grunted, turning to the glowing dial of the digital alarm clock. "It's eleven-fifteen," she said. Her voice was sleepy. "Who'd call us at eleven-fifteen?"

She didn't like getting calls this late. Usually they were drunks who misdialed.

"Is Joey there? Uh, can I speak to Joey?"

There's no Joey here.

"Where's Joey?"

And then—the real dumb ones dialed the same wrong number again.

"Hello, Joey?"

Will sat up. The phone rang one last time.

And even then—somehow—he knew that his life was about to change forever.

He picked up the receiver.

21

The voice said, "Hello."

There was a pause. Then, again, "Hello, Will."

As if I should know who this dingbat is, Will thought. As if it was someone I know . . .

No one *I* know calls at 11:15 at night.

Unless something was very wrong.

"Who is this?" Will said. "Do you know what time it is?"

Then the caller said his name.

He said: "It's Ted Whalen, Will. Ted. From St. Jerry's . . ."

Will paused. He turned and saw Becca watching him. Waiting for a reassuring smile, or for him to slam down the receiver, muttering about late night drunks who don't know how to touch seven buttons without screwing up.

But he didn't smile.

Who is it? she mouthed.

"Will?" the voice said again. "Are you still there?"

"Yes . . ." Then, with some difficulty, "Still here, Ted. Ted . . . it's kinda late." Will paused, dumbfounded. He always expected ghosts to rear out of his past. But he hoped some would stay away forever, melted into the woodwork.

History.

Ted Whalen was one of them.

I thought that was understood, Will thought.

I thought we all knew that.

"I wouldn't have called you if I didn't think it was important. I just got off the phone, Will. I'm in Los Angeles. And . . . I guess I just forgot the time."

For a second, Will almost said, How are you doing?

How the hell has your life been for the past twenty-five years?

But he said nothing.

Maybe he'll go away, Will thought.

Whalen's voice rumbled. He cleared his throat. "I just got off the phone with Jim Kiff."

At the name Kiff, Will immediately saw one image.

Saw it as if he were there—now—standing in the darkness.

Kiff, standing beside Narrio's body, laying claim to the blame while freeing the rest of them to run away. Kiff, claiming his heritage, his fucked-up life.

Tim Hanna once said that he had gone to see Kiff weeks later. Just for a few beers in Germantown. So did Whalen. But Will never did, never wanted to.

"Kiff . . ." Will said. "Let me put you on hold."

He pressed the button down and turned to Becca. She watched, playing their game of guessing who's on the phone. Playing this time, and losing.

"I'll take this downstairs," Will said, hearing how distracted his voice sounded. "I'll tell you about it later." He shook his head.

As if it were beyond fathoming.

And he walked out of the bedroom and downstairs to the phone in his small office just off the living room. Fumbling, he turned on the artist's light that craned over his cluttered desk. He picked up the phone and pressed the button below the blinking light.

"Still there?"

"Yes," Ted said.

Will thought he should say something, ask something . . . as if it were a normal call, at a normal hour.

"How are you?"

"Good. Not bad. I'm in insurance . . . annuities . . . tax shelters. That kind of thing. Doing well . . ."

"Great," Will said. "I'm always reading about Tim Hanna."

"Yes," Whalen said.

Tim Hanna had done better than well for himself. Tim Hanna had done so well that Will couldn't imagine that he might be the same person that they had gone to school with.

It was hard to imagine that one of New York's most pow-

erful businessmen and his old friend from school were the same
person. Tim Hanna owned real estate in three cities, primo
office complexes, shopping developments, and a small, up-
scale movie theater chain. He owned a piece of the Palace, in
Atlantic City.

He had powerful friends . . . He hung out with the glitter-
ati. At least once a week his face was in the paper. A fund-
raiser. A social occasion. Politics was rumored to be the next
step.

Good for him, Will thought.

Will never heard from him.

And he never called Tim.

"And you, Will?" Whalen said. "Are you okay?"

"I'm good, Wh—" He paused, about to call Whalen by
his last name, the pull of adolescence still strong . . . powerful. But instead he said, "Ted."

Another pause. Will heard the bed of static on the line.
Not a great connection.

He waited for Whalen to tell him what led him to call. Will
waited, growing more nervous, more upset at the way the
past can suddenly become the present, at the way a wall of
decades could just melt away.

As if it were yesterday . . .

"I tried calling Tim, but you know how things are with
him. Left a couple of messages. He was in Boston, maybe
Washington. They didn't know. But, well . . . Then I had
your number from the alumni directory."

"Uh-huh."

Whalen cleared his throat again. "It's about Kiff, Will. I
stayed in touch with him. A call now and then, just to see
what he was up to. Which wasn't much. I guess I felt a bit
guilty . . . responsible . . ."

Will noted that this man on the phone didn't sound much
like the Ted Whalen that he knew. Guilt? Responsibility?

Strange words coming from the cynical Ted Whalen.

Time does make for odd sea changes.

"He had a real bad time of it, Will. Real bad. He went to
Fordham for a year, dropped out, and then Uncle Sam
grabbed him."

"Vietnam?"

"Yeah. He had twenty-twenty vision and he was more ed-

ucated than most of the ghetto kids that they were feeding
into the meat grinder. So he made lieutenant and got to take
everyone out into the rice paddies looking for the enemy.''

"Poor bastard.''

There was one sorry platoon to be in . . .

"Yeah. Then he came to see me when he got out. He
came, and stayed for a week, then two, until finally I had to,
like, just tell him to leave. He was a mess. You know, a vet.
Hell, when he looked at me with those eyes—shit, Will, they
were like pie plates. I was scared. I didn't know. I thought
he'd kill me.''

But the point? Ted Whalen. What's the point? Why are you
calling me?

"But he left?''

"Yes. And then I'd get these cards, scribbled postcards
from Tempe, Arizona . . . then Mexico City . . . a donkey
wearing a big sombrero. I thought he was into drugs, dealing
stuff. But he wasn't . . .''

Will heard a sound upstairs. Becca walking around. Or
maybe one of the kids getting up to pee. Good night, Mommy,
Beth always trooped in to say. G'night, Daddy.

Except I'm down here now. Down here, listening to this . . .

Then, on the phone, Will heard Whalen take a drink. The
clink of ice cubes, a rattle followed by a slurp. Whalen cleared
his throat again.

A nervous tic. A habit. Or is Whalen scared?

And where is all this leading?

"The postcards stopped. And I was glad. I didn't want
him in my life. I was married at the time. I had a kid.''

From the tone of Whalen's voice, Will suspected that those
things were in Whalen's past.

"Then—about three years ago—I got another postcard. It
was a scrawl. Two sentences, barely decipherable. No address, but the postmark was clear enough. It was Peru. Fucking Peru! Can you imagine? And it said, 'I'm coming home.
Because there's no getting away, no running' . . .''

"What?'' Will laughed. He was losing interest in the ad-
ventures of Kiff.

Crazy men lead crazy lives.

"Running from what?''

Another clink, ice in the glass, and then, "I didn't know.

But I started thinking, and thinking, and I got kind of worried.''

Will doodled on a yellow pad in front of him. Mindless scribble, circles, and arrows, and—

"Shit, I thought about that night, Will. And Kiff taking it on the chin. And—I didn't know what the hell he was going to do. God, he was a fritzed-out vet at this point. He was capable of *anything*."

"And he had *your* address. I see what you mean."

"I thought that maybe he just wanted to tell the whole story, everything that happened back then." Will noticed that Whalen didn't mention Narrio's name. "They'd open the records, our names would be brought up again—a lot of hassle."

"That's ancient history," Will said, none too confidently. "No one's interested."

"I thought—I thought that maybe Kiff would want to get back at us."

More doodles, circles, and pointy things inside the circles. He flipped over the sheet of paper. Exposing another clean piece.

"Then he came back to New York. He called me. He tried calling Tim. He said he tried to reach you."

Will's number was unlisted, a necessity in his line of work. But the St. Jerome's directory had it, an option which he was glad hadn't occurred to Kiff.

"He sounded crazy, Will. He babbled on about someone following him, that he was being watched. That something was going to *happen* to him, to *all* of us soon. All because of that night—"

Will shook his head and moved the receiver to his other ear. "He's crazy, Ted. Crazy. Don't worry about him. Get a new phone number, keep it—"

"No. You're not listening, Will. He came *back*. He went to Brooklyn. I know where he is."

"So?" Will sighed, trying to keep this insanity as distant as possible.

"He sent me clippings . . . from the paper . . ."

"Clippings?"

"About those murders, those girls . . ."

"What girls?"

"Didn't you see them?" Whalen asked. "Don't you read the paper?"

Will laughed nervously. He was beginning to think that maybe Whalen was crazy too. "All the time. But what are you talking about?"

Whalen continued. "He sent me clippings, articles about the murders in the city, the girls being cut up in the streets . . . God, you must know about it. You're right there, for Christ's sake. I'm in California. But you're right there."

Will looked up. He was staring at photos of his family. Beth dressed as a bunny holding her Easter basket. And Sharon, a princess dressed in white from last Halloween. And a photo by the beach with Becca wearing a two-piece suit and looking beautiful, full of life.

Now he knew what Whalen was talking about.

Of course, everyone knew about those murders.

What was the body count? It was run as a banner headline by the *Daily News*. Nine dead since the summer began? Or was it up to ten?

And there were all these lively descriptions of how they were killed.

With surgical precision, the tabloids said, slavering over the detailed prose that let the readers imagine just how each woman was killed.

Slowly. That seemed to be the murderer's first concern. The women were cut laterally and vertically, from the chest to the abdomen, and the skin was peeled back. There was evidence that things were done to their insides, tiny tears, probes, and cuts to exacerbate the pain.

Their throats were cut, rendering screams or any cries for help impossible.

The *News* called him "The Madman."

The *Post* dubbed him "The New Age Ripper."

Calvin Thomas, the New York police chief, was trapped in a cycle of holding a news conference every few days, saying the same hopeless words, while the mayor looked discomfited, embarrassed, standing in the background.

We have nothing to report in our investigations . . .

Week after week . . .

The street hookers reported that business seemed to be off. *Live at Five* interviewed three of them, a titillating coup.

They said that they weren't scared. They had—smirk, smirk—protection.

Now for a look at the weather.

"He sent me all the clippings, the photos . . ."

Will heard Becca walking upstairs, maybe concerned because he had disappeared, summoned by this strange late night phone call.

She knew nothing of Whalen, or Kiff or Tim Hanna or poor Mike Narrio. None of it.

Nobody did.

Will stood up. He held the phone, standing, wearing his pajama bottoms and no shirt. He felt cold, then colder, as he started to flash on what Whalen was suggesting.

"Wait a second. Hold on. What is this? Are you saying that Kiff has something to do with these murders?"

Will felt trapped in his office, in his room. His pen slashed at the yellow paper, jabbing at it, filling it with pointillist dots.

"God, Will, no. He sounded too . . . scared. I just don't know. I got real worried for the poor bastard. Maybe he's gone nuts. He told me that he has to talk to someone, someone he can trust. He says he *knows* what's happening."

"I doubt that . . . But he wouldn't tell you?"

"No. He said he couldn't talk over the phone. That *he'd* find out . . ."

"Who 'he'?" Will smirked.

"I don't fucking know."

"Sounds like class-A paranoia, Ted. Why don't you call the NYPD. Call them, tell them about Kiff, the clippings. Let them deal with it."

"Could you wait a second?" Whalen said. And Will said sure. He heard Whalen get up. He heard the ice tumble into Whalen's glass, three thousand miles away. Whalen . . . getting more fortitude for his call. He came back, breathless.

"I thought of that. Don't you think that I thought of that? But what if he has nothing? What if it's all crazy Vietnam whammer-jammer, and I send the cops to whatever creepy place he's living? It wouldn't be right."

Will suspected that Whalen was lying. That wasn't the reason.

Nobody develops that much kindness late in life.

There's something else. Something he's holding back.

"And there's this. Shit, Will, what if the cops get him talking about Coney Island, and Narrio? The whole thing will come out again. There might even be hearings or something. I—I couldn't afford that."

Will looked at the photos of his kids. He wouldn't want them hearing the story either. In the tabloids, the newspapers. *Live at Five*. Dead at Six. Newscenter Nowhere.

Because the story—the scandal—would be big news. Real big.

Because Tim Hanna is big. A giant. What was the phrase natty Tom Wolfe used?

He's a Master of the Universe.

Boozy Ted Whalen was right.

It wouldn't be good for anyone.

And then Will had a creepy thought. Kiff could be a real embarrassment to Tim Hanna.

Maybe crazy Kiff has a good reason to be paranoid.

Will sat down. He shivered. It was cold, and he had had enough of this catching-up with Ted Whalen.

Enough . . .

"Ted, I think—"

"Will, I'd really like you to do something . . . I think that you gotta do it."

A car passed by the house, moving slowly, deliberately. A patrol car, Will guessed. On the hour, every hour. Keeping suburbia safe . . .

"Someone has to talk to Kiff. He needs help."

Will laughed. "And what if *he's* the killer, this madman? You know how to ask the big one, Ted."

"Listen!" Whalen ordered. "You can see him. And if you get any strange vibes, you don't even go inside his place. But shit, Will, *he's* the one that sounds scared. He babbles about these murders as if he's fucking terrified. He begged me for help. He pleaded with me to—"

A gulp. Will imagined Whalen drinking Stoli straight. A nice mellow drink for a quiet California evening.

"I—I can't do it. I would. If I was there. But you could. You owe it to him, Will. We all do. Christ, I wouldn't ask you if I was there. You got a family . . . kids . . . ?"

"Yeah."

"Great. But we owe a chunk of our lives to Kiff. He took it all, Will. He took it all. And if he's flipped now, we can try to help him."

Definitely hiding something, Will thought. I haven't spent two decades with slimeballs without my antennae going up. All the cards aren't on the table.

But he pictured Kiff, holed up in his apartment, scared out of his mind, needing an old face from the past.

And somehow, for some reason that he couldn't remember later, Will said, "Okay."

Whalen gave him the address. It was in Brooklyn near Livingston Street. It was near part of the Williamsburg section that hadn't been gentrified yet . . . maybe never would be.

Kiff lived over a bar.

Whalen gave Will his own phone number. His number at John Hancock. Whalen thanked Will.

And he hung up.

Will looked at the pad of yellow paper.

He looked at the circle, and the star inside it, and everywhere dots, tiny dots and larger dots, clustered together like spatters of paint.

Will crumpled up the sheet and tossed it into the trash basket.

22

She wanted to know all about the phone call, who it was, why the heck they called so late, talking until midnight, *past* midnight. Who could have called? What was the emergency?

Will was drinking from a cup featuring Minnie Mouse in a bathing suit playing with a frisky Pluto.

Half the glass was rum, left over from a party months ago, when summer began and everyone had too many daiquiris.

He thought about lying.

He thought about telling her it was a friend. With problems. An old school friend, getting divorced, needing someone to talk to.

But he looked at Becca, studying her, and he realized that he wanted to tell her, that he wanted to tell someone.

What really happened that night.

Everything about Manhattan Beach, about Steeplechase, and poor Mike Narrio getting killed because Will didn't stop him in time.

But he just told her about Kiff going crazy from the war, of bouncing around the country, a crazy man with tales to tell. A school friend, like Tim Hanna . . . Ted Whalen.

An old friend from school, in trouble, whacked out.

He didn't tell her about Kiff's clippings, about a connection with the neatly dissected streetwalkers in New York, about Kiff's jabbering fear, that he knew who was doing it . . . that someone was after him.

That would scare her.

For no reason. It was crazy stuff.

And when he was done, she told him to get in bed. It was late. She shut the light off.

And he lay very still, his face turned away from her, so she didn't know that his eyes were wide open.

Staring into the darkness.

23

Will groaned, turned in his bed. He grabbed at the sheet, tight, tighter, holding on to it as if it were a life raft on a churning, icy sea.

He opened his eyes.

In his dream.

Where is was a wonderfully sunny day, where the sun was brilliant and shining so brightly that it sparkled, a yellow diamond set against a rich, blue velvet.

His two daughters held him, one on each hand, tugging on him, pulling him along, squealing, "Oh, Daddy, look!" And, "Can we go there, can we try that?"

He looked up. Becca was beside him, looking at him holding their two girls, smiling, happy at this wonderful day and all this sun.

He looked up.

Yes. He saw where the girls were pointing. It was an amusement park. There were rides. And children in colorful sun suits, pale blue and crisp white. And fathers dressed in baggy, pleated pants eating hot dogs. And women in dresses and hats.

Dresses and hats. Splashy floral prints and white straw hats.

He looked at Becca, and saw that she was dressed the same way.

There was something odd about that style of dress. Odd.

He wasn't sure why.

He kept walking, his daughters tugging at him, pulling him further into the amusement park. The signs were colorful, bright reds and lime green. A hot-dog stand was just to the left, a ticket booth ahead, and all around the amazing peaceful sounds of the rides and the laughter.

What amusement park is this?

What place is this? he wondered.

He assumed that it was Playland, the colorful, clean amusement park in Rye, at the sleepy end of the Long Island Sound.

That's what he assumed.

But—he guessed—you should never assume things in a dream.

Ha-ha.

Never.

His girls—Sharon, Beth—pulled him up to the ticket booth. He laughed, a helpless prisoner, digging out his wallet. His wallet was so fat, overloaded with dollars, plenty of dollars to buy plenty of ride tickets.

His girls hopped up and down, and squealed next to him.

Will waited on the ticket line.

He waited. It crawled forward. He got annoyed, then mad. What's taking so long, what the hell is—?

Finally, Will was next. The person in front of him looked like—

—an old man, an old hunchbacked man. Now, why is he buying tickets? What would someone like him want with tickets?

Will watched the old man pick up his tickets and then the man turned around.

He looked and looked at Will.

His sallow face was grizzled, cut with lines and tired furrows. The man opened his mouth and a gummy residue of spittle stretched between his lips. A dry, cracked tongue moved inside the cavern of his mouth.

"Have fun," he croaked.

Will pulled his daughters back. The man nodded and shuffled off.

Will shook his head, shook away the feelings. He moved up to the counter.

He opened his wallet. Letting go of Sharon, of Beth. He opened his wallet. Looked at the sign . . .

One ride ticket: $13.

Very reasonable, he thought.

He dug out the bills, counting them out. A breeze sprouted around the booth and threatened to send his pile of bills swirl-

ing. He slammed down his fist—chuckling—imprisoning the
bills. Counting them out. Never looking up.

"Twelve," he said ponderously, like a small boy counting
marbles. "Thirteen," and he shoved the bills forward . . .
and looked up.

The person inside the booth reached down below, to a
drawer or a cache, and pushed a circular ticket to Will.

Steeplechase Park, the round ticket said.

No, Will thought in his dream. That's impossible. Steeplechase is closed. Gone.

He took the ticket.

The person in the booth leaned close. Out to the light.

Will saw his face.

The leering, grinning face. The teeth fixed in a sick grin,
a grimace that could only come from rigor mortis. The red
lips, from ear to ear, caught the light.

"Have fun," the Steeplechase man said.

Will looked around for his daughters, grabbing for them.

But they had run ahead, of course.

They had run ahead, inside the park, into the great white
wood and glass building.

He saw Becca chasing after them, falling behind.

Will held on to the round ticket, outlined with circles, one
circle for each ride.

You need a ticket to go on the rides, he told himself.

And he ran after his daughters . . .

You'll laugh till it hurts!

That's what the sign said, above the round, mouse-hole
entrance to the fun house.

This is the real entrance, Will thought. The way you're
supposed to go into the Steeplechase building.

Not like the way we did that night.

He saw all these people, in dresses and sun suits and baggy,
zoot-suit pants, walking with him, into the tunnel. A mechanical voice laughed all around him.

He didn't see his daughters . . . he didn't see Becca.

The hole opened up and everyone had to walk on these
slabs of wood that jiggled back and forth. People laughed,
fell down, got up again.

There were clowns on the sideline. Watching. Checking to see if anyone got hurt.

Safety clowns.

That's good, Will thought. That makes me feel better. He looked ahead, straining to see Beth and Sharon.

And he saw them, getting onto one of the spinning dishes. Locking arms with other people, strangers, everyone excited, breathless, waiting for the dish to start spinning. Will took a step.

The wood block moved, and he tumbled to the floor. His knees crashed hard against the wood. He started getting up.

The clown watched him.

The clown's oversized lips were frowning.

The clown looked angry.

Will took another step.

The dish, and his daughters, started spinning.

The wood block jigged.

"Oh, gee," he said, caught completely off guard again, and he fell again, harder this time. He looked over at one of the clowns. "Hey," he said. "Give me a hand. Help me off this thing." Will started to crawl to the side, to get an easy way off the wood blocks. He reached out his hand.

And the clown pulled a pole from behind his back. A long pole with a hook at the end. A sharp hook. The kind of thing you might use to grab at a tuna and pull it aboard a ship.

Will froze. Backed up a bit.

The clown reached out with the pole. Will shook his head.

Then the clown jabbed at Will, quickly, suddenly. He hooked Will right in his side. The clown twisted the pole, curling Will's skin, his muscle, around the hook.

Will screamed.

But everyone went on laughing.

Ha-ha-ha.

The Funny Place.

The hook popped free, and Will rolled backward, back to the center of the wobbly road leading further into the building.

His blood dripped off in big dollops that made noisy splats on the wood.

Be careful, he wanted to caution the other patrons. You don't want to go slipping on that.

I had a little accident . . .

He looked ahead, rocking side to side.

He saw the dish. His daughters, sitting together.

They waved to him. Becca stood on the side. She yawned.

While the clown with an air hose crept up behind her. Uh-oh. Watch out, Will thought in his dream. That nasty clown is going to shoot some compressed air under your dress. He's going to send your dress flying into the air, and everyone will see your cute bottom, your frilly panties. Uh-oh, watch out.

The dish started spinning. Slowly, calmly, as if there were nothing to fear.

But then faster.

And even back here, even standing here on the moving wood blocks, Will heard the screaming, the delighted, terrified squeals begin.

He grinned.

Ignoring another gummy chunk of blood splattering to the ground.

Just got to stay away from the clowns, that's all.

He heard a song from cheap speakers. Dion and the Belmonts.

Come-a-come-a-come-on, little angel . . .

Faster.

The dish moved faster. Beth looked scared. She was the youngest. Of course, she'd be scared.

He looked at Becca, at the wily clown creeping up behind her. She doesn't see, he thought. She's going to be surprised.

Faster. The people on the dish became a blur . . . except, there, at the center, he could still make out Beth's and Sharon's faces. He couldn't tell whether they were smiling or crying, but they were there.

People started spinning off the dish, rolling to the side, as they were supposed to.

Only.

He watched someone roll to the side. One person. Then another.

He saw what was wrong.

The dish was lined with sharp spikes, curbed, shiny hooks that surrounded it. As each person rolled giddily to the outside, they came flailing against the spikes.

Where they were skewered. Imprisoned.

"No," he mumbled.

He took a step and fell to the ground. He looked to the left. Another clown, another hook. Waiting for him to try to sneak off.

The only way was forward.

And when he stood up, he saw Becca, standing there. The clown with the air hose was just behind her. He reached under her dress.

And shoved the hose up, up, right into her. That's not what's supposed to happen. That's not how it's done. That's not funny.

Becca turned. Will saw her face. Blood started bubbling out of her mouth.

He heard her scream clear and pure above the others.

It wasn't an air hose. It was something else.

Will took another tottering step. The wood was whipping wildly back and forth. He crashed to the ground again.

He watched someone go flying off the dish. Some kid.

The kid rolled into the spikes, caught neatly by the spikes ramming to his chest, his gut.

Will saw the face.

It was Jim Kiff. Looking the way he did the last time Will saw him.

Another body, right next to that one.

No, he thought.

Ted Whalen, as Will remembered him. Rolling over and over, until he rammed the metal spikes and sent a shower of blood flying over the heads of the people watching the ride, laughing, waiting their turn.

Then—

God, no.

Please, no.

Beth.

His baby.

The one that could always make him laugh.

He heard her "Dad-eeee!" from all the way over here, nice and clear.

Becca was on her knees, watching too, while the clown pulled out the hose, the drill, whatever it was, and started working on her skull.

Will closed his eyes.

He heard a small thud, a squishy sound. He turned to the side.

The clowns stood with their hooks, waiting.

He went there anyway.

Just like they wanted him to.

A clown, in green and orange stripes, with a tuft of red hair and giant blue nose, hooked Will even before he got to the edge.

Hooked him, and then started digging around in his chest, scraping past the skin, the muscle, the bone, into some unfathomable pit within.

The wood blocks shimmied back and forth.

And Will cried, harder and harder. He heard Sharon's scream.

He reached out to grab the pole . . .

Will knocked the end-table light over.

He sat up.

Breathing hard. The room was dark, just the glow of the clock. He felt the sweat on his brow.

Becca snored beside him.

A low, almost comical rumble. She said she never snored.

Will kept breathing in and out, fast, in and out.

He brought his hand up to feel his side, to feel the place where the hook, the clown's fishhook, had been.

The air was cold, chilling him.

The clockface advanced to the next minute.

It all started melting away. The building, the ticket taker, the clowns, the dish, everything.

That was a bad one, he told himself. Crazy stuff. A real bad nightmare.

He knew why he had dreamed it, of course.

Because of Whalen's call. Of course. That's what did it. Just a nightmare, he told himself.

He shook his head.

No. There was something about it.

He got out of bed.

He wife snarled at the air, gulping it, and then she settled down into a rhythmic growl. Will got up, walked to the door and out to the hall.

A Mickey Mouse night-light cast a yellow glow from the

bathroom. He peeked into Beth's room. He saw her, all curled up at the foot of the bed, her head facing the wrong way, a menagerie of plush toys standing guard.

Then across to Sharon's room, so neat and orderly it put the rest of them to shame.

He looked in.

She slept perfectly, a princess awaiting a prince. He was tempted to give her a kiss on her brow.

He shook his head.

It's four o'clock in the morning.

I had a bad nightmare and now I want to go waking everyone up.

He thought about going downstairs. Getting a glass of milk. Turning on the big bright fluorescent light. Put the radio on to some all-news station.

But all he wanted to do was get back into bed with Becca. Pull her warm body close.

He closed Sharon's door and walked back to his room.

Past the spill of light from Mickey.

Inside, taking care to slide into bed easily, not creating any wind to awaken Becca.

He draped an arm over her.

He shut his eyes.

He opened them.

He thought of the dream. The screams. The bodies. And then the strange part. Whalen . . . Kiff.

And he knew something.

He knew that he'd call Jim Kiff in the morning. Maybe even go see him.

I owe it to him, Will thought uneasily.

For now, he forced his eyes shut . . . and tried to keep all the thoughts away.

24

Jim Kiff crawled closer to the piece of green linoleum.

The green square sat there, right over the hole, just a thin piece of linoleum.

But he was afraid to move it.

Always was. Every day, every morning. But it had to be done.

No way around it.

He felt safe in the apartment. Of course, he had put things all around the apartment, things that would alert him . . . things to protect him.

There were bells. All kinds of bells: a Christmas ornament and a tiny bell from the top of a Smurf pencil. An old doorbell. A cowbell that clunked more than rang.

They were all over.

A porcelain bell that he stole from a Hallmark store.

Bells in front of the door leading down. At all the windows. At all the entrances.

He didn't know whether they'd work or not.

The experts were divided on that subject.

They weren't sure.

But he wasn't taking any chances.

The door was locked—little good that would do. He also had a chair, a cheap ratty chair with the stuffing ripped out of its plastic-covered seat—wedged tightly against the door.

The window *was* a problem. He had a bar crossing the top pane, locking it. But the glass could still be broken.

But I'd hear that, Kiff thought. Sure I would. I don't sleep too soundly. Not anymore. Not in years.

Only sleep a few hours a night.

If you can call what I do sleep.

I close my eyes. Then in a few hours I wake up. Like now. Thirsty, ready to go to work.

Even thought it's too early.

Even though there's no one downstairs. Even though the bar is empty—will be empty for a long time.

He couldn't wait until Jimmie came, and the gin mill opened and they came. People. I'm safe when there are people around.

At least Kiff thought he was.

His hand reached out to the piece of loose linoleum.

He licked his lips.

Then he backed up.

Another shot first, he told himself. Something quick.

He sprung to his feet. Backing up into a table. A little bell rang.

He nodded. Took a breath. I did that, he told himself. He turned to make sure that the bell, a tiny hand bell he found in Caldor's, was still hidden under the shoe box.

It was.

He snorted. Always so mucusy in the morning. Always a damn cold, or the flu, or something. Until he got a few under his belt. A few eye-openers.

He walked to the table. The tabletop was a cracked, red Formica. There were stains on it that looked as though they had always been there.

But he guessed that he had probably made them . . . and just never cleaned them.

He unscrewed the top of the bottle. He picked it up.

Don't need a glass, he thought. Just having a sip. That's all.

He took a chug, then another. Then another.

The Seagram's felt soothing going down. But then—feeling that the bottle had passed the halfway point—he was disappointed. Jimmie doesn't like me going through so many bottles, he thought.

"Take it easy, Kiff," Jimmie joked. "Leave some for the customers."

But Jimmie liked Kiff. Liked the way he got the place all swept up in the morning.

It was a good job. Got this small apartment right above the bar—so damn convenient. And drinks on the house.

Shit, it was a great job.

He put the bottle down. Then he picked it up again and took another swig.

This was breakfast.

He never got drunk anymore. Couldn't remember when he got drunk last. No matter how much he drank. And he drank a lot. Had to. Or he didn't feel so good.

He bled, all right. From his asshole. Sometimes from his nose. Now, why the fuck did that happen? And he coughed all the time, even when he wasn't smoking.

And sometimes his muscles, his legs, felt funny when he walked, as if they didn't have any strength anymore, as if they were ready to pack it in. But he didn't get drunk.

I can hold my liquor, he thought.

No problem.

He put the bottle down.

He saw the books on the battered bookcase . . . something he found on the sidewalk on trash day. Must be fifty books on the shelves, most of them ripped off from the library. They used to be in alphabetical order. But he kept digging them out all the time, checking stuff, reading things, so that they were all mixed up now.

The books told him what happened.

Told him about the bells.

Probably saved my life, Kiff thought.

He had some pages ripped out and taped to the wall. Things he wanted to remember. There was a prayer used by St. Etienne. Maybe it worked, Kiff thought. Maybe it didn't.

And lots of pictures of crosses. Russian crosses, and Greek crosses, and Catholic crucifixes with Jesus in agony. And even some plain, boring Protestant crosses, silver and gold.

He had two real crucifix crosses. One hung right on the door. Another at the window. They were blessed. He got a priest to do that. With holy water—the priest convinced him that the water had definitely been blessed too.

They might work.

Or they might not.

Jimmie said he didn't want any crosses in the bar.

The customers wouldn't like it.

"This ain't church that they come to." He laughed, talking to Kiff. "They come here to get away from all that shit."

Kiff nodded.

But he hid a small crucifix under the bar, off in a corner where Jimmie's meaty hand would never discover it.

All this, thought Kiff.

All this, and I know I'm not safe.

Never have been.

That's why I called Whalen. He can call the others. They can get some help, some real help.

He looked at his bedroom, more of a closet, all dark, with the window facing an alleyway, away from the morning sun.

The other pictures were in there.

The photos of the girls, the headlines. The articles describing the way it was done.

Just like in the books.

Kiff chewed his lip. He looked back at the hole in his floor.

I should get down there, he thought.

He walked back to the loose piece of linoleum. He knelt down. His bones creaked, and his muscles let him land hard on the floor. He knelt next to the linoleum.

It made him pat the pockets of his pants. He felt the rosaries. One in each pocket.

He reached out and took the cracked square of linoleum away.

Underneath, there was a hole. A ragged hole girded by splintery shafts of wood.

As if a giant rat had chewed right through the floor. It was the size of a softball.

But it hadn't been a rat.

Jimmie said someone once fired a gun. Another time he told Kiff that this guy had killed himself in the apartment.

Heh-heh. Don't go getting any ideas, Jimmie said.

Just never got it fixed.

Kiff pushed the linoleum to the side. And slowly, breathing hard, excited, thirsty—always thirsty—he leaned closer to the hole.

I have to do this, he told himself. Otherwise, how can I be sure?

He cautiously brought his face down to the hole so that he could look with his left eye.

He saw the bar.

Barely lit by the few neon signs that Jimmie left on all night long. *The Silver Bullet. Miller Lite. The King of Beers.*

He didn't smell anything.

That was good.

Just the smell of the bar, the deep, sweet smell of beer and booze, filled his apartment. That smell was his life. There was no difference between the smell of the bar and his apartment.

But he didn't smell anything else.

He knew from the books that was a good sign.

So he always sniffed before he looked.

Don't want to get tricked . . .

He heard a creaking noise behind him. At the window.

He shot up.

It came from his bedroom.

He turned. Suddenly cold. He snorted at the air.

He heard it again. But Kiff could see the window, see it, and he knew that it was just the wind, pressing against the window.

He went back to the hole. To finish his survey. He checked behind the bar, studying each shadow, each dark corner that could hide something. He looked at the booths, the few tables. Then up to the rest rooms.

Someone could always be hiding in there, he thought. But he had an answer for that problem.

As soon as he got down, he locked the doors with sticks, old broom handles. He locked the cellar door too.

If someone was hiding, they would be locked up.

They'd have to make a hell of a racket to get out.

He laughed at his choice of words.

Hell of a racket.

He did one more survey, knowing that he couldn't see every spot, every dark corner.

There was some unavoidable risk involved.

He knew that.

But then, satisfied—as satisfied as he could be—he pushed the square of linoleum back into place and stood up.

Kiff took another swig of Seagram's, marveling once again at just how fast a full bottle turns into half a bottle.

And how half a bottle begins an inexorable march to empty.

Until it was time to start all over again.

"Okay," he said to himself, screwing the cap back on.

It was time to go to work.

And he went to his door, the heavy wooden crucifix on the back. He opened it and went downstairs.

Kiff heard traffic outside. Cars gunning past the bar.

Soon Jimmie would come with a paper under his arm and a bag of rolls.

"Roll, Kiff?" he'd ask. And Kiff would smile and say no. Not hungry this morning, Jimmie.

He used the big broom to push together the piles of dirt and cigarette butts, catching stuff he missed last night. Then he'd wipe down the bar and the tables with soapy water. And if there was time—and he was sure that the basement was quiet—he'd bring up a new keg, though they got harder to lift. Maybe restock the bottom shelf, the Four Roses, the Seagram's. The stuff that moved.

The radio was on, just noise, in the background.

He pushed the broom.

The phone rang.

Once. Kiff stopped.

The phone rang again. He stood still.

For a strange reason, Kiff thought it might actually be for him.

And when he went and picked it up, he discovered—thank God, thank sweet Jesus!—that he was right.

25

Brooklyn has changed.

But I knew that, Will told himself. Brooklyn changed, the world changed. Everyone's run away. To Long Island. To Westchester. To the wasteland of New Jersey.

He looked at the neon above the bar.

Jimmie's Bar & Grill.

It was open. Through the smeary window, Will saw some men slumped over on stools, staring into their beers. The tube was on, glowing an iridescent blue and green.

The place was completely uninviting.

To get here, to free up this day, Will had to call in some favors to get his cases moved to another day on the docket. There was nothing major pending, a few DWIs, a small possession rap. A guy who likes to take out his frustrations by beating his wife.

Nice citizens in trouble with the law.

It was cloudy. The warm glow of yesterday's picnic, the flash of Indian Summer, had been replaced today with an almost icy chill. His leather jacket offered little protection from the nipping wind.

An old black woman walked behind him pulling a two-wheeled cart filled with groceries. He saw her steal a nervous glance at him, and then hurry on.

I look pretty strange out here, he realized. Standing outside the bar. Looking in.

So this is where you ended up, Jim Kiff . . .

And Will walked to the door and went in.

No one looked up when Will walked in.

This is the waiting room for hell, he thought. Pick a stool, sit down, and wait for the next express to Gehenna.

The bartender was leaning toward a customer, his foot rakishly resting on a shelf below the bar. His white apron, stretched by a full-sized gut, was speckled with the scars of too many weeks between washings.

Will walked up to the bar.

The bartender looked at him, raised his eyebrows, but still made no move to come over. Will waited politely, looking at him while he finished delivering whatever pearls of wisdom he was dropping in his customer's ears.

Two men next to Will were carrying on a form of conversation, an inchoate, disorganized babble. Will listened while the bartender—slowly—disengaged from his high-level confab.

"Shit, wha' ya gonna do? There's not enough fuckin' cops in the city." The philosopher to his left took a slug of beer. "Too many fuckin' murderers, not enough cops."

His companion nodded, sipping at a shot glass. Then, with the authority of an imprimatur, he said, "Too fuckin' right, Johnny."

"And the judges! Real scum bags, I tell you."

The bartender looked over again, his eyebrow arching even higher this time as if he had just noticed Will, just saw him—on time delay—wander in to violate the intimate social circle of his establishment.

He walked over to Will.

Put down a Bud Light coaster.

"What'll it be?" he said.

Will had entered the joint with the idea that he'd just ask where Kiff was. Get his missionary work over. Pay his debt, offer some advice, and escape from Brooklyn. But the gloomy, suspicious air of the place made him feel that he should—at the least—order a beer.

"A beer," Will said. "A light beer."

The bartender nodded. He grabbed a glass that—unless Will was mistaken—still bore the soapy sheen of a cursory washing. The bartender put it under a spigot and pulled back, the glass expertly tilted, cutting the head to a neat one-quarter inch.

A professional at work.

Will put down a dollar. The bartender scooped it up and slapped back a quarter.

Will took the beer and sipped it, cool but not cold. He looked at the TV. ESPN was on with a motorcycle race held in some Martian-like desert terrain dotted with sagebrush and cactus. With the baseball play-offs in full swing, afternoon baseball was over . . . and there was no joy in this particular Mudville.

Will took another sip of the beer, a big one, and then he craned around, looking at the bar. There was a scattering of tables, idle, as if awaiting a flurry of guests. And some booths, bathed in a stygian darkness. Anything could be happening over there and no one would see.

Anything.

He saw two rest rooms—Ladies and Gents—lit by two naked bulbs. Will bet that if he inhaled deeply, another odor would join the pungent smell of beer and whiskey.

He turned back to the bar.

The bartender was back with his customer, but he was also watching Will. His suspicious eyes met Will's and then he stood up straight. He rubbed his hands against his apron.

Will responded by taking another slug of his beer. Then the man ambled over. "Get you another?" he said.

Will smiled. He shook his head. "No. I don't think so."

The man prepared to withdraw.

"Say," Will said. "I'm looking for an old friend of mine."

He waited, letting the bartender draw closer.

"Yeah . . ." the bartender said.

"He's supposed to be working here, living near here." The bartender squinted. "His name is Jim Kiff."

The bartender rubbed his hands on his apron again. "You're his friend?"

"Yeah," Will said, smiling. "We went to school together."

The bartender's face turned grim, nasty, and Will guessed that Jimmie—if that's who this was—probably had a pretty interesting history himself. "A friend," the bartender said again. "You wouldn't be jerking me around?"

Will imagined that they got their share of process servers and back-rent collectors haunting the denizens of Jimmie's.

Will smiled. "Scout's honor. I just—I want to see Jim Kiff."

The bartender nodded. He walked to the end of the bar,

and for a moment Will thought that the bartender was going to go over to one of those black stalls and kick something hiding in the darkness. Force it to come awake.

Instead the beefy man, with a bald spot not really covered by a thin veneer of carefully combed hair, walked to the back of his establishment, near the rest rooms. He opened a door. Will saw light, steps.

"Kiff!" the bartender said. Then louder, "Kiff, you got some company."

The bartender backed away from the entrance.

And he smiled, as if a neatly placed trap were about to be sprung.

"You can go on up," the bartender said, grinning, then arching his eyebrows. "He lives up there."

The bartender waited.

And Will slowly slid off the stool and walked toward the door, the light, the stairs . . . to his reunion with Jim Kiff.

"Will, I can't believe it."

Kiff met him at the top of the narrow stairs, holding open a door to what unknown wonders Will could only guess. When he had spoken to Kiff on the phone, it had been brief. The phones aren't safe, Kiff had said. Right, Will said, already regretting his call. He gave the address, the name of the bar off Church Avenue.

And now here was Kiff.

He looked skeletal.

Even before Will stood next to him, just the way Kiff looked scared him. His skin was tight against his face, molded to his jaw and cheekbones, collapsing in on itself. Will feared the way Kiff's hand would feel when he reached out to shake hands.

Kiff still had red hair. It was thinner, standing up like lonely shafts of wheat blown apart by a twister.

Will got to the top of the stairs.

Kiff stuck out his hand. It shook in the air, almost blurring, wavering back and forth. Out of control.

Then Kiff's hand closed on his. It was cold and bony. But it held on with incredible strength, not letting go. Desperate was the word that occurred to Will, and he squeezed back, hoping Kiff would release him.

"Hi, Jim," Will said.

Kiff pulled him into his apartment, still holding on to him.

The first thing that struck Will was the smell, the stench that filled the place. All the bar smells were here, but there was more. There was the odor of food gone real bad, and the ferric sting of urine, from a toilet that had been abandoned to a rainbow of discolorations.

Will felt the beer churning around in his stomach.

He tried to pull his hand back.

"Oh, sorry. I—hey, Will, I'm real glad you came. Real glad. You look good, Will . . . real good." Kiff's face fell as if reminded that Will could no way in hell return the compliment. "Whalen told me that you're a lawyer. That's great . . . real great." Kiff paused. Then, hurrying, breathlessly, "And you got a family."

Will smiled. "A wife. Two girls."

Kiff didn't smile back.

"Yeah. Right. Hey, I told Whalen, I told him that I didn't think there was a lot of time." Kiff turned to the wall.

He's crazy, Will thought. Whatever was left of Jim Kiff was probably still back in what was now called the Nam.

He's a wreck.

Only one question, Will thought.

One crucial question . . .

Is he dangerous?

Will glanced at the bookshelves, the pictures taped to the walls. The drawings of crucifixes, and strange symbols, Egyptian squiggles, and fragments in Latin, in Greek.

"He tried to tell me to calm down," Kiff went on talking, but he was looking over at his shelves. He turned to Will. "Oh, sit. Here . . ." Kiff gestured at a ratty chair near a table. The table was dotted with the explosive remnants of food.

Kiff stopped.

The social amenities momentarily forgotten.

"Oh, sorry. Would you like a drink? I mean, something to drink. I have—"

Kiff left his shelves.

"No, Jim. I don't—"

But Kiff walked over to a sink. He picked up a bottle of Seagram's.

A full bottle. Kiff picked up two glasses with his other hand. He put them on the table.

"I'm a little jittery," Kiff said. "This whole thing has got me—" Kiff unscrewed the bottle and poured two drinks, one into a Fred Flintstone jelly jar, the other into a Sau-Sea shrimp cocktail glass.

Kiff took the larger glass. Drank half of it in one shot.

He grinned at Will. His teeth were brown. Will imagined that he could smell Kiff, smell his breath wafting across the table consuming him.

"Yeah, er, Jim, Whalen said that you were upset about something. That it had to do with us . . . with Mike Narrio." Will hesitated about bringing up the thing that had him really on edge. He laughed nervously. "And something about the murders in New York . . ." Will dared mention it. "That they have something to do with us . . ."

And Will found himself looking around for a weapon. I don't want this guy to grab a steak knife and play slasher film with me.

Will paused. And now he couldn't imagine whatever made him come here.

Kiff is crazy. Completely alcoholic. That was clear. And what the hell is it with all these crucifixes?

Five minutes, Will thought. That's all I'll give him.

Then I'll consider my debt repaid.

Kiff licked his lips. They were thin, shrunken to thin, emaciated strands of muscle. Cracked.

His tongue looked pretty gnarly too.

"Okay," Kiff said as much to himself as Will. "Okay. You see. I got to tell you what happened. I got to try to explain." Kiff spun around and pointed at the books. "It's all in here . . ." He grinned. "But you don't have the time, of course. None of us has the time." Kiff made another crazy grin.

Shit . . .

Kiff finished his drink. Poured another. A few seconds that stretched for an eternity.

Then he began his story . . .

"It started after I came back," Kiff said, almost casually, "after Vietnam. I was—I guess I was a bit fucked."

He left it to Will to imagine the horrors and weirdness.

"I—I started reading about the occult. About black magic.

About the spirit world. I got into Castenada, Crowley. You know them?''

Will nodded politely.

''And I began to think—a lot—about what happened to us that night . . . what happened to Narrio. And I was in Arizona living with Indians, real Indians, Will, who still had their ceremonies. And this magic man, this *brujo*, told me that he could see it. And it wasn't no accident. He could see it, in my face.'' Kiff took another sip. ''It was no accident . . .''

Will squinted. Four minutes left, and I'm out of here.

''What do you mean, 'no accident'? We were stupid, Jim. We shouldn't have gone into Steeplechase. Narrio died because we were just *stupid*. And you got screwed for it, Kiff. You took it for us, but—''

Kiff stood up, shaking his head angrily. ''No, that's just it. If something had happened to us there, on the beach, something we could have seen, then we might have known what was going on. But we were tricked. We were drunk . . . and when it happened later . . .''

''*What* happened later?''

Kiff's eyes went wide—at least as wide as they could. His bony hands cut through the air, seeking the convincing gesture . . . the confident stance.

''We called on something, Will. We really did . . . and then the deal was struck.''

''Deal? What—?'' Will laughed.

Kiff held up a hand. His nostrils flared in and out, and Will felt his fear. The apartment was icy, and Will looked to the right, where he had seen a window. He saw the gloomy room, a corner of an unmade bed. A metal bar holding the window shut. Another crucifix. Newspaper articles, photos, taped to the wall, barely visible.

''A *sacrifice*. A fucking sacrifice, Will. We didn't see it. We didn't know. But without a sacrifice, there'd be no deal,'' Kiff laughed. ''I mean, we should have seen it. I started reading up, and Will—I know. I *know* what happened.''

Two minutes left, Will thought. That's it.

''Which was?''

''Mike Narrio. He died. It was him. We called on something. And Narrio was the price.''

Will grinned. This was too much. It reminded him of a vacation he took with Becca, years before Sharon and Beth. They were out in Santa Fe playing—of all things—miniature golf. They were alone, on the Humpty Dumpty course, while another spectacular Southwest sun set. And then, when they got done somehow, they got to talking to the skinny man who ran the mini-golf.

The type of conversation bored tourists fall into.

And they found themselves talking about things . . . like UFOs, and spirits, and magic . . . and the guy said he had a job like this because it gave him time to explore things.

The man grinned, like a crazy cat that had a bag full of canaries.

Will and Becca left, laughing, searching for a Tex-Mex joint that wouldn't eat their stomach lining for dessert.

At dinner, Becca checked her watch.

It was stopped.

At the exact moment that they had left the Humpty Dumpty.

It never worked again.

Will took a breath now.

He longed for the sparkling new White Plains courthouse, with its polished blond wood and brilliant fluorescent lights.

Sanity . . .

Will looked at the shrimp cocktail glass filled with the liquor. He reached out and took the glass. A small sip might help . . .

"The price for *what*?" Will asked.

Kiff shook his head. "I—I don't know." Kiff made one hand fly out. "We did this—ceremony. And Narrio had to die."

Kiff looked up, his beadlike eyes boring into Will. "We set something loose that night." Kiff shook his head. "I know it." Kiff's wooden tongue tasted the air. "It's been after me every since I figured it out."

The whiskey burned Will's tongue, then his throat, trailing down into some unsuspecting corner of his gut.

Oh, boy . . . got a live one here . . .

"I don't know, Jim. I think that you're reading things into this. Too many books, too much supernatural mumbo jumbo."

Kiff backed away, back to the shelf.

"You don't see it?" Kiff said, sounding affronted. "You still don't see it. It was a setup. It had been *planned*."

"Planned? By whom?"

"Where did we get it from, Will? Where the fuck did we get the idea, the books, the sketch, the whole goddamned ceremony . . . where the hell did it come from?" Kiff was yelling, spiraling out of control.

Will remembered their breaking into Mr. Scott's apartment. The books he had hidden in the closet.

They got away.

Nothing bad happened.

For a second he thought he felt Kiff right there, following his thoughts . . .

"Right, from Scott," Kiff whispered. "Scott. He set it up. Probably had the thing planned all along. Getting the next installment running. I—I don't understand it all, but we were set up, that's obvious."

And—to Will—it was obvious that he had heard enough.

He stood up.

"Yeah. Well, I got to go, Jim. I'll give you a call, stay in touch—"

Kiff grabbed his arm and squeezed it. "No, Will. You don't understand. You see, I'm being watched. There are things watching me. I feel them. I know they're out there. Now they'll start watching you, Whalen, Tim Hanna—"

Will very much doubted anyone was watching Tim Hanna. Not without his permission, that is.

"They'll come for us soon . . . it's just not time yet. You see, they have to wait—"

Oh, boy . . . where's the Twilight Zone music? Will thought. Welcome to Paranoia Land, boys and girls.

Will started walking to the door leading down to the bar. He faced the crucifix. The wounds on the Christ were bright red against pale skin. The Christ's eyes looked up, searching for release from the hell of his pain.

"Will you listen?" Kiff said, yelling. "It's going to be time for the rest of us. All of us. It will take us. And anyone we love. All of us. That was part of it. You see, it's twenty-seven years later. Three times three times three." Kiff spun around, gesturing at the books. "It's there, in the books."

Will stopped.

Something Kiff just said. Take us . . . anyone we love . . .

"You have kids. It wants them. Needs them."

Will's hand was on the doorknob.

When he remembered his dream.

His family. At Steeplechase. The screams. Little Beth rolling toward those sharp spikes. Becca on her knees screaming.

And Will helpless, forced to watch.

The pain. The horrible, immense, overwhelming pain of it all . . .

He looked at the crucifix, just a piece of wood. With painted eyes.

He turned back to Kiff.

"I'll listen," he said to Kiff.

God help me for being so stupid, Will thought.

But I'll listen . . .

26

Kiff had his Formica table covered with books, open to pages, some with crudely highlighted passages, circled inscriptions and illustrations. He moved from one book to another, the mad scholar. He'd point at something and then move on.

Slowly Will began to understand what Kiff was saying.

His thesis, if you will . . .

Which ran like this:

What we did that night worked.

We called for something. It came.

And yes, a sacrifice was needed. That was Narrio. He died for our idle playing with the spirit world.

But it didn't end there.

What we called was set free.

And at some specified point it would have to take the rest of us. All of us. One by one. And anyone we loved.

Because, Kiff demonstrated by pointing at one book after another, it can't stomach love. Or self-sacrifice. Or any positive human emotion.

Will tried asking Kiff how he came to know this.

Thinking: Whatever made Kiff believe this . . .

Kiff talked about hiding, down South, then out in the desert of Arizona, knowing that he was the only one who understood. That made him dangerous. He took precautions, he said. Crucifixes . . .

"I see them," Will said, nodding and looking around.

And other things. Holy water. Prayers.

One night, Kiff said, he saw footprints outside a shabby tourist cabin in the mountains that he was staying at.

"*Footprints*," he said, grabbing Will. "In the snow, all

around the cabin. But they couldn't come in. Hoofprints. That's a sign. That, and the smell, and—''

''Probably mule deer,'' Will said. ''You were in the woods, Jim. Probably just the deer.''

Kiff shook his head.

''No. It's a sign. It was one of the demons . . . one of the servants of Astaroth. A sign. Like the smells. And the noise . . .''

Noise.

''What noise?'' Will asked.

Kiff was looking through the books, flicking the pages. ''That damned clicking sound. It's—it's like—''

Will finished the sentence. ''Teeth. Like teeth chattering.'' He took a breath. Oh, God. Why did he have to say that? Why?

''Like thousands of teeth chattering away,'' Will said quietly.

Kiff's face changed. For the first time he looked almost normal.

''You heard it?'' Kiff said.

Will thought. Heard it? Guess I did. Heard something that night. Thought it was my head, thought—

He nodded.

Oh, God, Will thought, I'm starting to buy into this. Why am I starting to swallow this?

Because of the dream?

Because of the sound?

Because—

He looked at Kiff. ''Jim, what do you have there, in your''—he used the word advisedly—''bedroom? What are those clippings?''

Kiff nodded. He stood up and gestured for Will to follow him. For the amount that Kiff had drunk, he seemed steadier than when Will first came.

Kiff was swallowed by the blackness of his room.

''This is why I came back . . . came back to New York . . .'' Kiff reached down and turned a pathetic gooseneck lamp on. The reflected glow made it possible for Will to look at the papers, see the photographs.

It was stories and pictures about the Madman. The New Age Ripper. There were photos from the cheap tabloids, gruesome pictures of girls' bodies half covered by blankets. And a shot of a face, frozen into a rigid mask of terror, a tongue protruding from full lips, eye shadow gone all blurry.

"It's his work," Kiff said from behind Will, startling him.

Will shook his head.

A crazy man's work, to be sure. But—

"It lives on pain, on terror, Will. It feeds off it, always needs more, and then gives it back." Kiff reached out and touched one of the photographs. "I knew this was his work . . . The way they're cut. The precision." Kiff sounded almost admiring. "Like a surgeon . . ."

Enough, thought Will. Whatever flicker of interest, whatever concern Kiff had stirred, suddenly died in the morgue-like bedroom surrounded by the grim stories, the pictures, the headlines yearning to shock.

"Whose work?" Will said.

"The Adversary, the Eternally Damned One," Kiff said, his face set. He waved his hand at the pictures. "Or it could be any one of his demons: Eurynome, Oonwe, Yaphan, Orobas, even Astaroth." He paused. "I *know* some of their names. Some . . . but they are legion."

Will nodded. He felt dizzy, ready to faint if Kiff's stinked-up sepulcher. "Yes, and I'm late. Gotta go, Jim. I have to—"

Kiff followed Will to the other room, to the table, the books.

"Okay. I know that. I knew you'd have to leave." Kiff smiled nervously. "I knew that you wouldn't believe any of this. You think I'm crazy—"

Will tried shaking his head.

"But you have to do something for me."

Will was still shaking his head. "Hey, I'll call you in a few days," Will said. "Just to—"

"No. You have to do this *one* thing for me. I found a way out. A way out for all of us. A way to do it. But we'll need help." Will didn't like the sound of that word, "we." He wanted an end to this sick nonsense. He regretted coming here.

Will didn't think about his dream now. He didn't think about the clicking. Those experiences had to be tossed out.

Inadmissible evidence. Hearsay.

Kiff picked up a heavy book. The worn leather covers were loose, detached from the body of the book. It looked at least eighty, ninety years old. He pushed it at Will.

Will took the pieces. He looked at the spine.

Experiments in Time. By T. W. Dunne.

"There's a way out, right in there. But we need help. There's someone. But I can't do it. Look at me. He'd never see me. No one respectable would see me. But you . . . you're a lawyer, you're respectable." Kiff rubbed his chin. His dry-gulch tongue poked out of his gummy mouth.

Will saw his point. "See who?"

Kiff handed Will another book. New, with a shiny dust jacket. And a photograph of a man on the back of the dust jacket wearing a sport coat and a turtleneck. Will looked at the cover.

The Demonic Realm. The author was Dr. Joshua James.

"Who's this—?" Will said, wanting to add the word "quack."

Kiff looked strained. "He's an ex-priest. He was at the Vatican. He's officiated at dozens of exorcisms. He's witnessed hundreds of documented cases of possession."

Will held the book up. "This is help you need?"

"*We* need. I want you to talk to him." Kiff rubbed his chin as if he knew that Will was only humoring him.

Got to get out of here, Will thought. The smell, the nutty ideas. It's making my head spin.

"He teaches at Fordham—"

"The Church didn't kick him out?"

"You can see him, tell him what happened." Kiff grabbed Will's wrist. "Tell him what I said about the murders. And then—if he's willing—I can see him. And we can stop this." Kiff looked up.

Like the pathetic Christ on the cross.

"Oh, God, I hope we can stop this," Kiff whispered.

Will nodded.

Humor him, he thought. Move to the door. Open the door. Go down the stairs.

Leave Brooklyn.

"Okay," Will whispered hoarsely.

"Promise, Will?" Kiff said. "You can't fuck up. It's too important."

Will opened the door. "I promise."

The door opened. He heard sounds coming from downstairs. Men at the bar, talking, cursing, grimly whiling away their late afternoon, their late lives. It looked darker down there. The sun was going down, starting its cheerless withdrawal as winter approached.

Will went down the steps, the two unwanted books tucked under his arm.

"Promise?" Kiff nearly shouted.

"I'll call him," Will lied. "And I'll call you. I'll let you know."

He felt Kiff watching him, wondering whether he could sense his lies, scared that Kiff might be nutty enough to hurt him.

I'll change our phone number. Just in case. Keep it unlisted.

Oh, yeah. And I'll call Whalen and thank him for this little sentimental journey.

He walked out of the bar, ignoring the bartender, who barely looked up.

And out, to where the wind whipped around his jacket and sent bits of newspaper and plastic dancing against the side of the bar.

Will walked to his car.

He wanted to toss the books in the trunk. Out of sight . . . Out of mind.

He felt as if they stained his hands, marred his life.

But Kiff might be watching from his window, might have followed him. Crazy people do crazy things . . .

So Will opened the back door and tossed the books onto the seat.

He got in and started his Camry—the sound of the engine wonderful, reassuring.

And Will pulled away, forcing himself to drive smoothly, slowly, reining his desire to floor it, to get the hell away from here as fast as he could.

27

Will didn't say much during dinner. He stuck some mashed potatoes onto his fork and then adhered some peas to it, knowing that Becca was looking at him.

Studying him.

Fortunately the kids were at the table, chattering away.

Sharon moaning about the California tests—a week spent filling in little circles on an electronically scanned answer sheet.

Beth talking about the new baby mice in her class, so pink, so cute, and why can't I have one?

Neither of them needed any parental encouragement to go on talking, two conversations at once, chaotic and disconnected but—somehow—perfectly logical at the family dinner table.

It was later, when the kids left the table and started filling the dishwasher, that Becca snared Will.

"You're not telling me everything about today," she said.

"No, I'm not," he said.

And then he got up and walked away to his office.

Where he hid until it was time for the sleepy ritual of goodnight kisses and bedside tales.

Becca didn't press. She was good at that. She'd give him time, space. One of the good carryovers from their own wonder years, the days of revolution and rock and roll.

Instead, when he finally shut the beside light off, she reached down and fondled Will, playing with him, while she nuzzled his cheek.

For a second he lay there. Unresponsive.

Thinking: Nothing's going to happen.

Not tonight.

Because of all the stuff that's in my head. All that crazy stuff. I'm in no mood to be turned on . . .

But Becca was nothing if not experienced, and her deft persistence paid off, as thoughts of Kiff—his rat-hole apartment, his books, his crazy paranoia—gave way to a sudden need.

28

It was near closing time, past two, heading toward three, and for a Monday, it was late enough.

Kiff sat slouched on a stool near the corner, watching the last slugs of beer go down. Jimmie had his apron off—a signal to his customers. He looked over and winked at Kiff, another sign. He even poured himself a cool one, the very last thing he did every night before closing.

You can't run a gin mill and be your own best customer, he always told Kiff. Jimmie never had a drink until it was time to kick the bums out.

Sometimes he had to get real direct, and tell them to move it, that it was closing time. But these guys were regulars . . . one a fireman on disability, the other an unemployed, divorced insurance salesman who told his sad story every fucking night, no matter who was there to hear it. Chained to his miserable story . . . trapped.

Sometimes, sitting here, Kiff felt like a vulture. I wait until they leave and then I swoop down and pick over the carcass.

Kiff was supposed to clean the whole place after Jimmie left.

That was his job.

But Kiff didn't do that. He did a quick run-through with the broom, and then he got all the lights off and made sure the doors—front and back—were locked.

The rest, he left until morning.

Until it was light.

Jimmie didn't know about that. But what the hell difference did it make?

The fireman left, pushing himself unsteadily away from the bar. Then the other guy, the insurance salesman, his eyes red and bloodshot—not just from booze. The poor sucker lived through his bad fortune every night.

They drifted out the front door, letting in a sudden gust of cold air, refreshing, but out of place amid the smoke and the beery stench.

Jimmie tapped the register, removed the money, and shoved it into a canvas night-deposit bag.

"Okay, Kiffer, guess we're all done for tonight."

Kiff stood up.

A soldier standing at attention.

Jimmie dug his jacket out of a shelf below the bar. He pulled it on and then finished his beer.

"Guess we'll see you tomorrow."

"Yeah, Jimmie . . ." Kiff offered. "You take it easy . . ."

Jimmie nodded, heading out the door.

Always an anxious moment for Kiff.

Always.

Because then he'd be alone. From now until ten in the morning.

Kiff half followed Jimmie to the door.

And Jimmie stopped. "Oh, right. Damn, I knew I forgot something." Jimmie turned around. "We're nearly out of cans. Just the light shit. Meant to tell you before."

Kiff cleared his throat. "I'll get them in the morning."

But Jimmie shook his head, disappointed. "No. We need to get them in the damn cooler tonight. The goddamn thing is working at half power anyway." He looked up. "Got to get them in tonight, Kiffer. Give them time to get cool." Jimmie smiled. "Just a couple of cases. That should do us until the morning." He turned. "Don't forget."

Kiff watched Jimmie open the door.

"Night."

"Good—" Kiff started to say, but the door slammed shut. Jimmie looked back at him and signaled for Kiff to lock it.

As if I need reminding, Kiff thought. As if that isn't the first thing I'd do.

He turned the Yale dead bolt and then twisted the door lock, all the time wishing he had one of those bars, one of those heavy metal bars that pressed against the door.

And Jimmie didn't have an alarm system. Too expensive, he said. Besides, you're here all the time.

Ha-ha. Who needs an alarm?

Jimmie disappeared into the darkness. A newspaper headline danced in the street, swirling from curb to curb.

Kiff turned around.

And for the longest time, he just stood there . . .

He stood there thinking that maybe he didn't have to do it. He almost convinced himself that he could do it in the morning. *That would be okay.* Jimmie wouldn't know, wouldn't give two shits—

It would be no big deal.

But that just wasn't true.

The beer would still be warm when Jimmie came in. He'd be pissed. And when he got pissed, he threatened to kick Kiff out, put him on the street.

And that wouldn't be good. Not at all.

No protection there. None.

So—Kiff took a breath—he knew he had to go down to the cellar and grab a few cases of beer. I can do it fast, he told himself. Real fast. And then hurry upstairs, lock my door.

And wait for morning.

He nodded.

Almost convinced.

The feeling was familiar. And he tried to place it, tried to search through his tired brain, navigating all the sharp turns and dead ends inside his damaged neural pathways. Searching for what event in his past felt like this.

He took a step, ready to give up the mental chase, when he remembered.

It was in Quang Tri, just outside another small, pathetic village that the lieutenant had ordered torched. Nobody asked the lieutenant *why* they torched the villages anymore. After the first few—with the mumbled stories about infiltrators and arms caches and spies growing harder to believe—no one asked.

They just did it.

Kiff got used to the way burning skin and straw mixed.

It smelled like a cookout.

We're doing our job, the lieutenant always said. Search and destroy.

The lieutenant always grinned at that point.

And we're destroying.

But then an old man, some lucky Cong sympathizer who happened to be out in the fields, told the lieutenant that there were *others* hiding in the caves, yes, way up one of the low hills that surrounded the province.

So they marched up to the hill, to the caves. The lieutenant split everyone into parties of two and three—there were just too many caves for everyone to stick together.

And Kiff remembered how he felt, how he prayed that some other lucky bastards would be the ones to find the hiding VC, that *they'd* get the punja sticks in their gut, or step on a land mine, or have *their* face riddled by an Uzi. Nobody hurried. Everybody listened.

Until Kiff was looking into the third cave. Standing between two back grunts, one from Atlanta with a indecipherable accent, the other from the wilds of Bed-Sty. Neither of them had much to say to Kiff. But that was okay.

It was that kind of war.

They looked into the dark pit of the cave.

Took steps inside.

Something flew out, a bat, a fucking flying squirrel, Kiff didn't know . . . They didn't fire at it.

They took baby steps into the cave.

And all the time Kiff felt that *for sure*—this was it. We're the bait. They'll shoot us and then the others will come and blow the VC to hell.

"I don't like this," the kid from Atlanta said.

Kiff hissed at him to be quiet.

There was a noise inside the cave. A rustling, a squawking sound. Kiff felt something go flying over his head.

Another bat, he thought. He held his M-16 in front of him, playing with the trigger, wanting to just let off and wail. Fill the fucking cave with bullets. Shoot until they didn't have any bullets left.

Another step. The clatter of rock.

And then Kiff heard gunfire rattling from light-years away, the sound distant, muffled by the thick stone of the cave.

He turned to the other two soldiers. He smiled. He guessed they smiled back, though he couldn't see anything.

"They're not here." Kiff grinned.

"Fucking-A," Bed-Sty said.

And as Kiff walked out, he had only one feeling. He was glad someone else had found the cave, that someone else got all shot up, ready to be sent home in a plain pine box.

That's what the war was all about.

Hoping the other guy got it.

This time, there *are* no other guys, Kiff thought. Just me.

But then, there are no Cong.

Go fast, he told himself. Just go down, do it, and get the hell upstairs.

Kiff forced his legs to start moving, and he was amazed that they obeyed. He coughed, wanting some sound to fill the bar other than the shuffling of his own feet. He walked straight to the back to the two rest room signs, and the brown door leading to Jimmie's cellar.

He grabbed the doorknob, his body still—incredibly— following his instructions. He thought: I'm halfway there. Halfway down, and then up, and then—

The door opened with a nasty shriek. An ancient spring attached to the door pulled against Kiff. He stepped in, fumbled for the light switch. The door slapped shut behind him.

He wished he could have left it open.

But the spring pulled it closed behind him.

The light switch turned on two lights, one at the top of the stairs that showed just how uneven each step was, and another, down in the cellar, that did little to light up the stacks of beer cases, liquor, and shining metallic kegs.

Kiff hesitated.

He never went down there except in the daytime.

I'm not crazy, he thought.

Fat chance. I'll be away from all my protection.

He took a step. And stopped.

I could go get a cross, he thought. Some water. Maybe one of the books, one of the Bibles I got blessed by every priest and minister that I could find. Charge up them batteries, he thought, get as much good shit working as possible.

He grabbed the handrail hard.

He shook his head. No. That's crazy. Go up to my room and get the stuff? And then come down again? To here?

No.

He could see the beer cases. Now just twenty, thirty feet away.

He forced himself to move down again. The steps creaked. The wood moaning about its age, its dryness.

Kiff looked left and right, scanning the cramped cellar. Maybe there are rats, he thought. He hated rats. Jimmie had an exterminator come once a month. The place was clean.

They never saw a rat.

Still. They could be here.

Could be hiding.

He got to the bottom, to the stone floor. He felt how cold it was. Damn, the beer would be just as cold if it was left here.

No need to come down, he thought. None at all.

He walked over to a stack of Bud Light. He slid three cases off, easing their weight onto his arms. He grunted, hefting them up.

He heard something.

At first the sound seemed to come from down here. He froze. Already cold, he now felt icy. Frozen. Holding the cool cans of beer up near his face. It was hard. He wasn't as strong as he used to be.

He turned, looked around.

The sound was a shuffling sound.

No, he thought, it was an electric sound. A spark.

No. That was in my head. There was no sound. Just my nerves.

He breathed in, started toward the steps.

Heard a sound again.

Kiff stopped.

There. That was it. I really heard it that time. Off in the corner. Near the sidewalk entrance to the cellar.

There were steps leading up to the sidewalk, and heavy metal doors, and giant bolts with heavy locks. Nothing could get in here.

He thought: I should put the cases of beer down. Drop them, maybe run. Up the stairs.

Thinking: Where's the crucifix?

Picturing in his head . . . where is it? How many steps to get to it?

But when there was no new sound, when nothing else bur-

bled over in that corner by the doors, Kiff scolded himself
again. *Just nerves.*

Or no nerves. Too damn wired from drinking. Can't tell
what's real or not anymore.

As he went up the stairs, he kept telling himself that. A
mantra, over and over.

Just nerves. Too wired. Too much booze. Gotta . . .

As he went up, listening for anything behind him.

There was nothing.

Looking ahead, thrilled to be almost back in the bar, happy
when he came to the door, and pushed against the door, and
heard the spring screech out its *boinging* protest.

And he pushed on through, not worrying about the light.

I'll shut the fucking light off tomorrow.

Fuck the light.

And now, standing in the doorway, almost breathing normally, almost done, almost safe . . .

When Kiff saw someone sitting at the bar, someone
hunched over—

As if waiting to place his order.

Kiff blinked. The man was still there, slumped over the
bar like a mannequin. There were just a few lights on, a
Miller sign, and a white light under the top-drawer liquor
bottles, the good stuff that rarely got tapped.

The guy was still there.

"Hey," Kiff said, still in the doorway.

He felt the weight of the cases in his arms, pulling on the thin
muscles of his forearms, digging into the skin of his hands.

And again, "Hey. We're closed. Closed. You gotta leave."

The man didn't move.

A mannequin.

And Kiff remembered. Jimmie left. I locked the door. All
the locks.

He remembered the sound downstairs.

And he thought: I could be in deep shit.

Kiff cleared his throat. He moved forward. And the cellar
door held open by his body now slapped shut. It made a
sound like a gunshot.

It's a robber, Kiff thought. A junkie looking for cash.

"There's no money here. The owner took all the money
away. And I—I—"

The man started turning in his seat. Sitting up straight.

"I got nothing."

The man turned.

The cases of beer hurt Kiff's arms so . . . but there was no place nearby, no place to put them down. And—

The man, in the shadows, spoke.

"That's not true, Kiff. You have a lot."

Kiff squinted. The voice. It was familiar. Somehow, Kiff thought, I *know that voice*. And he tried to think about anyone he might have fucked over, anyone he might have screwed.

Who'd want to come and get him.

"You'd better go," Kiff said. "Get the hell out of here. I'll call the cops."

The shadow man shook his head. He stood up. "No. You won't do that."

Kiff thought, What's happening here? What's going on?

And a terrible thought appeared. A horrible thought.

This is it.

This is it.

And I don't have my cross, or my water, or my books or anything.

Oh, God . . . oh, God . . . oh—

He looked at the bar. To where he had hid the cross, down low.

The man was there, between him and the bar.

"You know," the man said, the voice still oddly familiar, "you're a lucky one, Kiff. Because you know what's happening. Now, isn't that lucky? You know almost everything about it. Very . . . lucky. Except you don't know how to stop it. You screwed up there, didn't you?"

Kiff nodded.

He gagged.

Why am I gagging? he thought.

But then he knew. I'm scared. I'm so scared.

He heard a noise. On the ceiling.

A rat went scurrying across the ceiling. He watched it. Then another, then another. Across the ceiling.

'Cause there's no gravity.

More rats. Scurrying across the ceiling. Until the ceiling was *gray* with rats, a sea of wormlike tails. The ceiling dotted with the eyes looking at each other, then looking down at him.

Rats on the ceiling.

Wait a second, Kiff thought.

Wait a fucking minute. This is just the DTs. Yeah, that's all this is. The fucking DTs. Went a bit too far. Made my head too damn wet, and now I'm seeing things. All wet heads see things. He looked back to the shadow man. And I'm hearing things too. Like the chirping of the rats.

Kiff almost grinned.

"You're not real," he said. "This is just a fuckin' hallu—"

The beer cases slipped from his arms. His arms just gave out. And the cases tumbled to the floor, the six-packs splitting open, the cans rolling away. Some cans popped open, shooting their spray across the floor. Kiff looked down, at the sprawl of cans and boxes.

He saw some of the cans moving.

They were . . . Christ, *they were bulging*.

He heard the creak of the aluminum.

Creak. Creak. They bulged out, as if breathing.

Until they popped open. And something crawled out.

A head. With teeth. And eyes. And hair. A human head, but covered with the gore and slime of a new birth. Tiny, small. A stunted human head, slithering out of each can. One, two, three . . . dozens of them.

Kiff backed up against the door.

The heads slithered out because they were attached to bodies, snake bodies.

Of course snake bodies. Of course.

"No," Kiff mumbled. "No fuckinway." He looked up to the shadow man. "Just the DTs."

He felt something dripping on him from the ceiling. Something plopped on his head, onto his thin, almost vanished stand of red hair. It felt warm against his skull. Then another plop, hitting his eyebrow, then dripping down, onto his cheek, near his lips.

Close enough so that he could smell it.

Smell the rancid odor.

He looked up

Checking out the rats. They blotted out the ceiling, cov-

ering it with a gravity-defying living rug of brown-gray fur
and whiskery bristles. They were shitting exploding little turds
that landed like hail on the floor, on Kiff.

But not on the shadow man.

It's not real, Kiff repeated. Oh, God, this isn't real. I was
told this could happen. Like Ray Milland in *The Lost Weekend*. The walls would come alive, the VA doctors said. Happens to every drunk. A moment of reckoning. You enter a
nightmare land and you don't leave for a long time.

But I can prove that! Kiff thought. Sure, I can prove that
to myself.

Another can popped open. Another squirming human-thing
slid out, its snake body a baby-fresh pink, squirming, slithering around on the floor as if awaiting instructions.

I can make the dream go away, Kiff said, screaming inside
his head, making himself listen to reason, to logic.

Sure.

He knelt down.

Closer to the squirming things.

One was near him, writhing around with a newborn's
crazed inability to control its life, searching for something.

I'll touch it. Touch it, and it will go away, Kiff told himself.

Because it's not real.

Closer. Almost tottering forward, unbalanced on his heels.
His leg muscles worth shit.

He stuck out his bony hand.

Oh, please, God, he begged. Please—

Close to the mouth of one of them, open and shut, a tiny
adult head on the pink-worm body. Closer. Right next to it.

And it struck.

Yes, like a bass taking the lure, like a snapping trout jump-
ing in the air, it rolled and closed its jaws on two of Kiff's
fingers. It bit down with enough force that Kiff knew—even
as his eyes filled with red flashes that signaled horrible pain—
that it could easily bite his fingers off.

But it didn't do that.

Kiff fell backward, sliding on the rat offal, the rain of shit
that splattered down upon him.

The others sensed him. He saw them rolling and twisting,
making their way to him. He shook his hand.

But the human snake stayed locked on his fingers. And now, besides the incessant screeching of the rats and the popping of the beer, he heard something else. A high-pitched keening.

It was coming from his own mouth.

Something plopped into his open mouth.

"This is bad," the man said, walking close. Kiff saw just his black polished shoes. The crisp crease of his gray slacks. "But not as *bad* as what will happen to the others, Kiffer. And certainly not as bad as what will happen to Will and his family. Not even close . . ."

The man laughed.

The heads nibbled him, on his side, at his legs, through his shoes to his ankle, his toes—

This little piggy . . .

The pain didn't get any worse.

There is a threshold. I reached it. It can't get any worse. No matter what happens.

The man turned and walked away.

Kiff felt one of the sausage-sized things sliding up his thin chest, squirming, nearly at his throat, his dry tongue, his rheumy eyeballs.

Nearly there. Nearly over.

He heard a door slam. A laugh.

And then—this last bit of awareness.

I know who it is.

I know who it is.

And then the rats fell . . .

All of them. Onto the floor. Onto him.

29

The guard was a pleasant, rotund man who smiled too damn much considering how much time he spent listening to the howling prisoners in the county holding pen. And the guard always had a pleasant word for Will whenever he came down to confer with one of his "clients."

The guard always said, "Nice day, Counselor." And, "How's the wife and the kids?" And always the caveat, "Don't work too hard."

Will was leaving a half-hour conference with a man staring down the muzzle of his third DWI conviction. It was a hopeless case, and the now-sobered man would probably lose his license for a year, maybe more. And—as the guy just finished explaining, blubbering through his remorseful gasps and tears—there's no way he could get to his construction jobs without a car.

You'll have to beg rides, Will told him.

Not adding . . .

Tough shit. How long do you think we can let alcoholics pilot their cars like kamikaze pilots, ready to wipe out some poor sap with three kids who doesn't know he's sharing the road with a drunk?

Will waited for the electronic cell entrance to beep open, and then he hurried along the corridor. He had a court appearance scheduled in twenty minutes. There was just enough time for a hot dog in the new cafeteria upstairs.

He passed another electronic barrier, another guard, this one with an appropriately grim demeanor. And then past the last guard at a desk, and up the stairs to the courthouse and the cafeteria.

And his hot dog.

But the guard at the desk stopped him.

"Mr. Dunnigan. Your wife called. Left a message. She'd like you to call back."

Will nodded. "Thanks."

Will continued up the stairs. He turned left, at the top, heading toward the public toilets—always dicey places considering the clientele—and a bank of pay phones. He called home using his FON card.

After three rings, he assumed Becca was out. Shopping, doing something at Beth's school. He went to hang up the phone when he heard the click. A breathless "Hello?"

"Hi, babe. Got your message."

She was breathing hard.

"Had to run in," she said. Another breath.

Will heard clicking steps down the hall, near the stairs. He heard the sound and he turned around.

Funny . . .

It was a young lawyer, a cute blonde right out of *LA Law*. Working with the DA's office for now.

But not for long, Will knew. The private concerns will snap her up *prontissimo*. She didn't look at Will. Nobody saw public defenders in this place.

We're invisible.

"What's up?" he said to Becca.

"That guy called this morning . . . around nine."

"Yeah? Who?"

"Ted Whalen. He sounded upset, Will. Practically stuttering on the phone."

"Groan. It probably has to do with yesterday. God, I'm sorry I ever—"

"Wait, Will. He told me to tell you something." The cute lawyer disappeared around the corner. "He said . . . that Jim Kiff is dead."

The phone seemed to slip in Will's hands. Oops . . .

For a second he thought he again heard the clicking of high heels, lonely and forlorn, echoing in the hallway. But all he heard was the clank of a jail cell rumbling from below.

He took a breath. "What?"

"He said to tell you that Jim Kiff died. That he's dead. He wants you to call him."

Will didn't say anything.

"Will? Will, honey? What's wrong? Are you okay?"

Will cleared his throat. "Sure. I'm fine. Just a bit . . . shocked. I saw him just yesterday. Did Whalen say how it—?"

"No. He just said you should call him."

Call him. Sure.

I didn't really want a hot dog anyway, he thought.

He asked his wife to find Whalen's number, there on a Post-it above his desk. She gave it to him and he copied the number down on the corner of a yellow pad.

"Thanks, honey," he said to his wife.

She gave him a kiss on the phone, which he forced himself to return. It always seemed like a dumb thing to do.

Then he hung up and called Ted Whalen in sunny California.

Whalen was home. He picked up the phone after just one ring.

"What happened?" Will asked.

Whalen sounded a bit incoherent, a bit sloshed, even though it was pretty damn early in the California morning.

But Whalen had questions to ask first.

"D-did you see him? Did you go see Kiff?"

"Yes, Ted. I went yesterday. He was a wreck. A basket case. Lost to his own paranoid world of voodoo."

Whalen cleared his throat, a tic, Will guessed. Something he recognized from countless cell-side interviews. *I—er— didn't do it, Counselor. No way . . .*

"But, shit, did he talk about what happened?"

"A bit. Look, Ted, it was all this crazy talk. Stuff about human sacrifices and how Narrio *paid* the price and, look, I just wanted to get the hell out of there."

"Oh, Christ . . ."

"What happened?" Will said. "What happened to Kiff?"

"They found my number," Whalen said flatly. "The police. The guy Kiff worked for. He must have given it to him. I don't know. They had my number so they called."

Will looked at his watch.

He was due in court in five. No, make that four minutes.

"Yeah, go on, Ted. I'm running out of—"

"They called me, Jesus. I don't know why they'd call me. Just because the crazy fuck didn't have—"

He was babbling.

"Whalen! Could you cut to the chase! I don't have all day."

Will hated chewing off Whalen's head, but the meter was running.

"Jesus, Will, they found Kiff lying facedown on the floor, in the bar . . ."

Not surprising, Will thought. Nothing too spectacular about that. The guy was hanging by threads.

"Facedown, and his whole body—shit. It was all chewed up."

Will's breath caught in his throat.

"What?"

Two minutes.

"Chewed the fuck up. They found gray fur—*rat* fur—all over the place, and beer cans, and blood, and Christ, Will—"

One minute, fifty. Forty-nine.

I gotta go, he thought.

I got to—

"Look, Ted. I'll call you tonight. Will you be there?"

"I'm not going anywhere, Will. I'm not going—"

"Good. We'll talk. I spoke with Kiff. He gave me some stuff. I don't know . . . But I'll call you. Tell you all about it. Okay?"

Silence. A nervous, prolonged silence, and Will felt the tremendous distance that separated Whalen and himself. And Will thought, Kiff was alone. Whalen's alone. And who knows about Mr. Tim Hanna? Who knows what his rarefied life is like?

I'm the only one with a family, wife, kids . . .

He felt cold.

And Whalen said, whispering throatily, "Okay."

"Speak to you," Will said.

And then Will ran—late—to Courtroom C.

Whalen looked at the phone. He looked at it wishing that he could pick it up and call someone else.

But there was no one else to call.

I should have gone to work today, he thought. I shouldn't

have let myself get so rattled. Started drinking. It's just that
. . . just that—

What? Just because that somehow there's a connection between me and Kiff? That, yeah, because Kiff is crazy, because *he* gets himself killed, I have to let it ruin my day, my
life?

He stood up.

His beige pants were stained from the poached eggs he ate
this morning. That, and the drops of scotch that dribbled onto
his pants.

Whalen walked over to his vertical blinds and pulled one
strip aside to look out.

It was a brilliant, sunny morning. Another perfect fucking
day, with the sun, obnoxious and oppressive, insisting on
working its way into his house, through sliver-thin cracks in
the folds of the blinds, under the doorjamb, tiptoeing in from
other rooms not quite so perfectly sealed.

Why the *hell* am I so rattled? he thought.

What is wrong with me?

He saw an ant.

It was on his glossy black coffee table, almost camouflaged
by the black wood. The ant, a big fat carpenter ant, hesitated.
Whalen watched the ant do something to its antennae. Clean-
ing them. Or something. Then it continued moving across
the table, up the side of a bowl, leading to the crumbs of
some hard-as-wood Pennsylvania Dutch pretzels.

It kept going.

"Bastard," Whalen said. He slammed at the bowl with his
hand, not caring that he was using his fingers to smash the
insect.

He smacked at it.

He pulled back.

The ant was stuck to his fingers. Half of its body was
crushed, but the other half—including the head—was still
alive, still writhing.

"Goddamn—" he said, and he brought his hand *thwap!*
flat against the table. Definitely flattening the ant this time.

He tried to return to his thoughts.

What am I worried about? he asked himself.

What?

But a tiny, nagging voice at the back of his head suggested that he knew what he was worried about.

Oh, yeah.

He knew that Kiff wanted to tell the truth about that night. The fucking truth.

The truth that even Will didn't know.

But I do.

And I didn't say anything.

And now what was going to happen? Kiff was going to tell the world. There might have been new hearings.

Maybe it was no big deal, Whalen thought.

But it doesn't matter now anyway. Because Kiff is dead.

Chewed by rats.

What a way to go. Poor bastard. Poor haunted—

Another ant. And another! Christ, they were like crooks breaking and entering, darting across the tabletop, looking left, right, preening their antennae, probably dropping a chemical trail for the others to follow.

This way to the eats, gang. This way.

Whalen walked into his kitchen, sliced by sunlight spilling onto the windows. The brilliant light hurt his eyes.

He reached above the refrigerator and opened a cabinet. He moved some cans aside, until he found a big yellow and purple can of Raid ant and spider spray. Industrial strength.

I don't have spiders, Whalen thought. But I sure as hell have ants. He grabbed the can, gave it a test spritz to make sure that it was full and ready for action. He pressed the nozzle down and the perfumy toxin filled the kitchen.

Now we're ready for business.

Whalen walked back out to the living room.

Only now the pretzel bowl was *filled* with ants. They scurried around inside, some holding giant flakes of pretzel crust over their ant heads like trophies. Still more were climbing up the coffee-table leg, hurrying across the shiny table surface, ready to party.

''Oh, shit,'' Whalen said, and he pointed the canister right at the bowl and blasted away. The jetlike vapor blew some of the smaller, less facile ants flying right out of the bowl. Whalen muttered to himself, cursing, as he adopted a side-to-side motion with his hand, spraying the whole table now, in a great arc, back and forth.

He watched the ants stop dead in their tracks. If he saw any twitching, hanging on to their happily communal existence, he gave them a direct blast that left their black exoskeletons sopping with Johnson Wax's best bug-killing petrochemicals.

"Take that, fuckers," he said.

In a few seconds, the battlefield was still. The ants were dead.

But he looked at the floor.

God, there were some more! Damn! There were ants making their way to the table leg.

Maybe I need an exterminator, Whalen thought. Maybe this is a serious ant problem. But he remembered dealing with ants other years. They come in when it's too hot, or too cold, or too wet, or—

Too something.

If I can get the message out that they aren't going to fucking prosper here, why, then I'll have the problem licked.

Sure.

I just have to find out where they're coming from.

He licked his lips, thinking that he'd like another sip of scotch. But—he saw—unfortunately his glass had been in the bomb zone. However toxic it was before, it was far worse now.

So, Whalen thought, screw it. And he got down on his knees, on the plush blue rug, ready to follow the trail of ants back to their point of entry.

"Your Honor—" Will was standing, and he flipped through some papers he had, just to make sure that he knew what he was about to do to whom.

It was mighty easy to get screwed up when you carried a thirty-plus caseload.

"I'd like to ask for a continuance. The prosecutor's office has agreed to supply me with copies of the blood tests and—"

The judge, a rather glitzy-looking woman, held up her hand and consulted some oracular pages on her desk.

Will stopped.

And he thought:

About Kiff. And rats. He tried to imagine what happened,

how it happened, and came up with a blank. *Chewed to death*.
Now, there's a nice way to go. There's a nice one to tell the
folks at home. Your son was *chewed* to death, Mr. and Mrs.
Kiff.

We think it was rats.

Shit. But then—he thought about Whalen.

And he knew that there was something going on with Whalen, something secret that he wasn't telling Will. But Will
couldn't imagine what it could be.

Judge Feinstein looked up. "Counselor, could you ap-
proach the bench?"

A snag, Will thought. And he pushed aside the weird
thoughts, the strange pictures in his head. Thinking: I'll get
to the bottom of this later.

When I call Whalen.

It was the bathroom, no doubt about it, Whalen thought.
He held the can of Raid in front of him, ready to blast the
little black suckers right against the wall.

He had found the ants spaced evenly, every three or four
feet, trailing back to the small bathroom.

Somewhere here there's a hole. That's how they're getting
in, Whalen thought.

He crawled into the small room. He smelled the pungent
odor of urine, the result of his own sloppy aim.

But he didn't see any ants.

He looked up, to the ledge of the small bathtub. And he
saw an ant perched there, watching him.

"Damn," Whalen said. He slowly brought up the can—
and shot the intruder off the ledge and into the tub. Whalen
didn't bother getting up to see if he was dead.

I can gather up the bodies later.

But how were the ants getting in? There had to be a hole
somewhere, a crack in the tile or on the plaster. Some opening leading outside . . .

But everything appeared seamless.

He began to think that he had the wrong place. Maybe it's
the kitchen.

Then he looked at the cabinet below the sink. The place
where he kept the Vanish. And some Lysol, a sponge.

That's it, he thought. There's probably a crack in the wall
behind there. That's what's happening.

He got his can ready.

Whalen wanted to get as many of the ants as possible when
he pulled open the doors.

He crawled backward a bit.

He brought the can up.

Damn, I don't like ants, he told himself. Big, black, nasty
motherfuckers. And with these carpenter ants, they were big
enough for him to see their mouth parts, their—what? Man-
dibles. Pincerlike mouth parts.

Yeah, they were nasty little fuckers.

Okay, he said. Here we go, men.

Take no fucking prisoners.

He reached out and grabbed the doors to the cabinet.

Okay. He took a breath. Then.

"Ayah!" he said.

Whalen pulled open the doors. They popped open, spring-
ing from his hands, and then flew back, nearly closing again
before bouncing against the latch, coming to rest halfway
open.

Then, slowly, he pulled the doors fully open, expecting a
horde of the black suckers to be startled, scrambling for cover.

It was dark in there. But he saw that there wasn't any
movement. The Vanish, the Lysol, and some wizened sponges
were on guard, solemn, with no signs of intruders.

Whalen was disappointed.

Maybe this wasn't it. Maybe this isn't their way in . . .

But no, he thought, they might still be coming in this way.
Just can't see . . .

He put down the can of spray, got up, and ran out to the
living room. He opened a drawer in one end table and found
a small flashlight promotional item, a gift from the Exxon
gas station. He turned it on. The light was yellow, fading
fast. But enough, he thought . . . just enough.

He went back to the bathroom.

Now he stuck the light in and—like a suspicious night
watchman—he examined the inside of the cabinet. The fat
curves of the underside of the basin. The coppery-green pipe
snaking away from it, down, into the floor.

Yeah, that might be it, Whalen thought.

Sure. If there's a crack, why, that would be the perfect place.

But he couldn't see all around to where the pipe went into the floor.

I'll have to lean into the cabinet, he knew.

Okay. And get a better look.

He leaned in, feeling his ass sticking up in the air behind him. He felt the strain on his back, and now he smelled the stink in here. The chemicals, the mildew, the rust. God knows what. The light turned from yellow to a sick orange.

Just a few more seconds of light, he thought. Just gotta see, gotta check.

His head was all the way in the cabinet now.

All the way. He could only fit one arm inside—that's all there was room for—and he had to fiddle with the small black flashlight, trying to aim the light down, to the pipe, to where it met the floor.

And it fluttered out of his hands.

"Shit," he said.

The light fell against one wall.

Pointing straight up.

His hand had to wriggle to get near it, to try and grab it.

He heard something.

Above his head.

He wondered whether the faucet was dripping.

Drip. Drip. Drip.

But the sound wasn't quite like that.

It was more—

Gotta get the light. Grab it and—

His hand gained another inch as he hunched his shoulder to the left and—

The sound. More like a chirping . . . no, a rattling. A *tiny* rattling sound, lots of little sounds, but so faint.

He wanted to tilt his head and look. But he could barely move. Then—funny thought—he wondered: What if I get stuck in here? Wouldn't that be—

He tilted a centimeter. Another.

His hand forgotten—for the moment—in its quest for the light.

Another tilt.

The strain on his back passing discomfort, cruising right

into pain, a broad pain that trailed from the base of his spine all the way up to his neck.

Another centimeter.

And he saw what the flashlight was so dimly illuminating. At the top of the cabinet. Surrounding the basin.

Above his head.

Something black. Moving.

His mouth opened.

He mouthed the word, but he didn't say it.

Ants.

Hundreds of them. Maybe thousands. It was a colony, a whole tribe. There had to be a queen there, and soldiers and workers and—

He quickly shut his open mouth.

He jerked backward.

Right the fuck out of here, he thought.

But he moved only the tiniest bit before his shoulder pressed against his elbow, and then against the wall of the cabinet.

Locking him in there.

The sound. The chittering, the clicking sound. Excited now. Louder.

"Oh, hell," he said.

An ant fell on his forehead. He felt the movement of its legs, delicate, considerate, crawling on the world that was Whalen's skull.

It moved up.

Right, thought Whalen. That's better, keep moving. He jerked against the Chinese lock of his elbow and his shoulders.

The ant, finding nothing of interest, moved down, straight down, before deciding that it wanted to move left. Over Whalen's eyebrow. Onto his eyelid. Whalen shut that eye.

I'm Popeye the Sailor Man.

He felt the ant circling the eyelid.

Whalen was making noises now.

A terrified bleating. "Oh, oh, oh," he said. "Oh, damn. Oh, no." And he bucked against his lock, his stocklike trap as if he were a steer harnessed to a meat factory machine, sensing that its mooing days were over.

"Oh, oh, oh." And then, "Oh, shit."

The ant circled some more. And then it bit him. The pain was small. No big thing. But the ant—and Whalen pictured the pincers, the devil-like fork prongs—closed on the tender flesh of his eyelid.

It bit again. Whalen screamed. He closed his other eye.

And his scream—stupid thing, really stupid, he told himself—made the ants fall. Knocking them from their perch, their clever hiding place.

A bunch of them sprayed onto his face.

He felt dozens of legs now walking on his face. Across his lips. Up and around his ears. Into his ears, driving him crazy with the command to scratch.

Something that he couldn't do.

And now Whalen bucked as hard as he could, pushing his knees against the floor. Pushing at the cabinet wall with his hand. And again.

Not yelling anymore, he thought.

He saw what that did.

Don't want to yell anymore.

But the edge of the cabinet, the hinges, dug into the flesh of his trapped shoulder, now cutting to the bone.

And the new arrivals—the ants on his lips, his eyelids, all over his face, and some moving down to the tender flesh of his neck—all of them began to bite.

And dozens of those bites, snapping in unison, created a feeling like tiny painful firecrackers exploding on his face.

He tried to twitch, to move his face, shake them off.

His other hand, outside, flailed behind him.

It hit the Raid can.

An idea.

I'll spray them. I can find a crack and spray in here.

More ants fell on him. The dozens of legs turned into a living mask of limbs and he felt ants at his lips, trying to get in. Snipping at his lips. He was tempted to push at them with his tongue. Force them away. Maybe I could blow them off . . .

But that would mean opening his mouth.

That's what they wanted.

He felt a new sensation. And he knew that one ant had chewed through his eyelid and was now feasting on the eye itself.

Whalen cried.

His hand brought the can up to the side, looking for a gap to squirt the poison in.

He found a hole.

He couldn't resist—he pushed some ants off his lips with his tongue. Puffed at them quickly blowing just a little bit . . .

And immediately a squad of ants fell onto his tongue, following it in, swirling around inside his mouth. His mouth opened.

I got to spit them out.

He started spraying.

And now he inhaled the insecticide. It seared his throat, his lungs.

He felt an ant at the back of his throat, going down his gullet.

I'm killing myself, he thought.

Coughing, spitting up ants, sucking in new ones as the poisonous fog filled the cabinet.

I'm killing myself . . .

But I'll kill them too.

But then the bites, all over now, down his chest, in his mouth, on his eyes, in his ears, where he heard their scratching footsteps amplified, made him drop the can to the floor.

A truce the ants didn't recognize . . .

30

On his way out of the new courthouse, Will tried calling Whalen's number. He hung up after the fifth ring and redialed.

Again, no one answered.

He gave up and left for home.

Becca greeted him at the door with a nervous stare. He smiled back.

"Daddy!" Beth said, running down the stairs. Will made ready to scoop her off the ground and twirl her through the air.

"Did you call?" Becca asked.

Will shook his head. And then, "Yes, just for a minute. I was supposed to call back. I tried, but—umph—"

Beth careened into his waiting arms and he hoisted her up, giving her the special flight that only dads can deliver.

"He wasn't there," Will grunted.

Becca nodded, and then she drifted away. Will knew that she had other questions to ask, questions that she'd hold until later.

He looked at Beth. Her entire face was one giant smile. Her hair flew behind her and she shook with each convulsive giggle. Sweetness and light, thought Will. That's what she is. No troubles, and filled with complete trust.

He stopped swinging her around.

He heard Beth groan against his shoulder.

"No, Daddy. Swing me some more."

Will nodded. "Sure, honey. Sure." But he just stood there a moment and held her tight. Tighter . . .

Will peeked in Sharon's room. She had a tape on. It was a woman's voice, but one he didn't recognize. Not Cher. Not Olivia Newton-John. Who? Paula Abdul? k.d. lang?

Face it, he thought, the music world has passed you by.

"Hey, tiger," he said, "how are you doing?"

Sharon turned and smiled, a pencil held between her fingers, ready to do damage to her homework paper. She smiled back, a small, controlled grin. Ah, the difference that six years can make. Sharon was well on the way to being a woman. She had her mother's deep, penetrating eyes. And she also shared Becca's abiding concern for the world, from the rain forests and the homeless, to lost puppies in the rain.

"Hi, Dad," she said.

Will risked a step inside her chambers.

Sharon's pencil went back to the paper.

"What are you working on there, kiddo?" he asked.

She looked up and made a disgusted face. "Geometry." She shook her head. "Stupid stuff."

Will risked a few more steps. "Not *that* stupid. It can be kind of fun."

He stood behind her, leaning over her desk. He looked at her math sheet. "Ah, bisecting an angle. Piece of cake," he said.

"For you," she said.

Will shook his head and leaned over her desk. "No. I can get you bisecting angles with the best of them. In five minutes, tops."

Sharon sat back a bit, waiting and watching him perform his magic.

He screwed up on his first attempt, and Sharon giggled as he ended up creating a new angle instead of bisecting the one on her paper.

"A bit rusty?" she teased.

"Hey, that was my first swing. Let me have another go at it."

He picked up the compass and tried again and—to his own amazement—he ended up with a neatly bisected angle.

"There you go," he said.

"But how'd you do it?" Sharon said.

"Okay," Will said. "Now watch carefully this time . . . Nothing up this sleeve, and nothing . . ."

He retraced his steps carefully, letting Sharon see everything he did. And by the time he was done, Becca called them down to dinner.

Becca waited until the girls were gone.

"Maybe," she said, "maybe you should try to reach Tim Hanna."

Will nodded, still picking at his salad. "Yeah, I guess so. But I don't think I could get to him. He's an important man," Will said, embarrassed at his sarcasm.

"Still," Becca added, "you were friends. He knew this Jim Kiff—"

He smiled at her. The way she said "this Jim Kiff"—as though Kiff were an *objet bizarre* from the National Museum of the Strange.

"He'd probably want to know."

Will looked at her. It's funny, he thought, the things we keep from our spouses. Old girlfriends and their techniques. Secret fears, desires, hopes. That's probably where divorce came from, he guessed. When enough secrets build up, the gulf becomes unbridgeable.

And one day your marriage is over.

He looked at her, listening to her, thinking . . .

"Sure he's a big businessman, Will. But you could probably reach him . . . if you wanted to . . ."

Except, thought Will, I very much doubt Tim Hanna *wants* to be reached. Not by me. Not by anyone who was there that night.

"Yeah," he said at last. "Maybe I'll try."

He thought about telling Becca then. Telling her about that night. About the special tie that bound Kiff and Whalen and Tim Hanna and him together.

A regular little club, he thought.

He *thought* about telling her.

Letting go of the last secret.

But she sighed and stood up, clearing the table.

And he stood up to help.

Around nine o'clock, he went into his office and tried Whalen's number again. This time he let it ring eight times, hoping that if Whalen had an answering machine, it would click on.

But there was nothing.

He looked at the two books on his desk.

He looked at the new one first, *The Demonic Realm*, by Dr. Joshua James. The glossy white dust jacket had bloodred lettering. Flaky book, Will thought. He flipped the book around to the back, to the photo of Dr. James. A smiling and earnest-looking man looked out at his hoped-for multitude of readers. The staged shot had James holding his glasses in one hand while he sat rakishly on a stool.

Nearly bald at the top, James had bushy white eyebrows. The warm smile looked completely unauthentic. And, idly, Will opened the book to the back, and he read some of the author's credits.

Dr. James was a former Dominican priest who had served as a staff assistant to Pope Paul VI. He headed a special Vatican study group exploring the Christian concept of sin and damnation.

How cheery, Will thought.

There's a lot of scared, silly, and superstitious people in the world. They eat this stuff right up.

The last paragraph of Joshua James's short bio had the good stuff.

He had assisted or witnessed over 150 exorcisms.

Nice hobby, thought Will.

And Will imagined crazy Kiff reading this book, swallowing this baloney hook, line, and sinker. Somehow mixing it up with that nonsense from decades ago.

Poor bastard, he thought again. Poor—

He heard a sound from behind him.

He turned, startled.

It was Sharon. "Dad," she said, her face crinkled up into a perfect mask of confusion. "Do you know anything about constructing *equal* angles?"

Will smiled. "Constructing equal angles?" he said. "Hell, I wrote the book. I was the equal angle constructing champ of my high school."

She grinned, her cool façade melting under his goofy boast. And Will reached out for Sharon's math book, hoping that a few diagrams would, er, refresh his memory about yet another arcane secret from the wonderful world of geometry.

* * *

It was later. Sharon and Beth were asleep. A timid rain began throwing drops against the windows, as if it wanted to come in. The news was on the TV. Will, coming out of the shower, missed the first story.

"Miss anything important?" Will said.

Becca shook her head. "No. Just—another murder. Someone else was killed—another woman cut up in the city."

Will stopped rubbing at his wet hair. "Wow. How many is that, eight—?"

"Nine," Becca said. "And this one wasn't a hooker. Just a secretary, working late . . ."

"Poor girl," he said.

Will heard the bumptious news anchor team promise more updates on the City Slasher, their station's own pet name for the madman.

But afterward only the fat weatherman came on, joking about even more rain so don't forget your umbrellas . . . it was going to be real nasty in the tri-state area.

Then the dull-eyed sports reporter grimly reported the Mets' loss of the sixty play-off game at San Francisco. The news closed with a syrupy story on a man who raised puppies and gives them away to poor city kids.

There was nothing more. No update. Becca shut the tube off. And then they were both lying in bed, reading books.

Except that Will wasn't reading.

He put down his book, an overheated true crime story, a love triangle involving an overheated teacher and a possessive young heiress.

A nicely lurid tale of murder and lust in Westchester.

Becca looked over

"What's wrong?" she said.

He looked at her. "I think I'll try calling again," he said, smiling.

He saw her check the clock. It was 11:15. "What time there? Eight-fifteen, seven-fifteen?"

Will slid out of bed. The air was cold and unfriendly. He went to his bureau and pulled out a pair of socks. He threw on his ratty robe that he just couldn't part with. It was too warm and comfortable. Reassuring in a disposable world . . .

"It's eight-fifteen there. I'll just try one more time," he

said. "Then I'll say the hell with it. Whalen can call me back if he wants to."

Becca nodded. "It's funny. He said he'd be in. That he wanted to talk with you." Becca chewed her lip. "He sounded desperate."

"Right," Will said. And he went out the door and downstairs to his office. He threw on the living room light. The room looked startled by his intrusion.

He thought about getting a beer. But then he knew he'd be up half the night while his kidneys processed it.

He sat behind his desk and picked up the phone.

He dialed Whalen's number.

And he listened to it ring and ring.

Knowing that no one was going to answer.

And how do I know that? he wondered.

What the hell makes me think that?

Because—because—

He remembered how Whalen sounded, so scared, obsessed with Jim Kiff. Whalen's wires were frayed and ready to start a meltdown.

Though Will couldn't imagine why.

The rain spat at the window in front of him.

He heard the leaves in the big maple outside the house rustle. The fall sound was punctuated by the steady ringing from the receiver held up to his ear, followed by silence, followed by ringing. Over and over.

Whalen kept something from me, Will thought.

There's something that he knows . . . about Kiff, about— God knows what.

Will hung up the phone. He dialed again, the sound of the unanswered ring almost reassuring now.

The cat cried from the backyard, begging to be let in from the cold rain. Can't do that, Will knew. The damn cat wakes us up at dawn, or even earlier. Mewling to get out or to be fed, or—

Dr. Joshua James looked at him.

Currently, the bio stated, Visiting Professor of Canonical Law at Fordham.

Will shook his head. He didn't imagine that the Catholic hierarchy would let an ex-priest stay active in the family business.

Things change, Will guessed. Even in the old Roman Church.

Now he pulled the other book closer. The old book. And just moving it made the smell of the leather come to life. He felt the dry binding stick to his fingers, the leather decaying like ancient skin, lost to ravages of time and worms.

He looked at the title. Then he read it aloud, seeking reassurance in the goofy sound of it. *"Experiments in Time,"* Will read. "By T. W. Dunne."

And he wondered—how did Kiff get this book? It had to be pretty damn rare. Unless Kiff had looked up old Mr. Scott and made an offer for the teacher's copy.

Scott's got to be dead, though.

Sure. Has to be . . .

Will opened it, thinking: It doesn't sound like an occult book.

The paper was tissue thin, dense with words, enormous paragraphs. The language was scholarly, arcane, indecipherable.

Will read a paragraph at random.

> *The presence of physical manifestations only reinforces the concept that the material plane is both fluid and mutable, and the true nature of reality and time stands revealed only at their highest levels.*

Fer shur, dude, Will thought.

He flipped through the pages, past odd-sounding chapter headings, and diagrams that looked vaguely Egyptian, or Mayan, or—

He came to a loose piece of paper.

It was a single sheet of lined paper, with a drawing on it. A circle, a star inscribed. It was old. Not as old as the book, but the white lined paper was yellow with age, curled at the corners, with a tear growing through the middle.

I know what this is, Will thought.

God, this is the paper. The sheet that Kiff used to copy down the ceremony from Scott's book.

Kiff kept it . . . all these years.

Will was reluctant to touch it, to pick it up.

But he did.

And suddenly that night, the sea, the young faces of his friends, the rocks, the very salt air, all of it seemed as if it happened only minutes ago . . . seconds.

He rubbed his chin.

The cat cried from the front door. And Will took a breath, startled.

In answer, the wind pressed against the windows of his office, demanding entry.

Holding the paper up to the light, Will saw something on the back, something on the other side.

It was a drawing of a cross, filling the whole page. And at the top, in small, tiny letters barely visible to the naked eye, were three words.

God help us.

The inside of the cross was filled with those words, line after line, every bit of space. The minuscule letters were all jumbled together until the cross was black with those words.

God help us.

A hundred times. A thousand times.

God help us.

A branch scratched at the window. Will looked up. The wind was picking up.

Picking up.

He grabbed up the phone and dialed again.

"Come on," he said. "Answer the goddamn phone."

It was 11:31. The phone rang and rang.

Will stuck the piece of paper back inside the book.

Then he slapped the book shut, still holding the receiver to his ear.

When he thought he heard someone pick up the phone.

The ringing stopped.

Yes, he thought. Whalen picked up.

Someone's there.

"Hello," Will said. Then more loudly, "Hello?" His voice sounded strange in the empty downstairs. His voice was swallowed by the furniture, the sullen couch, the cheerless paintings, more family pictures that surrounded him in the office. Beth as a baby. Sharon in her class play, a beautiful Alice tumbling down into Wonderland.

The ringing stopped.

"Hello. Whalen, is that you?" Will said.

Come on, asshole, he thought. Don't screw around. "Whalen . . ."

Then—yes, he heard breathing. God, someone was there. Unless I dialed the wrong number, unless I made a mistake, woke someone up and—

The tree branch scratched at the window again.

Hello. Let me in. We want to come in, the trees, the wind, the rain.

Let us in . . .

"Shit," Will said.

Then, a last time, "Hello? Who's there?"

A sound answered him.

A high-pitched squeal. Faint, like an airplane soaring in the distance, but then its engine noise swelling, louder and louder, hurrying to full volume, screaming before Will could yank the phone away, away from his ear—

"Ow!" he yelled. The sound made his eyes cross. And even with the receiver away from his ear, he heard the screech, an electrical scream, unintelligible, mechanical. Piercing, filling the room.

They'll hear, Will thought. God, the noise was incredible, so *loud*! He covered his ears. They'll all hear. Becca, the girls. Even louder, so that the noise cut right through his hands cupped tightly against his ears.

He picked up the phone and slammed it down on the receiver.

Thinking that it wouldn't do any good.

He waited for everyone to come downstairs, to ask him what that sound was.

Will watched the stairs.

And no one came down.

He looked at the phone. That sound had been incredible. Some stupid phone error, a crazy switching noise . . . something . . .

He looked back at the stairs.

Nobody upstairs heard.

He pushed the books away.

He stared at his window. At the trails made by the rain, running down the glass, joining together, running to the ground, chased by the wind.

He watched and listened, and he knew.

Something was wrong with Ted Whalen.

He said he'd stay by his phone. And now he's been away all day.

Or—Will thought—maybe not. Maybe I'm getting carried away here.

He thought of the cross.

God help us.

And Jim Kiff.

Chewed by fucking rats.

Maybe not.

There was one way to put the issue at rest.

He used the area code to get information to give him the number of the Los Angeles Police. He called them.

Will explained his concern. He spoke to a sergeant with a name that Will missed completely.

But Will told him where his friend Ted Whalen lived. He hasn't been well, Will lied, though—for all he knew—it might be true.

"He doesn't answer his phone," Will explained. "Could you take a look?" Will said that he was a lawyer. He gave his phone number in case there was anything wrong.

No need to call back otherwise . . .

They'd be glad to check, the desk sergeant said from three thousand miles away.

Will said thanks. He hung up.

He waited ten minutes for a callback. Then fifteen minutes more. He looked at Joshua James's book.

But not the other one.

He told himself he'd wait five more minutes.

Will did. And then, thinking that everything was fine, that the LAPD didn't find a thing, he got up and went back upstairs. It was late and he should be asleep.

He left his light on in his office.

The dream again. Exactly the same. Sharon and Beth screaming, spinning, flying into the blades. Becca not seeing the clown, not seeing it creep up behind her with the hose. And Will, so wobbly on the blocks, falling down, dodging the meat hooks being waved at him.

Helpless. Totally helpless.

This time, he cried in the dream . . .

* * *

The phone rang. It jangled rudely in the black room.

"Wha?" Will said, shooting up. Becca had the phone. He heard her mumble something groggily into it. And Will thought, Who'd be calling us so late? What the hell time is it? Who'd call so—?

He remembered.

Becca handed him the phone, hitting his shoulder rather than his outstretched hand.

"Er, it's a policeman. I—" Becca said.

Will lay flat on the bed, his head against his pillow. It was so black in here, it was like space. Like a coffin. A call into the void.

From the void.

"Yes?" Will said.

"Mr. Dunnigan? This is Detective Swenson, Los Angeles Police."

Will felt the pillow, soft, incongruous.

From the void, from the tomb.

"Yeah," Will said.

"Mr. Dunnigan, can I ask you why you called us, sir? Why you wanted us to check on your friend, Mr. Whalen?"

"What is it?" Becca hissed in his ear. "What's wrong?"

Will shook his head. But she couldn't see he knew.

"I—I was supposed to call him. A friend"—he said the word, uncomfortable with it—"had died. Ted Whalen had the information. He didn't sound well when I—"

"I see, Mr. Dunnigan. Well, we went to his house, sir. And—" There was static on the line. The storm, thought Will. The storm. He lost the next few words. "We couldn't get an answer at the door. But we got a look through a back window. A bathroom window." The cop hesitated.

"Yes?"

"We saw Mr. Whalen. He was—he was caught, in a cabinet."

Will thought of a clown, and spinning disks. Around and around. *Here we go* . . .

"We knocked out the window. We got our flashlights on him. And, sir—"

Don't let the clown hook you through the neck. That can hurt. And be careful. When you go spinning off the disks.

"Sir, we saw Mr. Whalen and—"

Becca nudged him, hissed close to him, "What is it, Will?"

The cop told him how Whalen had died.

Told him about the moving black rug that covered Whalen's body, black and glistening, reflecting the light.

How they saw the *shape* of a man, his back bent over, one arm sticking out. The legs, kneeling. But that it was all black and glistening.

"Mr. Dunnigan, he was being eaten. The ants—big ones— were all over, every inch of him. They were eating him while we watched."

Will tried to recover a bit. "Was he dead?"

Silence. An interminable silence, stretching across the continent, then words, slow . . . measured. Then the cop said something that made Will gasp, made him turn into his pillow and want to yell, scream.

"No, sir . . . he wasn't. He had been alive. God help us—"

The words! He said those words!

"—alive . . . But by the time we got him out of there, the ants off him, he was dead. He was dead. He had no skin left. Nothing."

Another pause.

And madness danced around the bedroom.

God help us, Will heard.

God help us. God help us. God help us.

Except.

There is no God.

But Will knew now—at last—that he needed help. Of some kind. From somewhere.

Help.

31

The policeman went on talking, asking questions that Will couldn't answer, telling him things about Whalen—now called "the deceased"—that Will didn't want to know.

Then the cop was gone.

Will told Becca what happened.

First, just about Whalen.

She deserved to know, he thought. Sure she does. After all, she's in the dream too. She has a right.

Then, when he felt her, how cold she was, maybe trembling beside him, he told her the rest. *Everything* he knew.

About Manhattan Beach.

At first, she didn't see any connection.

Then she laughed.

"That's crazy," she said. "What are you saying?" She laughed again. "That something happened that night?"

"I don't know what I'm saying," Will said.

Which was true enough.

And he thought that Whalen died knowing something . . . something that he didn't.

What the hell is it?

"Maybe I need help."

She laughed again, a hysterical sound. "Help? What do you mean, 'help'?"

"I don't know." He took a breath. "There's someone Jim Kiff wanted me to call, a priest, an ex-priest—"

"What?" Becca said.

This isn't happening, Will thought. Not real. Not fucking verifiable. I'm just getting freaked out—

No. It's not just that. It's as if this is a script. A little play unfolding. *The Reunion.* And I have my fucking part, whether I want to play it.

Or not.

There's not a damn thing I can do about it.

"I want to go see this man," Will said.

"Stupid," Becca said. "Now you're just being stupid. And"—she took a breath and sighed—"you're scaring me."

Will grabbed her hand. His cold hand encircled hers . . .

A script. Everything scripted.

"What you should do is call Tim Hanna," she said. "Let him know . . ."

Will nodded in the darkness. "I'll try. I can try."

Sure. Because if there's a script, then Tim has a role too. Something that all his money, all his success building high-rent apartments and office complexes in the new Battery Park City, and in the new Boston Commons, and in the gentrified south Washington, won't keep him safe from.

Becca lay there quietly.

Will didn't hear the soothing rhythmic sound of Becca's breathing, slipping back into sleep.

He turned to her, and saw that she was lying beside him wide-eyed. He gave her hand a squeeze.

He said something, meaning it as a joke, a bit of black humor to break the grim night mood.

"Becca—babe—you haven't seen any ants around, have you?"

The dumb words were out, hanging in the air. Serious, devoid of even the feeblest shot at humor.

And she turned to him, only her eyes shining in the near-total blackness. "No," she said calmly, as if he had been checking their milk supply. "No, I haven't."

Will turned away.

He lay there a long time, wondering at how he suddenly felt trapped. And what he was going do about it.

1 A.M.

32

Will opened his eyes.

He felt the hand locked on his, the bone rubbing against bone. And the sound filled the concrete stairwell. The sound of skin splitting, tiny liquid sounds, bubbles and pops.

But he opened his eyes.

Don't look at it.

He knew that. I must not look at it—

—or it will be all over.

Instead, he looked at his bag. His bag of tricks.

He felt like a fearless vampire killer. A comic character out of a mock-horror film. Hey, Abbott . . . you're not going to *believe* what just came out of this lady here.

His hand fumbled with the latch of the bag.

James said to pray. So he did. Mumbling the words bereft of any meaning for him. Wishing that somehow he believed.

Dear God, have mercy. Guard my soul and protect me against evil.

The words reverberated in the suddenly empty corridors of his mind. *Protect me against evil. Protect me against evil.*

And a terrible question.

What's evil?

The latch popped open.

He felt the bony hand squeeze his wrist again. There was a sudden painful spike, the sound of something cracking.

It just crushed my wristbone, he thought.

But Will didn't turn. Instead he dug into the bag and grabbed the first thing his hand came to.

He pulled out the jar. He fumbled with the lid.

It was so damn hard to unscrew something with one hand. It didn't move at all. He brought it against his body.

The thing holding his arm yanked him. The jar slipped a few inches, tumbling onto his lap. It almost hit the stone, he thought. Almost hit the stone and broke.

But it wedged in his crotch and he squeezed it with his legs. He grabbed the lid with his free hand, holding tight. The lid moved. He twisted the lid off. And then—taking a breath—Will turned.

The water flew out toward the dissolving hooker, the abomination, this bubbling, oozing mass that held him imprisoned.

"In the name of God, may all evil—"

He saw it now. The girl looked like a rumpled suit, discarded, curled up on the ground. She was a mess of bone and muscle and blood. But *the head*, the giant domehead was out now. Peering out of her midsection. And at the word "God," he watched a dozen tiny mouths bloom all over its surface.

"All power of evil, every spirit—"

The watery splash landed, and a noxious vapor farted from the open pit that was the girl's midsection. The dozen sets of teeth started chattering hungrily.

Still it held on, squeezing and crushing Will's wrist, grinding bone against bone now.

"And let Lucifer be put to flight. By the power of God—"

He threw another splash. It howled. Out of a dozen orifices, it wailed, like a dozen mad babies, demented, screaming for their mother.

Will pushed back against the wall, kicking at the thing with his foot. He heard it ooze, he watched the Uncle Fester head wobble while he kicked at it.

"By the power of God!" he yelled. "By the power of God!" Begging. Screaming.

It let go of his wrist.

A tidal wave of pain crashed over him and Will moaned.

But now Will was able to stand up. He was free!

And the head with the mouths, all those teeth, was waving back and forth, suddenly acting like a balloon beginning to lose air.

He looked at the jar. The water was nearly gone. He backed up. And risked another splash, repeating his command.

Will backed up another step.

And the thing shriveled back into its hole.

In a second, it was quiet.

There was just the gentle, oozing sound of the dead hooker's body as her blood sought ground zero.

Will heard the cars again. Horns honking.

He backed up one step. And then another. Then he stopped.

Got to cover the jar of water.

He brought his one hand around and looked at the damage. He tried to move his fingers. The hand just sat there, a useless claw. But he used that arm to hold the jar against his body. He picked the cap off the ground and sealed the jar. Tossed it into his bag.

His bag of tricks.

He laughed.

It actually worked. Praise—geez—praise God, it actually worked . . .

He closed up the bag.

Thinking: Got to get out of here. Got to get away. This will look very strange if someone comes by. Sure . . . very strange if some cops pull up in their car.

Oh, yeah, that would be a hard one to explain.

I—er—I just sent something back to God knows where.

Something with a lot of mouths.

Got to go.

He jabbed his bleeding wrist into his shirt, hoping it would stop the bleeding.

Up another step. Another.

Until he was on the street again.

Thinking: It was too easy.

Something was wrong for it to be so easy.

It won't be easy if I find him out here.

He turned. Took a step.

And someone said something to him.

Someone said, "Hello, Will."

Joshua James

33

Dr. Joshua James moved the pile of books on his table. A few tumbled off the edge. He used both his hands like bulldozers plowing through the jumbled pile of books and papers, searching for the elusive treasure.

Which in this case was his lecture notes for his next class.

He made a few more runs through the pile before he stopped and thought . . .

Well, I guess I could wing it. Wouldn't be the first time.

He scratched his balding dome, as if remembering the curly dark hair that was once there. Now there were just the vestiges of a shocking black mane that had made him more than usually handsome, especially for a priest.

Now he was nearly bald—save for two silvery patches on each side of his head.

Now he was no longer a priest.

Not a day went by that he didn't evaluate his decision—weigh his choice of options. Run through his entire checklist of feelings to see if he had done the right thing.

And always ending up with the same answer.

I just don't know.

Who said ignorance is bliss?

He shook his head, abandoning the search for his lecture notes. How tough could it be? he thought. Ethics 101. The type of class I can walk through blindfolded . . .

Just as my materialistic students do.

Ethics. Was there any more endangered subject in the entire curriculum? On the whole planet?

He looked at the clock. Good, he thought, I have plenty of time before class begins. I can walk across the campus—

the ancient trees on the Fordham campus not yet bare. A little physical exercise, just like my doctor ordered.

He walked to a wooden chair by his office door. He picked up his Verdi attaché, the fine leather now worn to a rough rawhide by years of traveling to conferences, guest lectures . . .

Consulting.

A few of the nicks in the case had come in a more dramatic fashion.

He tended not to think about those nicks and tears.

Bad memories, he thought. You have to guard against such things. They can debilitate the soul . . . weaken your resolve . . .

James picked up the attaché.

He sniffed the air.

A habit.

The former priest reached for the doorknob.

And though he didn't smell anything—

He knew—just knew—that someone was waiting on the other side.

He pulled open the door and looked at the man. James didn't smile, didn't nod . . . he offered him no encouragement at all.

Go away, he wanted to say. I have a class to teach, students. Go away. Take your long confused face somewhere else.

Instead, James stood there. And said something—

"Yes. What is it?"

Will blinked. The man's voice was crisp and harsh. I've obviously interrupted him going somewhere.

He felt as if he could melt under Dr. James's withering stare.

"Dr. James, my name is Will Dunnigan, and—"

God, how do I even start this? Will wondered. I have a crazy friend who had your book. No, not even a friend. And now he's dead. And someone else died, and—you see—it's the *way* they died—

Dr. James shook his head, and Will realized that he hadn't said anything.

"I have class, Mr. Dunnigan. Perhaps you'd like to schedule an appointment with the department secretary.'' James leaned out of his door, took a step. ''Her office is right down—''

Will looked in the proffered direction and nodded. But then he said, ''No. I mean, I just need to ask you something . . .''

James came out of his office and Will felt guilty. He must get a lot of odd people stopping to see him. Weirdos who want to know about demons, spirits . . .

He looks so normal. Like any other professor . . .

Dr. James's eyes narrowed, studying Will. A woman walked down the hall and Will saw James look up, as if ready to summon assistance in removing a wandering nut case.

I can't tell him here, out in the hall, Will thought.

But James sighed.

''I really must—''

Will reached out and touched James's arm.

A simple gesture, he thought. No viselike grip to stop the man. Just a touch. But then—then—

James looked up and all of a sudden something different was in James's eyes. His gaze softened.

And Will felt as if he could tell this man anything, everything. It didn't matter.

''An old friend died . . .'' Will said. ''Killed by rats, Dr. James. They found him all chewed to death.'' More steps in the hall. ''And another friend was—God.'' Will looked away. I sound crazy. Nut. ''Something about ants. I—I don't know.''

He saw Dr. James shift his attaché from one hand to the other.

James didn't say anything.

But his eyes seemed to urge him on.

''One of them had your book . . .'' Will handed it to James, who nodded, and then threw his eyes back on Will. ''He was afraid. He said—I don't know—he said a lot of crazy things. It had to do with something we did a long time ago.''

Dr. James scratched at his bald head.

''Go on,'' he said quietly.

''He had this too. It—it seemed important.''

Will handed him *Experiments in Time*, the tattered leather sticking to his hands.

James looked at the book in Will's hand. He looked at it, but he didn't take it.

Then slowly, deliberately, as if the act itself were important, Dr. James took the book and he said quietly, reverentially, *"Experiments in Time."* He looked back at Will. "An exceedingly rare book." He looked down at it again, and turned the book so that he could see the spine. "One could almost say . . . impossibly rare. I know of only one other copy extant." James looked up. "Where did your friend get it?"

Will cleared his throat. For the first time since he came here he thought that he wasn't going to be immediately booted off the Bronx campus. "I—I don't know," Will said. "And he wasn't a friend really, not anymore. He was someone I once knew in school."

Joshua James looked at his watch.

Back up to Will.

"You have time for a walk, Mr.—?" The name escaped him.

"Dunnigan. *Will* Dunnigan."

"Walk me to my class, Will. And tell me everything."

Dr. James walked down the hallway, and Will followed, starting slowly, faltering . . . while James just nodded and listened to the whole story.

The wind scratched at the trees trying to violently shake off the last tenacious clusters of leaves. Already, dry, brownish-red leaves gathered in piles along the walkways that snaked through the campus. Everywhere it was red and gray, the leaves, the stone of the buildings, the gunmetal sky.

And Will told Joshua James everything, omitting nothing. James just listened.

Then, when Will was done, James turned to him and asked, "You're *sure* of the date, when that boy died?"

"Yes," Will said.

More steps. A large, new building loomed ahead, incongruous amid the old red stone and expansive courtyard and tree-lined walkways.

"And you've consulted no one else, no one except me?"

Will nodded. "I almost didn't come. It's just that—well, with the both of them dying so strangely . . ."

James stopped. He touched Will's arm again.

"You did well. You haven't read my book?"

"No. I—er—I'm not much for religion . . ."

James smiled. "You and a hundred million other people. No matter. Let me ask you something. The ceremony— whatever it was you did that night—do you remember anything about it, anything at all?"

The wind blew at Will's hair. A cluster of leaves rustled, growled at his feet, scratching the stone walkway. "Not much. But—"

Some noisy students went barreling past, laughing, talking in great bellows, like sea lions at mating season. But they quieted, and Will saw one of the students nudge the others, pointing at James.

They moved on.

"Not much," Will repeated. "But it's there . . ."

James's mouth went wide. His face scrunched up, not understanding. "What?"

"It's *there*. The sheet we used. Inside that *Time* book."

James's face suddenly looked ashen, his cheeks hollow. He held the book up and examined it. The sheet of paper was barely visible, stuck halfway into the text.

"Oh, God," James said. Then to Will, "That's it?"

Will nodded.

James looked at the sky and for a second Will thought of Melville's Ahab, braving stormy seas, searching for the great white whale.

And was the whale good or evil?

James looked around as if thinking. His lips moved, and Will wondered that maybe the professor was a bit *off*.

Maybe I'm just overreacting. Maybe it's nothing.

("Chewed to death, Mr. Dunnigan. Down to the bone," the detective said about Kiff. And Whalen, covered with ants, thousands upon thousands, chowing down on his body. Still alive . . .)

Finally James turned back to him. He took out a small memo pad and jotted something down. Then he ripped the piece of paper off and gave it to Will.

"I want you to do something. I want you to meet me this afternoon. There's the address. It's a small church in the Orchard Street section of the Bronx . . . a nice little Italian neighborhood. A small"—James smiled—"old-fashioned

church. Meet me there, say, at''—James looked at his watch—
''four. I need to look at this.''

He held up the book.

''To think things through.''

Why a church? Will wanted to know. Why there, why not
in the library or his office? But James interrupted the flow of
questions inside his head.

''I have to go now. Try not to think about any of this. In
fact, make yourself *not* think about any of it. I'll meet you
later . . . all right?''

Will took a breath. Sure, he thought. Maybe James might
have an idea about what it was that Kiff and Whalen had kept
from him. Their secret, maybe Tim Hanna's too. What do
they know that I don't?

He felt cold.

Colder, as the wind blew against his thin jacket.

''I'll see you there,'' Joshua James said, touching Will's
shoulder one last time.

Will nodded, and then the ex-priest hurried away, joining
the swirling dance of leaves.

An old nun, dwarfish, her back bent into a hook shape,
fluttered about the altar. Every time she crossed in front of
the great marble slab, she genuflected.

The church was dark except for the flickering racks of votive candles and a pair of dim lights way up near the top of
the small vaulted ceiling.

And everywhere there were statues, a soulful-eyed Christ.
A Kubrickian baby with its arms extended out to the missing
parishioners. A Virgin Mary looking up, her graceful hands
folded in a quiet pose of adoration.

The nun arranged white flowers on the altar while straight-
ening a bloodred cloth.

Once she looked at Will.

Will smiled.

She looked away.

This is a church from another era, Will thought. No altar
turned to face the people here. No room for guitars and ban-
jos and *kumbaya, m'Lord*. The air is permanently heavy with
incense, an eternal ward against the sinfulness of heathens.

Will felt dizzy, surrounded by the smells, the heavy wood. It's as if no fresh air gets in here.

He sat in a pew halfway to the back, just forward of the small choir loft.

And he waited.

The nun finished her altar arrangements and disappeared into the sacristy. There was the faint noise of water running, and the clink of metal. A chalice being cleaned, perhaps.

Will checked his watch.

It was after four. 4:10. 4:11.

My life's been put on hold, Will thought. My sad-sack clients are filling my office with desperate, angry messages. Another court appearance was put off, not a good thing to do. Becca wanted to know what was going on.

And Will knew he couldn't tell her . . . not about this.

She'd call a shrink.

He smiled. Maybe that's what I need.

Again, he checked his watch.

4:15.

He felt almost relieved that Dr. James wasn't here. He's bailing out. Gone on to other emissaries from the demonic realm.

Will began to feel like a sucker.

When he heard the heavy doors behind him swing open. Bang shut. He turned and saw Joshua James hurrying to him. The ex-priest genuflected and crossed himself. Then he slid into the pew, moving next to Will.

He patted Will's hand.

"Good to see you again," James said, smiling, the kind of buck-you-up grin bestowed on a pilot about to fly a suicidal run into enemy territory.

James knelt down. Closed his eyes. His lips moved.

Praying, Will thought, feeling uncomfortable.

Then James finished, crossed himself again, and sat back. He pulled a small chalkboard out of his attaché.

Then he dug out a piece of chalk. He set them on his lap and he turned to Will.

34

"What is evil?"

James's voice was a whisper, but still his question seemed to shatter the stillness of the small church.

"What? What do you mean?"

James repeated his question. "What is evil?"

Will smiled. Silly question. Silly answer . . .

"Bad things. And bad people who do bad things."

"Uh-huh," James said. "Just kind of faulty mechanisms, breaking down? Poor upbringing, environment, all that?"

Will nodded. "Yes, I guess so."

James shook his head. "Then you're saying that there is no evil, no objective evil?"

"No. I mean, there are people that do—"

James held up a hand and interrupted him. "Without evil, Will, there's no good. No Satan, no Christ. It's a package deal."

The old nun came out again, this time holding a white cloth across her arms. She genuflected and then struggled to her feet.

"Unfashionable words, I'm afraid. But very true. You see, Will, there *is* something called evil. It exists as surely as good exists. And its goals are"—James smiled, as if he were teaching a small boy his addition facts—"directly in conflict with life as we know it."

"What are those goals?"

"To destroy the power of God, the power of heaven, the force of *order* in the world . . . the force that made life appear on earth. And evil's power is in direct proportion to the status of the human soul."

Will shook his head. It's all too much, he thought.

"You can look around at our world and see that God is losing."

Yeah, thought Will. And I'm losing it.

"Here. Let me make it simple. The soul, the human spirit, can affect external events. Say you get discouraged. Down on yourself. And, presto, suddenly you start having a bad day. Very simple, but *that's* the process. Hopelessness and hatred feed off each other, growing around us. Weakening the power of God." James cleared his throat. "While the Adversary of existence grows stronger."

"The Adversary? Who's the Adversary?"

James answered him by handing him the chalkboard.

"That's what we have to find out."

James sat back and waited a second before beginning his ever-more-incredible explanation.

"Automatic writing, Will. We'll try it. We'll see if you know more than you think you do."

Will grinned. "You're losing me. I was just trying to get some help, some advice—"

James looked affronted. "You came to me? Correct? I didn't come to you. You came to me. And I believe in the power of God. *And* the power of evil. *You came to me*. If you don't have even the beginnings of some belief, then why in the world did you come to see me?"

Will shrugged. He looked at the chalkboard. He remembered something about automatic writing. A phony psychic's trick. It's in the same class with a Ouija board, a crystal ball.

James saw him looking down uncomfortably at the small chalkboard.

"If I called this psychometry, would that make you feel better?"

Will knew that term from his psych courses, years before. Psychometry was the unconscious reading of objects and events. It was the Jungian idea—later adopted by spiritualists—that objects would carry fingerprints of their past.

Will held the chalkboard. "I don't know. This seems—" He wanted to act polite.

Through the stained-glass windows, Will saw the light fading. The dismal afternoon was giving way to the early black shadows of a fall night.

The doors opened again. And Will turned to see a young

woman walk in. She dipped her hand in the holy water fountain and then sat in the last row.

The cheap seats, Will's father used to call them.

He turned back to James. James held out the chalk. Will shook his head. But he took the chalk.

"Close your eyes, Will. Close them and relax and listen to me."

Will made a face. But he followed James's directions.

"Now just listen to my voice, Will. Think about nothing else, nothing but what I say. I want you to write whatever words come to your mind as I talk to you, and nod if you understand."

Will made his head go up and down.

Ridiculous, he thought.

What did I get myself into here?

"Any words. I want you to picture all your friends from that night. Each of them, and—as you do—I want you to write their names . . . and any other words that occur to you."

Will made the chalk move on the board. It screeched, the horrible sound echoing in the nearly empty church.

James went on talking, quietly. "Good. Think about that night, what you remember, what you *see*, as if you were there, Will, right there, on the rocks, drawing on the rocks, saying the words."

As Will wrote, he felt James lean over and erase the board, clearing it for more words, and—

Will felt his hand moving. Just jiggling up and down. Like the needle on a seismograph, shooting up and down. He laughed nervously, almost opened his eyes.

"Don't open your eyes!" James commanded, his voice loud, surely scaring the woman in the last pew.

Will nodded.

"Remember it all," James commanded.

And Will did.

The salty wind. Standing in the circle, in the points of a star. The words, silly, making them laugh. All of them drunk with the booze, all of them wobbling on the star points, waiting for something to happen.

But nothing happened. Nothing at all.

Except—

Something did.

(I never remembered this. How could I forget this?)

There was a hole.

A monstrous, black hole at the center of his memory. He couldn't imagine the circle, the star anymore. There was just this *hole*. And the five of them standing around.

No one was smiling.

I don't remember this.

Yet it was there.

He went on writing.

Words upon words upon words.

James erased, hardly able to keep up with the flailing movements of Will's hand.

Something glistened from within the hole.

I see something, Will thought.

There—where the circle, the star should be. Lumbering out of the hole.

We all watch.

We all see it.

It didn't happen.

But why do I remember it? Why do I see this?

Out, until the black glistening skin revealed an iridescent rainbow of colors, moving swirls of magenta and purple, like a dark Jovian planet filled with giant storms traveling along its surface.

We all look.

Then it's there.

The smell fills his nostrils.

No one laughs. No one's drunk.

It's there. A shape with blackish eyes, or do we just imagine them? And a mouth, an opening. As if it would speak, as if it would talk to us.

It looks at each of us.

And I—and I—

Will cried out. He screamed.

"No! Oh, God, no!" He stood up, and the chalkboard slid to the floor.

Will looked at the altar.

The nun started back.

"No," he muttered.

"Will." James was up next to him, his arm around him,

strong, gripping him. "You have to continue, Will. You can't stop now."

Will shook his head back and forth. "Yes, I can. I can stop now—"

James knelt down and picked up the chalkboard.

He grabbed Will's hand and stuck the board in it, then the chalk. "No. Sit down. Finish it. You know you have to finish it now."

Will turned to him.

He thought of Becca. Setting the table for dinner. The chatter of their two girls. He thought of his house. Please, he thought. I want to go there.

Joshua James is a madman. He's going to make me lose it all.

But he knew that wasn't true.

Because he was beginning to know what the truth was.

"You'll continue?"

Will nodded.

He sat down. He heard the church doors open. The lady left.

Not a good night for quiet prayer.

"All right . . . close your eyes . . . continue . . ."

It turns and looks at each of us.

Each of us, fixing us with those eyes, sending messages, wonderful promises, with each amazing swirl of colors on its body.

Just a form, Will knew.

It can be anything. Anywhere. Anytime.

At any moment.

It looked at Will . . .

Will felt it then. Looking at him. Demanding.

Promising. Oh, the promises, the wonders, the power, the beauty . . .

Asking the question.

Will felt it.

And he felt his answer.

Will opened his eyes.

He was crying.

James cradled, held him close. Will sobbed, in a way that

made him think he was five years old again, watching his
mother leave home for the first time. Crying for her. Heaving, gasping at the incense air.

"Oh, God, oh, sweet God, I never—"

James pulled him close. "Go ahead," he whispered. "Call
on His name." James laughed. "It's okay here . . . it's all
right . . ."

And Will was allowed to cry until the feeling was over.

Then James released him and said, "You have to continue
now. You have to finish, Will."

But Will knew that. Knew it.

Because he was beginning to know how all this would
end . . .

It turned from him, and all that beauty and power, all the
promises of worlds and life to come vanished. There was just
the terrible stench and the cold and the crashing of the hungry
sea.

It turned from him.

Will's hand moved on the chalkboard slowly.

"Tell me," James said. "Tell me who it is."

It turned and Will watched it, saw it looking at the next
person on the point of the star. It stretched something out, a
hand from some part of its body, armlike, reaching out.

And someone reached back.

Will stopped his writing.

He gave the chalkboard to James. His eyes were red, puffy
from his tears.

The old nun was near the sacristy door, pointing at them.
A young priest stood next to her.

James looked at the chalkboard.

"The Adversary," James said. He turned to Will. "You
did well. We have the name. And there's power in names,
Will."

"It was like I was there," Will said.

James nodded.

"Yes, you were." He looked at Will and smiled sadly, as
if he realized the strange, hopeless thoughts running through
Will's head. "I can tell you now about time, what it really
is, but I needed you to do this"—he held up the chalkboard—
"first."

Will looked at it.

He saw letters, the words barely legible, scrawled across the board. *Zar . . . Osirin . . .*

"Its name," James whispered.

And below it another word, something that Will knew already, just one word. The letters all crooked, jagged, spiky, fighting the pressure of his fingers.

Tim.

Will shook his head.

James patted his hand. "I won't lie. You're in danger, Will. *Your family is in danger.*"

Will turned and shot a look at him.

I'll kill him, Will thought. I'll kill the goddamn—

But he knew that wasn't possible. It wouldn't be that easy.

James made a small smile, trying to be reassuring. "But there's time, Will. Always time. He can be stopped. If you do everything I tell you . . . if you trust me completely. Can you do that?"

Will nodded.

The young priest opened the gate that was part of the communion rail. He walked toward them.

"Good," James said. "There's time . . . and we have the name. God help us, we have the name."

35

"Hey, Dad," Sharon said, nearly barreling into Will as she went galloping up the stairs. She grinned. "Er, you like missed dinner."

But then her smile faded.

And Will knew that she must have seen that he didn't look okay. *Something's wrong with Dad . . .*

I must be showing the telltale signs of insanity. This is how madmen look just before they cart them off.

He saw a book tucked under her arm. *Mathematics Around Us.* There was a ruler and space shuttle on the cover. A reassuring statement about the world. *From the King's foot to deep space—all of it is understandable, manageable by the human mind. With the help of modern mathematics!*

Except for some things that just don't fit, Horatio.

"Hey, are you okay?" she asked.

Will shut the door behind him feeling like Willy Loman in *Death of a Salesman.* And what I'm selling today, they wouldn't buy even on cloud cuckoo land.

Beth ran into the room, wearing a happy smear of chocolate across her face. She grinned—the weird gap of her missing front teeth both comical and bizarre.

"Hi, Daddy," she said. Then, pensive, thoughtful . . . "Where were you?"

Will smiled at her. At least, he thought it was a smile. "I—er—I had things to do." He looked back to Sharon, but his oldest was already clomping up the stairs.

Away from me.

Away from the crazy man.

"How—how was school?" Will asked, taking a step toward Beth. But her snaggle-toothed smile was gone, and she

backed up, and—Christ—I need a shower. Something to burn
away, wash away, the church smell, the incense, the feelings—

Then Becca came out.

Looking as if she already knew some very bad news.

Becca watched him eat. Will felt her eyes follow the movement of his fork as he speared stringy bits of beef Stroganoff
and then brought the food up to his mouth. He dabbed at his
lips. Wanting to appear tidy while under such close scrutiny.

He didn't tell her the truth.

Not even close.

"I got tied up at work," he said between bites. "A big
drug-trafficking case—" He nodded to her. "Big for Westchester, that is. Sorry . . ."

He went on eating, feeling Becca's eyes studying him.

"What about your friends?" she asked slowly, as if afraid
to bring the subject up. "What's his name? Kiff?"

Will shook his head. "I don't know. Strange stuff, eh?
Pretty strange." Another forkful of noodles and beef.

Then he quoted a bumper sticker.

"Life's a bitch."

"You look like shit," she said.

"Thanks." He smiled. "I feel about that good too."

His fork scraped noisily against the plate. He looked up to
see Becca chew at her lower lip, the telltale sign of worrying.
A dead giveaway.

"You should get to bed. Early," she said.

Will shook his head, his mouth full.

"Can't," he said finally. "I can't . . . because . . ."

But she saw this coming, Will knew. All along, saw it
coming.

"There's someone coming here tonight," he said. He
couldn't make his mouth smile, too afraid of the sick, comical cast it would take.

"Thanks for telling me. Do you mind telling me who?"

Will nodded. He had practiced the fabrication in the car,
saying it out loud to hear how it sounded, to see if it was the
kind of lie that would encourage immediate disbelief.

"An old teacher of mine, from St. Jerome's." He cavalierly speared some food. "Going through some bad times. A divorce—"

"How old is he?" Becca asked, with an explosive laugh.

Will smiled back. "A young lady is taking him to the cleaner's. I told him I'd help him get the ball rolling. Protect his savings account." Will gestured with the fork. "That kind of thing."

"*And* stay here?"

Will nodded.

"Just for a night or two. That's all."

Becca pushed her chair back and stood up. "Well, as I said, thanks for telling me. How long do I have to get the guest room presentable before—what's his name?"

Will told her Dr. James's real name.

James had said it wouldn't matter. Not after it was all over.

"Okay, when is he coming?"

Will looked up. Becca wasn't too happy. She didn't like surprises, didn't like people drifting into her house, unsettling it like a huge stone plopping into a still lake.

"Late," Will said. "Very late. I'll wait up for him."

Becca walked away, shaking her head. And on the way out she passed Sharon, who had returned with her math book.

Sharon stopped at the entrance to the kitchen. She was a lean, sharp-eyed kid.

"Dad," she said.

Will listened to the word. Cherished it.

He turned to Sharon, still leaning against the entrance, tentative. "Dad, do you know *anything* about finding hypot—hypothen—"

"Hypotenuses?"

Sharon snapped her fingers and said, "Yeah. That's it. Well, do you?"

Will squinted and made his eyes look up to the heavens. "I did once . . . a long time ago. But I doubt that it's anything I can't pick up again." He stuck out his hand. "Here, let me take a look." Sharon stepped forward, holding out her math book. "It's like riding a bike. Something you never forget," he said.

Which, Will discovered, wasn't at all true.

And for a little while, he was lost to a quiet moment with Sharon and the wonders of elementary geometry . . .

* * *

Will flicked from the play-off game to the news, and back again. With a 5–1 score, it looked as if the Giants would tie up the series tonight. Then it would be three games each. Tomorrow night's game would be interesting.

The news wasn't on yet. He caught a bit of a sitcom, something about two guys living together with a teenage daughter—gimme a break.

Will waited for the news.

He heard Becca leave the bathroom and walk down the stairs, halfway, toweling her hair as if it were teeming with lice.

"Still not here?" she said.

Will shook his head. "No. He will be."

"Show him where I put the towels," she said.

"Sure."

"And make sure you lock all the doors."

"Don't I always?"

"No, you don't."

"I will," he said.

The sitcom ended.

"Good night," Becca said.

"Good night," Will said, turning to her quickly, and Becca disappeared upstairs.

Hard to look at her, he thought. She always was hard to lie to . . .

Jangling theme music. A lightning bolt, and then a bright-eyed news team came onto the screen.

He listened to the first story. A three-story tenement caught fire and killed everyone living inside it. A half dozen families, kids, old people. Neighbors were interviewed, talking inchoately about the smell of the smoke, the other smells. And how nice the people were. A shot of a sea of black faces standing around the building, wondering when it would be their turn to be caught in some ghetto inferno.

Then the world news. Footage of marchers in Estonia, celebrating its government's decision to seek admittance to NATO and alliance with the West.

There were also clips from an anti-Semitic demonstration in an Estonian city. And the Soviets were threatening military force to keep Estonia "independent."

The bright-eyed news team cut to another local story.

A press conference about the budget. And the mayor is asked about progress in tracking down the slasher . . . the ripper . . . the madman.

Each reporter uses his own pet name for the killer.

The mayor looks annoyed. But then—looking as if he felt the cameras were guns aimed at him—he says something reassuring. Bland.

The mayor says the police are following up numerous leads, investigating *every* possibility. And patrols have been doubled, even tripled in target areas in the city.

Will sees a few beads of sweat bloom on the man's brow.

Doesn't have a fucking clue, Will thought.

Another question—from good old Gabe Pressman, as annoyingly feisty as ever.

Are the police ready to ask for outside help . . . ready to admit that they have no leads?

The mayor stops Gabe.

And says no comment.

Then it's back to the Newscenter team, all hyped up and excited about the Giants tying the play-offs and yes, coming up, there's some cold weather in Big Al's five-day forecast.

So stay tuned.

But Will shut the TV off. To listen to the quiet streets outside, the safe streets. Listening for the sound of James's car.

But it was too early. Way too early.

The night is young. And he turned the TV back on.

Every car that roared up the block, even the improbable ones that sported souped-up engines and drop-dead mufflers, got Will to his feet. But he was left looking out at the deserted street, the dark side of Our Town, all shadows and maple trees heavy with leaves aching to join the frolic on the windy streets below.

His hand touched the cold glass.

And then Will would walk back to his chair and dredge up another fifties sitcom from late night TV—still actually funny almost forty years later—while he kept his vigil.

Until he heard a car that didn't thunder and roar up the street.

No, this one slowed as it came near the house, slower, and Will imagined someone trying to read the house numbers, always so well hidden. Slower, slower, and then stopped. Right there, right outside.

Will didn't get up this time.

Not until he heard the car door slam, heard the footsteps right outside the door.

He opened the door before James had a chance to ring the bell.

A sound that Will feared would wake up everyone in the house, everyone in the sleepy neighborhood.

Will opened the door and threw the light on.

And what he saw scared him.

James pushed his way into the house.

"Wh-what time is it?" he said, looking around for a clock. Will looked at the VCR.

"Two-fifteen," Will said. His own voice sounded dry and thin. It came from another galaxy. I'm groggy, just the way I felt in college after staying up all night trying to crack the wonders of calculus. Or playing Monopoly till dawn, greeting the breadman when he showed up at the frat house.

James looked at Will. He grabbed Will's hands and Will felt how cold James was. The leathery skin felt cold and dead. "Do you have something warm I could drink?" James sniffed.

Will knew that James had been outside a long time.

Then James looked around, at the stairs, leading to Becca, the girls.

I'm crazy, Will thought. Crazy to let this man inside my house.

But James—as if sensing Will's doubts—gave his hands a squeeze. "And someplace to talk, someplace where we won't wake your family."

And Will nodded.

Will put the teacup into the microwave and zapped it for three minutes.

"I saw him," James said.

The microwave hummed behind Will.

"You know it was him?"

James nodded, rubbing his hands together, fighting the chill.

"Yes. I mean, I've seen his pictures. I've seen Timothy Hanna in the newspaper. He came out of his building and—"

The microwave beeped.

Will opened it and removed the cup of Lemon Zinger.

"Honey . . . sugar?" Will asked.

James shook the question away. He took the cup from Will and wrapped his hands around it.

"I saw him and"—James looked up at Will—"he didn't see me." His eyes looked away again. "I was right. He didn't sense me. Not if he wasn't looking." James grinned. "I could follow him."

Will sat down in a chair facing James, watched him.

"It was Tim Hanna," Will said. "You're absolutely sure?"

James nodded. "Yes, he came out of his building as if he was just going to th corner for a newspaper. For a little walk. I saw him say something to his doorman. I thought he might look down the block and see me." James grinned, a crazy man, thrilled with his wonderful phantasm.

Why is he here? Will thought. How did this happen? How did it happen that *this* man is here, and I'm listening to him, just because—because—

Two old friends are dead.

Bought the farm.

In a real nasty way.

And I'm scared.

God, I'm scared.

Watch the clown with the hooks. Oh, watch them . . .

"I watched him. I stayed in the shadows of the buildings." James grinned again. "I thought the police would get me, find me, but I followed him. He couldn't sense me, you see. I'm nothing special to him. Nothing at all. So I could follow him, watch—"

Will nodded.

Another car went down the street, tires screeching, sneering at the peace of the neighborhood.

"I watched him." James nodded. "I watched him kill."

James paused. James's face twisted, disgusted, with something unspeakable.

Will looked away. "Oh, Jesus." Then back to James. "What? What the hell are you talking about?"

James sipped the tea. It had to be scalding hot but James sipped at it, his two hands wrapped around the cup, cherishing it.

"He followed a girl. A young streetwalker, I guess. I don't know. I was so far away. I followed him. He turned down a block. Thirtieth Street. Thirty-first, I'm not sure. There didn't seem to be any police around. None of those patrols. As if he knew that they wouldn't be there. As if he could keep them away."

Will took a breath.

He looked at the refrigerator. America's bulletin board. With Sharon's last spelling test, a 96. And Beth's picture of a pumpkin with a giddy toothless face that mirrored her own. A page from the Sunday *Times* about the Gauguin show at the Met. Yellowed, old, the show long gone.

Missed.

And a grocery list. Whole-wheat bread. Yogurt. Fles color. *Fles color?* What's that? Will wondered, an alien item suddenly on the list. He looked at it again, the scribbled word resolving into intelligibility.

Flea collar. Right. For the cat.

Will looked back to James.

The man hadn't gone away, he hadn't vanished while Will tried to absorb all the reassuring normalcy that filled the kitchen.

James was watching him.

"We have to start," James said. "I have to teach you everything you need to know. All this"—James's birdlike eyes scanned around the room, an unclean act that made the room seem sullied—"is in danger, Will. You must know that. Trust me." James's hands left his cup and grabbed for Will. "You're the last one left. You know that? The last payment. You will have to stop him."

James waited for an answer. It was quiet. Will waited too, sat there, listening, waiting, until he realized that he was the one that had to answer.

"Yes," he said. "I'm ready."

But he wasn't. Not really. Not for what he was about to hear . . .

36

Will insisted that they stop at dawn.

But first, James went out to his car and got the bag.

It was the first time Will saw the black bag, sitting on the kitchen table, right at the spot where Beth ate her Kix, where there probably were sticky stains from yesterday morning's juice.

James wanted to go through it all again. But now only bits and piece of what the man was saying stuck . . .

Disconnected phrases.

"It's like Rumpelstiltskin," James said, laughing to himself. "And of course he'd pick prostitutes. The tension, the emotional pain, is perfect . . . just what he needs."

Will asked few questions.

He asked, "What is it? What am I really fighting?"

"Evil," James said, as if describing the postman. "A demonic power. There are many. There are thousands—"

Will remembered the word Kiff used. Legion.

James nodded. "This one—this one, though—is special. Very powerful. Very clever."

Will rubbed his eyes.

The chunk of sky in the kitchen window, bordered by the blue gingham curtains, shifted from black to gray. There was no bright sun this morning. There were faint drops of water on the window.

"You *have* to be prepared for deceptions, for the paradox. Tricks. I can tell you about some of them. But you can't let them surprise you."

Will nodded, punch-drunk with nonsense.

But every time he thought of getting up from the table and ordering James out, he thought of Whalen. Covered with ants.

Crawling over his body, in his body, until he was completely flayed. Flayed. And poor crazy Kiff, kicking at the rats, dozens and dozens of rats.

He heard footsteps upstairs. Little ones. Beth, an early riser, was up. Tiny feet padding on the floor.

"We have to stop," Will said groggily. "For now. Get some rest. We can do more. This afternoon."

Will followed the sweet sound of the small footsteps. Trooping into the bathroom. Then out again. Stopping in her room. For a Barbie. Or maybe a softie to drag downstairs as a TV companion.

"Yes," James said, his voice overcome with exhaustion. "Yes. You're right. But Will—"

James waited. Until Will was looking at him.

"Will. You have to know this now. You have to know this." James licked his lips.

Footsteps coming down the stairs.

Will knew what was coming.

It had been there. At the corners, just hovering there, unsaid.

"Will. God help you. You may never see them again."

Footsteps. Down to the living room, hurrying out to the kitchen, hearing their voices.

Beth. Running in.

"Daddy!" she said. "Why are *you* up?"

She wore a pink quilted robe. Mickey Mouse slippers. She climbed onto his lap. "Huh, Daddy? How come?"

Will used a hand to cradle her head against his chest, pressing it tight against him.

"Because, honey," he said. His voice felt funny, his voice tight, closing up tight. He coughed. "Because, honey, Daddy has to do something."

The girl asked no other questions.

And Will's tears fell onto her hair, unfelt by Beth, who just enjoyed the warmth of being held close and tight.

37

Will woke up and he didn't know what time it was. The bed sheets twisted around his body, covering his head, and his right arm was numb.

He moved his head out from under the sheets.

He looked at the clock: 1:33.

He watched it a moment.

1:34.

It's afternoon, he thought. He sat up in bed. He rubbed his eyes. He saw the window, covered with rain. He heard the steady ping as the drops splashed against the window.

Then he heard voices. Downstairs.

He got up, slid on his pants, and hurried down.

Joshua James was sitting in the kitchen with Becca, smiling, chatting.

Just a neighborly visit.

"Well, good *afternoon*," she said. "Your day is pretty well shot. Coffee?"

"Yeah."

James looked different, refreshed, smiling.

But when he looked at Will, his eyes narrowed, as if sending a warning. Will drew a blank and then the message—obvious—appeared.

Act normally. It's important to act normally. *Everything is fine. Everything is okay.*

"Yes, your husband was a great help to me last night. I'm in a terrible way. All these legal things I don't understand . . ."

Becca put the coffee down on the kitchen table. "Well, I should hope he helped you . . ." She rolled her eyes at Will. "Because the public defender's office is getting curious where he's been.'' She stood next to him. ''You know you have a trial starting tomorrow?''

''Damn,'' Will said, sitting down. ''I—''

James interrupted. ''Oh, I'm sure your husband will be all prepared,'' he said affably. ''He's very good.''

Becca grunted noncommittally.

James turned to Will, his eyes still cut into slits, but now an easy smile on his face. ''I was telling your wife why I left the priesthood, Will.''

''Oh, really.''

James laughed. ''She thought that maybe I wanted to get married or something.'' James turned back to Becca. ''I'm afraid that wasn't the reason . . . not at all.''

Will sipped the coffee.

Becca had her coat on.

And keys in her hand.

''Leaving?'' Will said. My voice, he thought. It sounded— Worried.

She laughed. ''I'm helping with Beth's Halloween party. You and Dr. James can have some more time to—''

''Please,'' James said, ''call me Joshua. I feel old enough without the 'Doctor.' '' He turned to Will. ''I explained to your wife that I left because I wasn't allowed to write. Not what I wanted to write. Mother Church keeps such a tight control on the works that its clerics publish. I felt that I could be more effective freed of the collar.''

Becca scooped up her purse from the counter.

''You didn't tell me that Doc—Joshua—writes books.''

Will cleared his throat. ''No, I—''

''Well, I'm off. Give you some more time to work.'' Becca looked at Will, an unspoken plea that the houseguest must move along.

''See you,'' Will said.

Becca left by the side door. And when it slammed, Will asked, ''Is that really why you left?''

''That's not the whole truth. I made some enemies at the Vatican. An Order of Silence was handed to me, a very serious thing. Apparently someone in the Papal Nuncio didn't appreciate my writing and talking about my work.''

''Which was?''

James laughed. ''A consultant. A tactician. Fighting the

good fight against chaos. When I said that we were losing
that fight, some of the good cardinals asked for my resigna-
tion.'' James shook his head. ''That's when I knew that the
level of corruption—of influence, if you will—had reached
even there.''

Will nodded.

''I've been thinking,'' Will said. He waited for James to
interrupt, as if the former priest might anticipate his thoughts.
''I've been thinking that maybe this is all wrong. I'm getting
carried away. How do you know someone was killed last
night? How do you know it was—'' He smiled. ''Maybe it's
hysteria. That's all, and—''

James nodded. He unfolded the newspaper lying on the
table near him. He slid it over to Will.

It was the New York *Times*, its first page cluttered with
stories. But James pointed to the first column.

Another Midtown Murder.

Then, below it, in smaller type: ''More Signs of a Bizarre
Ritual.''

James's face was set, granite hard, unsmiling. ''You have
no choice, Will. You know that.''

Right, thought Will. No choice.

Free will was a thing of the past.

The past. Maybe the future. But not now.

James was quiet while Will read the dispassionate descrip-
tion of the ''suspected prostitute's grossly mutilated body.''

Then—when Will finished the article—James stood up.

''I'll stay with them, Will. I'll stay here tonight. You can
tell your wife you have to do some research, some work. I'll
be here. I'll try to make things easier.''

Will thought that he might start shaking, crying again.

Make it go away, he begged. Make this whole damn thing
just disappear.

''I've arranged for a rental car. It will help.''

Will nodded.

He rubbed at his cheeks, and he felt the bristles of a day-
old beard. I should shave, he thought. I should get myself
together.

But it didn't matter.

James looked at the kitchen clock.

Tick. Tock. The second hand moved noisily around the circle of numbers.

"Your wife won't be gone long, Will. We have to go over it all again. We have to make sure you're ready."

Will nodded.

Trapped. A prisoner.

No way out, he thought.

No way at all. My personal Vietnam.

There's only one escape—if James is wrong. And then what?

But that possibility was even more terrible.

He couldn't bear to even think about that.

Becca came home with Beth holding a construction-paper pumpkin. James was in the tiny guest room resting. He'd have a long night, a night when he'd have to stay awake.

And Will had been in the bedroom—dumb thing. Looking at the old photo albums. Summers at the beach. Holidays, so many holidays . . . Christmases melting into birthdays, year after year.

Beth trudged up the stairs and ran into her room to show her artwork to Barbie. Will stood in the hallway and watched his daughter—dressed in a yellow rain slicker—vanish into her room without even seeing him.

Daddy wasn't supposed to be home.

Daddy worked.

He was tempted to walk up to her doorway and just watch her play.

Watch her without her knowing it. But then Becca followed upstairs, carrying a basket of laundry.

"Oh," Will said, startled. "I can help you with that." He took the basket from her.

"Tanks, bub. It's all part of the challenging career of housewifery."

Will smiled. Becca bore the boredom and the chowder— but just barely.

He followed her into the bedroom.

Thinking it was best that he tell her now.

He dumped the basket onto the bed and Becca started to sort the clothes into four piles. He stayed beside her to help.

"I have to go out tonight."

His words hung there while he dug out his oversized shorts from the more petite articles of the rest of his family.

"What?"

"I've got to do some research. For that case tomorrow. I lost time today, and the law library is open until twelve."

She shook her head. "I hope your kindly old professor will be moving on. He's a nice old man and everything. But—"

Will didn't say anything, and he felt Becca turn and look at him.

"He's staying another night." Will made his face look sheepish. "Just one more night. He'll have someplace to go . . . tomorrow."

"Oh, brother. Well, thanks for the warning. He's a nice man . . . but he kind of scares Beth."

Will listened. But he drew close to Becca and put his arms around her.

"Hmmm . . ." she said. "In the mood for afternoon delight?"

It wasn't that, he thought. Not at all . . .

He pushed her straight hair aside and kissed her neck.

His hand went around to her front and cupped her breasts. She backed against him. He was already hard, and it felt so good to have Becca pressing against him.

"Beth is just next door," Becca whispered.

He pulled her closer.

"Shut the door," he whispered. "Shut it and lock it."

Becca pushed against him once more and he felt that wonderful pressure, the perfect way her body moved against his.

Then she moved away, to the door. Shutting it gently. Turning the lock.

Then back to him.

She unzipped her skirt. Kicked out of her shoes. She pulled her sweater over her head.

"Can't make too much noise," she hissed. "There's Beth . . . and Grandpa, downstairs . . ."

He smiled.

She came to him.

He pulled her tight while she worked at his belt, pushing his pants down. Pulling him out. Stroking him, urging him to move more quickly now.

Not knowing.

Not ever suspecting, he thought, poor girl.

That this was it.

The last time.

For them.

Such a terrible thought, a thought to make his stomach sick with the pain. But then there was just her hand, working on him, and her lips searching his face, pressing against him, until they found his lips. And her tongue dancing wildly inside his mouth.

And then that's all there was, as they tumbled back onto the bed, strewn with clothes.

For a few brief moments, that's all there was . . .

38

Beth was still up. Will knew that. He heard her chatting to herself, issuing severe instructions to the rambunctious crowd of softies that loitered on her bed.

Will walked into the room, dark and heavy with the sleepy smell of a small girl's bedtime.

"Good night, sprout," he whispered, leaning down close to her.

For a second Beth didn't answer—lost in her fantasy. But then she said sweetly—

"Good night, Daddy."

He leaned over and kissed her forehead. A few strands of her thin hair brushed his lips.

"Daddy," Beth said, "when will you be back?"

Will made a fist and reached up to his mouth, covering it, nearly moaning, nearly crying out.

Can't. He thought. Can't . . .

He waited until it passed.

"Soon, honey. Real—"

A sudden lurch. The dark room exploded in a fireworks display. He touched the bed to get his balance.

"Soon," he whispered huskily.

He backed out of the room. Wounded, bleeding, dying inside while his little girl snuggled against the pillow. She pulled her sheets up tight, safe and sound forever.

In the hallway, he turned around.

Will walked past Sharon's room.

He looked at her, bent over her schoolwork, the radio on low. Only the syncopated hiss of the rap music could be heard.

But Sharon's room was bright, and he couldn't hide his

feelings if he went in there. So he stayed in the shadows. "Good night, babe," he said.

Sharon looked out, into the darkness, and squinted. "Dad? Night." Nice and casual. Just one of a thousand good-nights to come. She smiled and went back to her work.

Then Will spun around. I'm going to fall down, he thought. I'll stumble right down the stairs. Already the house was an alien thing, a lost place, a place he dimly remembered.

He went down the stairs.

And—

There's no other way.

No other . . .

The bag was at the bottom of the stairs, right by the front door. Becca was doing something in the dining room. James stood by the door. The TV was on, masking what James whispered to Will.

"Are you all right?" the man said. "You look—"

Will grinned. "Yeah. I know. I look pretty bad."

James is worried. He's worried that I'm falling apart, that everything might fall apart. James has done things like this before. What was the figure—100, 120 exorcisms? He knows about this . . .

But then Will looked in the man's eyes, and he saw fear there too.

"You're shaking," James said. He reached out and grabbed Will by the shoulders. "Steady, Will. Steady. It's all right, Will. They'll be fine. They'll—"

Will was too embarrassed to explain that it wasn't his family—right then—that had him terrified.

I don't think—he thought—I don't think I'm cut out for this . . . sacrifice.

It's just a variation of the runaway-truck scenario.

Which went like this:

A runaway truck is barreling down the street, careening out of control, right at your blue-eyed toddler. Your sweet little girl. Your darling blue-eyed boy.

And you see that you can probably knock your kid out of the way. But that's about it. You'd be stuck there while eighteen gigantic wheels rolled over you.

So what do you do?

Every parent knew the one, correct answer.

You move. You save your kid. Without a thought for your own life.

And here I am, Will thought.

The truck roaring right toward my family.

"Will—" James said quietly, still holding on to him. "You're okay?"

Will nodded. "I'm—"

Becca came into the room.

"Oh, I thought you left already," she said. She looked confused seeing James standing there so close to him. He's propping me up, babe. Getting me out the door.

Then James backed away, smiling, and Becca came closer.

"Drive carefully," she said. "What time do you expect—?"

"Late," Will said. "Don't wait up."

She smiled, her eyes looking at him, the confusion fading. "Don't worry. I'm beat. Are you—okay? You getting a cold?"

Will forced a smile. "Sure. Maybe." He shook his head. "Just tired."

He turned away. He looked at the bag. By the door.

And walked over and picked it up. Then, like any traveling salesman, he walked over to Becca and gave her a gentle kiss on the lips.

"Good night," she said.

Will said nothing. Couldn't say anything. He nodded to her, then to James.

And he turned and opened the door, a zombie-man walking as straight as his wobbly zombie-legs could carry him. He shivered as if he were braving a January morning dressed in just his underwear.

Will kept walking, down the steps, not looking back.

Out to his car. Which he was about to drive a block away, and leave it for the rental car.

He looked at his block. This quiet street they lived on.

Sleepy and safe, already the pumpkins glowing from people's windows, trying to scare away winter.

He got into his car and turned on the ignition.

The digital clock flashed on.

It was nine o'clock.

And it was time he went to Manhattan.

39

Will wouldn't have recognized him.

People change. We shed our high school images like butterflies emerging from a cocoon. Or flies screwing out of their maggoty pupas . . .

Will's wrist throbbed.

But he knew the voice. It still had that clear, cutting edge. The perfect lawyer's voice. A debater's voice.

Will said his name.

Remember the power of names, James had said.

"Tim . . ."

Will backed up another step. The bag was heavy, dangling from his hand. His mangled wrist throbbed. He jabbed it into his leather jacket like Napoleon. He felt the wet sear, growing.

"Pretty messy down there, eh, Will? You're lucky—"

Was there a smile? Will wondered. Was that a smile there?

"Lucky no cops came by." Tim Hanna looked around at the buildings, at the night sky. "There are a lot of cops on the streets. Looking for me, I guess."

Another laugh.

Tim Hanna took a step forward. Another. Will backed up. "Which is a waste of time, of course." Another smile. Another step. Will wished his wrist would stop throbbing. Damn, if only it would just stop throbbing.

The pain flashing on and off, hot and cold, driving any chance for a clear thought away.

"But I guess you see how impossible that is, don't you?"

Will nodded.

At nothing.

Tim Hanna had disappeared.

Will heard movement from behind him. He turned around.
And there was Tim Hanna behind him.

"Impossible, Will. They're dealing with a"—a pause, a
grin that caught the light—"a higher power here. The only
fly in the ointment, the only bug in the plan, the only—"

Tim walked toward him again, and Will backed up. But
then he stopped.

What does it matter? What the hell does it matter? If he
can just appear behind or in front of me anywhere? What the
hell difference does it make?

"The only little kink in the plan is you. The others all
carried their weight, their *burden*, like good little soldiers.
You—you escaped free—"

"What—what are you talking about?"

The bag, Will felt it hanging down, heavy, useless.

But he listened, and tried to think about what he was going
to do . . .

Got to remember . . .

"I *knew* that Narrio's ride would end prematurely. I *saw*
the fucking rail, Will. No surprises there. None at all. And
so did Whalen, and Kiff—"

"They knew?"

Tim Hanna nodded. "Sure did, my boy."

And Will thought: Were they too drunk to stop him? Or
maybe drunk enough to want to see what would happen.

The bag. Got to get it. Pull it up.

Open it.

He looked at Tim.

"But why do you want me?" It sounded pathetic, a pitiful
plea.

Tim Hanna laughed. "You were part of it from the beginning . . ." Hanna took a step. "You're not so innocent—
never bullshit a bullshitter. And you had a family, children.
Untainted. They would finish it. That was part of it." Another smile. "From the beginning."

Will nodded. He knew that.

Now, thought Will, I've got to do it now, before he comes
closer and—

He yanked the bag up, pulled it tight against his body. The
latch was still open. He locked the bag in the crook of his
bad arm.

My bag of tricks.

Watch the signs, James had said. Watch for the stench, the noise, the signals—

He reached into the bag and touched the jar. The lid was loose and Will fiddled with the cap while it was still inside the bag, trying to twist it off.

Fiddling crazily, he looked up at Tim Hanna—a man with golden hair, piercing eyes. Dressed in a dark suit. His skin smooth and tan even under the crime-stopper tungsten lamps. He was right there, in front of Will.

The lid fell off. Will pulled out the jar.

"By the power . . . of God—" Will muttered.

Like some deranged idiot.

Will went to toss the water.

Only feet away, at Tim.

But the jar grew warm, then hot, hotter, and a plume of steam erupted from the open mouth. The water bubbled and Will had to let the jar, so damn hot, slip through his fingers.

"You didn't really think *that* would work, did you?" Tim Hanna laughed. Then he said, "By the power of Mickey and Donald, Goofy and Pluto, Goobers with peanuts, a Penis for Venus, and Walla-walla Bing-Bang!"

The words echoed off the asphalt, off the concrete, off the buildings.

Will pulled out the cross, shaking it free of its velvety wrappings.

Again, he yelled, "By the power of God, all evil shall go, all—"

Hanna sneered. And Will thought he smelled something. A wind that blew across his face, filled with the gaseous odor of methane, a sticky warm gust of foul air.

"Don't say that fucking name!" Tim Hanna screamed. He raised his fist. "You will *never* say that name to me!"

Will held the cross up, pathetically. His bad arm holding the bag, the other holding the cross aloft.

Then it burned. Grew hot. It's a trick, thought Will. Just a trick. It's not really hot, and I can—

Hotter, until the metal creaked, bending, and it went soft in his hand. Will cried.

His fingertips burned. He tried saying the words.

"Power . . . God . . . commands Lucifer, commands all evil, every spirit . . . put to . . ."

He had to let the cross slide through his fingers, crying out as it turned cartwheels in the air, spinning to the ground, splattering to the sidewalk.

Will cried.

He heard the noises.

The chattering, the clicking sounds.

Listen for them, James had said. Take hope from them. His control is not perfect. Then it's time.

"I saved the worst for you, Will. The absolute fucking worst. For you. And your goddamn family."

The clicking filled his ears, but beneath that he heard another sound.

And he looked to the side of the buildings. To where the noise, the cracking sounds, were coming from.

He saw long, blackish things moving back and forth, hugging close to the crack of the building.

No, Will thought, not blackish, brown. He saw a line of them emerge into the purplish light.

"Big, aren't they? The biggest fucking cockroaches, Will. Do you know how a cockroach eats? They're maniacs, absolute monsters. They tear at their food, eating everything." Tim smiled. "I'll let them save your brain for last . . ."

As above so below, thought Will.

It's all scripted. He heard James . . .

We can change the script. It's about time, Will, time and power . . .

He knew that he really shouldn't look at the building, to the sounds that now circled him. But God, he had to, couldn't avoid looking down, around—

At the sea of brown. At these giant roaches, moving fast, excited, climbing over each other, surrounding him, hundreds, thousands, millions.

Waiting for a signal.

"There's just one thing I have to add," Tim Hanna said, "before we begin—"

Now, thought Will. Turn away. Don't listen.

You must act, James had said. When you see the signs, smell them, hear them, you *must* act then. He won't expect it.

Will dug into the bag and pulled out the book. It had a black binding, and ribbons dangled from it.

James's own Bible.

Been through a lot, he'd said. A lot of battles.

You've got to wrestle with the devil . . . not in your name, but God's.

Will held it up. Tim Hanna seemed unalarmed.

The rest had been a lure. Show him that I have no weapons. That I'm defenseless.

Then the words. Memorized, repeated at almost unintelligible speed. The book held out. Keeping me focused on where the power, the strength come from.

Telling Tim Hanna. It's not me.

Telling his master.

Because . . . because that's who the game was all about.

The roaches seemed directionless, moving over his feet, suddenly unleashed from any control.

Will sputtered, babbling quietly, but loud enough to be heard over the clicking noise, the sound of teeth gnashing, eager for their earthly feast.

"I command you, whoever you are . . . unclean spirit, and all your companions who possess this child of God—"

Will kept his eyes on the book, off Hanna, away from his face. Can't get distracted. And then faster, running the words together at high speed, but louder now, starting to yell—

"By the mystery of the Incarnation. The Passion. And Resurrection and Ascension. Of Our Lord Jesus Christ!"

A howl. A mind-numbing scream. From just ahead. Will kept looking at the book.

He felt cold. A million voices hissed at him.

You don't believe anything, you shit. You goddamn atheist fornicating sonuvabitch. You don't believe anything and—

Right. That's right. And this won't work. This is nonsense. And it means nothing because there's no God, no life, no—

No.

He made himself say the words. "By the Holy Spirit, be summoned to judgment, *leave this soul*. Leave and obey the word of God."

He screamed the last words again.

"Obey the word of God. By the power of Lord Jesus Christ, leave and—"

Will took his eyes off the book. He looked at Tim Hanna.

Hanna backed up, staggering now, oh, yes, reeling like a fighter taking another smash to the head.

Will intoned the words again.

The book felt cool in his hand, impervious to anything Hanna would do. Will walked forward, through the sea of roaches. He heard them crunch and crack under his steps. Some crawled absently and undirected onto his shoes, a few big ones up to his pants leg, but Will just kept repeating the words.

Over and over.

Tim Hanna said, "You liar. You believe nothing, your soul is empty. A damned empty pit. You are a fucking liar."

Will repeated, "By the power of God, I command you to obey . . . obey God's word and—"

He lifted his eyes from the book.

Another smell filled his nostrils.

The signs. He'll grow desperate, James had said. He'll call for help. *Remember that.* Watch for the signs. They mean he's desperate. Don't lose your concentration, your thoughts . . .

Back, nearing the corner of the street, Hanna stumbled backward.

Will looked up. The smell was barnlike, the stink of animals.

And then, dropping around Will, on him, landing on his head, his arm, on the Bible, something . . . gooey wet glops of offal, the smell filling Will's throat. Burning his throat. Choking him.

Will coughed. The words sputtered to a stop as he hacked at the air.

I looked away, he screamed inside his head. Then he saw it all slipping away. His concentration. His belief. Everything melting—a dream.

Something bit his leg. He cried out.

I've lost it.

They were at the corner.

Will tried to start his chant again. But it didn't feel the same.

Liar, screaming in his ear.

Bullshit artist.

God-hater. Deceiver.

Dumb fuck.
Hanna spoke.
He said, quietly, calmly, "Listen."
Will thought: No. I won't do that.
But he did.
The pay phone rang.
Ring. Ring. Ring.
Over and over.
"It's for you," Hanna said.
"By God's power, obey and—" Will tried to say again.
The phone kept ringing. Hanna said, "I think you should answer it. It's for you, Will."
A cold spiky hand seemed to close around Will's heart. He moaned.
"It's for *you*," Hanna said, his voice garbled, as if coming over through a cassette player in need of batteries.
"Pick it up. Pick it the fuck up, Will!"
Will stopped his yammering.
"It's a call from home," Hanna said.
But Will knew that already. Oh, sweet Jesus . . . he knew that.
And he reached out for the phone . . .

Joshua James shifted in the seat. It was strange, sitting here in this quiet house, sitting watch over Will Dunnigan's family.
Not as strange as other places I've been, other vigils I maintained.
No, I've sat huddled in freezing-cold tenements surrounded by stale puke and feces. I've walked through tiny Amazon villages in search of someone who was said to be blessed with powers and abilities.
When blessed was the wrong word.
James felt sleepy.
And he thought—
I can't fall asleep. I have to stay awake.
Simple as that.
Until morning. Until it's over.
He rubbed his eyes. He had the TV on, very quiet, almost inaudible. And a book. Father Paone's *Meditations*. A simple book of simple prayers.
Easy does it.

And beside him, a Bible, its cover worn to a frayed and tattered black hide. My spare, he thought. And—

I must not sleep.

He thought of his lie.

When they asked him why he left the priesthood.

How that wasn't the truth. Not the whole truth. But he couldn't very well tell them the truth, now, could he? Couldn't very well tell Will that one time he buckled? I ran from it, scared, terrified beyond belief. My own worldliness thrown into my face, my own secret desires dredged up, dancing in front of me.

And I was lost.

I was useless against it. Because each time, this evil, this mocking abomination, would plunge into my soul and find the hollowness and desire there. It fed on it. *Like rats. Like ants.* Fed on it, growing stronger.

The state of the human soul feeds it.

And I had let mine grow weak.

No, he thought. I couldn't tell him that. Not to Will.

Just as he knew he couldn't tell Will how he feared the same thing might happen to him. That Will might face the Adversary, so much stronger than he was, that it would be no contest.

If he forgot in whose name he fought . . .

And I must fight this feeling of hopelessness, James scolded himself. That was the worst. That opened all sorts of doors. Bad doors.

He shut his eyes. They were so heavy with a terrible need for sleep that they ached. He shut them. Just a second. Then he quickly opened them.

The TV seemed to have no sound now. Fading.

Fading.

Must not sleep, he told himself.

Must.

Not.

Will's hand locked on the phone. It kept ringing.

"Go on," Tim Hanna said. His voice smooth, seductive. It was a voice of reason, a doctor asking you to breathe in and out while he listened to your lungs. Nice, normal breaths, please. Or the dentist pleading for you to stretch your maw open just a *bit* wider.

Then, a subtle change, "Pick it up, you stupid bastard."

"No," Will moaned.

It rang in his ear, electric and shrill. Again and again.

Tim Hanna again, oily now, victorious. "Reach out . . . and pick it up!"

And shaking, shivering, Will did . . .

James's eyes blinked open. The phone was ringing. And, and—

Becca Dunnigan was standing there, in her white nightgown, looking out the window at the street. A red light lit her face. Faded. Lit her face, and then faded.

"The police," she said quietly. "There's a police car . . . right out—"

The ringing again. Except, no—it's not the phone. It's the doorbell.

I'm asleep, James thought. This is a dream. Nightmare. Not happening.

Becca went to the door.

"What are the police doing here?" she said to James as if he might know.

Awake. James knew. I'm awake.

The doorbell rang again. It's not the phone. It's the door. Of course, it's—

"No," he said. James tried to get up. He pushed against the arms of the chair, but he was settled into the soft plush cushion, and his body didn't move. His legs tingled, the circulation cut.

"No, Becca. Don't open the door. Please—"

She undid the dead bolt. Then the chain. She opened the door.

A young cop stood there. He looked concerned.

James finally pushed himself up.

And then he thought, God, it's about Will. Something has happened to him.

The cop was saying something to Becca, but James couldn't hear it. He saw the young dark-haired cop's lips move. And Becca nodding. And then the cop took another step inside the door.

And from behind James, there were more sounds.

Too fast. Things are happening too fast here, James thought. What is going on?

Behind him. The oldest girl, Sharon, bouncing down the stairs. Her face was all scrunched up, but it picked up the rotating red swirl from the police car's light outside.

Then the little one, Beth, following her sister, coming down the stairs.

James looked at the cop.

Still not hearing anything.

Watching how his eyes moved so slowly from Becca, then up the stairs to Sharon, on to Beth, marking their positions. And—

Ringing.

The phone. Yes.

The phone ringing.

From the end table.

The cop gestures at it.

James shakes his head. No. No, he says. James thinks he says. But—funny thing—he doesn't hear anything.

I fell asleep, he thought. God forgive me. I fell asleep.

The cop takes another step in. The red light seems to flash more wildly, more excitedly.

The cop is moving toward the phone.

No.

Not the phone. I have to get to the phone.

It rings and rings and rings . . . while James takes a step. Then another lurching step toward the phone, on rubbery legs, falling, collapsing, reaching out for the phone.

His hand closes around the cord, grabbing it.

Yanking the cord.

Pulling the phone right off the end table.

Until it clatters off the table, and the receiver is right there, right by his head . . .

"Hello," Will said. "Hello."

An icy breeze cut up the street. There was no one in the entire city except for him and Tim Hanna.

We were friends. School buddies.

And now?

He's the darkest thing in the universe.

"Hello."

"Listen," Hanna whispered gently to him.

Will heard a gasp, a sound. Then a voice, gasping near the phone. "Will? Will!"

It was James. Then another sound.

Becca's voice. Crying out. Then screaming.

Will squeezed the phone tighter.

Then—oh, God, no—please no.

Sharon. And Beth. Crying out, their shrieks traveling from miles away. Right into his ear. Into his brain.

Will heard tearing, cutting, more screams, and more screams, and—

The cord was alive. It wrapped itself around James's throat like a sleepy snake curling up for a sleep on a sunny rock. James watched it, and pulled at it. But the wire was too strong, tightening too quickly against him.

And he could see the others. Becca grabbed Beth, holding her shoulders. Holding her daughter tight.

But the cop—wasn't a cop anymore.

He became this dark thing, this purple-black pile of excrement, this gigantic tower of shit, with hundreds, thousands, millions of squirming things moving around and through it. In and out, a feast for worms.

The cord tightened.

No more air.

James felt his eyes bulge.

The tower leaned close to Becca, backing up, holding her Beth tight, the little girl's fists raised to the air, cursing at the horror, screaming at it through her endless tears to go away.

Instead—so quickly—a dozen of the things inside it grabbed Beth. The shock stopped her tears.

They moved along her skin.

James closed his eyes.

Like a vacuum cleaner, they peeled away the skin.

James started praying.

The poor sweet baby.

James heard another terrible yell. And he knew Becca had tried to wrest her daughter from the thing.

Silly, futile—

And James kept muttering the prayers . . .

* * *

"It was all planned, Will. From the beginning, this is just how it was . . . in the plan. But then, you know that. You do know that—"

Will turned to him.

He recognized Beth's screams. He wanted to drop the phone and grab Tim Hanna. Just a man, standing in front of him.

But then Becca's plea reached his ears.

Her voice. A disgusting croak. But clear enough—through what must be, yes, blood gurgling in her throat—yes, clear enough for him to hear the word.

"Will," she begged.

And where is James? Oh, Jesus, what have I let happen?

"You were part of it, Will. You felt his presence and you agreed like all of us . . . You agreed . . ."

Hanna grinned in the darkness.

Another scream. Sharon.

Will screamed into the phone. "Sharon, honey, run away. Get out of there. Run, baby, run—"

Run. Run. Run.

The scream changed. A higher pitch. The human thread pulled even more taut. Playing another, more desperate song. Sharon begged it. Begging this thing. He heard her beg. Please, oh, please, oh. Tearing sounds. More yelling, and—

Please.

Will looked at Hanna, not hearing him, trying to remember.

What am I supposed to do?

What is it that I must do?

I've got to remember. I'm here to do something. Now, what is it, what is—?

I just can't . . .

"It got your agreement. Kiff. Whalen. And we all agreed. And Mike Narrio was given to it."

Will shook his head. Not true. Not true. I never—

"Kiff knew. He knew what he'd done. Spent his whole life trying to wipe it away." Hanna grinned. "Crazy Kiff . . . But you can't do that, you know. Not allowed, kiddo. And Whalen pushed it away. Even though he saw the broken rails of that ride, saw the way they just streamed into space. He knew. And he tried to run away.''

Hanna paused. And stepped closer. Just a step.

But there was something about it, something that Will could see. Even though Will was shaking, rocking on the sidewalk, back and forth, mumbling, biting his lip.

He saw it.

What happened to them? What happened to my family?

''Dr. James,'' he said quietly into the receiver.

He heard sounds on the phone. Sliding, the movement of something heavy dragging across the floor.

''Dr.—''

James's throat kept contracting, trying to suck air through his nose.

He saw bits of their bodies in the thing. A bit of bone, Sharon's hair, slowly subsumed into it. A single small blue eye looked out at him.

But now it moved toward him.

And—oh, forgive my weakness, James prayed—he hoped that he'd die before it reached him.

But that didn't happen.

A dozen things squirted out of its body and landed on him, and he felt every tear, every pull at his skin, until it was a blessing to join the horror of its body . . .

''You blocked it, Will. Blocked it right out. Simple as that. But you can't hide secrets forever.''

Will held the phone away from his ear. There was nothing more to hear. No.

Nothing at all.

But.

Must remember.

Have to remember.

Can't listen to this.

''You blocked out your . . . *agreement* to Narrio's death. Your part. I understand, but you know it's true, Will. You did it.''

Remember.

The wind made him shiver more. Icy cold. He let the phone

fall. The streetlight was a kaleidoscopic blur. I wonder why it's so blurry?

Of course. Of course.

My eyes are so wet.

The phone swung like a pendulum, banging into the pay phone's pillar.

The Bible was there, still clutched in his aching claw hand.

"You did it."

Will didn't move.

He's right, Will thought. I let it happen. I agreed. Just as I blocked out the memory of that black shape in the center of the circle. I let it happen—

Then he remembered James's voice.

Watch the lies. The deception. The tricks. The paradox. You'll be tied up before you know it. Lost in a maze of thoughts. And then it will be too late.

Tim Hanna took another step.

A cautious step, a shriveled part of Will's brain whispered. Hiding it. But cautious.

"You did it!" Hanna laughed gleefully.

Will shook his head.

It's just a trick.

I've got to remember. Got to remember what I have to do . . .

And now.

Oh, God, now I do.

Will staggered back, shaking like a drunk into the pay phone. He saw Hanna's grin broaden. Will's stomach heaved. Even though it was empty, it went tight like a rag being wrung dry.

But now *I* pull the trick, Will thought.

He staggered back some more, while his good hand reached down. Into his bag, his magician's bag of tricks.

"No," Will mumbled, shaking his head, hoping to keep Hanna's eyes on his. "No. You're lying."

His family's screams seemed to echo in the air. Becca shrill, faint, calling for him.

"Will."

He wanted to reach out and grab Hanna. Lock a hand around his throat.

But he waited.

Another cautious step by Hanna.

Hanna didn't notice anything odd.

Another.

And another.

And Will held up the book.

Maybe you won't even need it, James had said. Maybe it's not even important.

But take it, he said. Take it. While you do what only you can do. Only you can do it . . . because only you were there.

Will held the Bible. Just pages. Filled with words. And some of them were silly words.

Dumb words, stupid words, false words, idiotic—

No.

Hanna saw him holding the book. And he had jumped into Will's head, shoveling in thoughts and doubts on top of him like manure.

"No," Will said.

The Bible was there just to help.

Will had to do this himself. Because I was there at the beginning.

At the time that it happened.

He took a step toward Hanna.

What's precognition? James had asked, flipping through Dunne's book. *What is it but a jump in serial time? And why? Because serial time is merely a creation. There are many times, many possible selves. Time is a creation of our minds, a tool for our lives—*

Another step.

Hanna looked at the book. His face sneered, he spat. Again, and again, at the ground. And tiny smoky plumes erupted from the sidewalk, a miasma to protect him from the hated text.

And time can be changed, Will.

Will grabbed Hanna.

Hanna spat at Will, spraying acid droplets onto Will's face, dribbling onto the book. And a different smoke filled his nostrils.

Will felt a yawning expanse of chaos.

He touched Hanna. And he *felt* the hater, the annihilator, the Adversary Incarnate, the end of existence.

The words came out too slowly, swallowed by the foggy mist summoned by Hanna's spit.

Watch for the signs, the voices, the stench. It means he's growing desperate, trapped . . .

Will spoke.

"By the power of God, He commands you." Something clutched at Will's stomach, right into his insides. Clutched it and twisted it.

"God commands, oh, no," he moaned, doubling up. More spits. More smoke.

Things crawling on his leg.

Desperation.

"By the power of God, take me, a witness, to that time and place of your coming—"

Then, barely able to sputter out the senseless sounds, Will said the name.

"Zar . . . Osirin . . ."

Again. And again, louder, screaming it, hearing Hanna's scream in his ear, and shake, and quiver, rocking back and forth as if he might explode.

A mad dwarf in a kid's book, sputtering with frustration.

"The time and place of your coming! Show yourself. By the power of Our Lord Christ, the time and—"

The Bible slipped from Will's hand.

He heard it land.

The clouds of smoke choked him. There was no air, nothing to breathe. Nothing at all.

And then . . . there was.

Manhattan Beach

40

This place, the rocks, the beach, the washed-out night sky—it all was as if he had never left.

Will felt the odd tilt of the stone slab he was standing on. And the air was full with the stinging, ripe smell of the sea, crashing so close by.

And Will looked at the sea and remembered how it seemed to him.

How the ocean seemed hungry, eager to suck at the land, to pull it away. To reclaim everything.

He was at Manhattan Beach.

And he wasn't alone.

There was someone behind him, breathing, just out of range of his peripheral vision. He heard movement. Steps scraping against the stone.

I should turn around and face him. Yes, Will thought, I have to turn around and face him. To finish this—

He told himself that. And again. But he didn't move.

A hand landed on Will's shoulder.

"You cocksucking bastard . . . You stupid asshole—"

Hanna's voice—dry, an old man's voice—croaked in his ear. Then Will spun around and saw him. Hanna was dressed the same, but now he was bent over, holding his stomach as if his insides were ready to explode onto the ground.

And Will—like some torturer from the Inquisition—started in again—

His voice screaming above the wind, the waves . . .

"By God Almighty, by the power of Our Lord—"

A gust of smoke belched out of Hanna.

"Jesus Christ, appear. He commands you to leave this soul. God commands you—"

Then the name.

Names have power.

Rumpelstiltskin.

Mr. Mztplyx.

And—

"Zar . . . Osirin . . ."

Tim Hanna curled around, a snake speared by an invisible lance. He curled around, writhing in agony. He looked at Will. His eyes softened. Then a smile that was almost human.

But a sick look suddenly covered Hanna's face. And Will heard something louder than the crash of the waves. A cracking, creaking sound. Hanna's face split open, a ripe coconut, splitting right down the middle. The tear went all the way down the front. His skull, his lips, pulled apart.

Will gagged again.

But I've got nothing to throw up. Nothing except my own stomach acid.

But the smell overwhelmed him, a putrid, toxic stench that felt liquid, drowning him.

The splitting went on, until Hanna's body teetered to the side, discarded, hitting the stone.

And there was this thing in front of Will.

Will had only one thought.

This took my family.

It uncurled—a twisted birth—revealing its shape slowly. Will stepped back. He lost his balance on the stone. He started to fall. He yelled out while he fell to the ground.

While all the while, he kept his eyes on the thing that uncurled before him.

It was nearly invisible against the black musty sky. Its skin—if it was skin—gobbled up the light. Will saw small liquid pools moving near a headlike shape.

Black eyes looking out.

Will's knuckles clawed at the stone, ripping the skin off. While he cursed, screamed at the thing.

"No! Oh, no—damn you! Damn—"

He got to his feet. His ankle hurt.

In fact, it might fall right in, and I'll fall down right in front of this thing.

And it spoke.

"Your family," it said. An elephant sound, a trumpeting, honking blast. But it said words . . .

Will thought it said words . . .

"Your . . . family . . . they died so wonderfully. Do you want to hear how they screamed? Do you want to watch now, to see how the little one kicked at my servant, how she called for help, begged to be left alive? Do you want to see that? I can let you see that."

No, Will thought. Begged. Please. No.

Watching. Listening.

"No," he begged. "Oh, God. No. I can't—"

He closed his eyes.

Another trick.

There was a rustling sound.

Christmas packages being opened. Too fast. Always over too fast.

Or dry skin peeling away from a corpse left too long on the mortuary slab.

Will quickly opens his eyes.

Tissue-thin membranes now dangle from the thing's back.

And Will sees.

Beth pulled into it, her fists bravely up in front of her. Stay away from strangers, they told her. Watch out for—

In the blackness, he sees Becca, slowly sucked into this purplish mass, her skin peeling off like carrot scrapings.

She looks out at him.

She wonders why he won't help.

Why? Help me, Will.

Help.

And somehow he remembers.

Somehow he has the sense to remember.

The one chance he has to help his family. The one way.

Here. Now.

Twenty-seven years before they are killed.

The images stopped. As if it sensed that Will had turned away from the horror, the screaming.

It reached out for him, slowly, and Will knew it was still unsure.

"No," Will said. "You won't have them. Not now . . . not ever . . ."

He took a step closer to it.

But then he heard boys' voices behind him.

Will Dunnigan, sixteen and starting to feel quite drunk, saw two people down near the rambling jetty that meandered into the Atlantic. At first, he thought they were two old homosexuals, looking for a quiet spot. Maybe two drunks.

But no.

They seemed to be fighting, grappling with each other.

"Hey, Dunnigan," Whalen said. "Pay attention. It's showtime."

Tim laughed. And Kiff and Narrio collapsed into each other, giggling. Stewed to the gills. Really bombed. Will grinned at them.

But he still watched the two shapes, moving around the rock. "Hey," he said. "I see—"

He thought he heard a yell. A cry of some kind.

It was a scary sound.

"Will, are you going to fucking do this with us or not?" Tim said.

Will nodded, but he kept on watching the two people.

"Let's get to it!" Kiff said. "Bring on the demons!" Mike Narrio laughed.

Will looked back at the circle, the pentagram, the weird symbols drawn on the stone. A big wave crashed nearby, and Will felt a fine spray on his face.

Kiff was saying words. Silly stuff.

Will looked over his shoulder at the two men, the two drunks, the—

Two . . .

And gooseflesh sprouted on his arms and legs.

Will grabbed it.

It was like touching Beth's Play-Doh, or digging his hands into warm clay or into an elephant's turd.

Will grabbed it.

"Your wife," it roared.

A hole opened, and oh, God, Will could smell her. The way her hair smelled after a shower. The perfume she wore. The sweet, wonderful smell of her skin when they made love.

The hole closed.

"I can't—" he said to himself.

Closed. To the world.

The creature spoke again.

If it actually spoke at all.

"Your children . . ."

And Will heard them. Fighting with each other, bickering over absolutely nothing. Then laughing. Their squeals as they opened birthday presents. Their call to "Look at me, Daddy, look at *me*!", when they dove into the pool. Fearless of the cold water.

Fearless of everything.

Signs. Voices. Images.

Will thought. Watched.

Desperation.

He held the thing, his fingers plunged into its fecal-like body.

Will thought he heard it groan.

"By God's power . . ."

He looked for eyes, some sign of intelligence. But this thing, this mad spirit—if that's what it was—was completely alien. No eyes. No soul. Eternal emptiness.

The negative image of existence.

The end of life.

The chaos of death.

Will looked at it. Held it fast, muttered the words. Over and over.

Until he roared with the waves, drunkenly shouting at the thing, feeling it shrivel, watching it curl up before him, melting like the Wicked Witch of the North.

Until just he stood there.

His hands reaching into the air.

Grabbing at nothing.

Will heard a chirp.

A feral sound. A rat worming its way through the maze of jumbled bricks.

Then Will turned to face them.

The friends of his youth.

Still so young . . .

Funny.

Now there was only one there.

One man.

And Will Dunnigan thought: Where did the other guy go?

Kiff was still carrying on with his silly prattle. His mumbo jumbo.

But now—God, Will felt cold, and the high tide was spraying him, and the bourbon wasn't sitting so well in his stomach.

The man stood there watching them.

"Shit," Kiff said. "Nothing's happening."

"Yeah, like you really expected something would happen?" Whalen said.

Will looked at the man, feeling creepier and creepier, and watched *him* looking at them. He's watching us, Will thought. Just standing there . . . and watching us.

And what happened to the other guy?

Maybe it isn't too safe here. He stepped out of the circle. Off the star point.

I'm cold and I want to go home.

And he knew he'd do that. No matter what crazy ideas Kiff came up with . . .

Narrio giggled. Drunk as a skunk. And then he too wobbled away from the circle.

Will looked back to the man.

But the man . . . ?

He was gone.

Will climbed up to the street.

I won, he thought. I won.

It never happened.

Nothing happened at Manhattan Beach. We never went to Steeplechase. Narrio never climbed onto the ride.

It all never happened.

He reached the corner, the row of small houses with unkempt lawns, unmowed for months. The breeze made the grass dance. The light let him see something that he hadn't been sure of.

My clothes, he thought. Blue jeans. Leather jacket. Sure, I'm dressed the way I was.

But now . . . now I'm here.

Before men like me wore blue jeans.

It was just as Dr. James had said it might turn out.

A one-way trip, Will. You have to know that. You have to *accept* that.

You may never come back.

And now Will knew that it was true.

He kept on walking, following the street to some faint neon lights in the distance.

But he also knew this:

If it all never happened . . .

Then Becca . . . and Sharon . . . and Beth were safe.

Time is a mental construct, Will, James had said. *Something to keep us sane, to give order to a universe more complex and chaotic than we can ever begin to imagine.*

Time can be changed.

And—

Will took a breath, sucking the air, clean, fresh.

I did it.

I changed what happened . . . what will happen. I was the only one who could.

With only one small problem.

I have to stay here.

This is my life now. My time.

Will kept on walking. The lights grew brighter. He saw people. Stores. Someplace to stop, perhaps. And think.

About the irony, the terrible irony.

To think that I saved them. That they'll live.

Only because I left them.

He laughed. And then because it seemed like the right thing to do, something he had to do, he started crying. Full out, crying, for joy, for sadness, for salvation.

Yes, by God.

Salvation.

1.

One of those lights, that night, had been a bar.

It was called the Bay Ridge Tavern. And Will went in looking for something to give him some sense of normalcy. A sink to wash the blood off his hands, the smell from his fingers . . .

But instead, what he saw and heard made him feel more lost.

The TV was on. Jack Paar was talking to a starlet with mile-high hair. But no one in the bar was listening. The men— there were only men in the bar—were talking loudly, laughing, ignoring the flickering colors on the set.

A purple blotch sat near the top of the TV screen.

Color TV had problems back then, Will knew.

Back then—

Which is now . . . for me.

He sat down on a vacant stool.

The bartender, a bowling pin of a man, with a loud laugh and sleeves rolled up, came up and asked what he wanted.

Will said, ''A beer.''

''Hey, speak up, mac. Can't hear you.'' Then the bartender turned to a bunch of guys at one end who were laughing as if they had just heard the funniest damn thing in the world.

''Will you fokin' guys pipe down!'' Then back to Will. ''Jeeez . . . What'll it be?''

''A beer,'' Will said. The bartender went in search of a clean glass.

Will saw a calendar. A cartoon cowgirl, all legs and perfectly rounded bottom.

October 1965.

"Here you go," the bartender said, returning with a glass with a foamy inch-tall head.

Will reached for his wallet.

Which wasn't there.

James had told him that too.

Bring nothing that ties you to this time.

Nothing that could keep you here.

A wallet could do that. It holds your life, your identification, your money, your credit cards. Photos.

"Oh, sorry," Will said. "I—"

The bartender's smile faded. He saw Will's arm slinking back from the futile grab at his back pocket. He noticed the crusty blood on Will's knuckles.

"I don't—" Will started to say.

But then the bartender—as if seeing something in Will's eyes—said, "Hey. Don't worry, mac." The bartender tapped the heavy wood bar. "It's on th' house."

Will nodded and said, "Thanks."

He took the sip.

He let the beer rest on his tongue, burning. Then he swallowed it.

The Paar show ended and the news came on. The newscasters were unfamiliar, and both looked goofily modish. The man was dressed in a suit with flaring lapels way too wide, and his tie glowed an otherworldly red. His hair was long, cut into a silly-looking page boy.

His woman partner had perfectly straight hair pulled back and she wore brilliant red lipstick.

The first story was about Americans bombing the Ho Chi Minh Trail. And a videotape of General Westmoreland flashed onto the screen, his shirt sleeves rolled up, arms folded in front of him.

He explained that the raid was "surgical."

That it would end any Cong initiative for the rest of the year. No doubt about it.

We could be out of here by Christmas, he said, grinning.

Right, Will thought. Will took another sip of beer.

I feel like laughing, Will thought. A giddy feeling. Right, sure . . . out of here by Christmas . . .

He felt the bartender looking at him, standing at the other end of the bar talking to his regulars.

Best move on, Will thought.

He looked down at his jeans. He looked at his leather jacket. Nothing too out of the ordinary there, he thought.

But I better leave . . .

He finished the beer.

Got up and started for the door.

The bartender called out to him.

"Hey, fella? You looking for a job?"

Will stopped. Turned around.

And—he rubbed his chin. He guessed he was.

So Will nodded, and he walked back to find out what he'd be doing the rest of his life.

2.

It was a life, he guessed.

The job was clerking in a small grocery, a small market not much larger than a deli. Stock work at the beginning, but then—as the owner got to know and trust him—Will ran the store. He got friendly with the customers. They liked him.

He was paid cash. And that made things easy.

The only difficult times were when people got too close, like the owner or regular customers. And they wanted to know where he came from. Where had he been? What had he done?

Will guessed what they suspected.

They think I'm an ex-con.

And that was pretty useful.

So he'd just smile and say, "Oh, I've worked out West, did lots of things. I was married once . . ."

And the sad look in his eyes was usually enough to close down any further questions. Most people assumed that he was divorced.

There were women, just friends mostly, but women near his age who were looking for someone just to talk to, and perhaps sleep with.

He'd take them fishing out on Sheepshead Bay, and he almost enjoyed this lost world, a safer world, before graffiti, before crack, before the world changed.

But there was one thing he had promised himself that he'd never do. James had told him that it would be wrong. Perhaps dangerous. Will figured he was just trying to spare his feelings.

Will couldn't keep that promise.

So as soon as he had a license and a car, he started watching.

Becca, in college at Russell Sage.

Sometimes he'd drive up and watch her on the streets of Troy, New York, walking with her friends, laughing, years before she would meet him.

And sometimes she'd stop and look in his direction.

He'd slide down in the car seat, hoping that the sun's glare on the windshield would hide him. Hide the man watching her.

Then she'd move on.

And he watched himself.

A young man. Carousing through the sixties. So full of life that he couldn't relate to that person at all.

That's not me, he thought. That's someone else. *But he was wrong.*

And when he came back to his small studio apartment in the Bay Ridge section of Brooklyn, only a block from the elevated subway, he'd sit in the dark and think about the life he'd lost.

He got older. Middle age took a firm hold, and he was fifty.

Will and Becca got married . . .

And he was amazed that all the details were the same.

As if nothing had changed.

But he knew it had. He knew it, because this Will still saw his old school friends. He went to reunions where Kiff was still a crazy man, and Tim Hanna was doing pretty well in real estate—no great shakes, but not bad. Whalen and Narrio both moved to California, but they flew back for the occasional reunion.

I changed it all, Will thought.

Things were different.

And his apartment grew to be filled with the history of

these people's lives . . . photographs that he took secretly . . . the articles from local newspapers, while the seventies unrolled like an old, badly scripted movie.

Then one night, drunk, sick with the pain that never went away, he pulled all the pictures down and threw his collection into a big box, intending to throw it into the garbage.

Which he never did.

Instead he put everything in a closet.

Knowing that he'd have to stop this shadow life, watching the others, the real people, live their lives that he had given them.

He stopped spying on Becca and Will. Feeling too sick every time he did it.

He stopped.

3.

But when the first baby was born—

When Sharon was born—

Will went to the hospital and he walked up to the giant window that showed the parents and the relatives a sea of squirming babies, all of them identical.

He had to tilt his head to read the card.

Sharon Dunnigan.

He put his hands against the glass.

That's my baby, he thought.

His lips pressed against the glass.

My little girl.

And he sobbed against the glass, heaving, looking at the tightly swaddled infant asleep.

And he was there for Beth too.

Now he couldn't stop.

He went to their school plays, seeing them again, rows behind their parents, and he felt crazy, loonish.

Once he thought about visiting Joshua James.

Because—all the time—he felt this need to talk with someone, anyone, about what had happened. Someone who would understand, who could say, ''You did good, Will Dunnigan.''

He went so far as to go to the Fordham campus.

A place that the other Will would never have to visit now.

And sometimes, after a lot of drinking, Will hoped that

maybe, if he went to see him, Dr. James would *know* him, that somehow he'd have this memory of what he and Will had done.

But that was impossible. Absurd.

When I changed everything, it changed for James too.

And so he never went to visit James.

And his days passed.

Until he was an old man.

4.

He turned sixty-eight.

And though he still worked, the new owner of the food store, a bright-eyed Latino named Hector, just had him operate the cash register.

Hector forgave Will when the register turned up a few bucks short. Will had trouble reading some of the prices, and the bodega didn't have a scanner.

Hector asked Will why he didn't retire. Why not live on Social Security, use Medicare?

Will smiled. He explained that he couldn't do that.

He didn't tell Hector that—as far as the government was concerned—he didn't exist.

Hector still paid him in cash and food.

It wasn't so bad, even if Will felt tired and empty.

He was alone now, most of the time. The people he had known in the neighborhood were gone, or dead. Many of them moved out to the suburbs, the sticks, before the neighborhood "changed."

Others went to live with children, grown, with their own families.

Will hadn't seen them—hadn't seen his family—in years.

It was harder to make the trip up to Westchester. His driving wasn't so great.

And somehow, he was always left shaking afterward. Shaking like a leaf.

He took medicine. For his heart.

He still had his box of pictures and clippings, sitting in a closet. That was important to him.

And he still watched baseball.

Though it had been boring knowing who was going to win

the World Series each year. And how many times had he been tempted to place a bet with the local bookie?

Too many times.

But that seemed all wrong.

I've been given a gift, he thought.

Life for those I love.

To bet on the things that I know . . . that would be all wrong.

But today . . . today was a special day.

Today there was an important baseball game and he didn't know who won.

It was the last play-off game. The Mets vs. the Giants.

Because today . . .

It was the day he left.

Twenty-seven years, he thought. Such a long time. To end up back where you started from.

Twenty-seven years.

And nothing would happen tonight. There was no slasher, no demonic ripper.

Had there ever been?

And the other Will would watch the ball game with Becca curled up on the couch with him. He'd have a few beers. Eat some popcorn, and see whether the Mets pulled it off.

And I'll watch too, thought Will. I'll watch, and I'll think about them, and—finally—I'll taste some time that I haven't lived through before.

His apartment was cold when he got to it. The landlord didn't recognize the chilly winds of fall. There would be no heat for a while. So Will—as soon as he went in—turned on the gas stove and left the oven door open. It was a smelly heat, stinky with the gas smell. But it kept him warm.

He opened a can of hash. Maybe I'll fry an egg and put it on top, he thought.

Why not celebrate?

And though he tried to watch his beer intake, he had a six-pack of Bud Light cooling.

I'm going to enjoy this game tonight, he thought.

It's a special night!

And he almost believed that.

5.

He fell asleep before the game ended.

And he woke up in his apartment with the TV yammering at him. An old movie, a World War II film. He saw Van Johnson, Ronald Reagan. It looked colorized.

A half-empty beer can was wedged in the pillows.

He looked at the clock on his cheap Korean VCR that didn't work anymore.

1:13.

He rubbed his chin.

I missed my game, he thought. I still don't know who won the game, now, isn't that something? Isn't that a pisser? Isn't that—?

1:14.

He looked at the digital readout as if it were a beacon into another world, another time.

He tried to tell himself: It's nothing. I'm about to pass the time I left. It's nothing at all.

No big occasion.

It's not New Year's.

What's the big deal? What is the damn deal?

Just moving from one minute to the next.

His legs hurt.

They often did now, some kind of circulation problem, the young doctor told him. You need more exercise. You need to walk around.

Around here? Will laughed. At night?

Right. Sure. That would be a good way to end my life. Sure . . .

He tried to push himself off the chair. He pushed against it.

He grunted. His body didn't seem to want to move.

He reached for the arms of his easy chair. Reached out—

To pull himself up.

He saw the clock.

1:15.

6.

And someone touched him.

He still saw his small apartment, the cluttered kitchen table, the TV flickering, the old war movie—

And then he didn't.

Instead, he saw who was tugging at his sleeve.

Pulling at it. Standing there in her bare feet, her nightgown with purple flowers—her favorite—touching the floor.

It was Beth.

"Daddy, what are you doing? What are you doing down here?"

This is not real, Will thought. It's another one of them cursed dreams, teasing me all the time, driving me half crazy when I wake up.

A sweet, lost dream.

But the Beth ghost tugged harder.

"Dad-dee!"

The TV was on. The same movie.

Will looked around.

At his house.

"Beth," he said. A whisper. The tiniest sound.

She cocked her head, as if aware that something strange was going on.

"Beth—my baby, my—" he said.

His hands moved to hers. So nervous that it would all disappear.

You can't touch things in dreams. They just disappear. They just vanish like cotton candy shriveling in your mouth to sweet nothingness.

He covered her hands.

She still looked sleepy and unsure.

Then Beth smiled, a toothless grin. "*Daddy*, you should be in bed. I wanted a glass of water and you didn't hear me."

Will nodded. "Yes, honey. Yes. I—I didn't hear you."

And Beth, reassured, pulled at him and Will stood up, easily.

His legs didn't hurt.

He saw himself in the living room mirror.

He saw who he was.

Who he was *now*.

And his mind tried to deal with this incredible change, this amazing gift.

And all he could guess, could only dream . . .

When I reached the point that I left, when I finally got to that spot on the circle of time, then it was all over . . .

My life could be mine again.

My life *was* mine again.

Beth tugged at him.

"It's bedtime, Daddy."

"Yes, honey," he said. And he followed her.

Knowing that Sharon would be upstairs, her math homework done. And Becca would be asleep on her side of the bed, her steady breathing a guardian against all the bad things that the world might send at him.

Up the stairs, a giant led by a little girl.

An image came to mind.

Frankenstein's monster being led to a little lake by a small girl who knew no fear because she was innocent and full of love.

Up the carpeted stairs until he reached the top.

And, beside her door, Beth turned to him and said, "G'night, Daddy."

She kissed his hand.

And before she could scurry away, Will crouched down close to her and held her tight, tighter, planting a million kisses in her curly hair.